Romance readers around the world were sad to note the passing of **Betty Neels** in June 2001. Her career spanned thirty years, and she continued to write into her ninetieth year. To her millions of fans, Betty epitomized the romance writer, and yet she began writing almost by accident. She had retired from nursing, but her inquiring mind still sought stimulation. Her new career was born when she heard a lady in her local library bemoaning the lack of good romance novels. Betty's first book, *Sister Peters in Amsterdam*, was published in 1969, and she eventually completed 134 books. Her novels offer a reassuring warmth that was very much a part of her own personality. She was a wonderful writer, and she is greatly missed. Her spirit and genuine talent live on in all her stories.

BETTY NEELS

Dearest Love
& Love Can Wait

 HARLEQUIN SPECIAL RELEASE

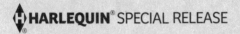 **HARLEQUIN**® SPECIAL RELEASE

Recycling programs for this product may not exist in your area.

ISBN-13: 978-1-335-00843-5

Dearest Love & Love Can Wait

Copyright © 2020 by Harlequin Books S.A.

Dearest Love
First published in 1994. This edition published in 2020.
Copyright © 1994 by Betty Neels

Love Can Wait
First published in 1997. This edition published in 2020.
Copyright © 1997 by Betty Neels

For questions and comments about the quality of this book, please contact us at CustomerService@Harlequin.com.

Harlequin Enterprises ULC
22 Adelaide St. West, 40th Floor
Toronto, Ontario M5H 4E3, Canada
www.Harlequin.com

Printed in U.S.A.

CONTENTS

DEAREST LOVE

Chapter 1

Dear Sir,
With reference to your advertisement in this week's *Lady* magazine, I wish to apply for the post of Caretaker/Housekeeper.

I am twenty-seven years of age, single with no dependants, and have several years' experience in household management including washing, ironing, cleaning and cooking. I am a Cordon Bleu cook. I have a working knowledge of minor electrical and plumbing faults. I am able to take messages and answer the telephone.

I would wish to bring my cat with me.
Yours faithfully,
Arabella Lorimer

It was the last letter to be read by the elderly man sitting at his desk in his consulting-room, a large apartment on

the ground floor of a Regency house, one of a terrace, in
Wigmore Street, London. He read it for a second time,
gave a rumble of laughter, and added it to the pile before
him. There were twelve applicants in all and Arabella
Lorimer was the only one to enclose references—the
only one to write legibly, too, neatly setting down all
the relevant facts. It was a pity that she wasn't a man…

He began to read the letters again and was interrupted halfway through by the entry of his partner. Dr
Titus Tavener came unhurriedly into the room, a very
tall man with broad shoulders and a massive person. He
was handsome with a high-bridged nose, a firm mouth
and rather cold blue eyes. His hair, once fair, was pep-
per and salt, despite which he looked younger than his
forty years.

Dr James Marshall, short and stout and almost bald,
greeted him with pleasure. 'Just the man I want. The
applications for the caretaker's post—I have them here;
I've spent the last hour reading them. I've decided which
one I shall accept. Do read them, Titus, and give me
your opinion. Not that it will make any difference to
my choice.' He chortled as Dr Tavener sat himself down
and picked up the little pile of letters. He read them
through, one after the other, and then gathered them
neatly together.

'There are one or two possibles: the ex-bus driver—
although he admits to asthma attacks—then this Mrs
Butler.' He glanced at the letter in his hand. 'But is she
quite the type to open the door? Of course the joker in
the pack is Miss Arabella Lorimer and her cat. Most
unsuitable.'

'Why?'

'Obviously a maiden lady down on her luck. I don't

think I believe her skills are quite what she claims them to be. I'd hesitate to leave a stopped-up drainpipe or a blown fuse to her ladylike hands.'

His partner laughed. 'Titus, I can only hope that one day before it's too late you will meet a woman who will turn you sides to middle and then tramp all over you.'

Dr Tavener smiled. 'Unlikely. Perhaps I have been rather hard on the lady. There is always the possibility that she is an Amazon with a tool-kit.'

'Well, you will soon know. I've decided that she might do.'

Dr Tavener got up and strolled to the window and stood looking out on to the quiet street. 'And why not? Mrs Lane will be glad to leave. Her arthritis isn't getting any better and she's probably longing to go and live with her daughter. She'll take her furniture with her, I suppose? Do we furnish the place?'

'It depends—Miss Lorimer may have her own stuff.' Dr Marshall pushed back his chair. 'We've a busy day tomorrow; I'll see if your Amazon can come for an interview at five o'clock. Will you be back by then?'

'Unlikely—the clinic is overbooked as it is. In any case, I'm dining out.' He turned to look at his partner. 'I dare say you've made a good choice, James.' He strolled to the door. 'I've some paperwork to deal with. Shall I send Miss Baird home? You're going yourself? I shall be here for another hour yet—see you in the morning.'

He went to his own consulting-room, going through the elegant waiting-room with a smile and a nod for their shared receptionist Miss Baird, before going down the passage, past the stairs to the basement and his separate suite. This comprised a small waiting-room, a treatment-room where his nurse worked and his own room facing

Dearest Love

the garden at the back of the house. A small, narrow garden but well-tended and bright with early autumn flowers. He gave it a brief look before drawing the first of the patients' notes waiting for his attention towards him.

Dr Marshall read Miss Arabella Lorimer's letter once more and rang for Miss Baird. 'Send a note by special messenger, will you? To this address. Tell the lady to come here at five o'clock tomorrow afternoon. A pity she hasn't a telephone.' He got up and switched off his desk light. 'I'm going home, Miss Baird. Dr Tavener will be working for some time yet, but check that he's still here before you leave.' He nodded and smiled at her. 'Go as soon as you've got that message seen to.'

He went home himself then, to his wife and family, and much later Dr Tavener got into his Rolls-Royce and drove himself home to his charming house overlooking the canal in Little Venice.

Arabella read Dr Marshall's somewhat arbitrary note sitting in the kitchen. It was a small, damp room, overlooking a weary-looking patch of grass and some broken fencing, but she preferred it to the front room where her landlady sat of a Sunday afternoon. It housed the lady's prized possessions and Arabella hadn't been invited in there because of her cat Percy, who would ruin the furniture. She hadn't minded; she had been grateful that Billy Westlake, the village postman, had persuaded his aunt, Miss Pimm, to take her in for a few days while she found a job and somewhere to live.

It hadn't been easy leaving Colpin-cum-Witham, but it had been necessary. Her parents had died together in a car accident and only then had she discovered that her home wasn't to be hers any longer; it had been mortgaged to the hilt and she had to leave. There was almost no money. She sold all but the basic furniture that she might need and, since there was no hope of working in or near the village and distant aunts and uncles, while full of good advice, made no offer to help her, she took herself and Percy to London. She had no wish to live there but, as the postman had said, it was a vast city and somewhere there must be work. She had soon realised that the only work she was capable of was domestic. She had no skills other than Cordon Bleu cooking and, since she had never needed to work in any capacity, she had no experience—something which employers demanded.

Now she read the brief letter again; she had applied almost in desperation, anxious to get away from Miss Pimm's scarcely veiled impatience to get rid of her and Percy. She had agreed to take them in for a few days but it was already a week and, as she had said to Arabella, she was glad of the money but she was one who kept herself to herself and didn't fancy strangers in her home.

Arabella sat quietly, not allowing herself to be too hopeful but all the same allowing herself to picture the basement room which went with the job. She would furnish it with her own bits and pieces and with any luck there would be some kind of a garden behind the house where Percy could take the air. She went up to her little bedroom with Percy at her heels and inspected her small stock of clothes. To be suitably dressed was important.

She arrived at Wigmore Street with two minutes to spare—the clocks were striking the hour as Miss Baird ushered her into Dr Marshall's consulting-room. He was sitting behind his desk as she went in and put down his pen to peer at her over his glasses. Just for a moment he was silent, then he said, 'Miss Lorimer? Please sit down. I must confess I was expecting someone more—more robust...'

Arabella seated herself without fuss—a small, nicely plump girl with mousy hair pinned on top of her head, an ordinary face and a pair of large grey eyes, thickly fringed. Anyone less like a caretaker it would be hard to find, reflected Dr Marshall with an inward chuckle, and just wait until Titus saw her.

He said pleasantly, 'I read your letter with interest, Miss Lorimer. Will you tell me about your last job?'

'I haven't had one. I've always lived at home—my mother was delicate and my father was away a good deal; he had his own business. I always did the house-keeping and dealt with minor repairs around the house.'

He nodded. 'Why do you want this job?'

She was sitting very quietly—no fidgeting, he no-ticed thankfully.

'My parents were killed recently in a car accident and now my home is no longer mine. We lived at Colpin-cum-Witham in southern Wiltshire; there is no work there for someone with no qualifications.' She paused. 'I need somewhere to live and domestic work seems to be the answer. I have applied for several jobs but they won't allow me to have Percy.'

'Percy?'

'My cat.'

'Well, I see no objection to a cat as long as he stays in your room—he can have the use of the garden, of course. But do you suppose that you are up to the work? You are expected to clean these rooms—mine, the reception and waiting-room, the passage and the stairs, my part-ner's rooms—and polish all the furniture and brass, and the front door, then answer the bell during our working hours, empty the bins, lock up and unlock in the mornings… Are you of a nervous disposition?'

'No, I don't think so.'

'Good. Oh, and if there is no one about you will answer the telephone, run errands and take messages.' He gave her a shrewd glance. 'A bit too much for you, eh?'

'Certainly not, Dr Marshall. I dare say I should call you sir? I would be glad to come and work for you.'

'Shall we give it a month's trial? Mrs Lane who is retiring should be in her room now. If you will go with Miss Baird she will introduce you. Come back here, if you please, so that we can make final arrangements.'

The basement wasn't quite what Arabella had imagined but it had possibilities. It was a large room; its front windows gave a view of passing feet and were heavily barred but the windows at the other end of the room, although small, could be opened. There was a door loaded down with bolts and locks and chains beside them, leading out to a small paved area with the garden beyond. At one side there was a door opening into a narrow passage with a staircase leading to the floor above and ending in another heavy door and, beside the staircase, a very small kitchen and an even smaller shower-room. Mrs Lane trotted ahead of her, pointing out the amenities. 'Of course I shall 'ave ter take me things with me, ducks—going up ter me daughter, yer see; she's got a room for me.'

'I have some furniture, Mrs Lane,' said Arabella politely. 'I only hope to be able to make it as cosy as you have done.'

Mrs Lane preened. 'Well, I've me pride, love. A bit small and young, aint yer?'

'Well, I'm very strong and used to housework. When did you want to leave, Mrs Lane?'

'Just as soon as yer can get 'ere. Bin 'appy 'ere, I 'ave, but I'm getting on a bit—the stairs is a bit much. 'Is nibs 'as always 'ad a girl come in ter answer the door, which save me feet.' She chuckled. ''E won't need 'er now!'

Back with Dr Marshall, Arabella, bidden to sit, sat.

'Well, want to come here and work?'

'Yes, I do and I will do my best to satisfy you, sir.'

'Good. Fix up dates and so on with Mrs Lane and let me know when you're going to come.' He added sharply, 'There must be no gap between Mrs Lane going and you coming, understand.'

Outside in the street she went looking for a telephone box to ring the warehouse in Sherborne and arrange for her furniture to be brought to London. It was a matter of urgency and for once good fortune was on her side. There was a load leaving for London in three days' time and her few things could be sent with it and at a much smaller cost than she had expected. She went back to Mrs Lane, going down the few steps to the narrow door by the barred window and explaining carefully, 'If I might come here some time during the morning and you leave in the afternoon, could we manage to change over without upsetting your routine here?'

'Don't see why not, ducks. Me son-in-law's coming with a van so I'll clear off as soon as yer 'ere.'

'Then I'll let Dr Marshall know.'

'Do that. I'll 'ave ter see 'im for me wages—I'll tell 'im likewise.'

Back at Miss Pimm's, Arabella told her that she would be leaving in three days and ate her supper—fish and chips from the shop on the corner—and went to bed, explaining to Percy as she undressed that he would soon have a home of his own again. He was a docile cat but he hadn't been happy at Miss Pimm's; it was a far cry from the roomy house and garden that he had always lived in. Now he curled up on the end of her narrow bed and went to sleep, instinct telling him that better times were in store.

Dr Marshall sat at his desk for some time doing nothing after Arabella had gone. Presently he gave a rich chuckle and when Miss Baird came in he asked her, 'Well, what do you think of our new caretaker?'

Miss Baird gave him a thoughtful look. 'A very nice young lady, sir. I only hope she's up to all that hard housework.'

'She assures me that she is a most capable worker. She will start in three days' time and I must be sure and be here when Dr Tavener sees her for the first time.'

It wasn't until the next morning, discussing a difficult case with his partner, that Dr Marshall had the chance to mention that he had engaged a new caretaker. 'She will start in two days' time—with her cat.'

Dr Tavener laughed. 'So she turned out to be suitable for the job? Let us hope that she is quicker at answering the doorbell and emptying the wastepaper baskets.'

'Oh, I imagine she will be.' Dr Marshall added slyly, 'After all, she is young.'

'As long as she does her work properly.' Dr Tavener was already engrossed in the notes in his hand and spoke without interest.

Despite misgivings that her furniture wouldn't arrive, that Percy would disappear at the last minute or that Dr

Marshall would have second thoughts about employing her, Arabella moved herself, her cat and her few possessions into the basement of Wigmore Street without mishap. True, empty it looked pretty grim and rather dirty, but once the floor had been cleaned and the windows washed, the cobwebs removed from the darker corners, she could see possibilities. With the help of the removal men she put her bed in a corner of the room, put a small table and chair under the back window and stacked everything else tidily against a wall. Her duties were to commence in the morning and she conned Mrs Lane's laboriously written list of duties before she made up the bed, settled Percy in his cardboard box and rolled up her sleeves.

There was plenty of hot water and Mrs Lane had left a variety of mops and brushes in the cupboard by the stairs. Arabella set to with a will; this was to be her home—hers and Percy's—and she intended to make it as comfortable as possible. Cleanliness came before comfort. She scrubbed and swept and polished and by evening was satisfied with her work.

She cooked her supper on the newly cleaned stove—beans on toast and an egg—gave Percy his meal and sat at the table, well pleased with her efforts, while she drank her tea and then made a list of the things she still needed. It was not a long list but she would have to buy a little at a time each pay-day. Her rather muddled calculations showed her that it would be Christmas before she had all she wanted but that didn't worry her—after the last awful months this was all that she could wish for.

She washed her dishes and opened the back door with Percy tucked under one arm. The garden was surrounded by a high brick wall and ringed by flowerbeds but there was a good-sized strip of lawn as well. She set Percy down and watched him explore, at first with caution and then with pleasure. After Miss Pimm's little yard this was bliss…

She perched on a small rustic seat, tired now but happy. It had been a fine day but it was getting chilly now and dusk had dimmed the colourful garden. She scooped up Percy and went back indoors and then, mindful of Mrs Lane's instructions, went up the stairs and inspected each room in turn, making sure that the windows were closed and locked, the doors bolted and all the lights turned out. The two floors above her were lived in, Mrs Lane had told her, by a neurologist and his wife. They had a side entrance, a small door at the front of the house, and although he was retired he still saw the occasional patient. 'But nothing ter do with us,' Mrs Lane had said. 'Yer won't ever see them.'

All the same it was nice to think that the house wasn't quite empty. She took her time in locking up, looking at everything so that she would know where things were in the morning and, being of a practical turn of mind, she searched until she found the stopcock, the fire-extinguisher and the gas and electricity metres. She also searched for and eventually found a box containing such useful things as a hammer, nails, spare light-bulbs, a wrench and adhesive tape. They were hidden away in a small dark cupboard and she felt sure that no one had been near it for a very long time. She put everything back carefully and reminded herself to ask for a plunger. Blocked sinks could be a nuisance, especially where people would be constantly washing their hands. Satisfied at last, she went back to her room, had a shower and got into bed, and Percy, uninvited but very welcome, climbed on too and settled on her feet.

She was up early, tidied the room and made the bed, fed Percy and escorted him into the garden, ate a sketchy breakfast and took herself off upstairs, wearing her new nylon overall.

There was everything she might need—a vacuum cleaner, polish and dusters. She emptied the wastepaper baskets, set the chairs to rights, arranged the magazines just so, polished the front door-knocker and opened the windows. It looked very nice when she had finished but a little austere. She went back downstairs and out into the garden; she cut Michaelmas daisies, dahlias and one or two late roses. She bore them back, found three vases, arranged the flowers in them and put one in each of the consulting-rooms and the last one in the waiting-room. They made all the difference, she considered, and re-alised that she had overlooked the second waiting-room. Back in the garden, she cut asters this time, arranged them in a deep bowl and put them on the table flanked by the magazines.

She hadn't met Dr Marshall's partner; she hoped he was as nice as that gentleman.

She went back to the basement then, tidied herself, made sure that her hair was neat and when the door-bell rang went to answer it. It was Dr Marshall's nurse, who had introduced herself as Joyce Pierce and then exclaimed, 'You're the new caretaker? Well, I must say you're a bit of a surprise. Do you think you'll like it?'

'Well, yes. I can live here, you see, and I don't mind housework.'

She was shutting the door when the second nurse ar-rived, small and dark and pretty. 'The caretaker?' she asked and raised her eyebrows. 'Whatever's come over Dr Marshall?' She nodded at Arabella. 'I'm Madge Simmons. I work for Dr Tavener.' She spoke rather frostily. 'Come on, Joyce, we've time for a cup of tea.'

The first patient wouldn't arrive until nine o'clock so Arabella sped downstairs. There was still a tea-chest of bed-linen, table-linen and curtains to unpack. As soon as she could she would get some net and hang it in the front window, shutting off all those feet...

At a quarter to nine she went upstairs again. There was no sign of the two nurses, although she could hear voices, and she stood uncertainly in the hall—to turn and face the door as it was opened. The man who entered seemed to her to be enormous. The partner, she thought, eyeing his elegance and his good looks and was very startled when he observed, 'Good lord, the caretaker!' and laughed.

The laugh annoyed her. She wished him good morning in a small frosty voice and went down to her room, closing the door very quietly behind her. 'He's what one would call a magnificent figure of a man,' she told Percy, 'and also a very rude one!'

The front doorbell rang then, and she went upstairs to admit the first patient. For the next hour or so she trotted up and down the stairs a dozen times until finally she shut the door on the last patient and Miss Baird came to tell her that Dr Marshall wanted to see her.

He eyed her over his specs. 'Morning, Miss Lorimer. Where did you get the flowers?'

The question surprised her. 'From the garden—only the ones at the back of the beds...'

'Nice idea. Finding your feet?'

'Yes, thank you, sir.'

'Miss Baird will tell you what to do when we've gone. We'll be back this afternoon, one or other of us, but not until three o'clock. You're free once you've tidied up and had your lunch, but be back here by quarter to. We sometimes work in the evening, but not often. Did Mrs Lane tell you where the nearest shops were?'

'No, but I can find them.'

He nodded and looked up as the door opened and Dr Tavener came in. 'Ah, here is my partner, Dr Tavener. This is our new caretaker.'

'We have already met,' said Arabella in a chilly voice. 'If that is all, sir?'

'Not quite all,' said Dr Tavener. 'I owe you an apology, Miss…'

'Lorimer, sir.'

'Miss Lorimer. I was most discourteous but I can assure you that my laughter was not at you as a person.'

'It was of no consequence, sir.' She gave him a fierce look from her lovely eyes which belied the sober reply and looked at Dr Marshall.

'Yes. Yes, go along, Miss Lorimer. If you need anything, don't hesitate to ask.'

A practical girl, Arabella paused at the door. 'I should like a plunger, sir.' She saw that he was puzzled. 'It is used for unstopping sinks and drains. They're not expensive.'

Not a muscle of Dr Tavener's handsome features moved; he asked gravely, 'Have we a blocked sink, Miss Lorimer?'

'No, but it's something which usually happens at an awkward time—it would be nice to have one handy.'

Dr Marshall spoke. 'Yes, yes, of course. Very wise. We have always called in a plumber, I believe.'

'It isn't always necessary,' she told him kindly.

'Ask Miss Baird to deal with it as you go, will you?'

Dr Tavener closed the door behind her and sat down. 'A paragon,' he observed mildly. 'With a plunger too! Do we know anything about her, James?'

'She comes from a place called Colpin-cum-Witham in Wiltshire. Parents killed in a car crash and—for some reason not specified—she had to leave her home. Presumably no money. Excellent references from the local parson and doctor. She's on a month's trial.' He smiled. 'Have you got flowers in your room too?'

'Yes, indeed.' He added, 'Don't let us forget that new brooms sweep clean.'

'You don't like her?'

'My dear James, I don't know her and it is most unlikely that I shall see enough of her to form an opinion.' He got up and went to look out of the window. 'I thought I'd drive up to Leeds—the consultation isn't until the afternoon. I'll go on to Birmingham from there and come back on the following day. Miss Baird has fixed my appointments so that I have a couple of days free.'

Dr Marshall nodded. 'That's fine. I'm not too keen on going to that seminar in Oslo. Will you go?'

'Certainly. It's two weeks ahead, isn't it? If I fly over it will only take three days.' He glanced at his watch. 'I'd better do some work; I've that article to finish for the *Lancet*.' He went to the door. 'I've two patients for this evening, by the way.'

As for Arabella, she went back to her room, had lunch, fed Percy and, after a cautious look round, went into the garden with him, unaware that Dr Tavener was at his desk at the window. He watched her idly, admired Percy's handsome grey fur, and then forgot her.

Miss Baird had been very helpful. There were, she had told Arabella, one or two small shops not five minutes' walk away down a small side-street. Arabella put on her jacket and, armed with a shopping-basket, set off to discover them. They were tucked away from the quiet prosperous streets with their large houses—a newsagents, a greengrocer and a small general store. Sufficient for her needs. She stocked up with enough food for a couple of days, bought herself a newspaper and then went back to Wigmore Street. On Saturday, she promised herself, she would spend her free afternoon shopping for some of the things on her list. She was to be paid each week, Miss Baird had told her and, although she should save for an uncertain future, there were some small comforts she would need. She would have all Sunday to work without interruption.

After that first day the week went quickly; by the end of it Arabella had found her feet. She saw little of the nurses and still less of Dr Marshall, and nothing at all of his partner. It was only when she went to Miss Baird to collect her wages that she overheard one of the nurses remark that Dr Tavener would be back on Monday. 'And a good thing too,' she had added, 'for his appointments book is full. He's away again in a couple of weeks for that seminar in Oslo.'

'He doesn't get much time for his love-life, does he?' laughed the other nurse.

Arabella, with her pay-packet a delightful weight in her pocket, even felt vague relief that he would be going away again. She had been careful to keep out of his way, although she wasn't sure why, and the last two days while he had been away she had felt much more comfortable. 'It's because he's so large,' she told Percy, and fell to counting the contents of her pay-packet.

While her parents had been alive she had lived a comfortable enough life. There had always seemed to be money; she had never been spoilt but she had never gone without anything she had needed or asked for. Now she held in her hand what was, for her, quite a large sum of money and she must plan to spend it carefully. New clothes were for the moment out of the question. True, those she had were of good quality and although her wardrobe was small it was more than adequate for her needs. She got paper and pen and checked her list…

It took her until one o'clock to clear up after the Saturday morning appointments and then there was the closing and the locking up to do, the answering machine to set, the few cups and saucers to wash and dry, the gas and electricity to check. She ate a hasty lunch, saw to Percy's needs then changed into her brown jersey skirt and the checked blouson jacket which went with it, stuck her rather tired feet into the Italian loafers she had bought with her mother in the happy times she tried not to remember too often, and, with her shoulder-bag swinging, caught a bus to Tottenham Court Road.

The tea-chests had yielded several treasures: curtains which could be cut to fit the basement windows and make cushion covers, odds and ends of china and kitchenware, a clock—she remembered it from the kitchen; a small radio—still working; some books and, right at the bottom, a small thin mat which would look nice before the gas fire.

She needed to buy needles and sewing cottons, net curtains, scissors and more towels, shampoo and some soap and, having purchased these, she poked around the cheaper shops until she found what she wanted: a roll of thin matting for the floor—it would be awkward to carry but it would be worth the effort. So, for that matter, would the tin of paint in a pleasing shade of pale apricot. She added a brush and, laden down with her awkward shopping, took a bus back to Wigmore Street.

Back in the basement again, she changed into an elderly skirt and jumper and went into the garden with Percy. It was dusk already and there were no lights on in the rooms above. The house seemed very silent and empty and there was a chilly wind. Percy disliked wind; he hurried back indoors and she locked and bolted the door before getting her supper and feeding him. Her meal over, she washed up and went upstairs to check carefully that everything was just as it should be before going back to lay the matting.

It certainly made a difference to the dim little room; the matting almost covered the mud-coloured flooring, and when she had spread an old-fashioned chenille tablecloth over the round table its cheerful crimson brightened the place further. It had been at the bottom of one of the tea-chests, wrapped around some of the china, and the curtains were of the same crimson. It was too late to start them that evening but she could at least sew the net curtains she had bought. It was bedtime by the time she had done that, run a wire through their tops, banged in some small nails and hung them across the bars of the windows. She went to bed then, pleased with her efforts.

She woke in the middle of the night, for the moment forgetful of where she was and then, suddenly overcome with grief and loneliness, cried herself to sleep again. She woke in the morning to find Percy sitting on her chest, peering down at her face—part of her old life—and she at once sat up in bed, dismissing self-pity. The walls had to be painted and if there was time she would begin on the curtains…

'We have a home,' she told Percy as she dressed, 'and money in our pockets and work to keep us busy. It's a lovely morning; we'll go into the garden.'

There was a faint chill in the air and there was a Sunday morning quiet. She thought of all the things she would do, the places she would visit in the coming weeks, and feeling quite cheerful got their breakfasts.

She had covered the drab, discoloured wallpaper by the late afternoon and the room looked quite different. The pale apricot gave the place light and warmth and she ate her combined tea and supper in great content.

The smell was rather overpowering; she opened the door to the garden despite the chilly evening and cut up the curtains ready to sew, fired with enthusiasm. As she wielded the scissors she planned what to buy with her next pay-packet: a bedspread, a table-lamp, a picture or two—the list was neverending!

Chapter 2

Dr Taverner, arriving the next morning, saw the net curtains and grinned. Unlike Mrs Lane, the new caretaker disliked the view from her window. Mrs Lane, on the other hand, had once told him that she found the sight of passing feet very soothing.

There were fresh flowers on his desk and there wasn't a speck of dust to be seen; the wastepaper basket was empty and the elegant gas fire had been lighted. He sat down to study the notes of his first patient and hoped that such a satisfactory state of affairs would continue. She was quite unsuitable, of course; either she would find the work too much for her or she would find something more suitable.

Arabella, fortunately unaware of these conjectures, went about her duties with brisk efficiency. Miss Baird had wished her a cheerful good morning when she had arrived, even the two nurses had smiled as she opened the door to them, and after that for some time she was opening and closing the door for patients, ignored for the most part—a small, rather colourless creature, not worth a second glance.

She had no need to go to the shops at lunchtime— the milkman had left milk and she had everything she needed for making bread. She made the dough, kneaded it and set it to rise before the gas fire while she started on the curtains. She was as handy with her needle as she was with her cooking and she had them ready by the time she had to go back upstairs to let in the first of the afternoon patients. She would hang them as soon as everyone had gone later on.

By half-past five the place was quiet. The last patient had been seen on his way, the nurses followed soon afterwards and lastly Miss Baird. Dr Marshall had already gone and she supposed that Dr Tavener had gone too. It would take her an hour to tidy up and make everything secure for the night but she would hang the curtains first...

They looked nice. Cut from the crimson curtains which had hung in the dining-room of her old home they were of heavy dull brocade, lined too, so that she had had very little sewing to do. She admired them drawn across the hated bars, and went upstairs to begin the business of clearing up.

She had a plastic bag with her and emptied the wastepaper baskets first—a job Miss Baird had impressed upon her as never to be forgotten. She went around putting things in their proper places, shaking the cushions in the waiting-room chairs, turning off lights, picking up magazines and putting them back on the table. She went along to Dr Tavener's rooms presently and was surprised to find the light on in his consulting-room.

He was at his desk and didn't look up. 'Be good enough to come back later, Miss Lorimer. I shall be here for another hour.'

She went away without saying anything and went back to the basement and began to get her supper. Percy, comfortably full, sat before the fire and the bread was in the oven. She whipped up a cheese soufflé, set the table with a cloth and put a small vase of flowers she had taken from the garden in its centre. She had been allowed to take essential things when she left her home—knives and spoons and forks and a plate or two. She had taken the silver and her mother's Coalport china plates and cups and saucers; she had taken the silver pepper-pot and salt cellar too, and a valuable teapot—Worcester. She would have liked to have taken the silver one but she hadn't quite dared—though she had taken the Waterford crystal jug and two wine-glasses.

She ate her soufflé presently, bit into an apple and made coffee before taking the bread from the oven. By then almost two hours had elapsed. She put her overall on once again and went upstairs to meet Dr Tavener as he left his rooms.

He stopped short when he saw her. 'Something smells delicious...'

'I have been making bread,' said Arabella, cool and polite and wishing that he would hurry up and go so that she could get her work done.

'Have you, indeed? And do I detect the smell of paint? Oh, do not look alarmed. It is very faint; I doubt if anyone noticed it.' He stared down at her. 'You are not afraid to be here alone?'

'No, sir.'

He wished her goodnight then, and she closed the door after him, bolting it and locking it securely. He paused on the pavement and looked down at the basement window. She had drawn the curtains and there was only a faint line of light showing. He frowned; he had no interest in the girl but living in that poky basement didn't seem right... He shrugged his shoulders; after all, she had chosen the job.

A week went by and Arabella had settled into a routine which ensured that she was seldom seen during working hours. Tidying Miss Baird's desk one evening, she had seen the list of patients for the following day, which gave her a good idea as to the times of their arrival. Now she checked each evening's list, for not all the patients came early in the day—once or twice there was no one until after ten o'clock, which gave her time to sweep and dust her own room and have a cup of coffee in peace. Nicely organised, she found life bearable if not exciting and, now that her room was very nearly as she wished it, she planned to spend part of her Sundays in the London parks. She missed the country. Indeed, come what may, she had promised herself that one day she would leave London but first she had to save some money before finding a job near her old home.

'We will go back,' she assured Percy, 'I promise you. Only we must stay here for a while—a year, perhaps two—just until we have enough money to feel safe.'

Only Dr Marshall came in on the Monday morning. Dr Tavener would be in directly after lunch, Miss Baird told her. He was taking a clinic at one of the nearby hospitals that morning. 'He's got a lot of patients too,' she warned Arabella. 'He probably won't be finished until early evening—he doesn't mind if he works late; he's not married and hasn't any ties.' She added kindly, 'If you want to run round to the shops I'll see to the phone and the door.'

'Thank you. If I could just get some vegetables? I can be back in fifteen minutes.'

'Don't hurry. You do cook proper meals for yourself?'

'Oh, yes. I have plenty of time in the evening.'

It was a cheerless morning, not quite October and already chilly. Arabella nipped smartly to the row of little shops, chose onions and turnips and carrots with care, bought meat from the butcher next door and hurried back. A casserole would be easy, she could leave it to cook gently and it wouldn't spoil however late she might have her supper. A few dumplings, she reflected, and a bouquet garni. It would do for the following day too.

She prepared it during the lunch hour, gave Percy his share of the meat and tidied herself ready to open the door for the first of Dr Tavener's patients.

The last patient went just before six o'clock and Arabella, having already tidied Dr Marshall's rooms, started to close the windows and lock up. There was still no sign of Dr Tavener when she had done this so she went down to the basement, set the table for her supper and checked the casserole in the oven. It was almost ready; she turned off the gas and set the dish on top of the stove, lifted the lid and gently stirred the contents— they smelled delicious.

Dr Tavener, on the point of leaving, paused in the hall, his splendid nose flaring as he sniffed the air. He opened the door to the basement and sniffed again and then went down the stairs and knocked at the door.

There was silence for a moment before he was bidden to enter—to discover Arabella standing facing the door, looking uncertain.

Neither of them spoke for a moment. Arabella was surprised to see him—she hadn't known who it was and had secretly been a little frightened—and as for Dr Tavener, he stood looking around him before remarking, 'Dear me, you have been busy and to very good effect.' He glanced at the table, nicely laid with a white cloth, the silver, one of the Coalport plates, a Waterford glass and a small vase of flowers. Their new caretaker was, indeed, a little out of the common. 'I hope I didn't startle you; something smelled so delicious that I had to see what it was. Your supper?'

She nodded.

He said with amusement, 'Are you a Cordon Bleu cook as well as a plumber?'

'Yes.'

'Surely if that is the case you could have found a more congenial post?'

'No one would have Percy.'

Dr Tavener studied the cat sitting before the little fire staring at him. 'A handsome beast.' And then, since their conversation was making no progress at all, 'Goodnight, Miss Lorimer.' As he turned away he added, 'You will lock up?'

'I have been waiting to do so, sir.' Her voice was tart.

His smile dismissed that. 'As long as you carry out your duties, Miss Lorimer.'

He had gone then, as quietly as he had come.

'He isn't just rude,' Arabella told Percy. 'He's very rude!'

When she heard the front door close she put the casserole in the oven again and went upstairs to clear up his rooms, close the windows and turn the key in the door before the lengthy business of locking and bolting the front door. Only then did she go back to her delayed supper.

Sitting by the gas fire later, sewing at the cushion covers, she allowed her thoughts to dwell upon Dr Tavener. He didn't like her, that was obvious, and yet he had come down to her room—something Dr Marshall would never think of doing. Perhaps she should have been more friendly, but were caretakers supposed to be friendly with their employers? She doubted that. He unsettled her. While her parents had been alive she had had friends, cheerful young men and women of her own age, but none of the young men had fallen in love with her, nor had she been particularly attracted to any of them. Dr Tavener wasn't like any of them. It wasn't only his good looks—perhaps it was because he was older. She gave up thinking about him and turned her attention to her work.

She had only brief glimpses of him for the rest of that week and beyond a terse greeting he didn't speak to her. On the other hand, Dr Marshall, while evincing no interest at all in her private life, was always friendly if they chanced to encounter each other.

Then Dr Tavener went to Oslo, his nurse took a holiday and Arabella found herself with less to do. True, she checked his rooms night and morning, but there was no need to Hoover and polish now he was away. There were fewer doorbells to answer too, so she had time to spare in which to make apple chutney from the wind-

falls dropping from the small old tree at the bottom of
the garden. She had, of course, asked Dr Marshall first
if she might have them and he had said yes, adding that
he had had no idea that they could be used. So for several
evenings there was a pleasant smell of cooking apples
coming from the basement. She made bread too, and a
batch of scones; and buns with currents—nicely iced;
and a sponge cake, feather-light. The tiny old-fashioned
pantry, its shelves empty for so long for Mrs Lane had
only fancied food out of tins, began to fill nicely.

Dr Tavener was due back on the following day, Miss
Baird told her. Not until the late afternoon, though, so
there would be no patients for him. 'And I dare say he'll
go straight home and come in the next morning.'

So Arabella gave his rooms a final dusting. There
were still some Doris pinks in the garden; she arranged
some in a glass vase and added some sprigs of lavender
and some veronica. The room was cool so they would
stay fresh overnight—she must remember to turn the
central heating on in the morning and light the gas fire.
She put everything ready for the nurse too, so that she
could make herself a cup of tea when she arrived, then
she went round checking the windows and the doors,
and went downstairs again.

Dr Marshall had a great number of patients the next
morning; she was kept busy answering the door and Dr
Tavener's nurse, short-tempered for some reason, found
fault with her because the central heating hadn't been
turned on sooner. In the afternoon it began to rain—a
steady downpour—so the patients left wet footprints
over the parquet flooring and dropped their dripping
umbrellas unheeding on to the two chairs which flanked
the side-table. Arabella had taken a lot of trouble to

clean them and polish them and now they were covered in damp spots. She would have liked to bang the door behind them as they left…

The house was quiet at last and she fetched her plastic bag, her dusters and polish, and lugged the Hoover from its place under the stairs. There had been no sign of Dr Tavener; he would have gone straight home as Miss Baird had suggested. Arabella bustled around, intent on getting back to her own room. Tea had been out of the question and she thought with pleasure of the supper she intended to cook—a Spanish omelette with a small salad. She had made soup yesterday, with bones and root vegetables, and she would have an apple or two and a handful of raisins. Bread and butter and a large pot of tea instead of coffee—what more could anyone want?

The weather had turned nasty, with a cold wind and heavy rain. It was a lonely sound beating on the windows; she wondered why it sounded so different from the rain on the windows of her home at Colpin-cum-Witham. There the wind used to sough through the trees—a sound she had loved. She had finished her tidying up when she remembered that the nurse had complained about the light in the waiting-room. The bulb wasn't strong enough, she had been told, and another one must replace it. She fetched it and then went to haul the step-ladder up from the basement so that she might reach the elaborate shade hanging from the ceiling.

She was on the top step when she heard the front door being opened, and a moment later Dr Tavener came into the room. He was bareheaded and carried his case in his hand. He put it down, lifted her down from the steps, took the bulb from her hand and changed it with the one already in the socket. Only then did he get down and bid her good evening.

Arabella, taken by surprise, hadn't uttered a sound. Now she found her voice and uttered a stiff thank you.

He stood looking at her. 'It's a filthy night,' he observed. 'You wouldn't be kind and make me a cup of tea or coffee—whichever is easiest?'

She started for the little kitchenette leading from his rooms but he put out a hand. 'No, no. No need here—may I not come downstairs with you?'

She eyed him uncertainly. 'Well, if you want to,' she said matter-of-factly. 'I was going to make tea.'

She went down to the basement, very conscious of him just behind her. The room looked surprisingly cosy; she had left one of the little table-lamps lit and the gas fire was on. She went to turn it up and said rather shyly, 'Please sit down, the tea won't take long.'

He sat down in the small shabby armchair and Percy got on to his knees. 'Have you had your supper? Do I smell soup?'

'Are you hungry?' She warmed the teapot and spooned in the tea.

'Ravenous. My housekeeper doesn't expect me back until the morning.' He watched her as she made the tea. 'I could go out for a meal, I suppose. Would you come with me?'

She looked up in surprise. 'Well, thank you for asking me but I've supper all ready.' She paused to think. 'You can share it if you would like to, though I'm not sure if it's quite the thing. I mean, I'm the caretaker!'

He smiled and said easily, 'You are also a splendid cook, are you not?' He got up out of his chair. 'And I don't believe there is a law against caretakers asking a guest for a meal.'

'Well, of course, put like that it seems quite...' She paused, at a loss for a word.

'Quite,' said Dr Tavener. 'What comes after the soup?'

She laid another place at the table. 'Well, a Spanish omelette with a salad. I haven't a pudding, but there is bread and butter and cheese...'

'Home-made bread?' And when she nodded he said, 'I can think of nothing nicer. While you are cooking the omelette I shall go and get a bottle of wine. Five minutes?'

He had gone. She heard the door close behind him and the car start up. She broke three eggs into a bowl and then a fourth—he was a very large man.

The omelette was ready to cook when he got back, put a bottle on the table and asked if she had a corkscrew. It was a good wine—a red burgundy of a good vintage, its cost almost as much as half of Arabella's pay-packet. He opened it to let it breathe.

Arabella was ladling soup into the large old-fashioned soup plates which had belonged to her grandmother. Dr Tavener, sampling it, acknowledged that it was worthy of the Coalport china in which it was served.

He fetched the wine and poured it as she dished up the omelette and, warmed by its delicious fruitiness, Arabella forgot to be a caretaker and was once again a well brought-up young lady with a pleasant social life. Dr Tavener, leading her on with quiet cunning, discovered a good deal more about her than she realised. Not that he asked questions but merely put in a word here and there, egging her on gently.

They finished the omelette and sat talking over coffee and slices of bread and butter and a piece of cheese. If he found the meal a trifle out of the ordinary way of things he gave no sign. Bread and butter, he discovered, when the bread had been baked by his hostess, was exactly the right way to finish his supper. Being a giant of a man, he ate most of the loaf and a good deal of the butter. She would have to go to the shops the next day...

It was almost ten o'clock when he went, taking her with him so that she could lock up after him. He stood on the pavement, thinking of her polite goodnight and listening to the bolts being shot home and the key turned in the lock. He had never worried about Mrs Lane being alone in the house for the simple reason that she frequently had had various members of her family spending a few days with her, but Arabella had no one. The idea of Arabella being alone at night nagged at him all the way to his home.

It was on the following Saturday afternoon that Arabella added another member to her household. She was returning from the shops, laden with a week's supply of basic food, taking shortcuts through the narrow streets which would bring her into Wigmore Street. It had been a dull, chilly day and bid fair to lapse into early dusk bringing a fine drizzle of rain. Head bowed against the damp wind, weighed down with her shopping, she turned down a short alleyway which would take her close to Dr Marshall's rooms.

She was almost at its end when a faint movement in the gutter caused her to stop. A puppy lay there, rolled up and moving to and fro, its yelps so faint that she could hardly hear them. She put down her plastic bags and bent to take a closer look. It was a pitiful sight, thin and very wet, and someone had tied its back legs together. Arabella let out a snort of rage and knelt down the better to deal with it. The cord was tight but roughly tied; it took only a moment to untie it and scoop up the small creature, pop him on top of her shopping and carry him back to her basement.

He was a very young puppy and, even if well fed and cared for, would have had no good looks. As it was he was a sorry sight, with tiny ribs showing through his dirty coat and sores on his flanks. Notwithstanding, he lay passive on the table while she gently examined him, and even waved a very long and rat-like tail. She dumped her shopping, fetched warm water and some old cloths, and cleaned him gently, wrapped him in an old curtain and set him before the gas fire where he lay too tired to move when Percy went to examine him in his turn.

'Bread and warm milk,' said Arabella who, living alone with only a cat for company, frequently uttered her thoughts out loud, and suited the action to the words. It was received thankfully and scoffed with pathetic speed so she gave him more warm milk with some vague idea about dehydration and then, aware of Percy's indignant stare, offered him his supper too, before taking off her jacket and putting away her shopping. She got her own tea presently, pausing frequently to look at the puppy. He was sleeping, uttering small yelps as he slept, and presently Percy stretched out beside him, with the air of someone doing a good deed, and curved himself round the small skinny creature.

'That's right, Percy,' encouraged Arabella. 'He could do with a good cuddle. He'll be a handsome dog if we look after him.'

He woke presently and she gave him some of Percy's food and took him into the dark garden, and when she went off to bed she lifted him on to its foot beside Percy. He looked better already. She woke in the night and found him still sleeping, but Percy had crept up the bed and was lying beside her.

It was then that she began to wonder what Dr Marshall was going to say when he discovered that she had a dog as well as a cat. Why should she tell him? The puppy was very young—his bark would be small and until he was much stronger he might not bark at all. Indeed, he would be no trouble for some time; he was far too weak to behave as a normal puppy would. Things settled to her satisfaction, she went back to sleep until Percy's nudges woke her once more.

Being Sunday, she had the place to herself and nothing could have been more convenient. The puppy, shivering with terror, was borne out into the garden again and then given his breakfast while Percy ate his, afterwards curling up before the fire and allowing the puppy to crouch beside him. Presently Percy stretched his length before the warmth and the puppy crept even closer and went to sleep.

He slept and ate all day and by the evening he cringed only occasionally, waving his ridiculous tail in an effort to show his gratitude.

'I shall keep you,' said Arabella. 'Percy likes you and so do I! And you're more than welcome.'

The puppy, unused to a kind voice, gave a very small squeaky bark, ate a second supper and went to sleep—this time with his ugly little head on Percy's portly stomach.

Monday came and with it a nasty nervous feeling on Arabella's part, but she went about her duties as usual and by the end of the day was lulled into a sense of security by the exemplary behaviour of the puppy who, doubtless because he was still very much under the weather, did nothing other than eat the food she offered him and sleep, keeping as close to a tolerant Percy as possible.

By the end of the week he had filled out considerably although he was still quite content to curl up and sleep. He went willingly enough into the garden before anyone was about and, although the dark evenings scared him, provided Percy was nearby he ventured on to the grass and even scampered around for a few minutes.

It was carelessness due to her overconfidence that was Arabella's undoing. On the Friday evening everyone left as usual and, after a quick reconnoitre upstairs to make sure that that really was the case, she went into the garden before she tidied the rooms. It was a fine clear evening and not quite dark and she took her torch and walked down the path while the animals pottered on the grass.

Dr Tavener, returning to fetch a forgotten paper, trod quietly through the empty rooms and, since there was still some light left, didn't bother to turn on his desk lamp. He knew where the paper was and he had picked it up and turned to go again when he glanced out of his window.

Arabella stood below, her torch shining on the animals.

'Well, I'm damned,' said Dr Tavener softly and watched her shepherd them indoors before going silently and very quickly back to the front door and then letting himself out into the street. He got into his car and drove himself home, laughing softly.

As for Arabella, blissfully unaware that she had been discovered, she gave her companions their suppers and went upstairs to clean and tidy up, then cooked her own meal before getting on with another cushion cover.

Saturday morning was busy. Dr Tavener, Miss Baird told her, had only two patients but he was going to the hospital and would probably not be back until after midday. 'So I'm afraid you won't be able to do your cleaning until he's gone again.'

Arabella, who turned the place upside-down on a Saturday, changed the flowers and polished everything possible, said she didn't mind. Secretly she was annoyed. She would have to do her weekly shopping and she didn't like to go out and leave him in his rooms—supposing the puppy were to bark? The shops closed at five o'clock— surely he wouldn't stay as late as that?

It was a relief when he came back just before everyone else went home, shut himself in his room for a while and then prepared to leave. Arabella was polishing the chairs in the waiting-room since Hoovering might disturb him and she heard him coming along the passage.

She had expected him to go straight to the door and let himself out but instead he stopped in the doorway, so she turned round to wish him good afternoon and found him staring at her. Her heart sank; he looked severe— surely he hadn't discovered about the puppy?

It seemed that he had. 'Since when have we had a dog in the house, Miss Lorimer?' His voice was silky and she didn't much care for it.

She put down her duster and faced him. 'He isn't a dog—he's a very small puppy.'

'Indeed? And have you Dr Marshall's permission to keep him here?'

'No. How did you know?'

'I saw him—and you—the other evening in the garden. I trust that he isn't rooting up the flowerbeds.'

She was suddenly fierce. 'If you'd been thrown in a gutter with your legs tied together and left to die you'd know what heaven it is to sniff the flowers.'

His mouth twitched. 'And you found him and of course brought him back with you?'

'Well, of course—and I cannot believe that, however ill-natured you are, you would have left him lying there.'

'You are quite right; I wouldn't. Perhaps if you could bear with my ill nature, I might take a look at him? He's probably in rather poor shape.'

'Oh, would you?' She paused on her way to the door. 'But you won't take him away and send him to a dogs' home? He's so very small.'

'No, I won't do that.'

She went ahead of him down the stairs and opened the basement door. Percy, asleep on the end of the bed, opened an eye and dozed off again but the puppy tumbled on to the floor and trotted towards them, waving his ridiculous tail.

Dr Tavener bent and scooped him up and tucked him under an arm.

'Very small,' he observed, 'and badly used too.' He was gently examining the little beast. 'One or two nasty sores on his flank...' He felt the small legs. 'How long have you had him?'

'Since last Saturday. I thought he was going to die.'

'You have undoubtedly saved his life. He needs a vet, though.' He looked at Arabella and smiled—a quite different man from the austere doctor who strode in and out of his consulting-room with barely a glance if they should meet—and she blinked with surprise. 'If I return at about four o'clock would you bring him to a vet with me? He is a friend of mine and will know if there is anything the little chap needs.'

Arabella goggled at him. 'Me? Go to the vet with you?'

'I don't bite,' said Dr Tavener mildly.

She went pink. 'I beg your pardon. I was only surprised. It's very kind of you. Only, please don't come before four o'clock because I've the week's shopping to do. It won't take long, will it? Percy likes his supper...'

'I don't imagine it will take too much time but you could leave—er—Percy's supper for him, couldn't you?'

'Well, yes.' She took the puppy from him. 'You're very kind.'

'In between bouts of ill nature,' he reminded her gently. Then watched the pretty colour in her cheeks. He went to the door. 'I will be back at four o'clock.'

Arabella crammed a lot into the next few hours. There was still the rubbish to take out to the dustbins outside and the brass on the front door to polish; she would see to those later, she told herself, changing into her decent suit and good shoes and doing her face and her hair. It was important to look as little like a caretaker as possible—she wouldn't want Dr Tavener to be ashamed of her. She took all the money she had with her, remembering the vet's bills for the dogs when her parents had been alive and, the picture of unassuming neatness, she went to the front door punctually at four o'clock.

He came in as she put her hand on the doorknob. He didn't waste time in civilities. 'Well? Where is the little beast?'

'In the basement. He's not allowed up here. I'll fetch him and bring him out to the car from my front door.'

'Do that. I'll be with you in a moment.' He went along

to his rooms and she heard him phone as she went downstairs.

He was waiting by the car as she went through the door and up the steps with the puppy tucked under an arm and ushered her into the front seat, got in beside her and drove off.

The puppy was frightened and Arabella, concerned with keeping him quiet, hardly noticed where they were going. She looked up once and said, 'Oh, isn't that the Zoo?' and Dr Tavener grunted what she supposed to be yes. When he stopped finally and helped her out she looked around her with interest. She didn't know London very well—in happier days she and her mother had come up to shop or go to a theatre, and birthdays had been celebrated by her father taking them out to dine.

'Where is this?' she asked now.

'Little Venice. The vet lives in this house. His surgery is in the Marylebone Road but he agreed to see the puppy here.'

'That's very kind of him.' She went with him up the steps of the solid town house and, when the door was opened by a sober-looking woman in an apron, followed the doctor inside.

'He's expecting us, Mrs Wise,' said Dr Tavener easily. 'Are we to go up?'

'Yes, sir, you're expected.'

They were met at the head of the stairs by a man of the doctor's age, tall and thin, already almost bald. 'Come on in,' he greeted them. 'Where's this puppy, Titus?'

Dr Tavener stood aside so that Arabella came into view. 'This is Miss Arabella Lorimer—John Clarke, a wizard with animals.' He waited while they shook hands. 'Hand over the puppy, Miss Lorimer.'

They all went into a pleasant room, crowded with books and papers. There were two cats asleep on a chair and a black Labrador stretched out before a cheerful fire. 'Sit down,' invited Mr Clarke. 'I'll take a quick look.' He glanced at Arabella. 'Titus has told me about his rescue. At first glance I should imagine that good food and affection will soon put him on his feet.'

He bent over the little beast, examining him carefully and very gently. 'Nothing much wrong. I'll give you some stuff to put on those sores and I'll give him his injections while he's here. There's nothing broken or damaged, I'm glad to say. What's his name?'

'He hasn't got one yet.' She smiled at Mr Clarke, who smiled back.

'You can decide on that as you go home.' He handed the puppy back and she thanked him.

'Would you send the bill or shall I...?'

'Oh, I don't charge for emergencies or accidents,' said Mr Clarke cheerfully. 'Bring him for a check-up in a month or so—or earlier if you're worried. There will be a fee for that. Titus knows where the surgery is.'

'Thank you very much. I hope we haven't disturbed your Saturday afternoon.'

He flicked a glance at Dr Tavener's bland face. 'Not in the least. Nice to meet you and don't hesitate to get in touch if you are worried.'

Getting into the car again Arabella said, 'It was very kind of you, Dr Tavener, to bring us to the vet. Mr Clarke is a very nice man, isn't he? We've taken up a lot of your time. If you would drop us off at a bus stop we can go home...'

'Have you any idea which bus to catch?'

'Well, no, but I can ask.'

'I have a better idea. We will have tea and I will drive you back afterwards.'

'Have tea? Where? And really there is no need.'

'I said, "have tea", did I not? I live in the next street and my housekeeper will be waiting to make it. And don't fuss about Percy—we have been away for rather less than an hour and tea will take a fraction of that time.'

'The puppy?'

'Is entitled to his tea as well.' He had turned into a pleasant street bordering the canal and stopped before his house. 'Let us have no more questions!'

Chapter 3

Clutching the puppy, Arabella was swept into his house, one of several similar houses with their backs overlooking the canal and their fronts restrainedly Georgian. The hall was square with a curved staircase to one side and several doors leading from it. Out of one of these emerged a large, bony woman with a severe hairstyle and a long thin face.

'Ah, Alice. Miss Lorimer—this is my housekeeper, Mrs Turner. Alice, I've brought Miss Lorimer back for tea; could we have it presently?'

Arabella offered a hand and Mrs Turner shook it and said, 'How do you do?' in a severe manner and cast a look at the puppy. 'In five minutes, sir. And perhaps the young lady would like to leave her jacket.'

'No need,' he said cheerfully. 'She won't be staying long—it can stay on a chair.' He took the puppy as he spoke and Arabella took off her jacket and laid it tidily on a rather nice Regency elbow chair and went with him into the drawing-room.

It was large, running from front to back of the house, the back French windows opening on to a small wrought-iron balcony which overlooked the canal. She crossed the room, dimly aware of its beauty but intent on looking out of the window. 'It isn't like London at all,' she declared, 'and there's a garden...'

As indeed there was, below the balcony—small, high-walled, screened from the houses on either side by ornamental trees and shrubs, with the end wall built over the water.

Dr Tavener stood watching her and saying nothing and presently, aware of his silence, she turned to look at him. 'I'm sorry, I've been rude, but it was such a lovely surprise.'

He smiled then. 'Yes, isn't it? I've lived here for some years and it still surprises me. Come and sit down and we'll have tea.'

She looked around her then, at the comfortable chairs and the wide sofa before the fire; the Chippendale gilt-wood mirror over the fireplace and the rosewood table behind the sofa; the mahogany tripod tables with their lamps and the Dutch marquetry display cabinets each side of the fireplace. It was a beautiful room, furnished beautifully. There was a rosewood writing-table under the windows, its surface covered by silver-framed photos. She would have liked to have examined them but good manners forbade that so she sat down composedly in one of the armchairs as Mrs Turner came in with the tea tray.

Cucumber sandwiches, muffins in a silver dish and a rich fruit cake. She sighed silently and swallowed the lump in her throat; it was a long time since she had seen such a tea, eaten and drunk from fine china with the tea poured from a silver pot.

'Be mother,' invited the doctor, and sat down opposite her. He still had the puppy in his arms.

'Shall I have him?'

'No. No, he is no trouble. It is a pity that my own dog isn't here. She's a gentle creature—a golden Labrador—she would have mothered him.'

Arabella opened her mouth to ask him where she was and stopped just in time. Perhaps he would tell her. He didn't, but asked if he shouldn't be given a name.

She bit into a sandwich. 'Well, yes. Something rather grand, I thought, to make up for the beastly time he's had.'

'What a good idea. Have some of this cake—Mrs Turner is a good cook.' He smiled a little. 'But I'm talking to one, aren't I?'

She wasn't sure about the smile—perhaps he was being a bit sarcastic.

'What kind of a dog is he?'

'Rather mixed, I fancy; the ears are very like a spaniel's and I imagine he will grow to some considerable size—look at his paws. I'm not sure about that tail. As to the name…how about Bassett?'

She gave him a thoughtful look and then laughed. 'Of course—how clever you are. Bassett's Allsorts!'

When she laughed she looked almost pretty, he decided. It would be interesting to find out more about her; when she forgot to be the caretaker she was someone quite different.

However, she hadn't forgotten. She put down her cup and got to her feet. 'I've stayed longer than I intended. I hope I haven't spoilt your afternoon, sir.'

He didn't try to keep her but fetched her jacket and settled her with Bassett in the car, making pleasant conversation as he did so. He went with her into the rooms at Wigmore Street when they arrived, checking that everything was as it should be, before bidding her a coolly friendly good evening and opening the door. He was closing it behind him when she cried, 'Stop, oh, do stop. Must I tell Dr Marshall about Bassett?'

'Of course. On Monday morning before his patients come.' He stared down at her troubled face. 'I will have a word with him first—he is a very kind man and besides, you are a very good caretaker.'

'Oh, will you? You promise? You won't forget?'

His eyes were cold. 'I keep my promises, Miss Lorimer, and I have an excellent memory.'

'Oh dear, I've annoyed you.'

'No, you don't annoy me; you surprise me, vex me and intrigue me, but that is all.' He nodded and this time the door closed firmly behind him, leaving her in the hall, her thoughts in a fine muddle.

She had forgotten to thank him for her tea too. She went down to her room and attended to the animals' wants and then went back to finish her cleaning. Tomorrow, if it was fine enough, she would take Bassett for a walk—Regent's Park wasn't too far away. She would have to carry him, of course, for she had no lead and he had no collar. She dismissed Dr Tavener from her thoughts. He had been kind and helpful but he didn't like her—worse, she doubted if he had formed any opinion of her at all. She was of no interest to him whatsoever, although he was prepared to help her if necessary—just as he would help a stranger who had stumbled in the street, or an old lady to cross a road. It was mortifying but it made sense.

She enjoyed her Sunday, walking briskly in the park with Bassett tucked under her arm and going back to her dinner—lamp chop, potato purée, sprouts and carrots cooked with sugar and butter. The three of them ate their meal and settled down for the afternoon before tea by the fire. Really a very pleasant day, decided Arabella, getting ready for bed later, and she was so lucky to have a home of her own and a job. She had managed all day to forget about seeing Dr Marshall in the morning but she woke in the night and worried about it, dropping off again at last with the thought that Dr Tavener had said he would have a word. 'I dare say,' she said, addressing the sleeping animals, 'he is a very nice man under that distant manner. If I knew him better I might even like him.'

Dr Tavener, driving himself home in the early hours of the morning after an urgent summons to a patient's bedside, was thinking about her too. He had telephoned Dr Marshall and told him about Bassett, and James Marshall, good-natured and amused, had agreed to allow the puppy to stay.

They had laughed about it together but now, driving through the silent streets, his thoughts were more serious. Arabella was a nice girl; she shouldn't be a caretaker in the first place. She might have no qualifications but she came from a good background; he remembered the nicely laid table when he had had his supper with her and her unselfconscious assurance at his house that afternoon. This wasn't her kind of life at all but he could see no way of bettering it. Finding something more suited to her would be difficult because of the cat and puppy

and he knew enough about her to realise that she would
never give them up.

He let himself into his house and Beauty, whom he
had fetched that afternoon, came to meet him and went
with him to the kitchen while he made himself a cup
of coffee.

He sat, a tired man, drinking it with her at his feet.
'The answer is to find her a husband,' he told her. Beauty
thumped her tail and he rubbed her ears gently, saw her
into her basket and went back upstairs to his bed—there
were still two or three hours before he needed to get up.
His last thought before he slept was that finding exactly
the right man for Arabella would be a difficult task.

Arabella, very neat in her overall, presented herself
at Dr Marshall's desk as soon as he was sitting at it.
His good morning was kindly. 'Problems?' he wanted
to know.

She didn't beat about the bush, but she didn't mention
Dr Tavener either. He might have forgotten to speak to
Dr Marshall and that might be awkward. He hadn't forgotten. Dr Marshall smiled at her. 'Ah, yes, Titus tells
me that we have acquired a dog. Splendid, I have no
objection just as long as you don't let him loose on our
patients. Quite comfortable, are you? Settled in now?'

She could have flung her arms round his neck. 'Yes,
thank you, sir.'

'Run along, then, the doorbell will be ringing at any
moment now.'

As she was leaving he stopped her. 'I think it would
be more suitable if we called you Arabella. You have
no objection?'

'No, sir.' They could call her anything they liked; Bassett was hers.

She was admitting a patient when Dr Tavener arrived, nodded a good morning and went straight to his room. The next patient to arrive was for him—a tall, good-looking girl, dressed expensively and skilfully made-up.

No one bothered to give Arabella more than a fleeting glance and sometimes a vague smile of thanks and she was about to do the same but stopped short. 'Arabella—whatever are you doing here? Good gracious—that frightful overall and your hair all screwed up.'

Arabella closed the door. 'Hello, Daphne. I work here. You're here to see Dr Tavener? He's down the hall...'

Daphne laughed. 'Oh, my dear, I know where he is—we're old friends. But what do you do exactly?'

'I'm the caretaker.'

Daphne pealed with laughter. 'My goodness, what a marvellous joke.' She would have said more but the doorbell was rung again and Arabella went to answer it. When she turned round Daphne was gone.

Presently, ushered into Dr Tavener's room, Daphne sat down opposite his desk. 'Hello, Titus. It's ages since we saw you—Mother was asking what had happened to you. I'm not ill but I do wish you'd give me something for my headaches.' She crossed an elegant leg. 'I've had such a surprise—Arabella, a girl I know, opened the door. She said she was the caretaker, of all things! A caretaker—I ask you. I expect you know she was left penniless when her parents were killed some months ago. A bit of a come-down from living in comfort. Not a great friend, of course,' she laughed. 'We lived some miles away from each other but we had mutual friends...' She smiled charmingly. 'Now, what about my headaches...?'

He had sat quietly while she talked, now he said blandly, 'You tell me where the pain is exactly. Perhaps you are worried about something or doing too much?'

'Parties, you mean? Well, I do enjoy life—why not? We're only young once and besides, it helps one from getting bored.'

'The boredom probably accounts for the headaches. I suggest that you miss a few late nights and take a long walk every day. Cut down on the drinks and go to bed at a reasonable time.'

She pouted prettily. 'Oh, Titus, you stuffy old thing! And I was going to invite you to come home for the weekend but now I shan't.'

'I'm not free in any case,' he told her blandly. He stood up and handed her the prescription he had written. 'Take these for a week and see how you get on. If you're no better we'll delve deeper. I'm sure it's nothing for you to worry about.'

He held the door open for her and she smiled up at him as she went past. A lovely face, he reflected, but nothing behind it. If he was to marry it would have to be a woman of intelligence, who would listen to him without twiddling her earrings or examining her nails. She had no need to be beautiful or even pretty—the right clothes would take care of that... It was only recently that he had wished for a companion. He was, he considered, past the age of falling in love and besides, a marriage founded on liking and compatibility was more likely to succeed than one plunged into in the heat of the moment.

He sat down at his desk, dismissing the matter from his mind, and picked up the next patient's notes.

His day's work done, his thoughts reverted to Arabella. It was unthinkable that she should remain as a caretaker—polishing and Hoovering and cleaning windows and doors, dragging out the rubbish to be collected, polishing the brass and, above all, being alone at night with no protection save that of a very small puppy and a cat. The matter needed urgent consideration.

As for Arabella, she avoided him as much as possible while at the same time wishing that she knew more about him. The small glimpse she had had of his life had intrigued her. She had supposed him to be a dyed-in-the-wool bachelor but, listening from time to time to the nurses gossiping, she had formed the opinion that he was much sought-after socially—a matrimonial prize several women were after. Hadn't she seen with her own eyes how her erstwhile friend Daphne had smiled up at him? She thought that it might be rather nice to be married to someone like him, to live in a lovely house and meet people again. To have clothes—new clothes, bought without having to look at the price-ticket first. That, she told herself, was no reason for marrying. She finished tidying the rooms and went downstairs to get her supper and take the animals for their evening stroll in the garden.

Saturday came round once more. Arabella did her shopping, gave the rooms their usual turn-out and went into the garden to pick some fresh flowers. Bassett had filled out and lost most of his timidity and followed Percy's dignified progress from one flowerbed to the other. Tomorrow, she promised him, he would wear his new collar and walk beside her on his lead in the park.

The evenings were getting colder; they all went indoors presently and had their suppers and then shared the warmth of the gas fire. The cushion covers were finished so she had brought some of the magazines down from the waiting-room and curled up to read them.

Before going to bed she went back upstairs once more to check that everything was closed and locked. The upstairs flat was empty again but she had grown used to being on her own.

She enjoyed every minute of Sunday. The walk in the park had been a great success; Bassett had behaved well, trotting along on his lead, chasing the fallen leaves and barking his small treble bark. They had gone back to Percy's welcome and had their tea and afterwards she sat down and did her sums for the week.

Even with three mouths to feed she was saving a little money each week. The future was uncertain; even if she stayed with the doctors for the rest of her working life, she would still need money when she retired. It seemed a long way ahead, but she might be ill, lose her job, need a home while she found something else. In a month or two, when she felt more secure, she would start looking for a post as a cook. Surely there was somewhere and someone who wouldn't object to a cat and a dog? It was going to be difficult and she was happy enough in her basement but she was aware that both the doctors felt an uneasiness about her working for them. She suspected that Dr Marshall had given her her job on a sudden whim and while he might not be regretting it he could be having second thoughts...

She finished the sums, gave Percy and Bassett their

suppers and went into the garden with them and, once indoors again, bolted the door before beginning to get her own supper. That eaten, she decided to check the rooms upstairs and go to bed early. Life, she decided, though dull, was at least secure.

Before she slept she allowed herself to daydream a little. Being a practical girl, she didn't allow her thoughts to dwell on the prospect of some young man falling head over heels in love with her and marrying her out of hand, but on the miraculous offer of a job as cook—a highly paid job in some stately home—with a cottage in the grounds and no objection to pets…

The partners had arrived early on the Monday morning and Dr Marshall had wandered along to Dr Tavener's rooms. 'Nice morning,' he observed affably. 'The garden looks pretty good too.' He glanced at the small chrysanths arranged on the desk. 'Keeps the place looking nice, does our Arabella.'

Dr Tavener had been writing; now he put down his pen. 'James, we shall have to do something about her. We ought never to have given her the job in the first place. I had a patient the other morning—she had been at school with Arabella, known her for years, saw a lot of her before the parents were killed.'

'And this friend, was she shocked at Arabella working in such a lowly capacity?'

Dr Tavener frowned. 'I believe she was rather amused…'

'Hardly a friend. I imagine Arabella is very proud, not wishing to be an embarrassment to her friends, going it alone.'

Dr Tavener said deliberately, 'I don't like the idea of her being alone here at night.'

His partner peered at him through his specs. 'No? Perhaps you are right; she's rather small although not at all nervous, she told me.'

'She would have said anything to get a roof over her head.'

'So what are we to do about it? Other than finding her a husband...'

'She is a Cordon Bleu cook. If we could find someone who would accept those animals she would be safe and secure and living in surroundings more suited to her.'

'Until she finds a husband. She would make a good wife and a handy one too— no need to call out the plumber or the electrician. Come to think of it, Titus, she would suit you very well and it's time you had a wife—patients like a married man!'

Titus didn't answer and Dr Marshall said hastily, 'Only joking. Time I went back, I suppose. Are you fully booked this morning?'

'Yes, and this afternoon. I've a clinic this evening.'

'You must come to dinner soon—I'll get Angie to phone you.'

'I'd like that, thanks.'

Dr Tavener opened the case sheets before him but made no effort to read them. That was the solution, he decided: to find a job for Arabella. In the country—because she was a country girl at heart. The place would be very empty without her, though.

Arabella, unaware of the future being planned for her, went about her chores, bought some wool going cheap because of the colour—a serviceable brown which wasn't selling well—and started on a sweater, keeping a loving eye on Percy and Bassett.

Dr Tavener, a man of considerable wealth, owned a pleasant small manor house in Wiltshire which had been in the family for more than two hundred years. Whenever his work permitted he drove himself back there, taking Beauty with him, spending his days gardening and walking. His parents were dead but his grandmother lived there with a meek companion, looked after by Butter and his wife who had also looked after his mother and father and probably, if they lived long enough, would look after him in his old age. He couldn't imagine the place without them.

He went there the following weekend, on a blustery autumn day. Twenty miles or so beyond Swindon he turned off the motorway to take a minor road towards Tetbury. Then, turning off again, took a narrow lane which brought him eventually to a small village and, beyond it, to his home.

There were lights in the windows and smoke coming from several of its elaborate brick chimney-pots, and as he stopped before the door it opened to allow a dog to rush out and race to the car, barking happily. Beauty's brother, Duke. He circled the car, delighted to see its occupants, and the three of them went indoors to where Butter was waiting.

'Good to see you again, Master Titus,' said Butter. 'Mrs Butter has tea all ready and waiting. I'll take the dogs along to the kitchen for their meal. Mrs Tavener is in the drawing room.'

Dr Tavener crossed the polished wood floor of the hall and went into the room—long and low-ceilinged,

its strapwork still perfect, with windows at either end of
it—lattice windows set in square bays—and the heavy
velvet curtains blending with the dark green and russet
of the vast carpet.

It was furnished with a clever mixture of Jacobean
and early Georgian chairs and tables and the fireplace
was of the Queen Anne period—ornate and heavily or-
namented with a vast mirror above it. On either side of
it there were comfortable armchairs and a great sofa but
the two ladies in the room were sitting in upright Regency armchairs with a small table between them upon
which lay playing cards.

Dr Tavener crossed the room and bent to kiss his
grandmother—a handsome old lady, sitting very upright, her features severe. She smiled as he greeted her.
'Titus, my dear, how pleasant to see you again. You don't
come home enough.'

'My home is in London,' he pointed out mildly. 'At
least while I'm working.'

'Yes, yes and I'm sure it is a very handsome house,
but this is the family home.' She paused. 'It is time you
had a family, Titus.'

He only smiled and went to shake her companion's
hand. Miss Welling was a thin lady of uncertain age
with a sharp nose, myopic brown eyes and an anxious
expression. There was no need for the anxiety—she received nothing but kindness and consideration from her
employer—but meekness and anxiety seemed to be her
nature and old Mrs Tavener might look severe but she
would never tax her with questions and over the years
had come to accept Miss Welling's cautious approach
to life.

Miss Welling greeted Dr Tavener in a pleased voice,

for she liked him, then excused herself with the plea that she would see if the tea tray was ready and slid out of the room.

'The dear creature,' said Mrs Tavener, 'anyone would think that I beat her. Come and sit down and tell me what you have been doing lately.'

He drew up a chair and embarked on a brief account of his days. The tea was brought in presently and afterwards he took the dogs for a walk in the deepening twilight. When he returned it was to find his grandmother alone. 'Miss Welling has gone to tidy herself, my dear. We have half an hour to ourselves—time in which to tell me what is on your mind.'

When he gave her a half-smiling look she said, 'You are very like your father—the bigger the problem, the more bland the face. Fallen in love at last?'

'No. No, I believe that I shall never do that seriously enough to marry. But I do have a problem…' He told her about Arabella, his voice placid and disinterested, and when he had finished he asked, 'Have you any ideas, Grandmother?'

'The young woman seems to be in most unsuitable work. On the other hand, Titus, she has a home of sorts, independence and is able to keep her pets with her. A sense of security must be very important to her—to be pitched out without warning into poverty and loneliness must have been such a shock. To subject her to an unknown future seems unkind, even if the work was more congenial, and who knows if she would be happy? Besides, you would lose touch with her. You like her?'

'Yes, I do. Surprisingly we have a good deal in common; she is undemanding as a companion and not above treating me with a tart tongue.'

Mrs Tavener hid a smile. 'She sounds as though she is very well able to look after herself, although I do agree with you that being in that place alone at night isn't quite the thing.' She glanced at him. 'But I will ask around, my dear, and if I hear of anything at all suitable I will let you know at once. The girl's presentable?'

'Yes—good clothes but out of date, nice manners, no looks to speak of but nice eyes—beautiful eyes—and a pleasant voice.'

Mrs Tavener considered this reply and decided not to comment upon it. Instead she said, 'I shall be coming up to town next week to shop. Will you give us beds for the night? Miss Welling will come with me, of course, but I promise you we will be no trouble to you.'

'That will be delightful. Would you like to go to the theatre? There are some good plays on. I'm afraid I shall be away from home all day but I can make sure I'm free in the evenings.'

'A play would be most enjoyable. Something romantic with music if possible. Will three days be too much for you?'

'Make it longer if you wish, Grandmother. You know you're always more than welcome.'

'Yes, my dear, I do know. We will come up on the Tuesday and return here on Thursday evening. Butter shall drive us up and fetch us again.' She paused. 'There's no reason why Mrs Butter shouldn't come up with him, then they could drive up early in the morning and she could go to the shops for an hour or two before he picks us up.'

'A good idea. Make any arrangements you like with Mrs Turner.'

'Thank you. Would it bother you to take a look at

Miss Welling while we're there? She can go along to your rooms—I'll put her in a taxi. She won't admit it but I don't think she sleeps very well.'

'Yes, of course. I'll get Miss Baird to make an appointment and phone you.'

Miss Welling came into the room and they talked of other things.

He took the old lady to church on Sunday morning and after lunch spent the rest of the day reading the Sunday papers, taking the dogs for a walk, having his tea and then driving himself back to his house in Little Venice. He made a detour when he reached town so that he could drive along Wigmore Street. The basement curtains were closed but there was a fringe of light showing round them and he stifled the urge to knock at the door and spend an hour with Arabella, telling her about his weekend. 'Ridiculous,' he told himself sharply so that Beauty, sitting beside him half-asleep, gave a sleepy bark.

Mrs Tavener was driven up to London on Tuesday and by the time Dr Tavener got home that evening she was settled in, sitting in his drawing-room playing Racing Demon with Miss Welling. They spent a pleasant evening together and he told her that he had got tickets for a long-running musical which he hoped that she would like. He had seen it himself in the company of an old friend's daughter who had been visiting in London. He hadn't liked the show particularly but perhaps that was because he had found his companion a singularly vapid girl with no conversation who was everlastingly fidgeting with her hair or her lipstick.

As for Miss Welling, she was to see him the next

morning despite her timid objections that he was a busy
man and she was perfectly well. 'Well, of course you
are,' he had told her kindly, 'but since you are here it is
a splendid opportunity to have a check-up. It won't take
too long and I'll put you in a taxi afterwards so that you
can come straight back here.'

Arabella, checking Miss Baird's list of patients, noticed that Dr Tavener had added a name at the end of
Miss Baird's list. A Miss Welling—and not until eleven
o'clock. Usually on Wednesday he left soon after ten
o'clock to take an outpatients clinic at one of the hospitals. She had seen him only briefly on Monday and Tuesday and he had acknowledged her good morning with a
brisk nod; she would try to avoid him in future since he
seemed to dislike her so much. She puzzled over that,
for he had been kind about Bassett and when she had
had tea with him he had been so friendly that she had
quite forgotten that she was his caretaker...

Wednesday morning was dark and cold and driz-
zling with rain, and those patients she admitted were
short-tempered as a result. To her pleasant good morning they either grunted or let loose a string of complaints
while they shook umbrellas over her pleasingly polished
floor or hung their damp raincoats over her arms. It
was a bit depressing, so when the bell rang once again
and she opened the door it was a pleasant surprise to be
greeted cheerfully by the elderly lady wishing to enter.
She was accompanied by a lady considerably younger
with a woebegone face who none the less answered Arabella's cheerful greeting with a smile.

'Miss Welling? If you would see the receptionist and

then go down the passage to Dr Tavener's waiting-room. Shall I take your coat?'

The elderly lady gave her companion a poke in the ribs. 'Yes, go along, do. I'll be in the waiting-room.'

She turned to Arabella. 'A wretched day, is it not? London can be horrid in this weather. You live here, I expect?'

'Oh, yes. I'm the caretaker. Would you like me to have your coat too?'

'No. No, thank you. You don't look very much like a caretaker.'

Arabella blushed but the lady was old and perhaps she was just being inquisitive. 'I'm very content; it's a good job. Shall I show you to Dr Tavener's waiting-room?'

'By all means, and here is Miss Welling back again. Good day to you.'

Mrs Tavener swept away with Miss Welling at her heels and Arabella went downstairs. Miss Welling was the last patient; she would have a quick cup of coffee before seeing her out presently.

Miss Welling, emerging from Dr Tavener's consulting-room some twenty minutes later, was accompanied by him to the door. 'I'll arrange a taxi—' He broke off at the sight of his grandmother sitting very erect in the waiting-room. Her 'Good morning, Titus,' was graciously said but she smiled as she spoke.

He said nothing for the moment but smiled a little in his turn before crossing the room and taking her hand. 'What do you think of her?' he asked. 'For that is why you are here, is it not?'

'Of course, you are quite right, Titus, she is most unsuitable. You will have to think of something else. As you said, she is quite without good looks. Although, of course, good looks don't matter if one is a good cook.' She stood up. 'Did you find Miss Welling in good health?'

'On the whole, yes. May we discuss that this evening? I'm late for my clinic.'

His nurse was in the examination room so he saw the two ladies to the door and a few minutes later left himself, so that when Arabella came upstairs again there was only his nurse there, grumbling because he intended to come back that afternoon and she had hoped to be free to go home early.

Arabella, nipping through the rain to the shops, reflected that Dr Tavener probably worked too hard. She hoped that he had time to eat proper meals and had enough sleep. It was difficult to tell because he was always beautifully turned out and he had the kind of face which gave away nothing of his feelings.

Choosing carrots and turnips with a careful eye, she reminded herself to stop thinking about him—it was such a waste of time.

Chapter 4

Dr Tavener did not know when the preposterous idea first entered his head. Perhaps at a dinner party as he sat with a charming woman on either side of him, both looking for a husband and both divorced. Not a conceited man, he was aware all the same that he had good looks, a splendid physique and more than enough money to satisfy the greediest of women. Or it might have been one early morning, when he had gone to his manor for a weekend and taken the dogs out into the garden before breakfast. It had been a cold night and the frost had iced every blade of grass and twig and he had wanted Arabella there beside him to enjoy it too. 'Not that I am in love with her,' he had told Beauty. 'It is merely that she is a good companion.' She would stand between him and the tiresome women who were introduced to him by his friends in the mistaken idea that he might like

to make one of them his wife. She would be restful to
come home to…

Because the idea was so preposterous, he avoided
her as much as possible. Arabella wondered what she
had done to annoy him, for if they did meet the look he
cast at her was thunderous. It made her unhappy, for he
had been kind, and from time to time had smoothed her
path. She did her best to forget it.

It was in the middle of the week, in the morning while
she was still getting the rooms ready for the day, that the
electricity failed. A fuse probably, she thought, and since
it was still dark groped her way to the hall where she had
had the forethought to put a torch in the table drawer.

The electrics were in a cupboard at the back of the
hall. She peered inside, saw what had to be done and,
since the fuses were in a box tucked away behind everything else, she got down on her knees the better to
get at them.

Dr Tavener, arriving early, had come in silently and
stopped short at the sight of Arabella's shapely person sticking out of the cupboard but before he could
speak she had crawled out backwards and got to her
feet, clutching the new fuse. She spoke tartly. 'Well, you
might have rung the bell or something—I might have
known it would be you.'

She wiped a dirty hand over a cheek and left a
smudge.

'How did you know that it was I?'

'Your feet…'

'My feet?' He had put down the bag and taken the
fuse from her.

She went a little pink. 'Well, I get to know the sound of people's feet.'

He nodded and went past her, fixed the fuse, and came back to where she had resumed Hoovering. She switched off to thank him and when she would have switched on again he put out a hand and stopped her. 'A moment, Arabella. There is something I wish to say to you. Unfortunately there is not time to explain fully but I should like to make you a proposal.'

At her look of astonishment he added kindly. 'Don't look so surprised. I should like you to consider marrying me. If you will think about it we can discuss it sensibly at a later date.'

He smiled then. 'Don't let me keep you from your work.' He had gone into his room and shut the door quietly behind him, leaving her with her mouth open, a white face and a rapid pulse.

As for Dr Tavener, he sat down at his desk and wondered if he had gone mad.

Arabella had no doubts about it—he had been overworking and had had a brainstorm, whatever that was, and hadn't known what he was saying. She would ignore the whole thing, let him see that she hadn't taken him seriously.

The last patient had gone by five o'clock that afternoon and everyone else followed him within half an hour. Arabella collected her cleaning things and went upstairs to tidy up. She had finished and was tying up the plastic bag of rubbish when Dr Tavener returned.

He had a bottle under one arm and a box with a Harrods label in his hand. 'May I come to supper? You can't leave the place, otherwise I would have given you dinner at home.'

She put the sack down. 'Look, I do understand. I expect you've been working too hard and thought you were talking to someone else. It doesn't matter a bit...'

He took the sack from her. 'No, you don't understand and I'm perfectly sound in my head. Shall we have supper and talk?' He smiled suddenly and she found herself smiling back. 'I have a great deal to explain.'

'Very well.' She led the way downstairs and he took the sack outside to the refuse bins, giving her the bottle and the box to hold. He hadn't been mad at all, he reflected, washing his hands at the sink—this was going to be one of the sanest things he had ever done.

Arabella peered into her small pantry. She had decided to have an egg and a baked potato for her supper but that wouldn't do for her guest. She measured macaroni and put it on to cook, grated cheese and beat an egg, scrubbed two more potatoes and put them in the oven and all the while he sat with Percy on his knee and Bassett curled up on his shoes, saying nothing. It was unnerving. She thought of several things to say but none of them seemed suitable. She held her tongue and laid the table.

He had brought a bottle of claret with him this time. He uncorked it and left it to breathe and presently he poured it and gave her a glass.

She sipped. 'Delicious,' she said. 'What's in the box?'

'Fruit pies. Can you sit down for a while or must you stay by the stove?'

She had put the macaroni cheese in the oven—it and the potatoes would be another half-hour and there was only a lettuce to dress.

She sat in the armchair and he took a chair from beside the table and sat opposite her. 'I appreciate the fact that I must have taken you by surprise but I do assure you that I was serious.' When she would have spoken he went on, 'No, please, let me explain. I am forty years old, Arabella—not a young man. I have been in and out of love on numerous occasions but I have never found the right woman and so I preferred to stay single. Lately, however, I have wished for a wife, someone to come home to each day, a companion for my leisure and someone who would put an end to my well-meaning friends vying with each other to marry me off to a succession of suitable young women. You see that I wish to marry for the wrong reasons, although perhaps they are no worse than many others. However, those are my reasons. I like you too much to pretend there are others. I am not in love with you and yet I enjoy your company so much that I have begun to miss you when you are not here. It worries me that you are living here alone, doing menial work, and having no friends or fun. We could get along very well together, I think, Arabella, to our mutual advantage.'

Arabella said quietly, 'This isn't…? That is, you are not suggesting this out of pity? Because if you are I shall probably throw something at you.'

She had, she reflected, had several proposals in happier times, but never one as forthright and unsentimental as this one.

Dr Tavener gave her an austere look. 'I do not pity you—never have pitied you. You interest me, frequently annoy me, amuse me, agree with me over the things which matter.'

'You're very outspoken…'

'Would you have me otherwise? Would you have believed me if I had told you that I was in love with you?'

'Of course not! The idea's absurd.' Her nose twitched. 'Supper's ready.'

She liked him for getting up at once to pour more wine and carry the plates to the table, talking now of a variety of matters and never once speaking of themselves. It gave her time to get over the shock.

They ate the macaroni cheese and potatoes and salad, and the fruit pies, all the while carrying on an unforced conversation—arguing about books, disagreeing amicably over the right cultivation of roses, agreeing about the pleasures of having animals to look after. 'I had a pony,' said Arabella wistfully, 'and a donkey.' She paused.

'And?' said Dr Tavener quietly.

'They wanted to sell them, but I took them to an animal sanctuary. They are still there, I hope. I simply hated leaving them.'

'Somewhere near your home?'

'Oh, yes. You must have heard of it.'

When she told him the name he nodded. 'I have heard of it. They have a fine reputation.'

She made coffee presently, while he washed up. He made a good job of it so she asked him if he looked after himself. 'Although you have a housekeeper, haven't you?'

'Mrs Turner took me in hand when my parents died. I admit that I seldom need to do household chores but I'm perfectly able to do so if need be.'

They took their coffee to drink by the fire and the animals pushed and shoved each other as near its warmth as possible.

Arabella took a sip of coffee. She had drunk too much wine and it had gone to her head. It had given her a pretty colour too. She was aware of Dr Tavener's eyes searching her face and buried her nose in her mug.

'Well—' he sounded brisk '—how long do you need to make up your mind?'

'I think,' said Arabella carefully, 'that I won't be able to make it up until I'm alone. You see, while you are here, you distract me.' She added hastily, 'That sounds rude but I don't mean to be; it's just that I have to think about it from a distance, if you see what I mean.'

'Yes, I see. You may have a week, Arabella, and then I shall ask you again. During that week I shall take no notice of you at all—not because I wish to avoid you but so that you can decide for yourself.'

He got up and drew her to her feet, holding her hands between his. They felt cool and comforting and undemanding. 'Thank you for my supper.' He bent and kissed her cheek. 'Goodnight, Arabella.'

She stared up into his faintly smiling face. 'But you might have second thoughts...'

'No, I can promise that I won't.' He went to the door. 'No need to come up, I'll lock the door after me—but remember to bolt it after me later, won't you?'

She sat for a long time doing nothing, her head in a turmoil, but it was no good thinking about it any more. In the morning she would be able to reflect upon her surprising evening with her usual good sense.

She went upstairs and bolted the door and checked the place as she always did and then went back to shower and go to her bed. 'I shan't sleep,' she told Percy, already perched on the end of the bed and giving Bassett a thorough wash. And she slept as soon as her head was on the pillow.

In the half light of a dull November morning the

whole thing seemed like an impossible dream. By the end of a busy day peopled by ill-tempered patients, a crusty Dr Marshall and only glimpses of Dr Tavener's broad back it didn't seem quite as impossible.

She was unable to make up her mind. She had argued, with Percy and Bassett as a more or less attentive audience, each evening, weighing up the pros and cons. But however matter-of-factly she put her problems it wasn't the same as talking to someone. With the end of the week looming she decided that something would have to be done. As Dr Tavener, last as usual, left that evening she stopped him as he went to the door.

'Could you spare five minutes? I need someone to talk to and ask advice, only I don't know anyone except you. I wondered if you would mind. It's about us, but if we could pretend that we're discussing two other people, if you see what I mean…'

'A sensible suggestion. Come into my room and we will see what can be done.'

She was relieved to hear nothing but a pleasantly detached voice and accompanied him back to his consulting-room, where he threw his overcoat on to a chair, offered her a seat and went to sit at his desk once more. Arabella, momentarily diverted by the thought that the overcoat—a splendid one of cashmere—should have been hung up properly and not cast in a heap, gathered her wandering thoughts and faced him.

'It's like this,' she explained. 'I—that is, the girl I'm asking you about isn't sure that she would be doing the right thing if she married this man. She doesn't know what will be expected of her. Does he go out a great deal? Would his friends like her? Perhaps she wouldn't like them. She wouldn't want to shame him; she's not clever or witty or anything like that. She might make a mess of the whole thing, and the thing is she's out of date about getting divorced and all that—' She eyed him with a severe look across the desk. 'If you're married, you do your best to make a success of it.'

She was watching his face and seeing nothing but placid interest there.

His voice was quiet. 'The girl is worrying needlessly. She has, if I might say so, too small an opinion of herself. She is perfectly able to fulfil the duties of a professional man's wife. She would be surprised how tiring clever and witty women are after a hard day's work and a marriage undertaken in mutual liking and respect is unlikely to come to grief. Indeed, the fact that there are no strong feelings involved should ensure its success.' He smiled at her. 'Does that help?'

She nodded. 'Yes. I think so. There's one other thing, though. You're rich.'

He said apologetically, 'I'm afraid I am, rather, but I have never let it bother me, nor would I allow it to bother you.'

'No—well, you see, I wouldn't marry you for your money.'

'No, no, I'm sure you wouldn't.' He spoke gravely; she didn't see the gleam of amusement in his eyes.

She got up. 'Thank you for letting me talk and for giving me advice. I hope I haven't made you late for anything.'

He assured her that she hadn't, bade her a cheerful goodnight and took himself off home where Mrs Turner met him with the warning that he would be late for his dinner engagement with the Marshalls. 'Forgot the time, I suppose,' she observed. 'Head buried in your books as like as not.' She went back to her kitchen saying over her shoulder, 'Time you were married, Doctor. And if I've said that once, I've said it a hundred times!'

He laughed as he went up the stairs two at a time. 'One day I'll surprise you,' he promised her.

'I told you to come early, Titus,' complained Angie Marshall as he offered apologies and an armful of roses.

'Got held up?' asked Dr Marshall easily. 'Come in and have a drink. There's no one else coming so we can talk shop if we want to. You'll come to Angie's dinner party at Christmas, won't you? She's rooting round for a suitable young woman to capture your attention.' He didn't wait for a reply. 'We had a busy day. Stayed behind to catch up on the paperwork?'

'No.' Titus had sat down opposite his host and hostess in the comfortable drawing-room. 'I had a talk with Arabella.'

'Nice little thing. Worried about something, is she?' He glanced at his wife. 'You'd like her, Angie. A pity you can't find her a good husband.'

'No need. She's going to marry me,' said Dr Tavener.

'Bless my soul! She's exactly right for you, Titus. You should have brought her along with you this evening.'

'I left her Hoovering and muttering about dripping taps.'

Mrs Marshall laughed. 'Titus, she sounds a dear and just your sort. Not in the least sentimental, and practical as well. Is she very in love with you?'

He answered calmly. 'Not in the least. Nor I with her, but we like each other and agree about everything which we consider important. I have every expectation that our marriage will be an enduring success.'

'We've known you for a long time—years and years,' said Mrs Marshall, 'and I was beginning to think that you would never marry. We're so happy for you both, Titus.' She added, 'She will be nice to come home to, my dear.'

He smiled. 'Angie, what an understanding woman you are. A good thing James appreciates you.'

'We've been married for sixteen years.' Dr Marshall sounded smug. 'Bring Arabella here for dinner and let her see how successful marriage can be.' He added, 'Oh, lord, we'll have to find another caretaker.'

'How about the ex-bus driver?'

'A good idea. I'll get Miss Baird on to it first thing in the morning.'

The three of them spent the rest of the evening in undemanding talk and later the two men went to Dr Marshall's study to discuss their various patients. It was late when Dr Tavener arrived back at his house; Mrs Turner had gone to bed. He put the car away in the mews garage and took Beauty for a walk through the quiet streets, feeling content.

Arabella was content too. Her mind was made up and she had no intention of altering it. She had seen enough sad results from friends who had married in a blaze of romance and come to grief within a few years to know that liking the same things—books, music, a way of living—as well as pleasure in each other's company were more likely to last even if they lacked excitement. Of course, she admitted to herself, being in love would be marvellous too, but it was obvious to her that Dr Tavener wasn't a man to waste time over romance and, since both of them had nothing but liking for each other, she could see no reason why their marriage shouldn't succeed.

True to his word, Dr Tavener made no attempt to speak to her, the weekend came and went, and suddenly the week was up.

Everyone but the two doctors had gone home. They stood in the hall talking; Arabella could hear them as she collected her cleaning things from under the stairs. Perhaps he wouldn't come—perhaps he expected her to go upstairs... She heard Dr Marshall laugh and the front door bang shut and a moment later Dr Tavener came down the stairs. He took her broom and dusters from her and ushered her back into the room. 'Never mind that now,' she was told briskly. 'Will you marry me, Arabella?'

He could have been asking her to post a letter for all the emotion in his voice. But what else had she expected? She sat down and waved him to a chair. She said, 'Yes,' and, since that sounded a bit terse, added, 'Yes, thank you. I will.'

'Splendid. We can go ahead with our plans. You can leave here at the end of this week—there's a caretaker lined up to start on Sunday. I'll get a special license— James Marshall will give you away—we can be married quietly...'

She said tartly, 'You said our plans—you seem to have taken it for granted that I would agree to everything you have arranged.'

'I'm sorry—oh, I'm sorry! That was unforgivable of me. All this week I have been planning and plotting. Say what you wish to do, Arabella, and you shall have your way.'

She said seriously, 'Well, actually, it all sounds very sensible. Where am I to go?'

'I have a house in the country—in a village midway between Tetbury and Malmsbury. My grandmother lives there—would you go and stay with her for a few days while I arrange things? Would you object to being married in the village church?'

'No. I'd like that very much, but perhaps your grandmother… I'm a stranger…'

'Not quite, you have met her—she brought her companion to see me.'

'Oh, so she knows who I am?' She sighed. 'That I'm the caretaker?'

He nodded. 'Oh, yes. She also knows that you're a very nice girl who will make me a good wife.'

'I shall do my best.'

He leaned forward and took her hands in his. 'We are agreed that there will be no false sentiment between us? Friends, companions, willing to allow each other to enjoy privacy without rancour, enjoying each other's company, spending our leisure together if we so wish.'

'If that is what you want,' she said steadily. 'You will help me, won't you? You have friends—perhaps you entertain sometimes?'

'Fairly frequently.' He smiled suddenly. 'And now I shall be able to enjoy that…'

'No more marriage-minded ladies to vex you!' She gave a chortle of laughter. 'They will think that you have gone mad when they see me.'

'In that case they will no longer be our friends. Tell me, Arabella, have you enough money? You will want to buy some clothes perhaps?'

'I've enough to start with. I expect I shall want more

clothes after we're married if I'm to look like a consultant's wife. You want me to go and stay with your grandmother—but I must do some shopping.'

'Of course you must. Let me see. If I can get the new caretaker to take over on Saturday instead of Sunday would a couple of hours on Saturday morning be enough? I'll drive you down in the afternoon. When you're there you could get to Bath—Butter could drive you there.'

'Who is Butter?' It was like turning the leaves of a book, discovering something fresh on every page.

'Oh, he and Mrs Butter run the house.'

'Then if you don't mind I'd rather shop there and spend Saturday morning packing up here. What about Percy and Bassett?'

'They will go with you, of course. You have some things you would like to keep from here?' His cool eyes swept the room. 'The china and silver and so on? I'll have the tea-chest delivered and it can be taken round to Little Venice. The furniture?'

'There's nothing I want to keep, only Mother's work table.' A dainty mahogany stand with a faded silk bag. 'When—when do you think we should marry?'

'A week—ten days' time? But only if you agree to that… If you have no objection we might marry on a Saturday morning and come back here on the Sunday.'

'So that you can see your patients on Monday? That seems a sensible idea.' She saw the look of relief on his face and reminded herself that their marriage was to be a friendly arrangement which mustn't interfere with his work.

He went presently. At the door he said, 'I very much dislike leaving you here, Arabella. Must you dust and clean?'

'Well, yes, it's my job, which I must do while I'm here…'

He threw an arm round her shoulders. 'When we are married you need never touch a duster or a dish-mop for the rest of your days.'

'A prospect no girl could resist. Will you let me know when the new caretaker is coming so that I can be ready for him?'

'Tomorrow. Take care, my dear.'

She bustled through her chores—there were only two days to Saturday and there were things to be done. Her clothes would pass muster until she could go shopping; they weren't in the forefront of fashion but Titus wouldn't need to feel ashamed of her. There were her precious bits and pieces to pack carefully and the place to set to rights so that the new caretaker would get a good impression. She told the animals about it while she got their suppers and then she started to wrap up her china and silver with the exception of necessities for the next day or two. She went to bed much later than usual, happily planning what was still to be done.

Dr Marshall sent for her the next morning. 'Well, well,' he said jovially, 'so you are to leave us, although I hope that we shall see a great deal more of you in the future. Of course I never thought that you would be with us for long, Arabella, and may I say that I am truly delighted for you and Titus. I'm sure you will be very happy together. Titus has arranged for the new man to call this morning so that you can show him round and explain things. You can let Titus know when it is convenient for you to be fetched on Saturday. You must come to dinner and meet my wife, although I'm hoping you will ask me to give you away at your wedding in which case perhaps she might accompany me?'

'Of course,' said Arabella warmly. 'And thank you for saying you'll give me away. I—I haven't any family living nearby and in any case I don't think they would be interested.'

The new caretaker was a middle-aged man, a cheerful cockney who had been made redundant from the buses and was delighted to have a job and a home again. He was a widower, living in a room near the Elephant and Castle and only too happy to move away from there.

He inspected the basement and pronounced it first-rate. 'I'll 'ave ter get some bits and pieces of furniture,' he told her. 'I suppose you wouldn't leave the curtains and the matting? I'll pay yer, of course.'

'You can have them for nothing,' said Arabella, liking the man, 'and I'd be glad to leave the furniture and the saucepans and so on. You see, I'm going to marry and don't need any of them.'

'Cor, bless my soul—yer really mean it?'

'Yes, of course I do. I'm going to make us a cup of coffee and explain the job to you and presently, when the last morning patient has gone, I'll take you round and show you everything.'

'That's a nice little dog you've got there—and a cat. I've got a cat meself. No objection to 'aving 'er 'ere, I suppose?'

'Well, I was allowed to have Percy. Bassett isn't really allowed, only I found him and he hadn't anywhere to go. A cat's company though, isn't it?'

'That she is.' He looked around him. 'This is a bit of all right, I can tell you.'

'It's a good job and everyone's very kind. If you've finished your coffee we'll go upstairs. Could you come on Saturday morning about eleven o'clock? I'll leave the bed made up with clean sheets and there'll be milk and bread and some food in the pantry. After you've cleaned up you are free on Saturday. I went shopping then—there are all the shops you'll need five minutes' walk away. The narrow road on the left as you leave the house. The doctors like the doors to be shut and locked and bolted when they are not here and I check each evening before I go to bed. I expect Dr Marshall told you about answering the door? You'll find the receptionist, Miss Baird, very kind and helpful.'

He went away presently and she gobbled a sandwich and had more coffee before going upstairs to answer the door to the afternoon patients.

There had been no sign of Dr Tavener. It was Miss Baird who told her that he had gone to Birmingham and would not be back until Friday.

'I haven't had the chance to congratulate you, Arabella,' she said kindly, 'and wish you happy. Dr Tavener is a splendid man. I'm sure you will deal excellently with each other.'

Arabella thanked her. 'I don't quite know when we are to be married.'

'We shall miss you—all of us…'

'Thank you. I have been very happy here, you know. The new caretaker seems to be a very nice man, and so delighted to have work again.'

She was up very early on the Saturday morning, dusting and Hoovering and putting fresh flowers in their vases, and after a quick breakfast she changed into her suit, tied her overall over it and checked that everything was ready for Mr Flinn, before going upstairs ready to open the door.

He came punctually and since there was a lull in the stream of patients she took him downstairs to show him the pantry, explain about the milkman, and point out the list of usual directions she had left on the table.

Dr Tavener hadn't been in and despite her good sense she felt a prickle of apprehension that he had forgotten all about her or, even worse, had second thoughts about marrying her. The idea was absurd, she admitted to herself, and it was only because she was excited and uncertain—a fact borne out by his quiet arrival just before noon.

His hello was friendly and the placid enquiry as to whether she was ready ruffled her feelings. Anyone would think, she reflected crossly, that getting married was a fairly regular event in his life.

He was in no hurry to go either, but stood talking to Mr Flinn before remarking that he would send Butter round for the tea-chest some time that afternoon, scooping Bassett up under one arm and picking up Percy's basket with the other hand. 'Said goodbye to everyone?' he wanted to know.

'Yes,' said Arabella and shook Mr Flinn's hand and wished him well. In the car she said, 'I thought you said that Butter lived in your other house?'

'Quite right, he does. He's coming up today so that he can drive you down this evening. I've an appointment I must keep this afternoon but I'll come down later tonight. My grandmother is expecting you and Butter will take good care of you.'

If I were beautiful and charming and well-dressed, thought Arabella crossly, I would throw a tantrum, make a scene and have him grovelling for treating me like a parcel.

She went red when he said, 'I'm sorry I can't drive you down—this is something which cropped up this morning and it really must be dealt with.'

He glanced at her pink cheeks and smiled a little. 'Would you agree to the wedding next Saturday? Will that give you enough time to do your shopping?'

'Yes, thank you. Are Percy and Bassett to come with me to your other house?'

'Of course, and we'll bring them back with us on the Sunday. Bassett is turning into a very well-mannered dog and Percy is happy wherever you are, isn't he?'

'Yes. You don't think they'll run away?'

'At the manor? No. There's a high brick wall around the grounds and Beauty's brother, Duke, will keep an eye on them.'

Mrs Turner met them at the door and Arabella, who had been secretly nervous of her reception, was relieved at the warmth of her welcome.

'I've been telling the doctor he should take a wife these years past,' said Mrs Turner, leading her away to tidy herself. 'And with respect, Miss Lorimer, I think he's chosen well. I'll be glad to serve you.'

'Why, thank you, Mrs Turner.' Arabella stopped and held out a hand. 'Shall we shake on that? I'm sure you know exactly how the doctor likes things done.'

'Indeed I do. Easygoing he may be, but he likes things just so, as you might say. When will you be marrying, Miss Lorimer?'

'Next Saturday. I hope you'll come to the wedding; it's to be very quiet.'

'Nothing would keep me away, miss.'

Arabella was left to pat her already neat head to even more tidiness and add a little lipstick, and since she was feeling a little nervous she didn't hurry over it. Presently she went back into the hall and was instantly hailed by the doctor from a door at the end of it.

'In here, Arabella. We'll have a drink before lunch.' He held the door open for her as she went into the room. It was small and cosy with a bright fire and easy-chairs and rows of bookshelves. The window overlooked the garden and the canal and there was a round table under it with two mahogany dining chairs on either side of it.

'I have my breakfast here and you must use this room as your sitting-room—your mother's work table will look exactly right here, won't it?'

He pulled up a chair for her to one side of the fire-place and nodded to the three animals sitting in a tidy row before the fire—Bassett in the middle. 'I dare say Beauty will adopt him if Percy allows her to.'

He handed her a glass. 'Champagne—for we have something to celebrate, do we not, Arabella? Here's to us and our happy future together.'

Arabella drank. 'Oh, I do hope so,' she said fervently.

Chapter 5

It was mid-afternoon when Arabella left with Butter in the dark blue Jaguar car which he had driven up. He had greeted her with obvious pleasure and gone away to the kitchen to have a quick lunch before taking her back and now she sat beside him, with the animals on the back seat, conscious that she should be feeling happy and content and aware of a faint prickle of unease. Titus had been kind and thoughtful of her comfort, putting her at ease in what might have been an awkward situation, but all the same she had sensed that he was relieved to see her go. Whatever it was—or whoever it was—he had to deal with that afternoon must have been important. A girlfriend? she wondered uneasily. After all, he had told her that he had fallen in and out of love many times. Perhaps whoever it was was unable to marry him? Married already, or just not wanting to be his wife. He would be going to say goodbye… She brooded over this sad fact of her imagination until it seemed to be true and, being a romantic girl at heart, she could have wept for him. Indeed, if she had been by herself she would have done so but Butter, after a lengthy silence, took it upon himself to tell her about the house they were going to.

'The house in Little Venice is nice enough,' he conceded, 'but the manor's a real home, as you might say. Not all that big but plenty of ground around it and a garden to be proud of, miss. Me and Mrs Butter, we've lived there for years. Served the doctor's father, we did. Very well-liked in the village he is, too. Old Mrs Tavener lives there too—got a companion and has rooms to herself. Under one roof, as it were, but independent, like.' He overtook a huge transporter and kept on in the fast lane.

He was a good driver; she had been surprised at that. He looked to be a very ordinary middle-aged man who would drive a family car at a steady forty miles an hour, and here he was whizzing along at almost twice that speed.

'Not going too fast for you, miss?'

'No, no, I like speed.'

'Now the doctor—he's one for speeding in that Rolls of his. Do you drive, miss?'

'I used to. A Rover.'

'Nice little car. There's a Mini in the garage at the manor, just right for getting around on your own.'

She supposed that she would be on her own for a good deal of her days. She tried to visualise her future and couldn't.

They were almost there and she longed for a cup of tea and at the same time wished that they could drive on for a long while yet because she was nervous of meeting

Titus's grandmother. That they had already met wasn't any help for then she had been the caretaker, answering the door and hanging up coats and taking umbrellas. The old lady might hate the idea of her grandson marrying a working girl, never mind what he had said.

The village came in sight, small and red-roofed and stone-built, tucked away in a narrow valley between the hills, the church—much too big for its size—standing in the centre, the one road running past it, uphill a little and turning sharply at the top.

She caught her first glimpse of the manor then, and sighed with delight. It made a lovely picture in the winter twilight, its windows lighted, and as Butter came to a stop before the door it was thrown open and a small, stout woman, oblivious of the cold, stood on the steps.

Arabella, helped from the car by Butter, clasped Bassett to her and crossed the sweep with him, carrying a muttering Percy in his basket.

'There now.' The little woman took Arabella's free hand and shook it. 'I'm Mrs Butter, miss, and very happy to welcome you. Come on in out of the cold—you'll be wanting a cup of tea, I'll be bound. Mrs Tavener and Miss Welling have had theirs this hour past but I'm to see that you have a cup before you do anything else, so let me have your coat and I'll fetch the tea tray. Butter, take the little dog and the cat into the garden and then they can be with Miss Lorimer before they have their suppers.'

'There's a lead tied on to Bassett's basket,' said Arabella, 'and Percy's harness. Shall I do it?'

'Leave it to me, miss,' said Butter comfortably. 'Just you go and have that tea and then Mrs Butter'll take you to Mrs Tavener's rooms.'

So Arabella found herself in no time at all in a small panelled room, softly lighted by wall sconces and table lamps, furnished in great comfort with easy-chairs and with a brisk fire burning in the old-fashioned grate.

'The master uses this room a great deal,' Mrs Butter told her as she arranged the tea tray on one of the tables. 'Comes in from walking the dogs, he does, "Mrs Butter," he says, "I'm famished." And he sits down in his chair and he and the dogs between them eat enough for a giant. Well, I mean to say he is a giant, isn't he, miss? And a good man, never better!'

She paused on her way out. 'We're that pleased that he's getting married. This house needs a mistress and a pack of children.'

Arabella, slightly overwhelmed, smiled and nodded and murmured and, left alone, drank her tea and then ate the scones and jam. She was beginning to worry about Bassett and Percy when the door opened and Butter came in with Bassett prancing at his heels and Percy under his arm. A black Labrador came in too, nudging Bassett gently and going to Arabella to stare at her with a mild eye. She scratched his head and he sighed heavily with pleasure and then sat down before the fire, and presently the puppy settled beside him. Then, much to Arabella's surprise, Percy, after a few tentative advances, sat down too.

'Now, if you are ready, miss,' said Butter, 'I'll take you along to see Mrs Tavener. We can close the door and leave these three to make friends.'

He noticed her hesitation. 'Never fear, miss, Duke's as mild as milk and he loves cats too.'

The house, she discovered, was larger than she had thought, with a great many passages and steps and unexpected staircases. Mrs Tavener's apartments were on the first floor, at the end of a passage at the back of the house. Butter knocked on a door at its end and Miss Welling answered it, greeting Arabella with a smile and invited her in. 'Mrs Tavener is so looking forward to seeing you again, Miss Lorimer. May I wish you every happiness? We are all so delighted that the doctor is to marry.'

She led the way along a small passage with several doors and opened the end one. The room beyond was large with a bay window at one end and rather over-full of furniture. It was also very warm for there was a great fire burning in the elegant fireplace. Mrs Tavener was sitting upright in a tall-backed chair, a book on her lap.

'Ah, Titus's bride. My dear, I am so happy to welcome you to our family—come here and kiss me.'

Arabella weaved her way carefully through the tables, chairs and display cabinets and kissed the elderly cheek and, bidden to sit down, sat.

'Titus telephoned not half an hour ago. Wanted to know if you had arrived. He was on the point of leaving—such a nuisance that he couldn't drive you down himself. But I believe this was a matter which he wished to deal with personally. It will be delightful to have you here for a few days, my dear. You must treat this house as your home, for that is what it will be. I live here with Miss Welling, but I promise you that I don't interfere or intrude into Titus's life—nor will I with you.' She smiled. 'I hope that if you want advice or just someone to talk to you won't hesitate to come and see me.'

Arabella liked the old lady. 'I expect I shall need a great deal of advice. You see, I know very little about Titus's private life.'

Mrs Tavener gave her a thoughtful look. 'Well, dear, I'm sure that he will tell you anything you want to know. I don't suppose you have had much opportunity to talk together.'

Which was true enough, reflected Arabella.

Presently Mrs Butter came to fetch her. 'I'll show you your room, miss, for the doctor will be here within the hour and you'll want to be ready for him. I've taken the liberty of unpacking your things.'

Her room was charming, furnished with yew and applewood, its curtains pastel chintz, echoing the pale colours of the carpet and the bedcover. She bathed, resisting the wish to lie for ages in the warm water and allow her thoughts to wander, and then, wearing her only dress— needlecord in teal-blue, several years out of date but still elegant—her face nicely made-up and her hair neatly coiled, she went downstairs to the small room again to find the animals still sitting, apparently on the best of terms and very content. The carriage clock on the mantelpiece chimed the hour—seven o'clock, she saw with something of shock—and she wondered how much longer Titus would be.

He came in a few minutes later, Beauty with him. 'I'm sorry I wasn't here when you came down,' he said cheerfully. 'I got here half an hour ago and I've been in my study. You're quite comfortable? You've seen Grandmother? Good. Butter and Mrs Butter are looking after you, I hope?'

He sat down opposite her and Beauty edged her way past him to sit beside Percy.

'They seem to have settled down very well—I hope you will do the same, Arabella.'

She took care to sound pleasantly satisfied as well

as friendly. 'Oh, I'm sure I shall. This is a very beautiful house, isn't it?'

'Yes. Tomorrow I'll take you over it and show you the grounds. Will you come to church with me in the morning?'

'Yes, I'd like that. Did you have a good drive down?'

'Excellent. We must try and come here as often as possible and it would be very pleasant for me if you will come with me when I have to keep appointments out of town. I must go over to Leiden at the end of the month—just for a couple of days. I have friends there whom I think you will like.'

'They're Dutch?'

'He is—his wife is English. We'll come here for Christmas, of course.'

Her head on the pillow and half asleep, several hours later Arabella decided that even if she had had doubts she had them no longer. Being with Titus was like being with an old friend. He had been quite right—without deep feelings for each other they were able to behave towards each other like old and tried companions.

She woke in the night and just for one moment thought that she was in her basement room. She sat up in bed, worried because she couldn't feel the animals on her feet, and then remembered that they had settled to sleep quite happily with Titus's two dogs in the kitchen and that she was in a quite different room.

The rector came back with them after church the next morning and his wife came too, frankly curious about Arabella and full of questions about the wedding. Over sherry Titus parried her artfully put questions and when they had gone told Arabella that she was a splendid rec-

tor's wife but eager to know everyone's business. 'She'll
be at the wedding, of course. You won't find ten o'clock
in the morning too early? We will have lunch here with
Grandmother afterwards and drive up to town in the
afternoon.'

He crossed the room and took her arm. 'Come and
look round the house before lunch.'

It was a roomy old place. Besides the vast drawing-
room there was a dining-room, his study, the little room
the animals seemed to consider was theirs, and a room
overlooking the garden at the back and opening on to a
conservatory. They stood at its open door for a few moments, surveying the wintry gardens. 'There's a swim-
ming-pool at the end behind those rhododendrons and
the kitchen garden is through that small doorway at the
end of the wall.' He turned away. 'Come upstairs—we'll
leave the kitchen for the moment or we shall get under
Mrs Butter's feet.'

At the top of the staircase he crossed the circular landing and opened double doors. 'This will be your room.'

It was large, with windows opening on to a small balcony, and carpeted in the colour of clotted cream. The
curtains were rose-patterned and silk, as was the bedspread. The bed was a four-poster with a cream canopy
highlighting the sheen of its mahogany. There was a vast
dressing-table in the same wood, bedside tables bearing
pink-shaded lamps and a chaise longue and small comfortable chairs in misty blue. It would be an enchanting
place in which to wake up each morning. 'Oh, it's beautiful,' said Arabella, rotating slowly. 'What's through
those doors?'

'Bathroom and beyond that a dressing-room. The
other door is a clothes closet.'

Beyond the bathroom and dressing-room there was another bedroom, smaller and rather austere. 'My room,' said Titus briefly, and led her through another door back to the landing.

She lost count of the bedrooms she was shown and followed him up a smaller staircase to the floor above. The rooms here were smaller but well-furnished and at one end of the passage there was a baize door.

'The Butters have a flat,' he explained. 'There are two housemaids but they come each day.'

He glanced at his watch. 'We had better go down to lunch. This afternoon if you would like to we will go round the grounds.'

On their way downstairs he stopped. 'I entirely forgot,' he told her gravely, and took a small box from his pocket. 'Your ring…'

She took it slowly and opened its velvet lid. The ring was a half-hoop of splendid diamonds in an old-fashioned setting. 'It's been in the family for a long time—gets handed down from one bride to the next. I hope it fits.'

He made no move to put it on her finger. Arabella told herself that would have been sentimental nonsense anyway. It fitted well and she held up her hand to admire it. 'It's very beautiful.'

However unsentimental the giving had been, she mustn't sound ungrateful. She added warmly, 'Thank you very much, Titus. I shall wear it with pride.'

She smiled up at him and surprised a look on his face which puzzled her, but even as she looked it had gone and been replaced with his habitual bland expression. She must have fancied it.

At lunch old Mrs Tavener said, 'Ah—you're wearing

the ring. You have pretty hands, Arabella. What do you think of your future home?'

They talked about the house and its history, the village and the people who lived there, and when the meal was finished the old lady went away to her room. 'Miss Welling goes down to the rectory for lunch on Sundays,' she explained, 'and Mrs Butter settles me for a nap. I dare say I shall see you at tea.'

After she had gone they sat for a little while over their coffee in the drawing-room, the animals stretched out before the fire, until Titus said, 'Fetch a coat and I'll take you round the gardens before the light goes.'

Even in the wintry weather the gardens were a great delight, and when he opened the door into the kitchen garden she said delightedly, 'Oh, it is—it reminds me...' and fell silent.

'Of your garden at home? I suppose that most of the country houses in these parts have these walled gardens. Come and see the greenhouses. I inherited the gardener with the house; he's old and crotchety and grows everything under the sun. I took on his grandson this summer—he will be just as good in time.'

'Only an old man and a boy for all this?' She waved an arm around her at the orderly rows, the bare fruit trees and the fruit bushes.

'A couple of men come in several times a week to give a hand with the heavy work. Come this way.'

She stayed where she was. 'Titus, I'm not sure...that is, I'm not sure if I can live up to you and all this.'

He took her arm and began to walk along the path bordering the rows of cabbages and leeks. 'Ah, now you can understand why I need a wife—someone to help me live up to it as well.'

'But it's your home.'

'And will be yours too…'

'You have an answer for everything.'

'No, no. The last thing I wish to do is coerce you. You have only to say, my dear, and you will be as free as air again.'

That brought her up short once more. 'You really want me to marry you?' she asked. 'You're quite sure?'

'Quite sure.' He bent and kissed her cheek and took her arm again. 'Come with me, I've something to show you.'

He flung an arm around her shoulders and her doubts melted away. Surely being his wife wouldn't be as difficult as caretaking. 'Not another garden?' she asked as he went through a second arched doorway. 'Oh, stables.' She peered around her in the afternoon gloom. 'Do you ride?'

'Yes, as often as possible.' He opened the first stable door and said, 'Come inside.'

There was a pony there, and there was a small donkey too, and both raised their heads as she went in. The pony whinnied and came to meet her, followed by the donkey.

'Why,' said Arabella, 'it's Bess—and Jerry too!' She went between them, hugging them, murmuring into their ears and stroking them.

'A wedding present,' said Titus quietly. 'Here—sugar for Bess and a carrot for Jerry.'

She ignored that. 'Titus, oh, Titus, how can I ever thank you? It's the most marvellous thing to happen to me since I left home.' She didn't see the lift of his eyebrows and his faint smile. She left the animals and stretched up to kiss his cheek. 'You have no idea…' she began, and burst into tears.

He put an arm around her and let her weep into his

shoulder. Presently she gave a great sniff and muttered in a sodden voice, 'Oh, I'm so sorry, what a way to behave. Only, I'm so happy.'

He offered a large snowy handkerchief. 'It's nice to meet old friends again,' he observed in a comfortable voice. 'They're in good shape—you don't ride Bess any more, I imagine?'

'No, not since I was about fifteen. She's very old—so is Jerry.'

'Yes, I suppose so. Well, they can enjoy the rest of their lives here. There's a paddock beyond the yard here—we've had them out for a few hours each day. Old Spooner's grandson—Dicky—is splendid with animals. You can safely leave them in his care.'

She gave him a wide watery smile. 'I can't keep saying thank you,' she began.

'No need. I am delighted to have pleased you. Shall we go back to the house? I have to go directly after tea.'

She gave the animals a final hug, assured them that she would see them the following day, and walked back to the house, happily unaware that her unremarkable face wasn't improved by tearstains and a very pink nose.

Back at the house she went to her room and was horrified at the sight of her face in the looking-glass. At least it had been almost dark outside; Titus would have noticed nothing. She repaired the damage, smoothed her hair and went down for tea—a meal taken in Mrs Tavener's company with Miss Welling sitting like a shadow beside her. She still looked apologetic but Arabella noticed that she ate a hearty tea. She thought that probably Miss Welling was perfectly happy despite her downtrodden expression—she was certainly treated as an old friend by the Taveners and she had beamed her delight when she had wished Arabella happy. It was a pleasant meal but soon Titus got to his feet. 'I must go, Grandmother. I'll be down next Saturday morning, early. I'll see Butter about that.'

He stooped to kiss the old lady's cheek, shook Miss Welling's hand and whistled to Beauty. From the look he gave her, Arabella guessed quite rightly that she was to see him out of the house. She followed him into the hall where Butter was waiting.

Dr Tavener's directions took only a minute or so before Butter tactfully withdrew, leaving Arabella and Titus facing each other at the door. If she had hoped for anything of even a slightly romantic nature, she wasn't going to get it.

'Take Duke for a run each day, will you? Butter usually takes him but I dare say you'll go at a pace to suit Duke better. Let Butter know what day you want to go shopping. Don't bother to buy too much; you can shop all you want to when we get back to London. Take care of that puppy of yours and Percy—they seem to have settled down very nicely.'

He didn't ask if *she* had settled down nicely. A flicker of resentment flamed inside her and died when she remembered Bess and Jerry.

'Drive carefully,' she said, and bent to pat Beauty's head.

He said, surprising her, 'You are happy, Arabella?'

'Thank you, yes, I am, Titus.'

He opened the door, kissed her briefly on a cheek, ushered Beauty into the car, got in himself and drove away with a casual wave as he went.

'After all, what did I expect?' Arabella asked herself, and went back to discuss a wedding outfit with Mrs Tavener.

* * *

Everyone was very kind; she was surrounded by warmth and comfort and people anxious that she should feel at home and happy. Although she had her meals with Mrs Tavener and Miss Welling she had the rest of the days to herself and despite the wintry weather she took Duke for long walks, getting to know the surrounding countryside. She had coffee with the rector and his wife too. The rector's wife was a dear little woman who took it for granted that Arabella and Titus were deeply in love. 'So very nice to have you at the manor,' she confided to Arabella. 'Titus has been single for too long. I look forward to you living there—it's a lovely old place, isn't it? Marvellous for children too.'

She misinterpreted Arabella's pink cheeks and smiled cosily.

Halfway through the week Butter drove Arabella to Bath, arranged to pick her up again in the late afternoon and drove off, leaving her to the exciting business of buying clothes. Every penny she possessed was in her purse—not a great deal of money but enough for what she intended to buy.

It was lunchtime before she had found what she wanted: a jacket and skirt in a fine wool in the blue of a winter sky. There was a matching silk top to go with them and, after a bit of poking around, she found a velvet hat with a high crown and a tiny brim. Pulled well down over her eyes, she fancied, it improved her looks…

It had been an expensive outfit so she went in search of the high street stores and found a pleated checked skirt with a three-quarter-length jacket to go with it, a couple of sweaters, some undies and a simple dress in stone-coloured cotton jersey—and she was almost penniless. She had pretty shoes and several pairs of good gloves salvaged from earlier days. She would have liked a handbag but that must wait. She ate a very overdue lunch in a small and cheap café and walked to where Butter was to pick her up.

Back in her room at the manor, she spread her purchases out on the bed. They were all right as far as they went but she would need to go shopping once she was married. Her wardrobe was woefully inadequate for the wife of an eminent physician. She tried on the hat and decided that it had been worth every penny of its price.

At dinner that evening she assured Mrs Tavener that she had had a most successful day shopping. 'I won't tell you what I've bought—I'd like it to be a surprise.'

Titus had telephoned once during the week. He would drive down with his best man—a friend of long-standing—and arrive for breakfast. Dr Marshall and his wife would arrive on the Friday evening—Butter had his instructions; they would stay the night at the manor. He would see her on Saturday morning at the church.

He had rung off with the kind of goodbye she might have expected from an older brother.

Mrs Butter, a great one for tradition, brought her breakfast up to her room on Saturday morning. 'The doctor's here, miss,' she said breathlessly. 'Dr and Mrs Marshall are having breakfast with him now. Do eat up—I'll be back in half an hour or so to run your bath. You mustn't be late at the church.'

Arabella ate her breakfast, for she had the good sense to know that she would be too excited to eat anything else for the rest of the day. She dressed carefully, wishing to make the best of herself; it was, after all, her wedding-day. She didn't look too bad, she considered, inspect-

ing herself in the pier glass. It would have been nice if
she had been pretty but since Titus wasn't in love with
her she supposed that that didn't matter very much, and
the right clothes, the right make-up and a visit to a good
hairdresser would certainly improve her looks.

It was time to go. Mrs Butter came to fetch her, wearing an overpowering hat and a buttonhole in her winter coat.

'You look lovely,' she said. 'Just like a bride should.
The master's gone to the church and Dr Marshall's waiting for you.'

Dr Marshall kissed her. 'You look beautiful—that's
a pretty thing you're wearing and I do like the hat. Let's
go.'

It was to have been a very quiet wedding but half the
village had crammed into the church. Arabella hesitated
at the door but Dr Marshall nipped her arm. 'Titus wants
you to have these,' he whispered, and handed her a little bouquet of roses and miniature lilies, pale pink, and
mixed in with them were lily-of-the-valley, miniature
daffodils and small sprigs of rosemary. She buried her
nose in its fragrance and then took Dr Marshall's arm
and walked serenely down the aisle, her eyes on Titus's
broad back. When they were almost by him he turned
to look at her and smile and she smiled back. Two old
friends meeting, she thought in a muddled way. Everything was going to be all right.

She made her vows in a small firm voice, meaning
to keep every word of them. The future was unpredict-
able but she intended to do her best to be the kind of
wife he wanted. She didn't hear a word of the rector's
short homily, so busy was she with her own thoughts.

The rest of the day passed in a dream; she smiled and

talked and shook hands and was kissed, drank a little
too much champagne, cut the cake with Titus's firm
hand upon hers and at length found herself in the Rolls
with the animals crowded in the back and all of them
covered in confetti.

Once they were clear of the village Titus pulled into
a lay-by.

'We should have brought a dustpan and brush with
us,' he observed. 'Come here and be brushed down.'

They laughed about it together while she did the
same for him and then the more difficult task of getting the confetti out of whiskery faces and furry coats
commenced.

'That's better,' said Titus. 'Now I can see you. I like
the hat!'

'Thank you, and thank you too for the beautiful flowers. It was a very successful wedding, wasn't it?'

'Indeed, yes. Now we will embark upon a successful marriage. Quite a different thing but one to which
I look forward.'

'Me too,' said Arabella.

Mrs Turner had been at the wedding and Butter had
left with her an hour or so before they had. She would
be at Little Venice by the time they got there, ready to
welcome them, and Butter would have started the drive
back to the manor, anxious not to miss the party to be
held in the village pub to celebrate the wedding.

Dr Tavener made good speed; there was very little
traffic and although dusk was falling the road was clear
but it was almost dark when he drew up before his house.
All the lights were on and Mrs Turner flung open the
door with a flourish.

'That's the best wedding I've ever been to,' she assured them as they went indoors. 'All the lovely flowers and the organ, and you, madam, looked a fair treat.'

Titus went to let the animals out and she said, 'Tea's all ready in the drawing-room. I'll see to the animals—you must both be needing a cup.'

'You're a jewel, Mrs Turner. Will you take Mrs Tavener up to her room first? I'll take the dogs and Percy into the garden—perhaps you would feed them presently?'

Arabella followed Mrs Turner up the staircase to a room at the back of the house, overlooking the canal. It was very large with doors opening on to a wrought-iron balcony and furnished in much the same style as her room at the manor—soft pastel colours, a wide four-poster bed and a dressing-table of applewood. There were a couple of comfortable chairs and pretty lamps on the tables, and delicate water-colours on the cream satin-striped walls.

'The bathroom's through that door and the dressing-room's on the other side, madam, and you've only to ask for anything you would like.'

'Mrs Turner, I'm sure everything is just perfect. I hope you will give me your advice...'

'That I will, with pleasure. Not lived in London before you went to the doctor's rooms?'

'No, my home was in the country, near Sherborne. Not anywhere as large as the manor but a nice rambling sort of house. This house is beautiful, though. It isn't like living in London at all and it's so quiet.' She turned from the window. 'You do have help in the house, Mrs Turner?'

'That I do. Maisie comes in each morning—a good girl, does her work as it should be done and always cheerful. I'll be going down to make the tea, madam, you must be fair parched.'

Later, sitting opposite Titus in the drawing-room, talking in a desultory manner while he went through his letters, Arabella had the strange feeling that they had been married for years, sitting in each other's company like an elderly married couple, easy with each other, comfortably silent if they wished. It was reassuring and what she supposed she had expected, only there was a vague doubt at the back of her head that Titus might discover one day that there was still a lot of life left before they reached the cosy stage. Supposing he met someone—some beautiful woman—and fell in love? He wouldn't be content to sit by the fire then, would he? She wasn't sure but she thought that he had never really looked at her, only as one would look at some familiar friend or a member of the family. He was comfortable with her, she was sure of that, and he liked her, but wouldn't he find that insufficient after a time? Would he miss his dinner parties and the divorced ladies bent on amusing him?

She frowned a little; she mustn't start thinking such thoughts on her wedding-day. She would make plans to improve her looks, buy clothes, meet people, give smart little dinner parties...

Dr Tavener, watching her, wondered what she was thinking. He said, 'It's been a long day. I dare say you are tired?'

'Well, yes, I am.' She uttered the fib with composure. 'You won't mind if I go up to bed?'

The alacrity with which he went to open the door was hardly flattering. She wasn't sure what she had expected;

it certainly wasn't his pleasant goodnight. 'Sleep well. Will breakfast at eight-thirty suit you?'

'Yes, thank you. Do we go to church in the morning?'

'If you would come with me I should be very glad.'

'Well, of course I will. Goodnight, Titus.'

He kissed her cheek. 'No regrets?'

'Not a single one. I'd like to go to the kitchen and say goodnight to Percy and Bassett.'

'Of course. Have them in your room if you would like that.'

'No, no. I'm sure they are happy with Beauty.'

She slipped past him on her way to the kitchen and she didn't look back.

Chapter 6

Arabella wasn't in the least tired. Curled up in the vast bed, she reviewed the day. It had gone without a hitch but then she had known it would; Titus wouldn't have stood for less than perfection. She had enjoyed the wedding and she felt at home here in this comfortable house by the canal although the manor house had her heart—besides, Bessy and Jerry were there. They would go there very often, Titus had said, and she knew him well enough to know that she could rely on him not to go back on his word. She wondered how she would fill her days, and went to sleep while she was still pondering that.

They breakfasted together, the two dogs and Percy lined up between them before the fire, discussing when they would go to the manor again, which day Arabella would like to go shopping, the best walks for the dogs—a pleasant, undemanding conversation. Arabella, notwithstanding her doubts of the previous night, felt very much at her ease.

'We'll take these two into the park this afternoon?' he suggested. 'Bassett needs a good run and Beauty will keep an eye on him.' He glanced at his watch. 'We can walk to church—it's only ten minutes or so. I've some telephoning—can we meet in an hour?'

She wandered round the house, getting to know her way around it, and then she went into the garden with the animals. It was a chilly morning and she was wearing her suit; her winter coat had seen better days and she hesitated to wear it to church. Probably Titus was known there and people might think her a very shabby sort of wife. It was fortunate that she still had a felt hat which would go very well with the suit—a dateless hat, plain and elegant and made by a well-known hatter.

He was waiting for her when she went downstairs. She was conscious of his eyes raking her person and went pink. 'Very nice,' he told her, 'but shouldn't you be wearing a thicker coat?'

She said simply, 'My winter coat is too old—you'd be ashamed of me.'

'Never. But you will be happier without it. Tomorrow you shall go to the shops and start to buy whatever you need, Arabella. I don't mean any shops—I've an account at Harrods; you'll go there, please, and buy anything and everything which may take your fancy.'

'That's a risky remark to make to a woman.'

'Not to you! As soon as I have time I'll get you settled with an allowance; in the meantime use Harrods.'

'It's a very expensive shop. I haven't been there for years.'

They were walking to church along the quiet streets.

'Well, now you can have a browse round and see if it still suits your taste. I'll give them a ring in the morning and let you have my account number.'

'Thank you, but you must let me know how much I can spend—I haven't the least idea.'

He mentioned a sum which brought her to a halt. 'You can't mean that—why, it's a small fortune!'

He took her arm and walked her along. 'My dear Arabella, you are now my wife and I am proud of you, therefore, like all husbands, I want you to have all the pretty things you would like. Besides, now that I am a safely married man we shall have to entertain and I warn you that before you know where you are you will find yourself sitting on committees, drinking coffee and organising bazaars. For all these occasions you will need clothes. You like clothes, presumably?'

'Like them? Of course I do. I shall run mad at Harrods—it will take more than one day's shopping, too.'

'Take as many days as you like. I've a busy week ahead of me. We will go down to the manor at the weekend, though, and the following week I have to go to Leiden and I would like you to go with me.'

'I'd like that very much. My passport's out of date, though.'

'We'll see about that in the morning.'

They had reached the church and sure enough a number of people there greeted Titus as they took their places in one of the pews. She enjoyed the service even if once or twice her thoughts strayed to the shopping delights ahead of her.

Mrs Turner was a splendid cook—the roast beef was done to a turn, the vegetables were just right and the queen of puddings which followed was deliciously light.

They had their coffee and since the winter days were getting short took the dogs into the park, walking until it was dusk, and Bassett was so tired that Arabella tucked him under one arm while Beauty raced to and fro, apparently inexhaustible.

They had tea round the fire and spent a pleasant evening discussing the week ahead. He would take her out to dinner during the week, he told her, adding with a twinkle, 'So that you will have a chance to air one of your new dresses.'

She sparkled. 'Oh, how lovely. Where?'

'Claridge's—we can dance.' He watched the colour come into her cheeks. 'I should be home early on Wednesday—shall we go then?'

'Oh, yes, please.' For a moment she was lost in a pleasant dream—transformed into a beauty overnight, wearing a gorgeous dress, making the kind of conversation which would set him smiling. She could at least have a try. Suddenly she wanted him to notice her, not just as a friend and companion but as an attractive woman...

'What plan are you hatching in that neat head of yours?' he wanted to know. 'We'll go down to the manor at the weekend and lay our plans for the trip to Leiden.'

Presently they dined, well pleased with each other's company so that later, Arabella, getting ready for bed, reflected that living with Titus was going to be a success. Of course it was early days yet but they had made a good beginning. They might even, she thought wistfully, become fond of each other in time. She had no illusions about his falling in love with her—if he hadn't lost his heart to all the charming females he must have known he wasn't likely to lose it to her. She chuckled about that and then went to sleep on a sigh.

They breakfasted together quite early and Arabella, aware that Titus wished to sift through his post, checking the various reports on his patients, did no more than wish him a cheerful good morning. Later, she thought hopefully, she would have post of her own. She had plenty to think about. She had wakened early and made a list of the clothes she would buy; now she reviewed it mentally, adding a few articles she had overlooked, trying to guess what everything would cost. She gave a guilty start when Titus said suddenly, 'Remember, Arabella, if you go shopping today, buy what suits you and don't look at the price labels.'

'Don't you want to know how much I've spent?'

'No. I'll pay the bills when they arrive and if they're too wildly extravagant I shall tell you so.' He smiled across the table. 'I gave you some idea of how much you might spend but I shan't cavil at a few hundred more.'

He left the house presently and she took the dogs and Percy into the garden. Beauty had already had an early morning run with Titus and Bassett was happy enough running around, teasing the patient Beauty and chasing an indignant Percy. They all went back indoors presently and Arabella went to the kitchen to talk to Mrs Turner.

'Will you take me round the house one day?' she asked. 'And tell me what the doctor likes and doesn't like—and I'd love to do the shopping sometimes if you would tell me what to buy.'

'Lor' bless you, madam, it'll be a pleasure to take you round the cupboards and pantry. There's china and linen and silver you must inspect and the tradesmen's bills. If you would come each morning we could discuss the meals for the day and make a list of the shopping if it's needed.'

'I'm going out now, Mrs Turner; I expect I'll be gone for quite a while. Would you please look after Beauty, Bassett and Percy?' She couldn't resist saying, 'I'm going to buy clothes.'

Mrs Turner looked positively motherly. 'And what could be nicer?' she wanted to know and added, 'But mind and have lunch, madam—shopping's tiring.'

Arabella wore the suit and felt hat; they were hardly high fashion but her shoes and gloves would pass muster anywhere. Mindful of Titus's request that she should take a taxi, she did so, feeling extravagant but it was a nice build-up to her day. She went through Harrods' elegant doors and began the delightful task of spending money.

By mid-morning she had acquired a winter coat—tobacco-brown cashmere—a brown and cream knitted three-piece, a jersey dress in copper, a beech-brown wool skirt, a cashmere cardigan and several blouses. She had a cup of coffee then, got her second wind, and went to look at dresses.

The choice was endless but she had a very good idea of what she wanted. By lunchtime she had tried on and bought a deep rose-pink dress in crêpe de Chine with a tucked bodice and a gored skirt which floated round her as she walked, a silk velvet dress in forest-green—very simple with a narrow skirt, long tight sleeves and a square neckline and, since she couldn't resist them, a wide midnight-blue skirt and an evening blouse with long full sleeves and a ruffled neck.

She went to the restaurant and had an omelette and coffee and decided that she had bought enough for one day. She had kept a rough check of the prices and although everything had cost a good deal there was still plenty over. Undies, shoes and a suit, she decided, as she was being taken back to her new home in a taxi loaded down with dress-boxes. It had begun to rain and she prudently added a raincoat to her list.

She had lunched late and Mrs Turner offered her tea as soon as she had got indoors. 'Well, just a quick cup,' said Arabella, 'before I take everything upstairs.'

'I'll see they go to your room, madam. Just you sit down and have that tea. Shopping can be tiring.'

So Arabella had her tea and presently, with the animals trailing stealthily behind her, went to her room. Here they arranged themselves tidily in a corner and watched her while she undid her packages and inspected what she had bought. She couldn't resist trying some of them on; she was twirling round in the pink crêpe de Chine when there was a knock on the door. It would be Mrs Turner, come to remind her that it had gone six o'clock and the doctor would be home presently. Arabella turned a guilty face to the door. 'Mrs Turner—do come in…'

Only it was Titus. She stopped in mid-twirl. 'Titus— I forgot the time—I thought it was Mrs Turner, come to tell me to come downstairs. I'm sorry—I did mean to be there, waiting for you…'

'Sitting with your knitting and the drinks poured?' He laughed then. 'My dear girl, you in that pink dress do me much more good than a soberly occupied wife.'

He cast his eyes round the room, strewn with clothes and tissue paper. 'You've made a start,' he commented drily. 'Will you wear this on Wednesday?'

She felt shy. 'If you would like me to. There are other dresses—I've bought an awful lot.'

'Splendid. I wondered where Beauty had got to. One of an admiring audience, I see.'

'Do you mind? I mean that they came upstairs with me? They were glad to see me.'

He crossed the room and took her hand. 'I'm glad to see you too, Arabella.' He kissed her briefly. 'Come down and have a drink before dinner. I'll take these three into the garden for a few minutes.'

He went away, whistling to the animals, who trooped after him, leaving her to get out of the pink dress and into the jersey dress, do her hair and do things to her face in a perfunctory way.

Dressed and ready on the Wednesday evening, she took stock of her person in the pier glass. The pink dress certainly gave an illusion of prettiness and between bouts of shopping on the previous day she had found time to buy the very best of face creams and powders and have her hair shampooed and cut. Indeed, fired by enthusiasm, she had tried out various new hairstyles but none of them seemed right. She ended up pinning her mousy locks on top of her head as she had done for years.

Perhaps it was the pink dress which made the evening such a success, although hardly a romantic one. Titus had had a busy day and she was a good listener. A good deal of their dinner was taken up with his comments and observations on treatments, medicines and the art of the physician as opposed to that of the surgeon. Arabella listened with interest, filing away some of the longer words she had never heard before so that she could look them up later and know what he was talking about next time.

The waiter had come to offer them coffee when Titus asked, 'Would you like to dance? It seems a pity not to display that pretty dress.'

She got up at once, making some cheerful remark about the band while under the pink bodice she seethed with a sudden ill-temper. He might have made some pleasant remark about her person, never mind if it wasn't true. She was no beauty but she was aware that she looked attractive against the luxurious surroundings. Never mind the lack of looks, she told herself, you know how to dance…

She certainly did. She was light on her feet, as pliant as a reed and a graceful dancer. Titus, a good dancer himself, after the first few moments bent his head to say quietly in her ear, 'It's like dancing with a moonbeam! What a treasure I have married—not only a first-rate plumber but a delightful dancer. We must do this more often before I get too middle-aged!'

She looked up at that. 'Middle-aged? Of course you're not. Aren't you supposed to be in your prime?'

'Why, thank you, Arabella, you encourage me to fend off the encroaching years.' He smiled down at her. 'Do you know you're attracting a great many admiring glances?'

'Oh, no, I didn't.' She had gone pink. 'I expect its the dress…'

He stared down at the top of her neat head, smiling a little. He found her company delightful; she was so very natural, so unassuming, so ready to fall in with his plans and wishes. She made no effort to attract him either, and that, after the scheming young ladies he had from time to time considered himself in love with, was something that he was already appreciating.

They went down to the manor at the weekend and, since it was cold clear weather, they walked for miles with Beauty and Duke bounding ahead and Bassett doing his small best to keep up with them. Arabella, scooping him up, said, 'Perhaps we should have left him with Percy—he's still so very small.'

'He has the heart of a lion. Let me have him; he can sit inside my jacket.' He slowed his stride so that she could keep up. 'We go to Holland on Thursday. I think it might be a good idea if we brought this lot down before we go. Butter can look after them and Mrs Butter dotes on Percy. Are you looking forward to going?'

'Yes, I am. Will you be away all day?'

'Most of it, but I'm sure you'll get on with Cressida. I've known Aldrik since we were students. Leiden isn't a large place but there are some good shops and plenty to see. You will be invited to the dinner which marks the end of the seminar—black ties and long dresses.'

'But everyone will be Dutch…'

'Well, I'm not, for a start. Besides, everyone there will speak English.'

'I think it might be fun.'

Titus, looking at her glowing face, found rather to his surprise that he agreed with her.

They had tea with Mrs Tavener before they went back to London. The old lady, with Miss Welling in close attendance, wanted a blow-by-blow account of their life there. 'It is a great deal more healthy here than in your London house,' she declared. 'Arabella's looks have improved a great deal since you arrived yesterday.' She broke off to take stock of Arabella, who blushed and looked into her teacup and thus missed Titus's long thoughtful stare. 'Of course,' went on the old lady, 'once the children come along, you will have to spend more time here; they'll thrive in the country air.'

Arabella went on looking into her teacup, while wishing it could give her a suitable answer. It was Titus who said easily, 'You are quite right, Grandmother, small children are happiest in the country. I hated leaving here when I was first sent to boarding-school.' A successful red herring which led the old lady to reminisce until it was time for them to leave.

If he even mentions it, thought Arabella, sitting silently beside him in the car, I'll throw something at him.

He never mentioned it, but talked easily of this and that so that by the time they were back at Little Venice she had managed to forget about it. All the same, she wished that they could have said something about it, laughed over it together, made a joke of it. It was the first time, she reflected, that they had avoided talking about something and she felt awkward about it. It was a good thing that Titus appeared to have forgotten about it, but perhaps he hadn't felt anything other than an amused interest in his grandmother's remarks.

They left early in the morning on Thursday to take the dogs and Percy to the manor, had a quick lunch there and then, after Arabella had raced down to the stables to make sure that the pony and the donkey were safe and well, they drove to catch the night ferry from Harwich. It was a long journey but Arabella, snug in her winter coat, her feet encased in fashionable boots, enjoyed it. They sped smoothly along the motorway until they reached the turning and circled round London to Watford, and then on to Hatfield, where they stopped for a late tea. It was a small café cosily lit and chintzy with very ladylike waitresses in flowered aprons; the tea was hot and plentiful and the buttered crumpets were delicious. Arabella sank her splendid teeth into them with a contented sigh.

'This is fun,' she said.

Titus found himself agreeing with her, reflecting that when he was with her he felt ten years younger.

They drove on presently and went on board the ferry. After dinner Arabella went to her cabin and despite the rough crossing slept soundly. Titus, watching her enjoying an early breakfast of rolls and coffee, smiled to himself. Their marriage was going to be a success; she was not only a good companion, she was sensible—accepting situations without fuss, undemanding of his attention and time and, he had to admit, really quite pretty now that she had new clothes. He studied her from lowered lids as she buttered a roll. What was more, she was dressed exactly as he would like to see her...

Leiden was less than half an hour's drive away. Arabella got glimpses of it as Titus drove through the town and presently turned into a narrow street lined with gabled houses, old and beautifully maintained. He helped her out, took her arm and urged her across the narrow cobbled pavement and pulled the wrought-iron bellpull beside an elegant front door. It was opened by an elderly rather bony-faced woman and a very large St Bernard dog, accompanied by a small insignificant beast. The woman smiled and the doctor said, 'Mies, how nice to see you again.' He patted the dogs' heads and added, 'Arabella, this is Mies—Cressida's housekeeper.'

She shook hands and was ushered inside as a small young woman came racing down the staircase. 'Titus— I should have been on the doorstep!' She lifted her face for his kiss and turned to Arabella. 'I'm Cressida—I'm so glad to meet you, Arabella.' She beamed happily, her lovely eyes sparkling from a very ordinary face. 'Aldrik has had to go to the hospital but he'll be back before lunch. Come on in and have some coffee. Titus, do go into the drawing-room—I'm going to take Arabella upstairs.'

Arabella followed her hostess upstairs, relieved at finding her so friendly. She had been a little worried that Cressida could have been a statuesque blonde and talked down to her. Instead here was this nice girl the same size as herself and certainly no beauty, although she looked so happy that she could have passed as beautiful.

'Titus said he would be late back each evening—seminars and things,' Cressida said vaguely, 'so I've put you in here and there's a dressing-room next door so that he needn't disturb you if it's the small hours.'

She sat down on the bed. 'This was my room—I mean when Aldrik brought me back here—just for a night, then he took me to Friesland to a friend's house to look after some children.' She smiled gently. 'He's nice—I do hope you'll like him. We think Titus is a dear too.'

Arabella had been poking at her hair and was sitting at the dressing-table, not saying much.

'Come and see the twins before we go downstairs. They're two months old—one of each. We are lucky, aren't we? A splendid start to the family.'

They were asleep—the little girl with mousy hair like her mother, the boy very fair. 'They're very good,' said their proud mother, 'and we've a wonderful nanny—my old housekeeper's niece.'

She led the way downstairs and into the drawing-room. 'Forgive me for talking so much, but I'm so glad to meet you. I've English friends, of course, but most of them live in Friesland—we've another house there...'

The room was warm and bright, with a brisk open fire and furnished with a nice mixture of antique furniture and comfortable chairs.

Titus got up as they came in, and the two dogs with him, staying politely on their feet until the three of them were seated and then collapsing into contented furry heaps before the fire. They talked over their coffee. It seemed that Titus knew many of the van der Linuses' friends and there was cheerful talk about St Nicolaas. 'I wish you could be here for that,' said Cressida. 'It's such fun for the children.' She jumped to her feet. 'Here's Aldrik…'

Arabella took to him at once. He was a year or two younger than Titus and his hair was already flecked with grey, but he was a handsome man—very tall and broad. He kissed his wife, then shook Titus's hand and smiled down at Arabella. 'I'm only sorry this is to be such a short visit,' he told her. 'Titus must bring you over for a week or two and come up to Friesland. That is our real home.'

Arabella thought privately that the one they were in now would do very nicely. 'Don't you work here?' she asked.

'Yes, but not all the time. Have you seen the twins?'

'Yes, they're adorable.'

He gave his wife a loving glance. 'We think so.' He went to sit down by Titus. 'There's a paper being read on asthma this afternoon. Do you care to come?'

They didn't linger over lunch and the men went away as soon as it was finished so, since it was a fine cold afternoon, the babies were wrapped up warmly, tucked into their pram and taken for a walk. They had been fed and played with and now they slept while the two girls gossiped. It struck Arabella that she had missed that during the last few months—cheerful chatter about clothes and husbands and babies, all of it light-hearted. They went back to tea and then to the nursery to help Nanny bathe the twins, feed them once more and tuck them up in their cots. The men came home then, to pay a visit to the babies, which meant lifting them out of their cots while Nanny clucked her disapproval. Not that they minded—they made small contented noises into their father's broad shoulder and had no objection when they were passed to Titus.

Arabella, changing for dinner, hummed a little tune as she dressed. This was a happy household and the babies were delightful. It would be nice… She wasn't going to think about that, she told herself resolutely, and went downstairs to drink her sherry and enjoy the roast pheasant and red cabbage, game chips and roasted parsnips. It was beautfully cooked and served in the splendour of starched linen and silver, delicate china and crystal glasses.

The seminar started at eight o'clock in the morning and although they all breakfasted together the two men wasted no time over it. Aldrik gave his wife a lingering kiss and Titus pecked Arabella's cheek with a cheerful, 'See you later, Arabella.'

Cressida noticed that out of the corner of her eye and checked a small doubt. It was obvious that Titus and Arabella got on well together, were at ease with each other, but there was something missing…

'After I've fed the babies at ten o'clock would you like to come into the town and see the shops? They are not bad at all although I go to den Haag for my clothes. I do like that suit…'

It was as they were having their lunch that Aldrik phoned to say that he was bringing Dr Tulsma to dinner. 'She met Titus last time he was over here, darling, and shares his interest in long-term medication. I'm sorry— I know you don't like her but she more or less invited herself and Titus seemed quite enthusiastic. It's a subject dear to him, you know.'

'Well, there's nothing to do about it, is there, darling? Only don't let her stay to all hours.'

'We'll be back around six o'clock. Are you having a pleasant day with Arabella? Are the babies all right?'

'I'm enjoying myself very much; she's a dear and the babies are fine.'

'Darling,' said Aldrik, and rang off.

'There's someone coming to dinner,' said Cressida. 'A doctor—she's frightfully clever and she'll talk about enzymes and antibodies and things. She's invited herself and I'm sorry—I was looking forward to a chatty evening. If she suggests coming again I'll say we're going out for the evening.'

They spent a lazy afternoon and after tea bathed the babies and put them to bed since it was Nanny's evening off, and then they changed. Arabella, going through the clothes she had brought with her, decided on the jersey dress. Simple, beautiful material and worth every penny she had paid for it. Doing her hair, she decided that when she got back home she would go to a good hairdresser and have a perm, even have it all cut off—anything as long as it was different from the mousy topknot she was now arranging so neatly.

She and Cressida were in the drawing-room when the men got back.

Aldrik opened the door with a cheerful hello and

stood back to allow a young woman to walk past him. Cressida hadn't said what she was like—arrestingly handsome, with large blue eyes and corn-coloured hair in little curls all over her head, and her dress, of some flowing silky stuff, was cut low over an opulent bosom. She didn't look in the least like a doctor but vaguely romantic and mysterious. Arabella, being introduced, smiled and held out a hand. The enemy, she thought silently, and wondered why she had thought that.

Titus had smiled at her as he came into the room but that was all. She felt resentment bubbling up and suppressed it; later she would give it full rein... 'How delightful to meet you,' said Arabella mendaciously. 'What interesting work you do, and you and Titus share a common interest, don't you?' She sat down on a small sofa and patted the place beside her. 'Do sit down and tell me something about it. Have you known Titus a very long time?'

Geraldine Tulsma eyed her carefully. 'On and off for several years. You and Titus haven't been married long, have you?'

'No—but of course we've been friends for some time.' Arabella spoke airily. 'You're not married? Titus says you're very clever.'

Aldrik had given them their drinks and Arabella settled against the cushions, aware that the dress was falling in very satisfactory folds around her person. After all, that was what she had paid for...

'No, I'm not married. I have refused offers of marriage many times; my work is very important to me.' She spoke sharply. Here was this plain girl asking her patronising questions. 'Has Titus never spoken of me to you?'

'Well, no. What I mean is, I dare say he might have

mentioned you—just to remark on your cleverness, you know. We have so many shared interests—nothing to do with his work or hospital.'

'I have come this evening so that I may continue to exchange views with Titus.'

'What a good idea. It's a pity you don't see more of each other.' She looked up as Cressida joined them.

'Getting to know each other?' she wanted to know. 'I'm sorry we haven't got a man for you, Geraldine, but it was such short notice.'

'I do not mind. It is Titus I wish to talk to.'

'Very well, why not? But shall we dine first?'

Arabella ate asparagus, coq au vin and chocolate and orange mousse piled high with whipped cream, and it all tasted the same—of nothing. Her keen dislike of Geraldine had taken away her appetite although she talked and laughed as everyone else did. Geraldine tended to carry on in a tedious fashion about herself, her aims and her ambitions and theories. They went back to the drawing-room for coffee and presently Geraldine suggested that she and Titus should have a quiet talk.

Arabella overheard her. 'I'm sure Titus is anxious to hear your views.' She gave him a smile as bright as a dagger's edge and he blinked at it before saying smoothly,

'Indeed I am, if you don't mind, Cressida? We don't want to inflict medical matters upon you.'

'Use my study,' said Aldrik. 'There'll be more coffee presently.'

When they had gone Cressida went up to the nursery to make sure that the twins were sleeping. 'I'm sorry that Geraldine invited herself here this evening,' said Aldrik, 'she's heavy-going.' He glanced at his watch. 'I'll suggest driving her back as soon as we've had some more coffee.'

'It's very nice,' said Arabella carefully, 'that Titus has met someone he enjoys talking to. I mean, I don't know anything about hospitals and medicine...'

'Nor does Cressida—you have no idea what a blessing and a joy it is to come home each evening to someone who doesn't know ichthyosis from nettle-rash...'

'I do know what nettle-rash is!' said Arabella. They were laughing about that as Titus and Geraldine came back into the room and Aldrik rang for more coffee.

Cressida came back and they sat around drinking it, chatting idly until Aldrik said, 'Isn't it time you saw to the twins, my love? I'll run Geraldine back home while you're doing that.'

'Don't bother,' said Geraldine. 'I've already asked Titus to drive me back. We can finish our discussion— there hasn't been enough time...'

Titus put down his cup. 'Then, shall we go?' he enquired mildly. 'We start early tomorrow morning, do we not?'

'Such a pity that you are only here for such a short time,' declared Geraldine in her rather loud voice. 'We really should meet more often...'

A little imp of mischief took over from Arabella. 'Then why don't you come and visit us?' she asked, and smiled at Titus. 'Wouldn't that be a good idea, Titus?'

His face was inscrutable; she had no idea if he was pleased or not. 'Oh, splendid,' he said. 'Shall we be going, then?'

Geraldine pecked the air above Cressida's cheek, offered a hand to Arabella and said, '*Tot ziens*,' to the room at large.

'See you all later,' said Titus as he followed her out.

Cressida and Aldrik went to the door with them and Arabella went to the window. The light from the hall streamed out into the street and she could see Titus and Geraldine standing by the car, holding a conversation in which she took no part, laughing at some joke which she couldn't hear.

The enemy, thought Arabella. Geraldine was modern to her fingertips, attractive and determined—divorce would mean nothing to her and Titus was a prize worth having. I'm exaggerating, thought Arabella, and why do I feel like this about her? It isn't as if I love Titus. She caught her breath, because of course that wasn't true. She did love him; she was in love with him. She closed her eyes for a moment and when she opened them the car had gone. A good thing too, she reflected, for I might have gone outside and thumped Geraldine and flung myself at Titus.

She wanted to cry at the hopelessness of it all. Instead she stitched a smile on to her face and turned to make some cheerful remark to Cressida, unaware that she was as white as a sheet and trembling.

Chapter 7

Cressida was on the point of asking Arabella if she felt ill but Aldrik touched her arm and said cheerfully, 'Come over to the fire, Arabella. We're going to have another cup of coffee—do have one too.'

He began to talk about the evening and then the various lectures and the seminar he and Titus were to attend. 'Next year it will be held in London and so we shall see something of you there.'

'You must come and stay.' Arabella had pulled herself together. 'We shall love to have you and the babies, of course.'

They sat for half an hour or so and since there was no sign of Titus Arabella went to bed, to lie awake until she heard Titus's tread long after midnight. This is a pretty kettle of fish, she told herself. Of course, now she thought about it, she had been falling in love with

Titus for weeks only she hadn't realised it. Would it have helped if she had known that before he had asked her to marry him? she wondered. She would have refused; being married to someone who didn't love you when you loved them would be an unbearable state in which to live. One in which she now found herself. But there is no reason, she reflected, why I shouldn't have a try at getting him to fall in love with me. The right make-up, a good hairdresser, attractive clothes, sparkling conversation and her feelings disguised under a friendly manner—but not too friendly. He must never think that she was trying to attract his attention or that she had no other interest in life but him.

A few tears escaped and trickled down her cheeks and she wiped them away impatiently. If she was to get the better of Geraldine and her like tears would be of no use. Suddenly full of determination to get the better of the enemy, Arabella went to sleep.

The men had already breakfasted and gone when she went down to breakfast with Cressida. 'I've been awake for hours,' said Cressida pouring their coffee. 'Aldrik read his paper to me—he always does, not that I understand any of it. He says it will bring him luck, not that he needs it. Did Titus wake you up to listen to his paper?' She didn't wait for an answer. 'We're a captive audience, aren't we?'

'I expect he's breaking me in gently,' said Arabella lightly. 'Do the twins let you sleep all night?'

'Oh, yes. Once or twice I've had to feed them in the small hours but now they're bigger they usually sleep right through until six o'clock. Aldrik's awfully good—we don't disturb Nanny and by the time they've settled the morning tea arrives.' She poured more coffee. 'Tell

me, what did you think of Geraldine?' She grinned. 'You
don't need to be polite.'

Arabella buttered some toast. 'I didn't like her. Far
too handsome for one thing and so pleased with herself.
All that bosom too…'

Cressida laughed. 'Frightful, isn't she? She's brilliantly clever, though. Aldrik can't stand her but even
he admits that he admires her brain.' She glanced at Arabella. 'Did Titus give you his opinion? She kept him long
enough—we heard him come in last night.'

'Yes, he was very late—I do hope he didn't disturb
you.' She added for good measure, 'He was far too tired
to talk about her.'

'You'll get the lot—chapter and verse. That's what's
so nice about being married, telling each other things
you would never dream of telling anyone else.'

Arabella agreed so quietly that Cressida made haste
to talk about something else. 'If you would like to go
sightseeing Nanny will have the twins until lunchtime.
We might take a look round the town—there's the university and the Pieterskerk and the Rapenburg Canal. We
can see the hospital from there too. There's Breestraat
and the Town Hall and the St Anna Almshouses…'

'All in one morning?'

'Well, it will be a quick peek here and there but better than nothing. We must find time for coffee at Rotis-
serie Oude Leyden too…'

The morning was passed pleasantly and rather to their
surprise the men came home for lunch.

'We didn't expect you,' said Cressida, lifting her face
for a kiss. 'But now you're here we're very pleased.'

'We decided that the whole day without seeing ei-

ther of you would be too long. What have you done with
yourselves?'

They came home again soon after six o'clock that
evening, and without Geraldine. Arabella, curling up
in bed that night, thought with pleasure of the cosy evening—a delightful dinner and then sitting round the fire
in the drawing-room talking about everything under the
sun. Titus had kissed her with a sudden and unexpected
warmth when she had gone upstairs with Cressida. Of
course it might have been because the others were there
watching them but she didn't think that he would pretend to something he didn't feel. They were going out
on the following evening, she remembered sleepily. She
would wear one of her new dresses…

She was glad that she had chosen to wear the pink
dress for they drove to den Haag where they dined at
the Bistroquet—small and exclusive and, she guessed,
wildly expensive. Afterwards they went to Schevenin-
gen, to the Steigenberger Kurhaus, to dance and visit
the casino. Titus had bought her some chips and she
had tried her luck and won, and so had Cressida. She
would have liked to put her winnings back on the table
but the men had swept them back to dance. It had been
a lovely evening and she had spent a good deal of it in
Titus's arms dancing and, just for the moment, happy.

The next day was their last, with a formal banquet in
the evening, and Arabella was glad that she had packed
the green velvet. Inspecting her person before she went
downstairs to join the others, she decided that she looked
like a consultant's wife. She wished that Titus had given
her a necklace as she fastened the double row of pearls
her father had given to her on her eighteenth birthday.

They were good ones and of course her engagement ring was everything a girl could wish for...

'Oh, very nice,' said Cressida as she went into the drawing-room. She looked quite delightful herself in a smoky grey taffeta dress. She wore a diamond necklace and an exquisite bracelet—Arabella caught a glimpse of them as Aldrik wrapped her lovingly in an angora wrap.

Titus held her evening cloak with the impersonal courtesy which he might have afforded an elderly aunt... Arabella, suddenly angry, thanked him politely, her cheeks pink. He might at least pretend.

Titus, watching her from under his heavy lids, thought what a very pretty girl she had become in the few weeks of their marriage. It was the clothes, he supposed. When they got back to England he would look around for some jewellery for her. He felt a surge of delight at the sight of her and bent to kiss her cheek, an action which pleased Cressida, who, in the privacy of their bedroom, had informed Aldrik that their guests didn't behave in the least like a newly married couple.

'My dear love,' her husband had observed, 'you cannot judge others by our own experience. Probably they—er—let themselves go when they are alone, just as we do.'

The banquet was a grand affair and very formal. Arabella had never seen so many large elderly gentlemen in black ties, smoking cigars and tossing off tiny glasses of *genever*, nor had she seen so many dignified ladies with severe hairstyles and large bosoms encased in black satin. There were younger people there, of course, but they were swamped by the senior members of the university and the hospital. They were nice, she discovered, these self-assured dignitaries, and Titus seemed to know all of them. She was handed round and smiled at and patted and told how glad they were to see dear Dr Tavener married to such a charming little wife.

She sat next to a younger man at dinner, with an older man on her other side, both of whom made much of her so that her lovely eyes sparkled and her face glowed—not entirely with pleasure, though. Titus, she noted, had Geraldine on his right on the opposite side of the long table. Geraldine, she had to admit, looked strikingly handsome in peacock-blue chiffon. A pity there was to be no dancing, she reflected. As it was, they sat for a long time over dinner and then listened for even longer to a succession of speeches—some in English but most of them in Dutch. It was hard to maintain a look of interest. When they rose at last little groups were formed while, coffee-cups or glasses in hand, people wandered from one to the other. The men were for the most part serious—swapping diagnoses, she supposed, listening with an air of great interest to an elderly professor detailing the history of the university to her.

It was as they were preparing to leave that she came face to face with Geraldine. 'Oh, there you are.' Her voice was patronising. 'I have hardly spoken to you all evening, have I?' She smiled in a self-satisfied manner and swirled the chiffon to show it to its best advantage. 'Titus and I have had a delightful evening—you don't mind, do you? We have known each other...'

Arabella interrupted her. 'Any friend of Titus's is a friend of mine,' she said sweetly, 'and do remember that we shall be delighted to see you if ever you come to England. Perhaps your work keeps you here, though?'

'No, no. I am well-known both in England and the States, as well as in Europe.' She gave a satisfied little laugh. 'I am free to take a holiday when I wish.'

'How nice,' said Arabella. 'It's been pleasant meeting you. We're going home tomorrow but of course Titus will have told you… So I'll say goodbye.'

Geraldine offered a hand. 'Shall we not say, *tot ziens*? That means—'

'Yes, I know what it means. I must go—I can see Cressida waiting for me.'

There was no sign of Titus. 'A good thing he came in his own car,' said Cressida. 'He's driving Geraldine back. Why that woman can't drive her own car beats me—anyone would think that she had already asked—' She stopped as Aldrik squeezed her arm.

'The trouble with Geraldine is that given an inch she takes an ell.' He took Arabella's arm. 'Did you enjoy your evening? It was all a bit serious, I'm afraid.'

'I enjoyed myself,' said Arabella, her eyes sparkling with temper. 'What a handsome lot of professors and medical people you've got living here.'

'Indeed, yes. I have to keep a tight rein on Cressy when we come to these gatherings; she's inclined to fall for bearded professors!'

'If you ever grow a beard I shall leave you,' declared Cressida as they went out to the car. 'When we get home I shall make a big pot of tea and we can drink it in the kitchen while we tear the women's dresses to pieces. There was one—you must have seen it, Arabella—purple crushed velvet, very tight in the wrong places…'

On this light-hearted note the evening ended, but although she sat for some time, drinking tea out of mugs and discussing the evening, there was no sign of Titus.

Arabella, with the excuse that she must do some packing if they were to leave in time for the ferry in the morning, went to bed, declaring that she hadn't enjoyed herself so much for years. 'You must all come and stay soon,' she said. 'I shall miss you so.'

After she had gone Cressida collected up their mugs. 'Darling,' she began, 'there's something not quite right…'

'My love, Arabella and Titus are grown people.' He smiled. 'Somehow I don't think we need to worry. Arabella is no fool, Cressy.'

'Does that mean that Titus is?'

'No, no—we men are notoriously blind, love, as you well know.'

She skipped across the kitchen into his arms. 'I'd like them to be as happy as we are.'

Titus was at breakfast looking well rested and impeccably turned out. He and Aldrik had been out with the dogs and were in some deep discussion while Arabella and Cressida talked of Christmas and what they planned to do. Presently they went upstairs to see the babies and then it was time to go. The men had joined them in the nursery but time was running out. They made their final goodbyes, got into the car and drove to the Hoek, boarded the ferry and, in due course, landed at Harwich.

They were home that evening to be greeted by Mrs Turner, a great pile of letters for Titus and a number of messages on the answering machine. Titus, coming from his study just before they were to sit down to dinner, came into the drawing-room.

'I have to go to the hospital—it's a matter of some urgency. I'm sorry, Arabella. Please don't wait up if I'm not back. Tell Mrs Turner to lock up; I'll let myself in.'

'We'll leave something for you in the kitchen; it'll keep hot on the Aga. I hope it's nothing too serious and that you can put it right.'

He came across the room and bent to kiss her. 'What a perfect wife you are, Arabella. This does happen from time to time.'

'Well, it's bound to, isn't it?' she said in a matter-of-fact voice. 'Be sure and have something when you get back if we are all in bed.'

She listened to the street door closing and went to tell Mrs Turner, reflecting that a doctor's wife could expect this—and not just once but over and over again.

She ate her solitary dinner, thinking about him. He was everything a girl could wish for and she loved him—two reasons to strengthen her resolve to make him love her. He liked her and perhaps he felt affection for her—but that wouldn't do. She would have to do something to make him see her with different eyes—not just as a quiet companion, ready at hand to listen when he wanted to talk or walk, but as a girl to take him by surprise so that he really saw her.

He hadn't returned by eleven o'clock; Mrs Turner had already locked up so Arabella went to bed.

'Was it all right?' Arabella asked at breakfast. Titus was already at the table but he got up to pull out her chair. He looked as though he had had a good night's sleep but her loving eyes could see that he was tired. 'Were you up all night?'

'Until just after four o'clock this morning. He'll pull through.'

'I'm glad. It must make you feel good.'

He smiled. 'Yes, it does. I'll be at my rooms until this afternoon, then the hospital. I expect to be home soon after five o'clock.'

'Oh, good. Shall we have tea together?'

'That would be delightful. What are you going to do today?'

'Well—I thought I'd go to the hairdresser. I wondered if I had my hair cut short and permed—'

He said with surprising sharpness, 'No, Arabella, I like your hair just as it is—don't let anyone touch it. Have it washed as often as you like but not an inch of it must be cut off.'

She stared at him round-eyed. 'All right, Titus, then I won't. Only I thought it would improve my looks.'

'Your looks are very nice as they are.'

'Thank you. I thought you liked short curly hair and I wanted to please you.'

'Well, I don't and that reminds me—why in heaven's name did you ask Geraldine Tulsma to come and see us?'

She looked meek. 'Titus, I thought you liked her, and she told me that you were old friends. You spent a lot of time together...'

She spoke so artlessly that he sat back and looked at her thoughtfully. He smiled then. 'So we did. She's very attractive, isn't she? Apart from her brilliant brain.'

'She's almost beautiful and it must be nice to be able to talk about things and know the person you're talking to understands exactly what you're saying.' She took a breath. 'She would have made you a splendid wife, Titus—if I'd known about her...'

'An interesting thought, my dear.' He got up, patted her on the shoulder in what she felt was an avuncular fashion and said, 'I must be off. See you this evening.'

She telephoned the manor when he had gone and talked for a long time to old Mrs Tavener and then spoke to Butter, who assured her that the dogs and Percy were fine and that Bess and Jerry were full of spirit. 'Looking forward to seeing you, ma'am—coming for the weekend, I hope?'

'I do hope so, but I don't know if the doctor will be free. I want to talk about Christmas with Mrs Butter...'

'We'll hope to see you, ma'am.'

It would be nice to be at the manor again, she thought, and went to put on her outdoor things. She hadn't thought about Christmas presents—it might be a good idea to look round the shops and decide on what to buy. It would have been fun to have had Titus with her.

When he got home he asked her what she had been doing.

'Looking at the shop windows, trying to decide what to buy for Christmas presents,' she told him.

'I'll give myself a half-day tomorrow—in fact I had arranged it some time ago. We'll go shopping together.'

'Oh, Titus, how lovely. I've made a list...'

She didn't think she would ever forget their afternoon together. He parked the car in the forecourt of a hospital near Brompton Road and walked her to Harrods to embark on the kind of shopping spree every woman would dream of. There were gloves for Miss Baird, a crimson dressing-gown for Mrs Turner, a charming tea-service for the Butters, a fine woollen stole for Miss Welling in rose-pink—to give her some colour, as Arabella said—the latest novels for Cressida, teething-rings for the twins, a hamper for Mr Flinn and a beautiful vase for the Marshalls.

'That takes care of the bulk,' said Titus. 'We give the nurses a bottle of wine and a cheque and the same for the maids and the gardener at the manor.'

'And the boy who helps in the garden?'

He smiled down at her. 'I happen to know that he

wants football boots—he's in the village team. The men who come up to help had better have cash. Now we have to find something for Grandmother.'

The jeweller's shop was like an Aladdin's cave. 'What do you suppose she would like?' asked Titus.

'Something she can put on easily,' said Arabella very sensibly. 'And something she can wear each day if she wants to. A chain perhaps?'

They had looked at chains of all types and chosen a fairly long one of gold links with a gold tassel. It was a beautiful thing and just right for the old lady. While it was being wrapped up Arabella went from showcase to showcase, admiring their contents, but only to herself. Titus was a generous man—if she evinced a desire for a diamond necklace she had no doubt that he would buy it for her. That wasn't what she wanted, though. She would rather have a bag of apples he had bought for her without any hint on her part.

They went home presently and piled the parcels on the sitting-room table. 'I'll leave you to wrap them up,' said Titus easily. 'I'm sure you'll do it beautifully. They will keep you occupied tomorrow—I'm going to Birmingham to a consultation; I may stay the night.'

He looked at her as he spoke and she quickly arranged her features to an expression of interested concern. 'Would you like me to pack a bag for you? You'll drive there?'

'Yes—you won't be lonely?'

'Good gracious, no.' She had spoken too quickly and added, 'Not with all those presents to wrap up. Besides, I've still a few more presents to buy and what about the Christmas cards?'

They had chosen them and ordered them to be printed

but she had no idea to whom they should be sent when they arrived.

'There is a list in the top right drawer of my desk in the study; you can safely send a card to each address on it. I usually get Miss Baird to do them but it would be much nicer if you were to sign them yourself for us both.'

'Very well. You will be free to go to the manor for Christmas?'

'Yes, unless something very urgent crops up. We'll go down next Saturday too, shall we?'

'Yes, please. It will be nice to see the animals again. Butter says they're all very well and happy and I talked to your grandmother—she was hoping you'd be free next weekend.'

He nodded. 'I've some work to do now—could dinner be put back for half an hour or so?'

'Of course. I'll go along and see Mrs Turner.' As they crossed the hall she said, 'It was a lovely afternoon, Titus, thank you for taking me.'

'I enjoyed it too.' He sounded remote.

In his study he didn't pick up the telephone immediately. It was quite true, he had enjoyed himself—perhaps because Arabella had been so obviously delighted with everything she saw. Her ordinary face under her charming hat had glowed with pleasure. She was, he decided, really a pretty girl and her new clothes had made no difference to her; she was still forthright and sensible and undemanding. A most agreeable person to live with and one he would miss—the very thought of that made him frown. Really he was getting quite fond of her.

His work forgotten, he allowed his thoughts to wander.

Arabella's thoughts were wandering too as she changed into one of her new dresses, but they wandered to some good purpose. Sternly suppressing her more loving thoughts of Titus, she concentrated them on the best way in which to encourage him to fall in love with her. Perhaps she was too much the taken-for-granted friend, rather like a favourite pair of comfortable shoes—hardly noticed but always there. A little coolness perhaps, a slight show of independence—although she had no idea how to set about that. Beyond his remarks that she looked nice from time to time, her beautiful new clothes hadn't had much effect upon him. It was a pity she couldn't alter her face. In the privacy of her room she had tried out various make-ups and decided that all of them made her look peculiar, and he had sounded annoyed when she had suggested that she should have her hair cut off.

'Oh, well,' said Arabella. 'I must leave Fate to take a hand.' She gave her hair a final pat and went down to the drawing-room.

Titus was still in his study but he joined her for dinner presently and spent the evening with her, talking idly about their plans for Christmas. There was an annual party for the children in the village, he explained, and they should attend. The carol singers would come early on Christmas Eve and be invited into the manor— a long-held custom.

Arabella nodded. 'Mince pies and hot drinks. Shall we have a Christmas tree?'

'Of course—Butter sees to that. There will be one or two of the family there.' When she looked up in surprise, for he had told her that his parents had been dead for some years, he said, 'An aunt or so—and a couple of cousins and their children. And a great-uncle to keep Grandmother amused...' He added gently, 'I didn't tell you before—I didn't want you to worry about meeting a number of strangers, but they are family; we meet seldom, but Christmas is a long-standing custom I don't care to break.'

'A house full of guests is lovely for Christmas,' said Arabella. 'It will be delightful to meet your family. If you'll give me a list of their names I'll look for presents...'

'Will you? I'm afraid I shan't have the time. We're not doing anything for the rest of the weekend, are we?'

'Just Dr and Mrs Marshall coming to dinner the day after tomorrow.'

'Ah, yes, of course.' He stretched out his long legs and picked up the newspaper.

'The week after next,' said Arabella in a no-nonsense voice, 'we are invited to a party at Mrs Lamb's. You told me to accept.'

'Oh, lord, I'd forgotten.' He looked at her over the paper. 'An indefatigable matchmaker on my behalf—she knew my mother well and seemed to think that it was her duty to find me a wife.'

'Oh, dear. Need I go? I could have a headache...'

'My dear girl, my main purpose in marrying you was to put a stop to Mrs Lamb's efforts to introduce me to those ladies whom she considered suitable.'

If that was meant as a compliment, thought Arabella, it had been rather ineptly put. She sighed. Not only had she to contend with Geraldine, the enemy, now there was Mrs Lamb too. She said merely, 'Is it a dress-up party?'

'Very much so. Black tie and long frocks. Buy something for it—you always look very nice.'

Who wants to look nice? thought Arabella and smiled sweetly at him.

She would find something to make him open his eyes—black velvet perhaps, with a tight skirt slit all the way up and a plunging neckline. She couldn't hope to compete with Geraldine but she had some nice curves.

Of course she didn't buy the black velvet, but a lengthy prowl at Harrods the next day brought to light the very dress she knew would be right for the occasion. Silver-grey chiffon over a satin slip, cunningly fashioned to emphasise and make the most of the curves. She studied herself in the long mirror in the fitting-room and nodded with satisfaction. It concealed what it revealed— or should that be the other way round? Anyway, it was a masterpiece and never mind the price.

Leaving the shop, the dress box in her hand, she felt guilty at spending money—so much money—when there were so many people who needed it so badly. She opened her purse and gave an elderly man selling cheap cigarettes and lighters its entire contents. She had to walk all the way home after that but at least she had made someone happy.

The cards had come and she went to Titus's study to look for the list he had told her to use. There was another list there too—charities, a dozen or more. She read it and felt a surge of love for him. He might have wealth but he was generous too. She sat down at his desk, in his big chair, and began on the Christmas cards.

The Marshalls came on Sunday evening. She and Mrs Turner had planned a special menu and she had set the table with lace mats and the silver and crystal and arranged a low bowl of holly and Christmas roses with silver candelabra on either side. They were to have watercress soup, rack of lamb and a mince tart with syllabub to follow. Arabella had itched to do the cooking but Mrs Turner's feelings would have been hurt. Besides, she was an excellent cook. Arabella went upstairs to shower and get into the silk jersey dress, well pleased with her preparations. Before she went downstairs she opened the closet door and took another look at the grey dress. It gave her a thrill just to look at it; she hoped that Titus would get a thrill too.

The evening was very successful; the Marshalls were good company and dinner was as good as she had hoped it would be. They had their coffee, idly gossiping in the drawing-room until the men went away to Titus's study to discuss a case, leaving Arabella and Mrs Marshall by the fire.

Mrs Marshall had known Titus for some years and had frequently urged him to marry. Now, sitting opposite his wife, she felt satisfied that Arabella was the right girl for him. No looks, of course, but charm and a pretty voice, a good figure and lovely eyes. They were easy in each other's company too, almost like very old friends. There were none of those sidelong loving glances she would have expected from newlyweds, although of course Titus wasn't a man to show his feelings and she didn't think Arabella would either. She began to talk about Mrs Lamb's party, an annual event which was always a success. 'You'll enjoy every minute of it,' she assured Arabella, happily unaware how wildly awry this statement would prove to be.

Arabella and Titus drove down to the manor on the following Saturday morning. It was a cold grey day but the house looked welcoming and as he stopped the car the door was opened by Butter and all three dogs came

pelting out to greet them. Percy, more prudent and dis-
liking the cold weather, had stationed himself in the hall
and Arabella, making much of all four of them, turned
a beaming face to Titus.

'Oh, it is nice to be home.' She paused. 'What I mean
is, London's home too, but this is different, isn't it?'

'I know what you mean. Let Butter have your things,
we'll go and see Grandmother, shall we?'

Mrs Tavener was in her room, sitting very upright beside the fire while Miss Welling read to her. She looked
round as they came in, Percy in Arabella's arms, the
dogs at their heels.

'My dears—how delightful to see you. Miss Welling, fetch the sherry—we must all drink to this happy
meeting.'

Which they did, while they told her about Leiden—
Arabella doing most of the talking while Titus sat,
watching her, putting in a word here and there. The day
went too fast after that and so did Sunday. They got into
the car after tea, this time with Beauty and Bassett—
Percy was to stay at the manor since he and Duke had
become firm friends.

'We will be down again next weekend,' said Titus,
eyeing her downcast face. 'If you would like to do so,
there is no reason why you shouldn't stay for a week or
two after Christmas.'

She spoke without thinking. 'And leave you alone in
London? I couldn't do that.'

He turned to look at her but she was gazing out of
the window.

He was away very early on Monday morning to take
a teaching round, leaving her to finish the cards and buy
the rest of the presents. When he got home in the eve-

ning she saw that he was tired. She gave him a second look—not tired perhaps, but worried about something. And when he wanted to know how she had spent her day she told him in her quiet voice.

His eyes were on her face. 'How restful you are, Arabella,' he observed, and when she looked up, surprised, he asked, 'Have the dogs been good?'

The party was the next day. Anxious to look her best, she creamed her face, did her nails, washed her hair and took another look at the dress.

When the day arrived she bade him goodbye after they had had breakfast and assured him that she would have a late tea ready for him before they needed to dress, and then she went off to the kitchen to talk to Mrs Turner and take the dogs for their romp in the garden. Glowing from the cold air, back indoors, she went upstairs to Titus's room to lay out his clothes for the evening only to be interrupted by a peal on the doorbell. She was at the head of the staircase when Mrs Turner opened the door and after a moment stood aside to admit someone. Geraldine Tulsma.

Arabella, hurrying down to the hall, saw that she had a suitcase with her and her heart sank.

Geraldine was in complete command of the situation. 'Here I am, Arabella. I have a day or two free and I know Titus will be delighted to see me.' She shook hands. 'We have known each other too long to stand on ceremony.'

'He's at the hospital,' said Arabella and added belatedly, 'How nice to see you, Geraldine.'

'He'll be home for lunch?'

Arabella led the way into the drawing room. 'Well, no, he won't be back until about five o'clock—we're going to a party this evening...'

'I'll come with you. We're bound to get a chance to talk there—you know what parties are, all noise and chatter, ideal for a quiet discussion. There's a theory I intend to tell him about...'

'How nice,' said Arabella, and felt foolish. 'Do sit down and have some coffee. I'll tell Mrs Turner to get a room ready for you.'

It was like being in a bad dream. Geraldine might despise her as a woman but Arabella was an audience; her ears were ringing by the end of the afternoon. Geraldine had a splendid opinion of herself and liked people to know it.

I don't think Titus will be pleased, thought Arabella as she heard the front door being opened.

Chapter 8

Arabella got up and went into the hall, anxious to tell Titus that Geraldine was there, but Geraldine came with her, hurrying past her and taking Titus's hand in hers.

'I've surprised you,' she exclaimed in her vibrant tones. 'I have a few days off and I came at once, knowing that you would be delighted to talk to someone with a mind compatible with your own.'

The doctor shook the hand on his arm and handed it back. Looking at him, there was no knowing what his feelings might be. He said pleasantly, 'This is indeed a surprise, Geraldine.'

'I knew that you would be delighted.' She waited impatiently as he crossed the hall to kiss Arabella's cheek. 'I hear there's a party tonight. I'm sure no one will mind if I come along too.'

Arabella found her voice and was pleased to hear

how pleasant it sounded. 'I'll phone, shall I, Titus? I'm
sure Geraldine will be welcome. After all, there will be
so many people there that one more won't be noticed.'

He hid a smile. 'Yes, by all means do that, my dear.
Now, if you will forgive me I have some phoning to do.
I'll be in my study if you should want me, Arabella.'

Geraldine looked disappointed. 'I suppose it is necessary for him to go away,' she observed to Arabella.
'I will go to my room and unpack and rest until he has
finished what he has to do.'

Arabella, the epitome of the perfect hostess, led the
way upstairs, offered refreshment, an extra blanket and
the assurance that she would be waiting to let Geraldine
know the moment that Titus was free.

'I hope those dogs will be quiet,' said Geraldine. 'I
do not care for them. And you have a cat…'

'Yes,' said Arabella equably, 'we both like animals.'

She went downstairs, her eyes sparkling with rage.
It wouldn't have mattered so much if Titus had looked
annoyed, even taken aback at Geraldine's appearance.
There had been no expression on his face— She paused.
Yes, there had. Faint amusement. She couldn't think
why.

She went to the phone then, to explain about their
unexpected guest, and was assured that their hostess
would be delighted to see any friend of Titus's. 'Friend,'
muttered Arabella through her teeth, and turned to find
Titus in the doorway, watching her.

'Geraldine's very welcome,' she told him airily. 'I'll
just go and talk to Mrs Turner.'

That lady's feathers were ruffled—the nice little dinner for two would have to be stretched to three. 'Coming

unexpected like that,' she grumbled to Arabella. 'How long will she be stopping, ma'am?'

'Well, not long, I think. She said something about a few days…'

Mrs Turner gave the sauce she was stirring a look which should have curdled it.

Titus was in the drawing-room when she went back there, stretched out in his armchair with Percy on his knee and the dogs drowsing by the fire. Arabella eyed him peevishly. 'I'll go and tell Geraldine that you're out of the study—she asked me to let her know. I'm sure you won't want to miss any time with her!'

She flounced to the door to be halted by his quiet voice. 'Am I mistaken in thinking that you are making it as easy as possible for Geraldine and me to be together, Arabella?'

'Well, that's what you want, isn't it? I hadn't noticed you discouraging her.' She swept out of the room and went to tap on their guest's door.

Dressing for the party, Arabella reflected that if Titus and Geraldine had wanted to be together she had given them every opportunity. After a token appearance with their guest she had excused herself on some household pretext and left them alone. 'And I hope they enjoy each other's society,' she observed to Percy, sitting on the end of her bed, watching her as she dressed.

Contrary to the normal desires of a woman in love, Arabella ignored the silver-grey dress and picked out a dress which hadn't been designed to catch a man's eye at all—an elegant mouse-brown silk crêpe, guaranteed to be eclipsed by the other gowns worn at the party. She had overlooked the fact that it fitted her quite delightfully and by its very quiet elegance would stand out in a crowd.

Her hair in a French pleat, her face nicely made up, she went down to the drawing-room to find Titus already there. He got up when she went in and took stock of her. 'Charming.' He took a box from his pocket. 'I would like you to wear this, Arabella...'

He had gently unclasped the pearls around her neck and fastened a diamond necklace in its place. He didn't say anything and after a moment she crossed to the great mirror over the fireplace and took a look. It was a delicate affair, the diamonds set in small flower-like sprays in gold, the necklace a series of fine gold loops between each spray. It looked like a spangled spider's web. She touched it gently. 'It's old...'

'Yes. It has been in the family for a great many years and is handed down from one bride to the next.'

She looked at his reflection in the mirror. 'So of course it is right and proper that your wife should wear it this evening.' She turned on him, her cheeks very pink. 'We have to keep up appearances, do we not?'

He had gone rather white. 'If that is how you choose to look at it...'

The door opened and Geraldine came in, wearing another floating chiffon creation in vivid pink.

'What a charming dress,' said Arabella. 'So—so colourful, don't you agree, Titus?'

'Extremely so.'

Geraldine viewed her opulent person with satisfaction. 'One doesn't want to look drab...' She smiled at Arabella. 'Time enough to dress in brown and black and grey when one is old. Are we likely to meet anyone interesting this evening?'

'I'm sure you will meet someone to interest you,' said Titus smoothly.

Arabella added sweetly, 'You can always fall back on Titus.'

A remark which earned her a cold stare from her husband.

The party was in full swing when they arrived. Arabella, Titus's firm hand steering her from group to group, smiled and shook hands and murmured party talk, all the while aware that breathing down her neck was Geraldine, intent on keeping as close to Titus as possible. If he minded this, there was no sign of it and presently, after the dancing had started and he had had the first dance with Arabella, he handed her over to an eager young man and as she danced away she saw him bending his head to hear what Geraldine was saying.

She saw them dancing together presently and then lost sight of them as she went from one partner to the other—a small graceful girl, the brown dress a splendid foil for the diamonds around her neck.

There was a buffet supper and briefly she found Titus with her again but, since there were half a dozen other people clustered around the table, talking was out of the question—besides, what did she have to say?

She danced for the rest of the evening while she laughed and talked and wondered if Titus would ever fall in love with her. Several of the men there had expressed their pleasure in her company, which was more, she reflected unfairly, than Titus had ever done. Memory could be a very convenient thing to lose when one was angry and unhappy and, she had to admit, jealous of the tiresome Geraldine.

Back at the house in the very early hours of the morning, that lady showed an alarming tendency to sit about discussing the evening. Arabella wondered what she should do. Urge the lady to go to bed? Go to bed herself and leave her with Titus? Make some graceful remark and sweep Geraldine upstairs with her? She might not go...

It was Titus who said presently, 'Well, I've some work to finish. I'll say goodnight, Geraldine.' He kissed Arabella very deliberately. 'I won't disturb you, my dear.'

Arabella saw Geraldine's instantly alert face. 'Oh, I'm a light sleeper, Titus—I dare say I'll still be awake,' she uttered in a voice dripping with sweetness while she glared at him.

Percy was at the top of the stairs, waiting for her.

'I believe cats to be dirty animals,' said Geraldine, sweeping past him.

'Have you ever watched a cat washing itself? A pity some humans aren't as thorough.' Arabella saw her guest to her bedroom door, wished her goodnight and, gathering up Percy, went to her own room.

The house was very quiet. She undressed, put on her dressing-gown and, bidding Percy stay where he was on the bed, tiptoed downstairs again. Bassett and Beauty would be in the kitchen; she always went to see them before she went to bed.

They were snoozing in their baskets but they woke as she went into the warm room. She bade them goodnight, sitting on the floor between them, an arm round Bassett's small body and the other around Beauty's massive neck. The day had been horrid and she was glad it was all over.

'Though mind you,' said Arabella, 'tomorrow may be a great deal worse.'

Presently she crept back through the house and up the stairs, unaware that Titus had opened his study door and was watching her.

Titus was getting ready to leave the house when she went down to breakfast. 'Geraldine not with you?' he wanted to know.

'She fancied breakfast in bed,' said Arabella, matter-of-factly. 'Did you want to see her? Shall I give her a message?'

His look made her feel uncomfortable. Was it amusement? What had he to be amused about?

'Would you tell her that I have arranged a visit to the Royal College of Physicians? Eleven o'clock—the main door. I'll be home some time after five o'clock, Arabella.' He turned at the door. 'Did I tell you how charming you looked last night?'

He had gone before she could think of a reply to that, which was as well for she was fuming at the thought of him and Geraldine strolling round the Royal College of Physicians. She was vague as to what functions were held there or for what purpose one would visit it—sufficient that the pair of them were going to spend the morning there and probably have lunch together afterwards...

She went upstairs to give Geraldine the message, noting with satisfaction that while her guest when fully clothed gave the appearance of a magnificent figure, in bed she was plain fat. She probably wore a strongly built foundation with bones...

'I shall be out to lunch,' said Geraldine, without bothering to thank Arabella for the message. She took a bite of toast. 'Titus enjoys my company.' She slid a sly glance in Arabella's direction. 'But of course you know about that.'

Arabella sat down in a pretty little armchair by the window. 'No, I don't—at least, not your version. Do tell?'

'Many men have loved me,' declared Geraldine smugly, 'but there is only one whom I wish to marry and that is Titus—he must have told you that he wanted to marry me?' She didn't wait for an answer, which was just as well. 'But I was a silly girl. I wished to make my mark in the medical world and so I continued to refuse him—each time he came to Leiden I would say no. I was wrong, of course—two brilliant minds such as ours are meant to become one. I cannot blame him for marrying you—there is nothing about you which could come between us. You are of no account; you are not clever, nor are you pretty. A very nice person, I am sure,' she added graciously, 'therefore I have no feelings of jealousy about you. You are Titus's wife but of course he has no love for you, that is obvious to my eyes—the eyes of a woman who loves him.'

Arabella found her voice. She could stand no more. 'How very interesting—but I mustn't keep you talking or you will be late. Have you finished your breakfast? I'll take the tray. Mrs Turner is busy and I'm going downstairs anyway.' She added politely, 'Do you know how to get to this place.'

'No.'

'No, nor do I. I should take a taxi or ask a policeman.'

She was in the garden with Percy and the dogs when Geraldine called to say, 'I am going now,' and added, 'I shall be back during the afternoon.'

Arabella went to the front door with her, wished

her a delightful day and closed the door after her. She would feel better if she had a nice quiet cry. She leaned against the door and sniffed and snivelled and sobbed, and then went and washed her face, powdered her pink nose and drank the coffee Mrs Turner brought her, carefully avoiding looking at her swollen eyes and ill-disguised nose.

'That woman,' said Mrs Turner viciously to Betty, one of the girls who came in daily to help. 'I'd like to get my hands on her. The doctor must be out of his mind. And don't you remember what I've just said, or breathe a word, or I'll take my rolling pin to you!'

Arabella took the dogs into the park and came back for lunch, which she pushed around her plate and didn't eat. There was no sign of Geraldine but she hadn't expected there to be. She got into her outdoor things again, told Mrs Turner that she was going shopping and would be back for tea, and let herself out of the house.

She had no idea where she wanted to go. A cruising taxi came along and she hailed it and said, 'Oxford Street,' because it was the first place she thought of. There were lights there and the pavements were thronged with people doing their Christmas shopping. She walked slowly, stopping to look at the gaily dressed windows, buying several things she neither needed nor liked particularly—a scarf which was of a colour she never wore, socks with Father Christmas and his reindeer embroidered on them, which Titus would receive with outward pleasure and never wear, and a pair of outsize earrings, glittering with imitation jewels, dangling almost to her shoulders. When she got home she put them all carefully in a drawer in her bedroom. The scarf at least would be just right for Betty, who loved bright colours. The socks she buried under a pile of undies but the earrings she put on. They looked absurd and she turned her head to and fro watching them swing and glitter. She kept them on and went downstairs to have her tea in the animals' company.

Mrs Turner brought the tea tray. 'That Dr Tulsma came back an hour ago. Said she needed to rest. Shall I tell her the tea's ready?'

'Please, Mrs Turner.'

Geraldine joined her five minutes later and Arabella handed her her tea, offered the cakes and enquired as to her day.

'A splendid day,' said Geraldine loudly. 'I have never enjoyed myself so much—so much to talk about and a delicious lunch. I do not know how I am going to tear myself away from you…'

'Oh, do you have to go back shortly?' Arabella did her best not to sound delighted.

'My dear Arabella, duty calls and someone in my position cannot ignore that. I go on an evening flight. I rang for a taxi just before you returned home.'

'Rang for a taxi?' repeated Arabella. 'You mean you're on the point of leaving now?'

'Indeed I am.' She glanced at the clock. 'In ten minutes or so.'

'Can't you wait for Titus? He'll be so disappointed and I'm sure he would drive you to Heathrow.'

Geraldine put her hand on her ample bosom. 'We have said goodbye. We have to be satisfied with these brief glimpses of each other—there will be other meetings.'

She went away to fetch her things and Arabella, rather dazed with the suddenness of it all, wished her goodbye and a safe journey.

'You are quite a nice little thing,' said Geraldine. 'I can understand that Titus finds you exactly the kind of wife he needs—undemanding and allowing him to lead his own life and lacking in childish romantic notions. Goodbye, Arabella.'

She went out to the waiting taxi and Arabella shut the door on her for the second time that day. Mrs Turner, coming into the hall, took a look at her face. 'I'll make a nice pot of tea, ma'am, and you just sit down and enjoy it. It's not my place to say so, but it's nice to have the house quiet once more.'

'She's very beautiful,' said Arabella in a small voice.

'Beauty is but skin-deep,' quoth Mrs Turner. 'Just you go back and sit by the fire and there'll be a fresh pot of tea in a brace of shakes.'

Arabella drank the tea and then sat back in her chair, Percy on her knee, the two dogs sprawled at her feet. The day's happenings had been strange and they had sounded the death knell over any hopes she might have had about Titus's feelings towards her. Geraldine had made it clear that she and Titus would have married save for her reluctance to give up her career, and although Arabella hated her she couldn't believe that she would tell a pack of deliberate lies about it. Titus had made it plain before they married that although she and he were friends there was no question of love.

She was still sitting there, the tea forgotten, when Titus came in. It was unfortunate that the first thing he said was, 'Hello, where's Geraldine?'

Arabella sat up straight; the dogs had run to meet him and Percy set indignant claws in her skirt at being disturbed. 'She left for Heathrow half an hour ago.'

He sat down opposite her. 'Rather unexpected—did she get a phone call to return, I wonder?'

Arabella said carefully, 'You don't need to pretend, Titus. She told me about you and her. You said goodbye this afternoon after you'd had lunch together, didn't you? You knew she was going back.' She swallowed the lump of tears in her throat. 'I'm only sorry that you must both be so unhappy. Of course it can all be put right, can't it? It's easy these days and it isn't as if…'

'Before you go on with this rigmarole, Arabella, let us put it into plain language.'

He had spoken quietly but his voice was cold and his eyes, when she looked at him, were hard and cold. 'Not to mince matters, you are telling me that Geraldine and I are in love, that we are unhappy and you are kindly planning to divorce me.'

'Well, that's what I said, didn't I? It was plain enough for an idiot to understand. I can quite see that you need a wife—I suppose all professional men do—but why pick on me?' She answered herself. 'I'm undemanding and allow you to lead your own life and I don't have any childish romantic notions—she told me that.'

'Did she, indeed? Geraldine seems to have told you a great deal. And you believed her?'

'I didn't want to, really I didn't, but someone like her—I mean, an important well-known doctor wouldn't tell lies, would she? Besides, you said that you wished to marry for the wrong reasons—for someone to come home to each day, a companion, someone to put an end to your friends trying to marry you off. I accepted all that but only because I didn't know about Geraldine, did I?'

'You don't want to hear my side of the story?'

'I wouldn't be human if I didn't, would I? But I don't want to—I'm sure talking about it would make you feel unhappy.'

'Not unhappy, my dear Arabella, but blind with rage, and if you persist in sitting there filled with sweetness and forgiveness I shall wring your little neck.'

'In that case,' said Arabella, 'I shall go and sit somewhere else.'

She whisked out of the room, clutching Percy, and went to the kitchen to say that she had a headache and would go to bed.

'A morsel of supper?' asked Mrs Turner.

'No—no, thank you. The doctor will dine at the usual time, please.'

The doctor had poured himself a drink and gone back to his chair. He sat for a long time deep in thought, but presently he laughed. 'What a pair of fools we are,' he observed to the dogs, who mumbled an understanding and went to sleep again.

'Madam's gone to her bed,' said Mrs Turner severely, serving him his soup. 'Got a headache and I'm not surprised. I may be speaking out of turn, sir, but that lady-friend of yours fair upset madam.'

The doctor tasted his soup. 'Delicious. Dr Tulsma and Mrs Tavener don't have much in common, Mrs Turner, and her visit was unexpected.' He glanced up at his faithful housekeeper. 'I think it unlikely that she will visit us again.'

'That's a good thing, sir, for I don't like to see madam upset—such a sweet little lady she is, as you well know, no doubt.'

'No doubt at all. Will you take a nice little supper up-stairs presently? A little food often helps a headache.'

'One of my omelettes,' breathed Mrs Turner, and went back to the kitchen with his soup plate.

Arabella, fortified by a delicious light supper, slept soundly and went down to breakfast. She had no wish to apologise and indeed she couldn't see why she should—he had wanted to wring her neck, hadn't he? He was the one to apologise. She sat down opposite him at the break-fast table and poured herself a cup of coffee, accepted the plate of scrambled eggs he fetched from the side-board and wished him good morning in a polite voice.

'Feeling better?' he enquired in a breezy manner which annoyed her at once. 'There's nothing like a good night's sleep to help one regain a normal view of things.'

She buttered toast and ate a mouthful of egg. 'My view of things is exactly the same as it was yesterday evening,' she told him frostily. 'I see no point in dis-cussing it any more.'

'Not at the moment, perhaps. You still persist in your absurd accusations, Arabella?' His voice was smooth but it had a nasty edge to it. She reflected with a tiny shiver that he must have a nasty temper beneath that calm visage. Not that he could frighten her, she told herself silently.

She said clearly, 'Yes—and they are not absurd. You told me yourself in Holland that Geraldine was one of the most honest and dependable doctors you had ever met. You're not going to accuse her of lying, are you?'

He glanced at his watch and didn't answer her. 'I must go, I've a good deal to get through today. I'll be home by six o'clock, barring accidents. We are to dine with the Marshalls, aren't we?'

'Yes.'

'Good. In a day or two, when you've calmed down, we can have a quiet talk.'

'I do not want a quiet talk,' said Arabella pettishly. 'I can think of nothing more to say.'

'That astonishes me. I, on the other hand, have a great deal to say. Time enough to say it when we are at the manor.'

He put a hand on her shoulder as he went to the door and the touch of it sent sudden tears to her eyes. She loved him so, and she was behaving in all the wrong ways. She wasn't sure quite *how* to behave; he hadn't been very nice about her being sweet and forgiving...

Christmas was very near now; she wrapped some more presents, arranged Christmas cards all over the drawing-room—for they had been sent any number—and spent a long time making a centrepiece for the table with holly and Christmas roses and trails of ivy and sweet-scented hyacinths. It looked pretty when she had finished it and so did the small Christmas tree standing in front of the window, with its twinkling lights and glass baubles.

Tomorrow, she remembered, several of the doctors' wives were coming for coffee; she had met them at the Marshalls' and at the party and they had offered to tell her about the various festivities which would take place at the hospital after Christmas—to have them in for coffee had seemed a good idea. She was aware that they were curious about her but too polite to show it, and it would be nice if she could become one of their circle.

She took the dogs for a walk then, and presently set out for the last of her shopping. A present for Titus. She had left it until last, hoping to gain some inspiration as to what he would like. He seemed to have everything; the only thing was to go and look in shop windows and hope to see something.

She might be angry with him and unhappy too, but she loved him despite that. It would have to be something very special. She went from one end of Bond Street to the other and down the arcades, peering in windows— what did one give a man who had everything?

She found it at last in a small bookshop, crammed to the ceiling with rare editions, old maps and prints. An early edition of Chaucer's *Canterbury Tales* in its original text; she remembered that he had mentioned his interest in the book and as far as she knew he had only a modern version of it. She bore it home, reflecting sadly that perhaps this would be the last and only present she would give him. She had an unpleasant feeling that the quiet talk he had suggested might disclose a future she had no wish to contemplate.

In the meanwhile there was the Marshalls' dinner-party that evening. She dressed with extra care—dark green velvet this time, long-sleeved and high-necked, and since she had the time she arranged her hair in a complicated topknot which was well worth the time it took to do.

Titus was home when she went downstairs to the drawing-room. He was sitting with the dogs, reading the afternoon's post, but he got up when she went in.

'I'll go and change. Have the dogs been out?'

She put Percy down by the fire. 'Yes, they've had their walk.'

'Good. Can I get you a drink?'

'No, thank you.'

She sat down and Percy got on to her lap and Bassett danced around her chair.

'You have enjoyed your day?' he asked.

'Yes, thank you. Several people are coming in for coffee tomorrow morning…'

'I shall be away all day, probably until late in the evening. Don't wait up for me tomorrow.'

'I expect you're busy,' she said politely.

'Yes, I have to go over to Leiden in the morning but I shall be back in good time to drive to the manor.'

He went out of the room, leaving her suddenly icecold with panic. He was going to see Geraldine, of course, and tell her what had happened, and when he came back they would have their talk and her heart would be broken.

The dinner party at the Marshalls' house was fairly small and she had met everyone there already. The house was decorated with holly and mistletoe and paper chains and an enormous Christmas tree and the atmosphere was decidedly festive. Dinner was leisurely and the talk was light-hearted and afterwards everyone gathered in the drawing-room, still talking. It was late when finally everyone went home, calling the season's greetings to each other as they went.

Back in the house Arabella said, 'That was a lovely evening; I enjoyed it.' She stood in the hall, looking at him. 'I'll go to bed. Will you be leaving early in the morning?'

'Yes. Shall I give your love to Cressida?'

'Oh, will you be seeing her?'

'Yes. Who did you suppose I'd be seeing, Arabella?'

'Well, Geraldine, of course.'

'Ah, yes, of course.' He turned away to go to his study. 'Goodnight, Arabella.'

There he sat, doing nothing behind his great desk. A brilliantly clever man, he hadn't been clever enough to know when he had fallen in love with Arabella. He supposed, since she had never been out of his mind for long since the moment they had first met, that he had loved her at first sight, unaware of it even when he had asked her to be his wife, knowing only that it was something which he wanted.

He gently pulled Bassett's small ears, for the little dog had climbed on to his knee, and then reached down to rest a hand on Beauty's head.

'When I get back,' he told them, 'we must talk, Arabella and I. Perhaps once we have cleared up this misunderstanding she could learn to love me.'

Arabella went down to her solitary breakfast, determined to fill her day so that there would be no time to sit and brood. There were the last of the presents to wrap and plans to make with Mrs Turner, who would stay in the house over Christmas. Not alone, however. Her married sister and her husband would stay with her and Arabella, prompted by Titus, had seen to it that there was an abundance of Christmas fare for them. Titus had several appointments for the day after Boxing Day and they had planned to return to Little Venice very late on Boxing Day. She wondered now, as she listened with half an ear to Mrs Turner's plans for a meal for them on their return, if it would be a good idea if she were to stay at the manor for a while. It would seem a natural thing to do and, in the light of the present situation, sensible too.

The day seemed long despite her efforts to keep busy.

She had just got back from walking the dogs when the phone rang. Titus's cool voice sounded very close. He would be unable to get back home that evening—he hoped to be back some time the following afternoon. He would go straight to the hospital where he had a clinic and see her later. 'You are all right?' he wanted to know.

'Yes, thank you,' said Arabella. Even if she could have thought of something to say he didn't give her the chance. His goodbye was brief.

She spent the evening deciding what to take with her to the manor, although her mood was such that packing a couple of sacks would have done very nicely. The day was neverending; the coffee morning had taken up part of it, of course, and she had laughed and talked and rather liked her guests and squirmed inwardly at their smiling remarks about brides and a rosy future. Medical men made rather good fathers, one of them had observed, amid laughter. She remembered that now.

Titus got home early the next afternoon, coming in unexpectedly on his way to the hospital. Arabella, tying an artistic bow on the parcel in which she had wrapped Mrs Turner's Christmas present—a handsome dressing-gown—looked up in surprise as he came in.

'I need something from the study,' he explained. 'I'll be home just after five o'clock. Will you be ready to leave shortly after that?'

'Yes. Would you like something before we go? Sandwiches and coffee? Tea?'

'I'll get tea at the hospital—we can have a meal when we get home. Phone Butter, will you? Tell him we'll be there about eight o'clock and will need supper.'

He had spoken pleasantly but she could see that he was impatient to be gone. Her, 'Very well,' was uttered in a matter-of-fact voice although her hands were shaking under the bunch of ribbons.

They left well before six o'clock after giving Mrs Turner her present, loading the boot with things for the manor and stowing the dogs and Percy on the back seat. The streets were crowded with Christmas traffic and it took some time to reach the motorway, and all the while Titus had nothing to say.

Arabella had tried once or twice to start up a conversation but since she received only pleasant monosyllables in reply she had lapsed into silence. Christmas, she thought bitterly. Last Christmas had been a terrible one, with her parents recently dead and the future bleak, but this one was even worse; the future was just as bleak. How could it be otherwise, loving a man who loved someone else?

Chapter 9

There was a Christmas tree ablaze with lights just inside the gates of the manor when they reached it, and lights streamed from the many windows of the house. As they stopped before the door Arabella could hear Duke's deep bark and then was almost deafened by the happy barks of Beauty and Bassett. Titus got out, opened her door and let the animals out of the back of the car, picking up Percy's basket at the same time. Just for a moment Arabella stood looking around her; the door had been opened and Duke had come pelting out to greet them and then tear round the garden with the other two. Butter stood at the door and beyond him she could glimpse another Christmas tree in the hall. She heaved a sigh and Titus gave her a quick look which she didn't see.

Butter stood with a beaming face. 'Welcome home, ma'am—and you, sir. There's a nice little supper waiting for you when you're ready and Mrs Tavener Senior hopes that she and Miss Welling may share it with you.'

'Why, of course,' cried Arabella. 'Nothing would be nicer. I'll just take off my things and say hello to Mrs Butter.'

Titus had been taking Percy out of his basket; she took the cat in her arms and went off to the kitchen, glad to get away from Titus's blue stare.

They all had supper together shortly after and even Miss Welling looked cheerful and drank two glasses of wine. Old Mrs Tavener was full of questions which the doctor answered readily enough, referring often to Arabella to bear him out; whatever their differences were in private, they were to be kept that way.

The old lady went to bed presently with the faithful Miss Welling, very slightly tipsy, in attendance.

'I should like to talk,' observed Titus, 'but I think you have no wish to listen for the moment.'

'Well, no.' She sat down near the fire in the drawing-room with Percy curled up on her lap. 'I think I am still angry and hurt—if you wouldn't mind waiting a few days, until I feel all right again, I'll listen...'

'But you will agree with me that the hatchet should be buried over Christmas. I would not like Grandmother to be made unhappy nor would I like the painstaking preparations taken by the staff to be overshadowed; they have been here for so long that they are quick to sense when anything has gone wrong.'

She said quietly, 'Of course I agree with you. I'll do everything to make it as you wish.' She paused. 'Titus, may I stay here for a few days after Christmas? Just until you come on the following weekend. I think it might be a good idea, don't you?'

When he didn't reply she added, 'It's easier—I mean looking at something from a distance. Do you see?'

'Oh, yes, but surely that depends on how you are looking at it? Clearly and honestly or blinded by all the wrong feelings?'

'Feelings? Feelings?' Arabella wanted to know in a lamentably shrill voice. 'And you're the one who's blind.' She got to her feet, dislodging Percy who stalked to the door. 'I'm rather tired. Goodnight, Titus.'

He was at the door before she could reach it. He was smiling a little and had kissed her before she could turn her head. 'Crosspatch,' he said, and actually laughed.

Which, naturally enough, caused her to burst into tears the moment she got into her room.

Feelings or no feelings, she woke on Christmas Eve knowing that they must be hidden. Besides the extra bustle in the house the carol singers would be coming in the early evening, she would be going to the church with an armful of flowers specially grown in the glass-house and there was a Christmas lunch for the children in the village hall at noon. A busy day and she thanked heaven for it.

She dressed carefully, knowing that it was expected of her, and Titus nodded approval when they met at breakfast. 'I'll see you at the children's party,' he told her pleasantly, for all the world as though they had parted the best of friends. 'I've one or two things to attend to first while you're in church.' He added, 'We go to the midnight service, Arabella. Grandmother and Miss Welling come too, and so do the Butters.'

She thought she detected a warning note in his quiet voice. 'I shall enjoy that. Do we go to the morning service as well?'

'Yes. It makes a full morning so we usually exchange our gifts when we get back here around noon, before lunch. I dare say you've already seen Mrs Butter?'

'Yes, she's arranged everything beautifully.'

'She was the kitchenmaid here when Grandmother came here as a bride. She must have been very young— thirteen or fourteen, I suppose. She has been here every Christmas since then.'

'But she married Butter...'

'There was a butler in those days—servants were two a penny—Butter worked under him until he learned to drive and he's been driving ever since and running the place for me. He's more than a servant, he's an old friend—so is Mrs Butter. She used to give me slices of bread and dripping—I was always hungry and dripping in those days was delicious...'

Arabella looked down at her plate, picturing a small hungry boy wolfing bread and dripping. 'You were happy here?' she asked.

'Yes. And I shall be again.' He added silkily, 'I cannot say that at the moment I am happy.'

'Well, nor am I,' said Arabella in what she hoped was a reasonable voice. Perhaps this was the right moment to talk—over a prosaic breakfast table in the cold light of the morning.

It seemed that it wasn't; Butter came in to say that the flowers had been brought up from the glasshouse and perhaps she would care to approve them when she had breakfasted.

'I'll come now. I've finished,' said Arabella, all of a sudden anxious to escape from Titus, sitting so close to her and yet so far away.

The flowers were beautiful and she was lavish in her

praise. 'I'll take them with me now. I'm going to church early—they'll need to be arranged.'

She put on the new winter coat and added the hat she had bought in a fit of extravagance. It was of the softest felt with a narrow brim which curved around her face and tilted very slightly sideways. It matched the coat exactly and she was well pleased with it. She was pleased with her boots too—of the very latest style, making the most of her small feet—and since it was Christmas she tucked a green scarf patterned with holly into the neck of the coat. Surveying her person in the pier glass, she thought that she didn't look too bad—not that Titus would notice, she reflected—and went downstairs.

He was in the hall, huge in his overcoat, waiting for her.

'Shall we walk down?' he asked her.

Since Butter was hovering, ready to open the door, she said at once, 'Oh, yes, I should like that. Will you take the dogs?'

'Of course. We'll part company at the church—I dare say you'll be some time there. We're expected for coffee at the rectory at eleven o'clock; we'll meet there.'

They went out together and Butter watched them go and thought what a splendid couple they made. Trust the doctor to get himself such a perfect little lady...

Arabella, walking beside Titus out of the gates and into the lane leading to the village, was surprised to find that despite their quarrel she felt quite at ease with him, listening to his easy flow of casual talk. And he, used to putting patients at their ease, watched her expressive face and was satisfied.

He left her at the church after a brief talk—his arm around her shoulder—with the rector, and she was led

away to see about the flowers while the rector enlarged
upon the doctor's splendid character. 'Takes after his
father,' he told her. 'Does a great deal for the village,
you know, and very much dislikes anyone finding out
about it.' He beamed at Arabella. 'But of course he has
no secrets from you, my dear Mrs Tavener.'

She and Titus met again at the rectory where they had
coffee, surrounded by the rector's son and daughter-in-
law and their children, all talking at once and plying
them with mince pies.

Arabella, led away to tidy herself before going to the
village hall, remembered that Titus's various aunts and
uncles would arrive at teatime and wondered if they'd be
as much fun as the rector's household. She adjusted the
hat, powdered her nose and accompanied Titus through
the village once more.

The children's lunch was noisy; the little boys tended
to fight among themselves and the little girls, in their
best dresses, were shy to start with and then noisier
than the boys. They ate everything on the long table and
drank enormous quantities of lemonade before pulling
the crackers, putting on paper hats and crowding round
the Christmas tree to receive the parcels Arabella was
to hand to each of them.

She was enjoying herself mightily; she had taken off
her coat, put a paper hat on top of her own elegant head-
gear and was singing along with the children in a small
clear voice.

Titus was enchanted. The world was a wonderful
place in which to be and only he and Arabella were in
it. He smiled a little—he was a little too old to have such
romantic thoughts. If only she would let him explain
about Geraldine—but he would have to wait for the right

moment to do that. In the meantime they must hide their differences for a couple of days, and perhaps her idea of staying at the manor for a few days was a good one…

They went back home presently, with the dogs running free around them, and had sherry with Mrs Tavener and Miss Welling. They ate their lunch with a good appetite and much cheerful small-talk then separated to go their own ways—Mrs Tavener to rest, with Miss Welling to read aloud to her, Titus to his study and Arabella to tour the guest-rooms to make sure that everything was just as it should be. There would be six guests staying over Christmas and eight more coming to lunch on Boxing Day.

She went to look out of the window of the largest room overlooking the grounds at the back of the house and saw Titus strolling around with the dogs. He looked very much at home in elderly, beautifully tailored tweeds, his hands in his pockets. He was whistling too. The wish to join him was very great. If she did, she reflected, he would greet her with apparent pleasure and set himself out to entertain her with a gentle flow of talk. He would probably wish her at Jericho. She went down to the kitchen and spent the next half-hour conferring with Mrs Butter.

The guests arrived for tea—first Mrs Tavener's son, a very upright grey-haired man with a reserved manner, who shook Arabella's hand and begged her to call him Uncle Tom, and his wife, Aunt Mary, who peered at her through thick lenses and murmured softly that it was a great pity that Jeremy Titus and Rosa weren't there to see their daughter-in-law.

'My father and mother,' said Titus briskly. 'Uncle Tom is the younger son. Come and meet the cousins.'

They were three young men and a girl of her own age. 'Josephine, Bill, Thomas and Mark.' She shook hands with them in turn, aware of their interested gazes.

It was Thomas who spoke, a serious-looking young man who looked as though smiling was an effort. 'We were beginning to think that Titus would never marry...'

'Head of the family and all that,' explained Mark. 'Wish I'd seen you first.' He was a cheerful young man with an engaging grin. 'I'm a medical man too—haven't had time to get married, let alone find a girl to love as yet.' He nodded towards Thomas. 'He's just got engaged and Josephine is on the brink. Before we know where we are the family gatherings will be littered with babies.'

Everyone laughed, even Thomas, and after that the talk became general over tea round the fire. Presently Arabella went away to help Mrs Butter with the dinner table; they had discussed the menu over the phone some time ago and had decided on smoked salmon, rack of lamb with several vegetables and sauté potatoes, and a trifle for dessert. The table looked charming with a starched linen cloth, the family silver, a centrepiece of holly, ringed around by red candles in silver candlesticks, and sparkling crystal glasses. She went away to change her dress, feeling well pleased.

It was after one o'clock by the time she was in bed. The church had been full and no one had hurried away afterwards but had stayed, exchanging good wishes, and old Mrs Tavener had had to be coaxed away and driven back. Arabella had accompanied her and Miss Welling to her own rooms and seen her safely settled with a warm drink.

'You're a dear child,' the old lady had declared. 'Titus is a lucky man.'

He might not agree with that, reflected Arabella in the morning, accepting a cup of hot chocolate from him and sitting down beside Aunt Mary, but he was behaving exactly as he should—the smiling glance, the hand on her shoulder—almost as if he meant it.

Breakfast was leisurely before church and it was only when they got back that the family, with the Butters, gathered round the Christmas tree. Arabella and Titus handed out the presents together and since everyone had brought a gift for everyone else the drawing-room was soon knee-deep in coloured paper. It wasn't until the last of the presents had been handed out that Arabella sat down to open her own pile.

'Move over,' said Titus and sat down beside her on one of the sofas while Butter went round with a tray of champagne. 'I wonder why one has such pleasure in opening parcels?'

'Natural curiosity.' Arabella was admiring a rose-pink silk scarf from Josephine. 'Exactly what I would like best,' she told her new cousin. They were going to get on well together, she and Josephine. They smiled at each other across the room and she picked up the next gift. She had seen quickly enough the little box with its label written in Titus's hand and deliberately left it until the last. There had been presents from the dogs and from Percy of course—chocolates, perfume, a little evening bag—and of course he had bought those, just as she had given him a Victorian ink-blotter for his desk from the four of them. Everyone else was still opening gifts and no one was watching them. She felt his hand on hers for a moment. 'How did you know,' he asked her quietly, 'that I collect rare books?'

'I looked round the library here and at Little Venice. I hope you'll like it.'

'I am delighted with it, Arabella. Thank you, my dear.'

She opened the little box then. There were earrings inside, diamonds set in gold, miniature replicas of the necklace.

She held them up. 'They're beautiful, and they match the necklace—' She looked a question.

'I had them made…'

'But you gave me the necklace only a week or two ago.'

He said patiently, 'I knew I would give you the necklace—oh, before we married—and it seemed that the earrings would go very well with it.'

'You did that before—' she paused and went on softly '—before you—before we went to Holland?'

She choked back tears and Mark called across the room, 'You two—what are you whispering about? Arabella, what has Titus given you? It must be something marvellous to make you look so bright-eyed.'

She got up and went to sit by him, taking the earrings with her, and everyone crowded round to see them. 'You must wear them,' cried Aunt Mary. So Arabella went to the Florentine mirror between the windows and put them on and someone cried, 'Aren't you going to thank him for them? Go on, it's Christmas.'

There was nothing for it but to go over to the sofa. Titus had got to his feet and she stretched up to kiss his cheek. At least, that had been her intention. Instead she found herself swept into his arms and kissed in a manner which took her breath away.

'Oh,' squeaked Arabella, and stared up into his face. His eyes were very blue and the gleam in them was no longer hidden.

'A pity we aren't alone,' he said softly, and let her go amid an outburst of cheerful teasing and laughter.

The rest of the day didn't seem quite real to Arabella. Lunch had been a buffet with everyone milling around—talking about their presents, recalling other Christmases, discussing the rest of the family who would arrive in time for tea. Tea had gone off well too, with a host of new faces and names to remember and the cake to cut, and then a brief peace while those staying in the house went upstairs to change for dinner. She had worn the brown dress with the diamond necklace and the earrings and there had been a lot more talk while they had drunk champagne cocktails and then gathered round the table to eat turkey with all the trimmings and one of Mrs Butter's Christmas puddings. She had sat opposite Titus at the oval table and tried not to look at him, something which she found very difficult.

Boxing Day, with a house overflowing with guests and several people from the village coming in for drinks, kept her so busy that she had no time to talk to Titus—which was a good thing. She was still feeling shy about his kiss and puzzled too, although perhaps he had kissed her like that because the family was watching. When they were alone again she would ask him—they still had to talk about Geraldine…

He went back to Little Venice after dinner on Boxing Day, leaving her there until he came to fetch her at the weekend. She went with him to the door after he had said goodbye to his family in the drawing-room.

'Well, we buried the hatchet very well, didn't we?' he observed, standing close to her, looking down on to the top of her head, smiling a little.

'Well, I think…' began Arabella, to be stilled by the ringing of the phone on the side table.

Titus picked it up. 'Mrs Turner? Is something wrong?' He listened a moment. 'From Leiden? You said I would be back later tonight—good.' He glanced at his watch. 'I should be with you in two or three hours.'

He hung up and Arabella said, 'That was Geraldine…'

He gave her a cold stare, his face expressionless. 'If you say so, Arabella…'

He went out to his car without a word, not looking at her, and because she loved him so much she knew instinctively that he was in a white-hot rage. 'Take care, Titus, oh, do take care…!'

He drove away without a glance and she stood shivering on the step until the tail-lights had disappeared. It was a good thing that when she returned to her guests her white face was attributed to her having to part with Titus. She was surrounded by people intent on cheering her up, plying her with drink and the suggestion that she should go to bed and have a good night's rest.

'All the excitement,' said Aunt Mary. 'You must be worn out. And you've made such a success of it, my dear. We all understand how you feel, it's hard to be parted, but doctors' wives…'

Everyone went home after lunch the following day and Mrs Tavener and Miss Welling retired to their own part of the house, which left Arabella with the three dogs and Percy for company. She had phoned Little Venice early that morning and Mrs Turner had told her that the doctor had left for the hospital not half an hour since. 'Looked worn out, he did,' Mrs Turner had said. 'A good thing when it's the weekend and he can fetch you back.

And all that telephoning just when he should have been going to his bed...'

'Oh, yes,' Arabella had said, 'the call from Leiden...'

'That's right, madam. Went on and on, it did. Must have been about a patient, I suppose, because I heard him say he'd ring later.'

It was a phone call Arabella wished she hadn't made, for it only made the day harder to get through. A long walk with the dogs made her feel better. She had tea by the fire in the little sitting-room with Percy on her lap and the dogs hugging the fire and, since the Butters were going to the village for an evening with friends there, she had undertaken to see to her own dinner.

She busied herself presently in the kitchen—making a salad, cooking scrambled eggs and making a pot of coffee. She ate at the kitchen table, tidied everything away and went back to watch TV, but after a while she switched off and, suddenly making up her mind, phoned Little Venice. Mrs Turner answered again.

She sounded puzzled when Arabella asked to speak to the doctor. 'He's gone to Holland, madam—in a terrible rush, he was. Expects to be back tomorrow some time. I expect he'll phone you from there.'

Her voice held a faint question, so that Arabella said at once, 'I'm sure that he will—if he had a plane to catch he wouldn't have had the time to do a lot of explaining. I shall hear all about it when he gets back and I'm sure he'll phone here once he has the chance. It might be something urgent.'

It was a good thing she was on her own, she reflected, for there was time to think. How he must have disliked having to spend Christmas here, being the perfect host and the perfect husband, she thought. I dare say he made the excuse of work at the hospital so that he could get back as soon as possible. I wonder what she said that made him go to Leiden in such a hurry?

Arabella picked up the magazine lying on the table beside her and began to tear it into ribbons. The exercise gave her a certain amount of satisfaction although she would have much preferred the magazine to have been Geraldine. It relieved her feelings a little, although a few good screams would have been a great relief.

There were two days to get through before Titus would come. She filled them with almost unceasing activity—grooming the pony and the donkey, going for long walks with the dogs, visiting the rectory to say what a delightful Christmas it had been, entertaining various ladies from the village anxious to enrol her in the WI, the first-aid classes, the committee for the annual church bazaar...

Friday came at last and no news from Titus. All the same she had a long session with Mrs Butter about meals for the weekend, saying lightly that she thought he would probably be home late that evening and arranging a light supper for him. She was filled with excitement at the thought of seeing him again even though a quarrel seemed inevitable and her heart, already badly cracked, would be broken completely. A good thing to get it over, she told herself, and took the dogs for yet another walk.

It was late afternoon when she suddenly decided that she couldn't face him. She would go out and walk up the lane behind the house from where she would be able to see the lights of the car. Only when he was in the house would she return. The Butters were in the dining-room so she went to the kitchen and through its doors to a passage lined with small rooms—the pantry, the old-fashioned still-room, the larder, the boot-room. At the end of the passage was another door, leading to the kitchen gardens, behind which were a variety of elderly coats, old hats and, ranged beneath them, a selection of wellies. She got into a jacket with a hood, pushed her feet into Mrs Butter's wellies and went outside.

It was still light although there was a bank of cloud beyond the hills. For a moment she wondered if she should fetch a torch, but supposing Titus was to arrive early and meet her? She buttoned the jacket tightly and set off.

The lane up the hill beyond the kitchen garden was a stiff climb, and she marched to it via the stables so that she might offer carrots pulled from the garden to Bess and Jerry. By the time she was almost at the top, with the thick crown of trees which topped the hill only a few yards away, it was dusk, the distant clouds suddenly overhead and the first few drops of rain falling. As she stood looking down the hill towards the village there was a sudden gust of wind and the trees behind her swayed and creaked as it soughed through them. Though not a nervous girl, she wanted to be home—secure by the fireside.

There was a shortcut down the hill, a narrow path which she and Titus had once taken; it would mean going a little way up into the trees but she thought that she could find it even in the gathering gloom. Somewhere on the right of her, she decided, as the first of the trees closed over her. The rain was coming down in earnest now and turning to sleet as the wind freshened. She took the path and at the fork a few yards further turned to the left, towards the village, took a step forward and rolled into a deep gully—right to the bottom.

It was filled with dead leaves and an inch or so of water. She lay where she was for a moment, too surprised to do anything, and then got slowly to her feet, brushed herself down and looked for a way to climb out. It wasn't a very deep gully but its sides were slippery with wet bracken and earth and when she took hold of a tuft of coarse grass it came away in her hand and landed her in a puddle of water. She would have to climb out before it got really dark so she went carefully all round it, feeling for a foothold in its sides, and came to the conclusion that there weren't any—nor were there any large stones which she could pile against its steep sides.

'How very unfortunate,' said Arabella. Not a panicky person by nature, she felt a nasty little pang of fear at the idea of spending the night there. Not that she would have to do that, she told herself robustly. They would miss her at the manor. A pity she hadn't brought a torch. If the wind would die down she could shout, but at the moment it would be a waste of breath. It just needs a rat or two, she thought gloomily.

The doctor stopped before his home with a sigh of satisfaction. Whether she liked it or not, Arabella and he were going to have that talk—but first of all he would wring her darling little neck and kiss her silent...

He was welcomed by the three dogs with delight and by Percy with dignity and then by the Butters in their turn, beaming at him, deploring the sudden onslaught of bad weather and at the same time offering tea, drinks and saying madam was in the drawing-room.

Only she wasn't. 'Well,' said Mrs Butter, 'she had a cup of tea here earlier, after she took the dogs out. She'll be upstairs. I'll call her.'

'Don't bother, I'll go,' said Titus and went up the staircase two at a time, knocked on the door and went in. Arabella wasn't there, of course; he went from room to room and then downstairs again. She wasn't there either.

'She wouldn't go out,' declared Mrs Butter. 'She took the dogs like I said, and I'd have heard the front door for we were both in the dining-room and you can hear it close from there.'

The doctor said, 'Ah, the back door,' and went to look, the Butters close behind. 'Is there anything missing?' he wanted to know, turning over the coats and capes hanging there.

'My boots,' said Mrs Butter suddenly. 'I had them on this morning—they were here, under that old jacket—I wear when I go down to the kitchen garden.'

'Take a torch, Butter, and go down to the village. See if anyone has seen Mrs Tavener. I'll go up the lane. Wave the torch if you find her—I'll do the same.'

He shrugged into an old mac, gave up the idea of boots since none of them were large enough for his feet, took the torch Mrs Butter had fetched, and opened the door. The wind took his breath as he stood there, the dogs crowding round, anxious to help. They all went up the lane at a great rate with frequent stops while Titus bellowed, 'Arabella,' in a voice to rival the wind.

Arabella heard it. She was numb with cold and her feet, despite the wellies, were blocks of ice although she hadn't stood still. Indeed she had been scrambling in a fruitless manner up the sides of the gully and slipping down to the bottom again. She was frightened now and her answering shout had been no more than a squeak, but she tried again and was cheered to hear his shout in answer. A long minute later she saw the torch shining

above her and looked up to see four pairs of eyes looking down at her.

The dogs barked, delighted to have found her, and the
doctor said, 'Oh, you silly girl,' in such a tender voice
that she very nearly burst into tears. She gulped them
back. 'Don't any of you fall in,' she said.

Titus was examining the gully by the light of the
torch. He bade the dogs sit and then said, 'Now, listen
carefully, Arabella. Go to the end—that's it, as far as
you can go—it's a little lower. I'm going to lie flat and
reach down to you. Lift your arms as high as you can
and I'll lift you out.'

'You won't be able to—I'm too heavy.'

He laughed. 'One of your more ridiculous remarks,'
he said cheerfully. He waved the torch in the air in the
hope that Butter would see it and stretched his considerable bulk on to the soaking ground. It was raining very
hard now but he hardly seemed to notice that. He put his
great arms down into the gully and caught Arabella's
cold hands in his.

She landed in an untidy heap beside him, covered in
mud and bits of bracken and grass and very wet. He got
up and lifted her to her feet and she said in a small polite voice, 'Thank you, Titus,' and burst into tears. He
held her close while she sniffed and snuffled in a manner
totally devoid of any glamour, then she blew her small
nose, mopped her face and said, 'Sorry.'

'My dearest darling girl,' said Titus, in a voice which
she had never heard before. He might have said a great
deal more only Butter came puffing up to join them. As
it was he contented himself with a kiss which took her
breath before observing, 'Mrs Tavener had fallen in the
gully, Butter—she's wet and cold. Would you go ahead

and ask Mrs Butter to get a warm bath ready? We'll be right behind you.'

Butter hurried off and Titus picked Arabella up as though she had been a feather duster and carried her back down the lane with the dogs trotting beside him.

'I can walk,' said Arabella. He had called her his dearest darling girl. Had that been to keep her spirits up? And what about that kiss? Something to remember lingeringly.

Mrs Butter was at the door and so was Butter, with glasses and a bottle of brandy. 'Ah,' said the doctor, putting Arabella down but not letting her go. 'Just what we all need.'

'I don't like brandy,' said Arabella.

A remark of which the doctor, quite rightly, took no notice. She drank it down under his impassive gaze before he picked her up again, this time without the jacket, and carried her upstairs.

Half an hour later, warm and dry and very clean, her still-damp hair hanging down her back, Arabella went downstairs. 'You're not to dress, madam,' Mrs Butter had said. 'Doctor says a warm dressing-gown and you're to go to bed early.' First, however, she had to face him across the dinner table.

Titus was waiting for her in the drawing-room. He looked as though he had never been near a gully in his life—the epitome of a well-heeled gentleman with time on his hands. She went slowly into the room. It would be hard to ask him about Geraldine but it had to be done. 'Titus…' she began.

He was across the room and she was in his arms before she could say another word. 'And before you say anything, my darling heart, I love you. I think that I always have only it didn't occur to me sooner… And before you fling Geraldine in my teeth, I do not care a jot for her—never have. If you hadn't been such a busy-body, flinging me at her head at all hours of the day, you would have seen that for yourself. And, yes, I went to Holland—because Aldrik's mother has had a stroke.' He looked down at her. 'Well, my darling?'

'Well,' began Arabella, 'I love you, you see, and I think I must have a jealous nature.'

'There are ways of curing you of that,' said Titus.

Neither of them saw the faithful Butter come to announce dinner and slide away again.

Presently Titus said, 'I shall always remember this day, my love.'

'Me too,' said Arabella and kissed him just once more.

She was remembering that just eighteen months later, sitting on the window-seat in the drawing-room, an open letter in one hand, a very small baby tucked under the other arm. 'He's coming home, my poppet—listen…'

She began to read the letter again, out loud this time so that their son could hear it too, even though it meant nothing to his very small ears…

Dearest love,
By the time you read this letter I shall be on my way home. I have missed you so—the week has seemed like a lifetime without you. I picture you and our son sitting in the drawing-room reading this—I wonder if I am right? I cannot wait to be with you again.

Why, I wonder, do VIP patients always choose to be ill in far-flung places? He is recovering; he will be flown home some time next week and I shall be able to treat him without having to leave you both.

I am not sure at what time we shall land but I shall be with you at the earliest possible moment. Titus—who loves you.

* * * * *

LOVE CAN WAIT

Chapter 1

Mr Tait-Bouverie was taking afternoon tea with his aunt—a small, wispy lady living in some elegance in the pleasant house her late husband had left her. She was seventy and in the best of health and, although a kind woman, very taken up with herself and that health. She had long ago decided that she was delicate, which meant that she never exerted herself in any way unless it was to do something she wished to do. She was his mother's older sister, and it was to please his parent that he drove himself down from London to spend an hour with her from time to time.

He was standing at the window overlooking the garden, listening to her gentle, complaining voice cataloguing her various aches and pains, her sleepless nights and lack of appetite—aware that her doctor had recently examined her and found nothing wrong, but nonetheless offering suitable soothing remarks when appropriate.

Someone came into the room and he turned round to see who it was. It was a girl—rather, a young woman—tall, splendidly built and with a lovely face. Her hair, a rich chestnut, was piled tidily on top of her head and she was dressed severely in a white blouse and navy skirt.

She was carrying a tea tray which she set down on the table beside his aunt's chair, arranging it just so without fuss, and as she straightened up she looked at him. It was merely a glance; he was unable to see what colour her eyes were, and she didn't smile.

When she had left the room he strolled over to a chair near his aunt.

'Who was that?' he asked casually.

'My housekeeper. Of course, it is some time since you were last here—Mrs Beckett decided to retire and go and live with her sister, so of course I had to find someone else. You have no idea, James, how difficult it is to get good servants. However, Kate suits me very well. Efficient and rather reserved, and does her work well.'

'Not quite the usual type of housekeeper, surely?'

'She is rather young, I suppose. She had impeccable references—Bishop Lowe and Lady Creswell.'

Mr Tait-Bouverie accepted a cup of tea and handed his aunt the plate of sandwiches. 'Someone local?' he hazarded.

'I believe so. She lives in, of course, but her mother lives locally—a widow, so I am told. Left rather badly off, I hear—which is to my advantage, since Kate needs the job and isn't likely to give her notice. I must say, it is most convenient that she drives a car. I no longer need to hire a taxi to go to Thame to my hairdresser each week—she takes me and does the shopping while I'm at Anton's. It gives her a nice little outing…'

Mr Tait-Bouverie, watching his aunt eating sandwiches with dainty greed, wondered if shopping for food could be regarded as a 'nice little outing'.

'And, of course,' went on Lady Cowder, 'she can cycle to the village or into Thame for anything I need.'

'A paragon,' murmured Mr Tait-Bouverie, and passed the cakestand.

He left half an hour later. There was no sign of the housekeeper as he got into the Bentley. He had half expected her to show him out, but it had been Mrs Pickett, the daily from the village, who had opened the door for him and stood watching him drive away.

Kate watched him too, from the kitchen window. She had to crane her neck to do so, for although she had looked at him in the drawing room it had been a quick glance and she wanted to fill in the gaps, as it were.

Tall, very tall—six and a half feet, she guessed—and a very big man. He had a clever face with a high-bridged nose and a thin mouth, straw-coloured hair going grey and, she supposed, blue eyes. He was a handsome man, she conceded, but there was nothing of the dandy about him. She wondered what he did for a living.

She went back to her pastry-making and allowed a small sigh to escape her. He would be interesting to meet and talk to. 'Not that that is at all likely,' said Kate, addressing the kitchen cat, Horace.

She went presently to clear the tea things away, and Lady Cowder looked up from her book to say, 'The chocolate cake was delicious, Kate. My nephew had two

slices. A pity he was unable to stay for dinner.' She gave
a titter. 'These men with their girlfriends.'

Kate decided that she wasn't supposed to answer that.

'You asked me to remind you to ring Mrs Johnson,
my lady.'

'Oh, yes, of course. It had quite slipped my mind.
I have so much to think of.' Lady Cowder closed her
book with an impatient frown. 'Get her on the phone
for me, Kate.'

Kate put down the tray and picked up the telephone.
She still found it difficult to be ordered about without
a please or thank you. She supposed it was something
she would get used to in time.

Back in the kitchen, she set about preparing dinner.
Lady Cowder, despite assuring everybody that she had
the appetite of a bird, enjoyed substantial meals. Kate
knew now, after almost three months, that her employer's order for 'a morsel of fish and a light sweet' could
be interpreted as Dover sole with shrimp sauce, Avergne
potato purée, mushrooms with tarragon and a portion
of braised celery—followed by a chocolate soufflé or,
by way of a change, crème caramel.

It was of no use to allow that to annoy her; she had
been lucky to get work so near her home. She suspected
that she wasn't being paid quite as much as the going
rate for housekeepers, but it included her meals and a
small, quite comfortable room. And the money enabled
her mother to live without worries as long as they were
careful.

Kate had plans for the future: if she could save enough
money she would start up on her own, cooking and de-
livering meals to order. It would need enough capital
to buy a van, equipment for the kitchen and money to

live on while she built up a clientele. Her mother would help, although for the moment that was out of the question—Mrs Crosby had fallen and broken her arm and, although she made light of it, it was difficult to do much with it in plaster.

When Mrs Crosby expressed impatience about it, Kate sensibly pointed out that they couldn't make plans for a bit—not until she had saved some money. If she could get a hundred pounds she could borrow the rest. It was a paltry sum, but would be an argument in her favour when she tackled their bank manager. It would be a risk but, as she reminded herself constantly, she was twenty-seven and if she didn't take that risk soon it would be too late. Being a housekeeper was all very well but it was a temporary necessity.

When her father had died suddenly and unexpectedly their world had fallen apart. He had given up his work in a solicitor's office to write a book, the outline of which had already been approved by a well-known publisher. He had given himself six months in which to write it— but within three months, with the research barely completed, he had fallen ill with emphysema and died within six weeks, leaving his wife and daughter with the remnants of the capital that they had been living on.

It had been a risk, a calculated risk which he had been sure was worthwhile, and it was no one's fault. Kate had set about getting their affairs in order and looked around for a job. A sensible girl, she had looked for work which she could do and do well—and when she'd seen Lady Cowder's advertisement for a housekeeper in the local paper she had presented herself to that lady and got the job.

She had no intention of being a housekeeper for a

day longer than was necessary; she intended to start a cooked-meals service from her home just as soon as she could save enough money to get it started. But she and her mother had to live—her mother's small pension paid the rent and the running costs of the little house, but they had to eat and keep warm and have clothes. Even with the frugal way in which they lived it would take a couple of years. There were better paid jobs, but they weren't near her home. At least she could go home for her weekly half-day off, and on her day off on Sunday.

It was Sunday the next day—a warm June day with hardly a cloud in the sky, and Kate got onto her bike and pedalled briskly down to the village, thankful to be free for one day. She sighed with content as she pushed her bike up the little path to the cottage where she and her mother lived. It was the middle one of three at the top end of the village main street. It was rather shabby, and the mod cons weren't very 'mod', but the rent was low and the neighbours on either side were elderly and quiet. Not quite what they had been used to, reflected Kate, propping the bike against the back fence and going in through the kitchen door, but it was their home…

Her mother came into the kitchen to meet her. Still a good-looking woman, her russet hair was streaked with grey but her eyes were the same sparkling green as her daughter's.

'You've had a busy morning,' she said with ready sympathy. 'No time for breakfast?'

'I had a cup of tea…'

'You need more than that, a great girl like you,' said her mother cheerfully. 'I'll make a pile of toast and a pot of tea and we'll have lunch early. Come and sit down, love. We'll go into the garden presently.'

Mrs Crosby frowned a little. 'I'm not sure that this job is good for you. Lady Cowder seems a very demanding woman.'

Kate sat down at the kitchen table and Moggerty, their elderly cat, got onto her lap. The room was small but very neat and tidy and the sun shone warmly through the window over the sink. It seemed so much nicer than Lady Cowder's gleaming white tiles and stainless steel. She said mildly, 'It isn't for ever, Mother. Just as soon as we've got a little money saved I'll give it up. And it isn't too bad, you know. I get good food, and my room's quite nice.'

She pulled the breadboard towards her and began to slice bread for the toast. 'How is your arm? Isn't it next week that you're to have another plaster?'

'Yes, dear. It doesn't hurt at all, and I only wear a sling when I'm out—then no one bumps into me, you see.'

When Kate started to get up her mother said, 'No, dear, I'll make the toast. It's nice to do something for someone other than me, if you see what I mean.'

Her mother was lonely, Kate realised, although she wouldn't admit that. Kate was lonely, too—and though they had a strong affection for each other neither of them were ever going to admit to their loneliness. She said cheerfully, 'We had a visitor yesterday. Lady Cowder's nephew came to tea.'

Mrs Crosby turned the toast. 'Young? Old? What does he do for a living?'

'Youngish—well,' Kate added vaguely, 'In his thirties, I suppose. Very pale hair going grey, and one of those faces which doesn't tell you anything.'

'Good-looking?'

'Yes, but a bit austere. One of those noses you can look down. Enormous and tall.' She began to butter the toast. 'I've no idea what he does. Probably so rich that he does nothing; he was driving a silver-grey Bentley, so he can't be poor.'

'One of those young executive types one is always reading about. Make their million before they're twenty-one, being clever on the stock exchange.'

'Perhaps, but I don't think so. He looked too—too reliable.'

Mrs Crosby regretfully dismissed him as a staid married man. A pity—Kate met so few men. She had had plenty of admirers while her father had been alive but once she and her mother had moved from their comfortable home in the Cotswolds they had gradually dwindled away, much to Mrs Crosby's regret. Kate hadn't minded in the least—she had felt nothing but a mild liking for any of them. She could have married half a dozen times, but for her it was all or nothing. As she had pointed out to her mother in her sensible way, if any of the men who had professed to love her had really done so they would have made it their business to find out where she and her mother had gone, and followed them. And done something about it.

Kate, who wanted to marry and have children, could see that it wasn't very likely that she would get her wish. Not in the foreseeable future at any rate. She did her best to ignore her longings and bent all her thoughts on a future which, hopefully, would provide her and her mother with a livelihood.

Presently they went into the tiny garden behind the cottage and sat under the old plum tree in one corner.

'Once I can start cooking,' said Kate, 'this tree will be a godsend. Think of all the plums just waiting to be bottled and turned into jam. Perhaps I could specialise in some kind of plum tart...'

'Not this year,' remarked her mother.

'No, no, of course not. But by the end of next year we might have enough money to persuade the bank manager.'

Moggerty had gone to sleep on Kate's lap, and presently Kate dozed off too.

She made light of her job, but she was up early and went to bed late and quite often did the work of two. Lady Cowder saw no reason to hire more help in the house—Kate was young and strong, and didn't complain. Besides, Mrs Pickett came up from the village each morning to help with the housework. That she was elderly, with arthritis in her knees which didn't allow her to do anything much below waist level, was something which Lady Cowder found unimportant; a hefty young woman like Kate had plenty of energy...

Kate awoke feeling much refreshed, ate a splendid lunch with her mother and later that evening cycled back to Lady Cowder's house, half a mile or so outside the village. She reminded her mother that in three days' time, on her half-day off, they would take the bus into Thame and have a look at the shops. They would take sandwiches and eat them on a bench in the pleasant green gardens around the church, and later treat themselves to tea in one of the teashops.

Taking Lady Cowder's breakfast tray up to her room the next morning, Kate found her sitting up in bed with a pad and pencil. She nodded in reply to Kate's polite good morning, accepted her tray without thanks and said,

with more animation than she usually showed, 'My god-
daughter is coming to stay—she will arrive tomorrow, so
get the guest room overlooking the garden ready. I shall
arrange a dinner party for her, of course—Wednesday
suits me very well…'

'My half-day off,' Kate reminded her quietly.

'Oh, so it is. Well, you will have to manage without
it this week—I'll see that it's made up to you later on.
I want Claudia's visit to be a happy one. We can have
a few friends in for tennis, tea on the terrace, and perhaps a little supper one evening. Certainly I shall ask
friends to come for a drink one evening. We must keep
her amused…'

And me run off my feet! thought Kate. She said, without visible annoyance, 'I shall need extra help.'

Lady Cowder looked startled. 'Whatever for? Surely
you're capable of a little extra cooking?'

'Of course I am, Lady Cowder, but I can't make beds
and dust and cook meals for dinner parties and suppers,
let alone teas. Of course, I could go to the supermar-
ket—they have excellent meals, all ready to warm up.'

Lady Cowder stared at her. Was the girl being impertinent? Seemingly not; Kate had spoken gravely and
stood there looking concerned.

'No, no, certainly not. I'll get Mrs Pickett to come
for the whole day.'

'She has a niece staying with her,' volunteered Kate,
straight-faced. 'I think she is in service somewhere in
Oxford—perhaps she would oblige for a few days.'

'Yes, yes, see what you can do, Kate.' Lady Cowder
buttered toast and piled on the marmalade. Feeling magnanimous, she added, 'I dare say you can get an hour or
so free in the evenings after dinner.'

Kate thought that unlikely. 'I should like to go home for an hour this evening, or perhaps after lunch while you are resting, Lady Cowder. My mother and I had arranged to go out on Wednesday, and I must tell her that I shan't be free.'

'Very well, Kate. As long as it doesn't interfere with your work.' Lady Cowder lay back on her pillows. 'You had better get on. I fancy a light lunch of cold chicken with a salad, and one or two new potatoes. Perhaps one of your jam soufflés to follow. I'll let you know later about dinner.'

Kate went back downstairs, dusted the small sitting room where Lady Cowder sat in the morning, got out the Hoover ready for Mrs Pickett and went to the kitchen to make a pot of tea and butter a plate of scones—Mrs Pickett needed refreshment before she started on her work and so, for that matter, did Kate—although a good deal of her day's work was already done.

Mrs Pickett, sweetened by the tea and scones, agreed to come for the whole day.

'A week, mind, no more than that. Sally will come up for a few hours whenever you need her. She'll be glad of a bit of extra money—the cash that girl spends on clothes… How about a couple of hours in the morning? Nine-ish? Just to make beds and tidy the rooms and clear the breakfast. You'll have your work cut out if Her Nibs is going to have parties and such. Sally could pop in evenings, too—help with laying the table and clearing away. I'll say this for the girl: she's a good worker, and honest.' Mrs Pickett fixed Kate with a beady eye. 'Paid by the hour, mind.'

'How much?'

'Four pounds. And that's cheap. *She* can afford it.' Mrs Pickett jerked her head ceilingwards.

'I'll let you know, and about your extra hours. Would you like to stay for midday dinner and clear up after while I get the cooking started?'

'Suits me. Puts upon you, she does,' said Mrs Pickett. 'Do her good to do a bit of cooking herself once in a while.'

Kate said cheerfully, 'I like cooking—but you do see that I need help if there's to be a lot of entertaining?'

'Lor' bless you, girl, of course I do. Besides, me and the old man, we're wanting to go to Blackpool in September for a week—see the lights and have a bit of fun. The extra cash will come in handy.'

Lady Cowder, informed of all this, shied like a startled horse at the expense. 'Anyone would think that I was made of money,' she moaned. She caught Kate's large green eyes. 'But dear Claudia must be properly entertained, and it is only for one week. Very well, Kate, make whatever arrangements you must. I shall want you here after tea to discuss the meals.'

Mr Tait-Bouverie took off his gloves, stood patiently while a nurse untied his gown, threw it with unerring precision at the container meant for its reception and went out of the theatre. It had been a long list of operations, and the last case hadn't been straightforward so there would be no time for coffee in Sister's office—his private patients would be waiting for him.

Fifteen minutes later he emerged, immaculate and unhurried, refusing with his beautiful manners Sister's offer of coffee, and made his way out of the hospital to his car. The streets were comparatively quiet—it was too late for the evening rush, too early for the theatre and cinemagoers. He got into the Bentley and drove himself home, away from the centre of the city, past the Houses of Parliament, and along Millbank until he reached his home—a narrow house wedged between two imposing town houses, half their size but sharing their view of the river and the opposite bank.

He drove past it to the end of the side street and turned into the mews at the back of the houses, parked the car in the garage behind his house and walked back to let himself in through the front door. He was met in the hall by a short, stout man very correctly dressed in black jacket and pin-striped trousers, with a jovial face and a thick head of grey hair.

His 'Good evening, sir,' was cheerful. 'A splendid summer evening,' he observed. 'I've put the drinks on the patio, sir, seeing as how a breath of fresh air would do you no harm.'

Mr Tait-Bouverie thanked him, picked up his letters from the console table and took himself and his bag off to the study. 'Any messages, Mudd?' he paused to ask, and braced himself as the door at the back of the hall was thrust open and a golden Labrador came to greet him. 'Prince, old fellow, come into the garden—but first I must go to the study…'

'Lady Cowder phoned,' said Mudd. 'Twice. She said she would be glad if you would telephone her as soon as you return home, sir.'

Mr Tait-Bouverie nodded absently and sat down behind his desk in the study, with Prince beside him. There was nothing in the post to take his attention and he went into the sitting room at the back of the house and out onto the small patio facing the narrow walled garden. A drink before dinner, he decided. He would ring his aunt later.

It was a pleasant little garden, with its borders stuffed with flowers and a small plot of grass in its centre. The walls were a faded red brick and covered in climbing roses, veronica and clematis. Mr Tait-Bouverie closed his eyes for a moment and wished he was at his cottage in Bosham—roomy, old and thatched, at the end of Bosham Lane beyond the avenue of oaks and holly trees, within sight and sound of the harbour.

He spent his free weekends there, and brief holidays, taking Mudd and Prince with him, sailing in the creek, working in his rambling garden, going to the pub and meeting friends there… Perhaps he could manage this weekend, or at least Saturday. He had a list next Monday and he had no free time at all until Saturday, but it was only Monday now—he had the whole week in which to arrange things to his satisfaction.

He ate the dinner Mudd set before him and went to his study to phone his aunt.

'James, I was beginning to think you would never telephone. I've tried twice to get you.' She paused, but not long enough for him to reply.

'Something so exciting. Dear Julia Travers's daughter, Claudia—my god-daughter, you know—is coming to stay for a week. Such a dear girl, and so pretty. It's all rather sudden.' She gave a little laugh. 'But I'm doing my best to plan a pleasant stay for her. I've arranged a dinner party for Wednesday evening—just a few friends, and you, of course. Do say that you can come…eight o'clock. Black tie.'

Mr Tait-Bouverie listened to this patiently for he was a patient man. A list of possible excuses ran through his head but he discarded them. He didn't want to go, but on the other hand a drive down to Thame in the middle of the week would make a pleasant break.

'Provided there is no emergency to keep me here, I'll accept with pleasure,' he told her. 'I may need to leave directly after dinner, though.'

'Splendid. I'm sure it will be a delightful evening.'

He thought it unlikely. His aunt's friends weren't his, and the evening would be taken up with time-wasting chat, but the drive back to London in the evening would compensate for that.

Lady Cowder talked for another five minutes and he put down the phone with an air of relief. A few minutes later he let himself out of his house with Prince and set off on his evening walk, Wednesday's dinner party already dismissed from his mind. He had several cases for operation lined up for the week and he wanted to mull them over at his leisure. Much later he went to his bed to sleep the sleep of a man whose day had gone well.

Kate, going to her bed, reflected that her day hadn't gone well at all. After she had given Lady Cowder her lunch and eaten a hasty snack herself, she'd got into the car and driven to Thame, where she'd spent an hour or more shopping for the elaborate food decided upon for the dinner party. When she got home she had been summoned once more—dear Claudia, she was told, would arrive before lunch on the following day, so that meal must be something special, and Kate was to make sure that there was a variety of cakes for tea. Moreover, dinner must be something extra special too.

Unlike Mr Tait-Bouverie's, Kate's day had not gone well.

* * *

Claudia arrived mid-morning, driving her scarlet Mini. She was small and slender and pretty—a chocolate-box prettiness—with china-blue eyes, a pert nose, pouting mouth and an abundance of fair curls. She looked helpless but Kate, carrying in her luggage, reflected that she seemed as hard as nails under that smiling face. She had wasted no time on Kate, but had pushed past her to embrace Lady Cowder with little cries of joy which made Kate feel quite sick.

Kate took the bags up to the guest room, fetched the coffee tray and retired to the kitchen where Mrs Pickett was cleaning vegetables.

'Pretty as a picture,' she observed. 'Like a fairy. And such lovely clothes, too. She won't stay single long, I'll warrant you.'

Kate said, 'Probably not,' adding silently that Claudia would stay single just as long as it took her to find a man with a great deal of money who was prepared to let her have her own way, and indulge every whim. And if I can see that in five minutes, she thought, why can't a man?

Her feelings, she decided, mustn't get in the way of her culinary art. She presented a delicious lunch and forbore from uttering a word when she handed Claudia the new potato salad and had it thrust back into her hands.

'I couldn't possibly eat those,' cried Claudia. 'Vegetables which have been smothered in some sauce or other; it's a sure sign that they've been poorly cooked and need disguising.'

Lady Cowder, who had taken a large helping, looked taken aback. 'Oh, dear, you don't care for devilled potatoes? Kate, fetch some plain boiled ones for Miss Travers.'

'There aren't any,' said Kate. 'I can boil some, but they will take at least twenty minutes…'

'Well, really… You should have thought of it, Kate.'

'If Miss Travers will give me a list of what she dislikes and likes I can cook accordingly.'

Kate sounded so polite that Lady Cowder hesitated to do more than murmur, 'Perhaps that would be best.'

When Kate had left the room Claudia said, 'What an impertinent young woman. Why don't you dismiss her?'

'My dear, if you knew how difficult it is to get anyone to work for one these days… All the good cooks work in town, where they can earn twice as much. Kate is a good cook, and I must say she runs the house very well. Besides, she lives locally with a widowed mother and needs to stay close to her home.'

Claudia sniggered. 'Oh, well, I suppose she's better than nothing. She looks like a prim old maid.'

Kate, coming in with home-made meringue nests well-filled with strawberries, heard that. It would be nice, she thought, serving the meringues with an impassive face, to put a dead rat in the girl's bed…

Claudia Travers wasn't the easiest of guests. She needed a warm drink when she went to her room at night, a special herb tea upon waking, a variety of yoghurts for breakfast, and coddled eggs and wholemeal bread—all of which Kate provided, receiving no word of thanks for doing so. Claudia, treating her hostess with girlish charm, wasted none of it on Kate.

Lady Cowder took her god-daughter out to lunch the next day, which meant that Kate had the time to start preparing for the dinner party that evening. She was still smarting from her disappointment over her half-day off.

No mention had been made of another one in its place, and over breakfast she had heard Claudia observing that she might stay over the weekend—so that would mean no day off on Sunday, either.

Kate, thoroughly put out, started to trim watercress for the soup. There was to be roast duck with sauce Bigarade, and Lady Cowder wanted raspberry sorbets served after the duck. For vegetables she had chosen braised chicory with orange, petits pois and a purée of carrots; furthermore, Kate had been told to make chocolate orange creams, caramel creams and a strawberry cheesecake.

She had more than enough to get on with. The menu was too elaborate, she considered, and there was far too much orange…but her mild suggestion that something else be substituted for the chocolate orange creams had been ignored.

After lunch she started on the cakes for tea. Claudia had refused the chocolate sponge and the small scones Kate had offered on the previous day, so today she made a madeira cake and a jam sponge and, while they were baking, made herself a pot of tea and sat down to drink it.

As soon as Claudia left, she would ask for her day and a half off and go home and do nothing. She enjoyed cooking, but not when everything she cooked was either criticised or rejected. Claudia, she reflected crossly, was a thoroughly nasty young woman.

The cold salmon and salad that she had served for dinner the previous evening had been pecked at, and when Lady Cowder had urged her guest to try and eat something, Claudia had smiled wistfully and said that she had always been very delicate.

Kate had said nothing—but in the kitchen, with no

one but the kitchen cat to hear her, she'd allowed her feelings to erupt.

Sally, Mrs Pickett's niece, arrived later in the afternoon. She was a strapping young girl with a cheerful face and, to Kate's relief, a happy disposition. She served tea while Kate got on with her cooking, and then joined her in the kitchen. Mrs Pickett was there too, clearing away bowls and cooking utensils, making endless pots of tea, laying out the tableware and the silver and glass.

Kate, with the duck safely dealt with and dinner almost ready, went to the dining room and found that Sally had set the table very correctly. There was a low bowl of roses at its centre, with candelabra on either side of it, and the silver glass gleamed.

'That's a marvellous job,' said Kate. 'You've made it look splendid. Now, when they have all sat down I'll serve the soup from the sideboard and you take it round. I'll have to go back to the kitchen to see to the duck while you clear the dishes and fetch the hot plates and the vegetables. I'll serve the duck and you hand it round, and we'll both go round with the potatoes and the veg.'

The guests were arriving. Kate poked at her hair, tugged her skirt straight and went to open the door. It was the local doctor and his wife, both of whom greeted her like old friends before crossing the hall to their hostess and Claudia who was a vision in pale blue. Following hard on their heels came Major Keane and his wife, and an elderly couple from Thame who were old friends of Lady Cowder. They brought a young man with them, their nephew. He was good-looking and full of self-confidence. And then, five minutes later, as Kate was crossing the hall with the basket of warm rolls ready for the soup, Mr Tait-Bouverie arrived.

He wished her good evening and smiled at her as she opened the drawing room door. Her own good evening was uttered in a voice devoid of expression.

Mindful of her orders, Kate waited ten minutes then announced dinner and went to stand by the soup tureen. Claudia, she noticed, was seated between the nephew and Mr Tait-Bouverie and was in her element, smiling and fluttering her eyelashes in what Kate considered to be a sickening manner. A pity Sally hadn't spilt the watercress soup down the front of the blue dress, thought Kate waspishly.

Dinner went off very well, and an hour later Kate helped clear the table after taking coffee into the drawing room. Then she went to the kitchen, where the three of them sat down at the kitchen table and polished off the rest of the duck.

'You're tired out; been on your feet all day,' said Mrs Pickett. 'Just you nip outside for a breath of air, Kate. Me and Sally'll fill the dishwasher and tidy up a bit. Go on, now.'

'You don't mind? Ten minutes, then. You've both been such a help—I could never have managed...'

It was lovely out in the garden, still light enough to see around her, and warm from the day's sunshine. Kate wandered round the side of the house and onto the sweep in front of it, and paused to look at the cars parked there: an elderly Daimler—that would be the doctor's—Major Keane's Rover, a rakish sports car—the nephew's no doubt—and, a little apart, the Bentley.

She went nearer and peered in, and met the eyes of the dog sitting behind the wheel. The window was a little open and he lifted his head and breathed gently over her.

'You poor dear, shut up all by yourself while everyone is inside guzzling themselves ill. I hope your master takes good care of you.'

Mr Tait-Bouverie, coming soft-footed across the grass, stopped to listen.

'He does his best,' he observed mildly. 'He is about to take his dog for a short stroll before returning home.' He looked at Kate's face, pale in the deepening twilight. 'And I promise you, I didn't guzzle. The dinner was superb.'

He opened the door and Prince got out and offered his head for a scratch.

'Thank you,' said Kate haughtily. 'I'm glad you enjoyed it.'

'A most pleasant evening,' said Mr Tait-Bouverie.

Kate heaved a deep breath. 'Probably it was, for you. But this was supposedly my half-day off, and on Sunday, when I should have a full day, I am not to have it because Miss Travers is staying on.' Her voice shook very slightly. 'We—I and my mother—were going to spend the day at Thame, looking at the shops. And my feet ache!'

She turned on her heel and walked away, back to the kitchen, leaving Mr Tait-Bouverie looking thoughtful.

Chapter 2

Mr Tait-Bouverie strolled around the garden while Prince blundered around seeking rabbits, his amusement at Kate's outburst slowly giving way to concern. She had sounded upset—indeed, he suspected that most girls would have given way to floods of tears. Knowing his aunt, he had no doubt that Kate was shown little consideration at the best of times and none at all when Lady Cowder's wishes were likely to be frustrated. He had been touched by her idea of a day's outing to Thame to look at the shops. The ladies of his acquaintance didn't look at shop windows, they went inside and bought whatever they wanted.

He frowned as he remembered that she had said her feet ached...

Back in the house, Claudia fluttered across the room to him. 'Where have you been?' she wanted to know, and gave him a wide smile. 'Are you bored?' She pouted prettily. 'Everyone here, except for Roland, is a bit elderly. I'd love to walk in the garden…'

He had beautiful manners and she had no idea how tiresome he found her.

'I'm afraid I must leave, I'm already late for an appointment.'

Claudia looked put out. 'You've got a girlfriend…?'

He answered her in a bland voice which gave no hint of his irritation. 'No, nothing as romantic, I'm afraid. A patient to check at the hospital.'

'At this time of night? It will be twelve o'clock before you get back to town.'

'Oh, yes. But, you see, people who are ill don't observe conventional hours of sleep.' He smiled down at her pretty, discontented face. 'I must say goodbye to my aunt…'

Lady Cowder drew him a little apart. 'You enjoyed your evening?' she wanted to know. 'Isn't Claudia charming? Such a dear girl and so pretty, is she not?'

'Oh, indeed. A delightful evening, Aunt. The dinner was superb. You have a treasure in your housekeeper, if she did indeed cook it. A big task for her, I should imagine—but doubtless she has ample help.'

'Oh, Kate can do the work of two,' said Lady Cowder airily. 'Of course, I allowed her to have a daily woman to help, and a young girl—she waited at table. Some kind of a niece, I believe. The best we could do at such short notice.'

'You plan more entertainments while Claudia is here?'

'Oh, yes—tennis tomorrow, with tea in the garden and perhaps a buffet supper. And on Friday there will be people coming for drinks, and I dare say several of them will stay on and take pot luck. Claudia thinks she may stay until early next week. I must think up something special for Sunday. A barbecue, perhaps. Kate could manage that easily.'

She would manage, thought Mr Tait-Bouverie, but her feet would be aching fit to kill her by then, and her longed-for day off would be out of the question.

'If Claudia is staying until Monday or Tuesday, why don't you bring her up to town on Friday evening? I'm free for the weekend. We might go to a play on Friday evening, and perhaps go somewhere to dine on Saturday. And she might enjoy a drive down to Henley on Sunday?'

'My dear, James, what a delightful idea. We shall both adore to come. I can leave Kate to look after the house—such a good chance for her to do a little extra work...'

'Oh, you're far too generous for that,' said Mr Tait-Bouverie suavely. 'Let the girl go home for a couple of days; your gardener could keep an eye on the house. I'm sure you will want to reward Kate for such a splendid dinner. Besides, why keep the house open when you can lock up and save on your gas and electricity bills?'

Lady Cowder, who was mean with her money, said thoughtfully, 'You know, James, that *is* a good idea. You have no idea how much this place costs to run and, of course, if I'm not here to keep an eye on Kate she might give way to extravagance.'

'I'll expect you around six o'clock,' said Mr Tait-Bouverie. 'And, if by chance I'm held up, Mudd will take care of you both. You'll come in Claudia's car?'

'Yes. She's a splendid driver. She does everything so well. She will make a splendid wife.'

If she expected an answer to this she was to be disappointed. Her nephew remarked pleasantly that he must leave without delay and embarked on his farewells, saying all the right things and leaving the house by a side door.

He was letting Prince out of the car for a few moments when he heard voices, and saw Mrs Pickett and her niece leaving the house from the kitchen door. They wished him goodnight as they reached him, and then paused as he asked, 'You're going to the village? I'm just leaving, I'll give you a lift.'

'Well, now, that would be a treat for we're that tired, sir.'

'I imagine so.' He opened the car door and they got in carefully.

'You will have to tell me where you live, Mrs Pickett.' He started the car and said over his shoulder, 'What a splendid dinner party. You must have worked very hard.'

'That we did—and that poor Kate, so tired she couldn't eat her supper. Had a busy time of it, with all the shopping and the house to see to as well as concocting all them fancy dishes. Now I hears it's to be a tennis party tomorrow—that means she'll have to be up early, making cakes. Missed her half-day off, too, though she didn't say a word about it.'

Mrs Pickett, a gossip by nature, was in full flood. 'It's not as though she's used to service. She's a lady, born and bred, but she's got no airs or graces, just gets on with it.' She paused for breath. 'It's just along here, sir, the third cottage on the left. And I'm sure Sally and me are that grateful,' she chuckled. 'Don't often get the chance of a ride in such a posh car.'

Mr Tait-Bouverie, brought up to mind his manners by a fierce nanny, got out of the car to assist his passengers to alight—an action which, from Mrs Pickett's view, made her day. As for Sally, she thought she would never forget him.

'I cannot think what possessed me,' Mr Tait-Bouverie told Prince as he drove back to London. 'I have deliberately ruined my weekend in order to allow a girl I hardly know to go and look at shop windows…'

Prince leaned against him and rumbled soothingly, and his master said, 'Oh, it's all very well for you to approve— you liked her, didn't you? Well, I'm sure she is a very worthy person, but I rather regret being so magnanimous.'

Lady Cowder told Kate the following morning, making it sound as if she was bestowing a gracious favour. She sat up in bed while Kate drew the curtains and put the tea tray beside her.

'There are some employers who would expect their staff to remain at the house during their absence, but, as I am told so often, I am generous to a fault. You may go home as soon as you have made sure that your work is done, and I expect you back on Sunday evening. Harvey, the gardener, will keep an eye on things, but I shall hold you responsible for anything which is amiss.'

'Yes, Lady Cowder,' said Kate, showing what her employer found to be a sorry lack of gratitude. Kate went down to the kitchen to start breakfast for the two ladies, who liked it in bed. More extra work for her.

It would be lovely to have two whole days at home; the pleasure of that got her through another trying day, with unexpected guests for lunch and a great many people coming to play tennis and have tea in the garden.

Mrs Pickett's feet didn't allow her to walk too much, so Kate went to and fro with pots of tea, more sandwiches, more cakes, lemonade and ice cream.

'It's a crying shame,' declared Mrs Pickett, 'expecting you to do everything on your own. Too mean to get help, she is. I suppose she thinks that having Sally last night was more than enough.' Mrs Pickett sniffed. 'It's the likes of her should try doing a bit of cooking and housework for themselves.'

Kate agreed silently.

That evening there was a barbecue, the preparations for which were much hindered by Claudia rearranging everything and then demanding that it should all be returned to its normal place—which meant that by the time the guests began to arrive nothing was quite ready, a circumstance which Claudia, naturally enough, blamed on Kate. With Kate still within earshot, she observed in her rather loud voice, 'Of course, one can't expect the servants to know about these things...'

Kate, stifling an urge to go back and strangle the girl, went to the kitchen to fetch the sausages and steaks.

'Now you can get the charcoal burning,' ordered Claudia.

Kate set the sausages and steaks beside each other on one of the tables.

'I'm wanted in the house,' she said, and whisked herself away.

She made herself a pot of tea in the kitchen, emptied the dishwasher and tidied the room. It was a fine, warm evening, and the party would probably go on for some time, which would give her the chance to press a dress of Claudia's and go upstairs and turn down the beds. First, though, she fed Horace, scrubbed two potatoes and popped them into the Aga for her supper. When they were baked she would top them with cheese and put them under the grill.

One more day, she told herself as she tidied Claudia's room. The drinks party the next day would be child's play after the last few days. She wished Mr Tait-Bouverie joy of his weekend guests, and hoped he was thoughtful of his housekeeper. She wasn't sure if she liked him, but she thought he might be a man who considered his servants...

The barbecue went on for a long time. Kate did her chores, ate her potatoes and much later, when everyone had left and Lady Cowder and Claudia had gone to their rooms, she went to hers, stood half-asleep under the shower and tumbled into bed, to sleep the sleep of a very tired girl.

Since Lady Cowder and her goddaughter were to go to London in the early evening, the drinks party the next day was held just before noon, and because the guests had tended to linger, lunch was a hurried affair. Kate whisked the plates in and out without waste of time, found Lady Cowder's spectacles, her handbag, her pills, and went upstairs twice to make sure that Claudia had packed everything.

'Though I can't think why I should have to pack for myself,' said that young lady pettishly, and snatched a Gucci scarf from Kate's hand without thanking her.

Kate watched them go, heaved an enormous sigh of relief and began to clear lunch away and leave the house tidy. Horace had been fed, and Harvey promised he would be up to see to him and make sure that everything was all right later that evening. He was a nice old man, and Kate gave him cups of tea and plenty of her scones whenever he came up to the house with the vegetables. He would take a look at the house, he assured her, and see to Horace.

'You can go home, Missy,' he told her, 'and have a couple of days to yourself. All that rumpus—makes a heap of work for the likes of us.'

*   *   *

It was lovely to sleep in her own bed again, to wake in the morning and smell the bacon frying for her breakfast and not for someone else's. She went down to the small kitchen intent on finishing the cooking, but her mother wouldn't hear of it.

'You've had a horrid week, love, and it's marvellous to have you home for two whole days. What shall we do?'

'We're going to Thame,' said Kate firmly. 'We'll have a good look at the shops and have tea at that patisserie.'

'It's expensive...'

'We owe ourselves a treat.'

They sat over breakfast while Kate told her mother about her week.

'Wasn't there anyone nice there?' asked Mrs Crosby.

'No, not a soul. Well, there was one—Lady Cowder's nephew. He's very reserved, I should think he has a nasty temper, too. He complimented me on dinner, but that doesn't mean to say that he's nice.'

'But he talked to you?'

'No, only to remark that it had been a pleasant evening.'

'And?'

'I told him that it might have been pleasant for some, and that my feet ached.'

Her mother laughed. 'I wonder what he thought of that?'

'I've no idea, and I really don't care. We'll have a lovely day today.'

A sentiment not echoed by Mr Tait-Bouverie, who had welcomed his guests on Friday evening, much regretting his impulsive action. After suitable greetings he had handed them over to Mudd and, with Prince hard on his heels, had gone to his room to dress. He had got

tickets for a popular musical, and Mudd had thought up
a special dinner.

Tomorrow, he had reflected, shrugging himself into
his jacket, he would escort them to a picture gallery
which was all the fashion and then take them to lunch.
Dinner and dancing at the Savoy in the evening would
take care of Saturday. Then a drive out into the country
on Sunday and one of Mudd's superb dinners, and early
Monday morning they would drive back.

A waste of a perfectly good weekend, he had thought
regretfully, and hoped that Kate was enjoying hers more
than he expected to enjoy his. 'Although, the girl is no
concern of mine,' he had pointed out to Prince.

Presently he had forgotten about her, listening to
Claudia's ceaseless chatter and his aunt's gentle complaining voice. A delicious dinner, she had told him, but
such a pity that she wasn't able to appreciate it now that
she suffered with those vague pains. 'One so hopes that it
isn't cancer,' she had observed with a wistful little laugh.

Mr Tait-Bouverie, having watched her eat a splendid
meal with something very like greed, had assured her
that that was most unlikely. 'A touch of indigestion?' he
had suggested—a remark dismissed with a frown from
Lady Cowder. Indigestion was vulgar, something suitable for the lower classes...

He'd sat through the performance at the theatre with
every show of interest, while mentally assessing his
work ahead for the following week. It would be a busy
one—his weekly outpatients' clinic on Monday, and a
tricky operation on a small girl with a sarcoma of the
hip in the afternoon. Private patients to see, and a trip
to Birmingham Children's Hospital later in the week.

In his own world of Paediatrics he was already making a name for himself, content to be doing something he had always wished to do, absorbed in his work and content, too, with his life. He supposed that one day he would marry, if he could find the right girl. His friends were zealous in introducing him to suitable young women in the hope that he would fall in love, and he was well aware that his aunt was dangling Claudia before him in the hope that he would be attracted to her. Certainly she was pretty enough, but he had seen her sulky mouth and suspected that the pretty face concealed a nasty temper.

The weekend went far too quickly for Kate. The delights of window shopping were followed by a peaceful Sunday: church in the morning, a snack lunch in the little garden behind the cottage with her mother and a lazy afternoon. After tea she went into the kitchen and made a cheese soufflé and a salad, and since there were a few strawberries in the garden she made little tartlets and a creamy custard.

They ate their supper together and then it was time for Kate to go back to Lady Cowder's house. That lady hadn't said exactly when she would return—some time early the following morning, she had hinted. Kate suspected that she would arrive unexpectedly, ready to find fault.

The house seemed gloomy and silent, and she was glad to find Horace in the kitchen. She gave him an extra supper and presently he accompanied her up to her room and settled on the end of the bed—something he wouldn't have dared to do when Lady Cowder was there. Kate found his company a comfort, and, after a little while spent listening rather anxiously to the creaks

and groans an old house makes at night, she went to
sleep—her alarm clock prudently set for half-past six.

It was a beautiful morning; getting up was no hard-
ship. She went down to the kitchen with Horace, fed
him generously, let him out and made herself a pot of
tea. She didn't sit over it but went back upstairs to dress
and then went round the house, opening windows and
drawing back curtains while her breakfast egg cooked.
She didn't sit over breakfast either—fresh flowers were
needed, preparations for the lunch that Lady Cowder
would certainly want had to be made, the dining room
and the sitting room needed a quick dusting…

Lady Cowder arrived soon after nine o'clock, driven
in a hired car, her eyes everywhere, looking for something she could complain about.

She had little to say to Kate. 'Dear Claudia had to
drive to Edinburgh,' she said briefly. 'And my nephew
had to leave early, so it seemed pointless for me to stay
on on my own. You can cook me a light breakfast; I had
no time to have a proper meal before I left. Coddled eggs
and some thinly sliced toast—and coffee. In fifteen minutes. I'm going to my room now.'

Lady Cowder wasn't in a good mood, decided Kate,
grinding coffee beans. Perhaps the weekend hadn't been
a success. Come to think of it, she couldn't believe that
she and Claudia and that nephew of hers could have
much in common. Although, since he had invited them,
perhaps he had fallen in love with Claudia. She hoped
not. She knew nothing about him—indeed, she suspected that he might be a difficult man to get to know—
but he had been kind, praising her cooking, and he might
be rather nice if one ever got to be friends with him.

'And that is most unlikely,' said Kate to Horace, who was hovering discreetly in the hope of a snack. 'I mean, I'm the housekeeper, aren't I? And I expect he's something powerful on the Stock Exchange or something.'

If Mr Tait-Bouverie, immersed in a tricky operation on a very small harelip, could have heard her he would have been amused.

It was some days later, chatting to one of his colleagues at the hospital that he was asked, 'Isn't Lady Cowder an aunt of yours, James? Funny thing, I hear her housekeeper is the daughter of an old friend of mine—he died a year or so ago. Nice girl—pretty too. Fallen on hard times, I hear. Haven't heard from them since they left their place in the Cotswolds—keep meaning to look them up.'

Mr Tait-Bouverie said slowly, 'Yes, I've met her. She seems very efficient, but overworked. My aunt is a kind woman, but incredibly selfish and leaves a good deal to Kate, I believe.'

'I must do something about it.' His elderly companion frowned. 'I'll get Sarah to write and invite them for a weekend.'

'Kate only has Sunday off...'

'Oh, well, they could spend the day. Have they a car?'

'Kate rides a bike.'

'Good Lord, does she? I could drive over and fetch them.'

'Why not invite me, and I'll collect them on my way and take them back on my way home?'

'My dear James, that's very good of you. We'll fix a day—pretty soon, because we're off to Greece for a couple of weeks very shortly and I dare say you've your own holiday planned. I'll write to Jean Crosby. They left very

quietly, you know; didn't want to make things awkward,
if you understand. A bit dodgy, finding yourself more or
less penniless. Kate had several young men after her, too.
Don't suppose any of them were keen enough, though.'

Mr Tait-Bouverie, overdue for his ward round, dismissed the matter from his mind. He liked Professor
Shaw; he was a kindly and clever man, but also absent-
minded. He thought it was unlikely that he would remember to act upon his suggestion.

He was wrong. Before the end of the week he was
reminded of their plan and asked if he could spare the
time for the Sunday after next. 'Sarah has written to
Jean and won't take no for an answer, so all you need
do is to collect them—come in time for drinks before
lunch. Our daughter and her husband will be here, and
she and Kate were good friends. Spend the day—Sarah
counts on you to stay for supper.'

Mr Tait-Bouverie sighed. It was his own fault, of
course—he had suggested driving the Crosbys down.
Another spoilt weekend, he reflected, which he could
have spent sailing at Bosham.

Kate, arriving home for her day off with barely time
to get to church, since Lady Cowder had declared in
her faraway voice that she felt faint and mustn't be left,
had no time to do more than greet her mother and walk
rapidly on to church.

She felt a little guilty at going, for she was decidedly
out of charity with her employer. Lady Cowder, cos-
seted with smelling salts, a nice little drop of brandy and
Kate's arm to assist her to the sofa in the drawing room,
had been finally forced to allow her to go. She was being
fetched, within the hour, to lunch with friends, and when

Kate had left she'd been drinking coffee and nibbling at wine biscuits, apparently quite restored to good health.

'This isn't a day off,' muttered Kate crossly, and caught her mother's reproachful eye. She smiled then and said her prayers meekly, adding the rider that she hoped that one day soon something nice would happen.

It was on their way home that her mother told her of their invitation for the following Sunday. 'And someone called Tait-Bouverie is driving us there and bringing us home in the evening...'

Kate came to a halt. 'Mother—that's Lady Cowder's nephew—the one I told about my aching feet.' She frowned. If this was the answer to her prayers, it wasn't quite what she'd had in mind. 'Does he know the Shaws? Professor Shaw's a bit old for a friend...'

'John Shaw and he work at the same hospital; Sarah said so in her letter. He's a paediatrician—quite a well-known one, it seems.'

'But how on earth did he know about us?'

'John happened to mention our name—wondered how we were getting on.'

'You want to go, Mother?'

'Oh, darling, yes. I liked Sarah, you know, and it would be nice to have a taste of the old life for an hour or two.' Mrs Crosby smiled happily. 'What shall we wear?'

Her mother was happy at the prospect of seeing old friends again. Kate quashed the feeling of reluctance at going and spent the next hour reviewing their wardrobes.

It seemed prudent to tell Lady Cowder that she would want to leave early next Sunday morning for her day off. 'We are spending the day with friends, and perhaps it

Love Can Wait

would be a good idea if I had the key to the side door in case we don't get back until after ten o'clock.'

Lady Cowder cavelled at that. 'I hope you don't intend to stay out all night, Kate. That's something I'd feel bound to forbid.'

Kate didn't allow her feelings to show. 'I am not in the habit of staying out all night, Lady Cowder, but I cannot see any objection to a woman of twenty-seven spending an evening with friends.'

'Well, no. I suppose there is no harm in that. But I expect you back by midnight. Mrs Pickett will have to sleep here; I cannot be left alone.'

Lady Cowder picked up her novel. 'There is a lack of consideration among the young these days,' she observed in her wispy voice. 'I'll have lamb cutlets for lunch, Kate, and I fancy an egg custard to follow. My appetite is so poor…'

All that fuss, thought Kate, breaking eggs into a bowl with rather too much force, just because I intend to have a whole day off and not come meekly back at ten o'clock sharp.

Lady Cowder, not intentionally unkind, nevertheless delayed Kate's half-day on Wednesday. She had friends for lunch and, since they didn't arrive until almost one o'clock and sat about drinking sherry for another half-hour, it was almost three o'clock by the time Kate was free to get on her bike and go home for the rest of the day.

'I don't know why I put up with it,' she told her mother, and added, 'Well, I do, actually. It's a job, and the best there is at the moment. But not for long—the moment we've got that hundred pounds saved…'

* * *

She was up early on Sunday and, despite Lady Cowder's pathetic excuses to keep her, left the house in good time. They were to be called for at ten o'clock, which gave her half an hour in which to change into the pale green jersey dress treasured at the back of her wardrobe for special occasions. This was a special occasion; it was necessary to keep up appearances even if she was someone's housekeeper. Moreover, she wished to impress Mr Tait-Bouverie. She wasn't sure why, but she wanted him to see her as someone other than his aunt's housekeeper.

Presently she went downstairs to join her mother, aware that she had done the best she could with her appearance.

'You look nice, dear,' said her mother. 'You're wasted in that job—you ought to be a model.'

'Mother, dear, models don't have curves and I've plenty—on the ample side, too...'

Her mother smiled. 'You're a woman, love, and you look like one. I don't know about fashion models, but most men like curves.'

Mr Tait-Bouverie arrived five minutes later, but, judging by the detached glance and his brisk handshake, he was not to be counted amongst that number.

Rather to her surprise, he accepted her mother's offer of coffee and asked civilly if Prince might be allowed to go into the garden.

'Well, of course he can,' declared Mrs Crosby. 'Moggerty, our cat, you know, is asleep on Kate's bed. In any case, your dog doesn't look as though he'd hurt a fly.'

Indeed, Prince was on his best behaviour and, recognising someone who had spoken kindly to him when he

had been sitting bored in his master's car, he sidled up to
Kate and offered his head. She was one of the few people
who knew the exact spot which needed to be scratched.

Kate was glad to do so; it gave her something to do,
and for some reason she felt awkward.

Don't be silly, she told herself silently, and engaged
Mr Tait-Bouverie in a brisk conversation about the
weather. 'It's really splendid, isn't it?' she asked politely.

'Indeed it is. Do you have any plans for your holidays?'

'Holidays?' She blinked. 'No—no. Well, not at present. I'm not sure when it's convenient for Lady Cowder.'

She hoped he wasn't going to talk about her job, and
he'd better not try and patronise her…

Mr Tait-Bouverie watched her face and had a very
good idea about what she was thinking. A charming
face, he reflected, and now that she was away from her
job she actually looked like a young girl. That calm
manner went with her job, he supposed. She would be
magnificent in a temper…

'Did you enjoy your weekend?' he wanted to know, accepting coffee from Mrs Crosby. 'Cooking must be warm
work in this weather.' He gave her a thoughtful look from
very blue eyes. 'And so hard on the feet!' he added.

Kate said in a surprised voice, 'Oh, did Lady Cowder
tell you that? Yes, thank you.'

She handed him the plate of biscuits and gave one
to Prince. 'I dare say he would like a drink before we
go.' She addressed no one in particular, and went away
with the dog and came back presently with the air of one
quite ready to leave.

Mr Tait-Bouverie, chatting with her mother, smiled to
himself and suggested smoothly that perhaps they should
be going. He settled Mrs Crosby in the front seat, ush-

ered Kate into the back of the car with Prince and, having made sure that everyone was comfortable, drove off.

The countryside looked lovely, and he took the quieter roads away from the motorways. Kate found her ill-humour evaporating; the Bentley was more than comfortable and Prince, lolling beside her, half-asleep, was an undemanding companion. She had no need to talk, but listened with half an ear to her mother and Mr Tait-Bouverie; they seemed to have a great deal to say to each other.

She hoped that her mother wasn't telling him too much about their circumstances. She suspected that he had acquired the art of getting people to talk about themselves. Necessary in his profession, no doubt, and now employed as a way of passing what for him was probably a boring journey.

Mr Tait-Bouverie, on the contrary, wasn't bored. With the skill of long practice, he was extracting information from Mrs Crosby simply because he wished to know more about Kate. She had intrigued him, and while he didn't examine his interest in her he saw no reason why he shouldn't indulge it.

The Shaws gave them a warm welcome, tactfully avoiding awkward questions, and the Shaws' daughter, Lesley, fell easily into the pleasant friendship she and Kate had had.

There was one awkward moment when she remarked, 'I can't think why you aren't married, Kate. Heaven knows, you had all the men fancying you. Did you give them all the cold shoulder?'

It was Mrs Shaw who filled the too long pause while Kate tried to think of a bright answer.

'I dare say Kate's got some lucky man up her sleeve.

And talking of lucky men, James, isn't it time you settled down?'

Mr Tait-Bouverie rose to the occasion.

'Yes. It is something I really must deal with when I have the time. There are so many other interests in life…'

There was a good deal of laughter and light-hearted banter, which gave Kate the chance to recover her serenity. For the rest of their visit she managed to avoid saying anything about her job. To the kindly put questions she gave a vague description of their home so that everyone, with the exception of Mr Tait-Bouverie, of course, was left with the impression that they lived in a charming cottage with few cares and were happily settled in the village.

Presumably, thought Mrs Shaw, who had been told about the housekeeper's job, it wasn't quite the normal housekeeper's kind of work. There was talk about tennis parties and a pleasant social life in which, she imagined, Kate took part. Not quite what the dear girl had been accustomed to, but girls worked at the oddest jobs these days.

Mrs Shaw, whose own housekeeper was a hard-bitten lady of uncertain age who wore print aprons and used no make-up, dismissed Kate's work as a temporary flight of fancy. There was certainly nothing wrong with either Kate's or her mother's clothes…

Mrs Shaw, who didn't buy her dresses at high-street stores, failed to recognise them as such. They were skilfully altered with different buttons, another belt, careful letting-out and taking-in…

Mr Tait-Bouverie did, though. Not that he was an avid follower of women's fashion, but he encountered a wide variety of patients and their mothers—mostly young women wearing just the kind of dress Kate was wearing today. His private patients, accompanied by well-dressed mothers and nannies, were a different matter altogether. He found himself wondering how Kate would look in the beautiful clothes they wore.

He had little to say to her during the day; the talk was largely general, and he took care to be casually friendly and impersonal. He was rewarded by a more open manner towards him; the slight tartness with which she had greeted him that morning had disappeared. He found himself wanting to know her better. He shrugged the thought aside; their encounters were infrequent, and his work gave him little time in which to indulge a passing whim—for that was what it was.

After supper he drove Kate and her mother home. It had been a delightful day and there had been plans to repeat it.

'We mustn't lose touch,' Mrs Shaw had declared. 'Now that we have seen each other again. Next time you must come for the weekend.'

Sitting once more with Prince in the Bentley, Kate thought it unlikely. As it was she was feeling edgy about returning so late in the evening. Even at the speed at which Mr Tait-Bouverie was driving, it would be almost midnight before she got to Lady Cowder's house.

Mr Tait-Bouverie, glancing at his watch, had a very good idea as to what she was thinking. He said over his shoulder, 'Shall I drop you off before I take your mother home? Or do you wish to go there first?'

'Oh, please, it's a bit late—if you wouldn't mind…'

The house was in darkness when they reached it, but that wasn't to say that Lady Cowder wasn't sitting up in bed waiting for her with an eye on the clock.

It was foolish to feel so apprehensive. She worked long hours, and Lady Cowder put upon her quite shamelessly in a wistful fashion which didn't deceive Kate—but she couldn't risk losing her job. She didn't need to save much more before she would be able to see the bank manager...

Mr Tait-Bouverie drew up soundlessly and got out of the car.

'You have a key?'

'Yes. The kitchen door—it's round the side of the house...'

Kate bade her mother a quiet goodnight, rubbed the top of Prince's head and got out of the car.

'Give me the key,' said Mr Tait-Bouverie, and walked silently beside her to the door, unlocked it and handed the key back to her.

'Thank you for taking us to the Shaws',' whispered Kate. 'We had a lovely day...'

'Like old times?' He bent suddenly and kissed her cheek. 'Sleep well, Kate.'

She went past him, closed the door soundlessly and took off her shoes. Creeping like a mouse through the house, she wondered why on earth he had kissed her. It had been a careless kiss, no doubt, but it hadn't been necessary...

Chapter 3

Kate found herself thinking about Mr Tait-Bouverie rather more than she would have wished during the next day or so. Really, she told herself, there was no reason for her to do so. They were hardly likely to meet again, and if they did it wouldn't be at a mutual friend's house. She told herself that his kiss had annoyed her—a careless reward, a kind of tip. Her cheeks grew hot at the very idea. She dismissed him from her mind with some difficulty—but he stayed there, rather like a sore tooth, to be avoided at all costs.

Lady Cowder was being difficult. She seldom raised her voice but her perpetual, faintly complaining remarks, uttered in a martyr-like way, were difficult to put up with. She implied, in the gentle voice which Kate found so hard to bear, that Kate could work a little harder.

'A big strong girl like you,' she observed one lunchtime, 'with all day in which to keep the place in good order. I don't ask much from you, Kate, but I should have thought that an easy task such as turning out the drawing room could be done in an hour or so. And the attics—I am sure that there are a great many things there which the village jumble sale will be only too glad to have. If I had the strength I would do it myself, but you know quite well that I am delicate.'

Kate, offering a generous portion of sirloin steak with its accompanying mushrooms, grilled tomatoes, French-fried onions and buttered courgettes, murmured meaninglessly. It was a constant wonder to her that her employer ate so heartily while at the same time deploring her lack of appetite.

Because she needed to keep her job, she somehow contrived to arrange her busy days so that she could spend an hour or so in the attics. There was a good deal of rubbish there, and a quantity of old clothes and pots which no self-respecting jumble sale would even consider, but she picked them over carefully in the hope of finding something worth offering. It was a thankless task, though, and took up any spare time she had in the afternoons. So it was that when Mr Tait-Bouverie called she knew nothing of his visit until he had gone again.

'Really,' said Lady Cowder in her gentle, complaining voice, 'it was most inconvenient, Kate. You were up in the attics and there was no one to get us tea…'

'I left the tea tray ready, Lady Cowder.'

'Yes, yes, I know that, but poor James had to boil the kettle and make the tea himself. As you know, I have had a headache all day and did not dare to leave the chaise longue.'

The idea of 'poor James' having to make his own tea

pleased Kate. Serve him right, she reflected waspishly. And there had been only thinly cut bread and butter and sponge cake for tea, since Lady Cowder had declared that her digestion would tolerate nothing richer. He would have gone back home hungry.

Kate didn't bother to analyse her unkind thoughts—which was a pity for he had gone to some trouble to do her a good turn.

Mr Tait-Bouverie had gone to see his aunt on a request from his mother, and he hadn't wanted to go. His leisure hours were few, and to waste some of them on a duty visit went against the grain—although he'd had to admit that the prospect of seeing Kate again made the visit more tolerable.

Lady Cowder had been pleased to see him, regaling him in a plaintive little voice with her ill-health, deploring the fact that Kate had taken herself off to the attics so that there was no one to bring in the tea tray.

Mr Tait-Bouverie had made the tea, eaten a slice of the cake Kate had left on the kitchen table while he boiled the kettle and borne the tray back to the drawing room. He was a kind man, despite his somewhat austere manner, and he had listened patiently while his aunt chatted in her wispy voice. Presently he had striven to cheer her up.

'I'm going to Norway in a week or so,' he told her. 'I am to give some lectures in several towns there, as well as do some work in the hospitals. I was there a few years ago and they asked me to go back. It's a delightful country…'

'Ah, you young people with your opportunities to enjoy yourselves around the world—how fortunate you are.'

He agreed mildly. There wouldn't be much opportunity to enjoy himself, he reflected—the odd free day, perhaps, but certainly not the social life he felt sure his aunt envisaged. Not being a very sociable man, except with close friends, he hardly thought he would miss that.

His aunt ate the rest of the bread and butter in a die-away fashion, while at the same time deploring her lack of appetite.

'Perhaps a holiday would improve my health,' she observed. 'I have never been to Norway but, of course, I couldn't consider it without a companion.'

Mr Tait-Bouverie, a man who thought before he spoke, for once allowed himself to break this rule.

'Then why not go? Surely a companion won't be too hard to find?'

'The cost, dear boy...'

He remained silent; Lady Cowder could afford a dozen companions if she wished, but, as his mother had told him charitably, 'Your aunt has always been careful of her money.'

Lady Cowder glanced at the empty cakestand. 'Really, I don't know what I pay Kate for—my wants are so simple, and yet she seems unable to offer me even a simple meal.'

Mr Tait-Bouverie wished that Kate would come down from the attics; he had no more than a passing interest in her but she intrigued him. He said, half jokingly, 'Why should you pay for a companion? Take Kate with you. She seems to be a woman of good sense, capable of smoothing your path...'

Lady Cowder sat up straight. 'My dear James, what a splendid idea. And, of course, I need only pay her her usual wages. She will be delighted to have the opportunity to travel. Tell me, where would you recommend that we should stay?'

Mr Tait-Bouverie hadn't expected his suggestion to be taken so seriously. 'Kate might not wish to go to Norway...' he said. 'Though at this time of year one of the smaller villages around the fiords would be delightful. Very quiet, of course, but by no means cut off from civilisation—these places attract many visitors in the summer months. Or you could stay in Bergen—a pleasant small city with everything one could wish for.'

'Could you arrange it for me?'

'I'm so sorry, Aunt. I'm not free to do that. My trip to Norway has been arranged, of course. I suggest that you get hold of a good travel agent and get him to see to everything. That is, if you intend to go.'

'Of course I intend to, James. I'll tell Kate in the morning and she can see to the details.'

'She might not wish to go.'

'Nonsense. It's the chance of a lifetime for the girl. A free holiday and nothing to do. I hardly think it necessary to pay her her wages at all—after all, she won't need to spend any money.'

Mr Tait-Bouverie lifted an eyebrow. 'I don't think that would be legal. You wouldn't wish to be involved in a court case.'

'Certainly not. She will, of course, have to make herself useful.'

'If she agrees to go with you...'

'She can have a month's notice if she refuses,' said Lady Cowder tartly.

Mr Tait-Bouverie, his duty visit paid, took himself off home. There had been no sign of Kate, and the thought crossed his mind that he might have done her a disservice. He reminded himself that she was a young woman capable of managing her own affairs. She had only to refuse to go and look for another job.

He dismissed the whole affair from his mind but, all the same, it returned to bother him during the next few days.

Kate, bidden to the drawing room by one of the old-fashioned bells which still hung in the kitchen, took off her apron, tucked an errant russet tress behind an ear, and went upstairs. The sack? she wondered. Or, far worse, another visit from Claudia. She opened the door, went into the room and stood quietly, waiting to hear whatever news her employer had for her.

Lady Cowder stared at her. Really, the girl didn't look like a housekeeper and certainly didn't behave like one; she didn't even look interested…

'I have decided to take a holiday, Kate. I need relaxation. My palpitations must be a sign of something more serious although, as you know, I am never one to worry about myself. I intend to go abroad—to Norway. You will come with me. I need someone to take care of me, see to travel arrangements and so on. It is a pleasant surprise to you, no doubt, to have a holiday which will cost you nothing. I shall, of course, continue to pay you your wages. You may consider yourself very fortunate, Kate.'

Kate said quietly, 'Are you asking me to go away with you, Lady Cowder?'

'Well, of course—have you not been listening?'

'Yes, but you haven't asked me if I wish to go, Lady Cowder.'

Lady Cowder turned a shocked gaze upon her. 'You are my housekeeper, Kate. I expect you to do what I wish.'

'If I am asked,' said Kate calmly. 'And I would prefer not to go, Lady Cowder. I am sure you will have no difficulty in finding a suitable companion.'

'And you expect to remain here, being paid for doing nothing?'

Kate didn't answer, and Lady Cowder spent a few moments in reflection. She didn't want to give Kate the sack—she was hard-working, a splendid cook and hadn't haggled over her wages. Nor was she a clock-watcher, everlastingly going on about her rights. To engage a companion, even for a month, would cost money—something Lady Cowder couldn't contemplate without shuddering…

There was only one solution. She said, in the wispy voice she used when she wanted sympathy, 'Please consider my offer, Kate. It would be for a month, and I am prepared to pay you the normal wages of a companion—considerably more than you get at present. Of course, when we return your wages will revert to the present amount.'

'What exactly would my wages be, Lady Cowder?' asked Kate pleasantly.

Lady Cowder closed her eyes and assumed a pained expression. She was thinking rapidly. Mrs Arbuthnott, a friend of hers, had just engaged a new companion and her salary seemed excessive, although Lady Cowder had been assured that it was the standard rate. Surely half that amount would be sufficient for Kate; that would still be almost twice as much as her present money.

Lady Cowder opened her eyes and told Kate.

Twice as much, thought Kate, and if she could save all of it she would soon have the money she needed. She said quietly, 'Very well, Lady Cowder, I will come with you. When do you intend to go?'

'As soon as possible, while I still have my health and strength. Go to Thame tomorrow morning and see the travel agents. I wish to fly—first class, of course—and stay at one of the smaller towns situated close to the fiords. A good hotel, not isolated, with all the amenities I am accustomed to.'

'You want me to bring back particulars of several places so that you may choose?'

'Yes, yes. And some possible dates—within the next two weeks.' Lady Cowder sank back against the cushions. 'Now bring me my coffee. I could eat a biscuit or two with it.'

Kate, watching the coffee percolate, weighed the doubtful delights of travelling with her employer against twice as much money for a month. She didn't expect to enjoy herself, but it would mean that she would be able to give up this job sooner than she had expected. It would also mean careful budgeting; her mother would have to manage on her pension while Kate was away so that every spare penny of her wages could be saved.

'The chance of a lifetime,' Kate told Horace, offering him a saucer of his favourite cat food. 'I shall become a famous cook and live happily ever after.'

She told her mother when she went home for her half-day.

'Darling, what a stroke of luck…' Mrs Crosby got a pencil and the back of an envelope and began to do sums. The result was satisfactory and she nodded and smiled. Then she frowned. 'Clothes—a hotel—you'll need clothes…'

'No, I shan't, Mother. There's that mole-coloured crêpe thing I had years ago. That'll do very well if I have to change for the evening. Lady Cowder wouldn't expect me to be fashionable, and no one will know us there.' She thought for a moment. 'There is also that black velvet skirt—if I borrow your silk blouse, that'll do as well. I'll only need skirts and blouses and sweaters during the day, and the navy jacket and dress will do to travel in.'

'One or two summer dresses?' suggested Mrs Crosby. 'It's July, love, it could be very warm.'

'I'll take a couple of cotton dresses. But I'm a bit vague about the weather there—for all I know it might even be getting cooler! I should have asked at the travel agents, but there was so much to discuss. I'm to drive us to Heathrow and leave the car there, and the flight should be easy enough. We're to be met by a taxi at the airport and taken to the hotel in Bergen that Lady Cowder has chosen. She wants to spend a day or two there before we go to Olden; there's a modern hotel there. It's a small village on the edge of a fiord. I do wonder if Lady Cowder is going to like it. A whole month…'

'Let's hope she will get to know some of the people staying there. She plays bridge, doesn't she? Hopefully so will they; that will give you some free time. I can't think why she can't go alone. She's elderly, but she's quite fit, and there would be plenty of help at the kind of hotels she stays at.'

'I'd much rather have been left to caretake—but don't forget all the extra money, Mother. And a month goes quickly enough.'

'Money isn't everything,' observed Mrs Crosby.

'No, but it does help…it *is* a stroke of luck.'

Something she had to remind herself of during the next ten days, for Lady Cowder's orders and counter-or-

ders were continuous. Her entire wardrobe had to be inspected, pressed, packed—and then unpacked, because
she had changed her mind as to what she would or would
not take. Kate's patience was sorely tried.

The ten days went quickly and Kate, busy from early
morning until late at night, had little time to think her
own thoughts. All the same, from time to time she
thought about Mr Tait-Bouverie. She had to admit to herself that she would have liked to know more about him.
'Not that he would remember me,' she said to herself as
she repacked Lady Cowder's cases for the third time.

Mr Tait-Bouverie hadn't forgotten her. The thought
of her wove through his head like a bright ribbon, dis-
rupting his erudite ponderings over the lectures he was
to give at the various hospitals to which he had been invited in Norway. Only by an effort was he able to dismiss her from his mind as he stepped onto a platform
and embarked on the very latest advances in paediatrics.
It would not do, he told himself firmly; the girl was dis-
rupting his work as well as his leisure hours. He even
dreamed of her…

Surprisingly, the journey to Bergen went smoothly.
Kate drove to Heathrow, deaf to Lady Cowder's back-
seat driving while she went over in her mind all the
things she had to see about in order to get them safely
to the hotel in Bergen. She guided her employer safely
onto the plane, assured her for the tenth time that the
car had been safely parked, that she had the tickets in
her handbag, that the plane was perfectly safe and that
they would be met at the airport in Norway.

Lady Cowder assumed the air of an invalid once on

board, and asked wistfully for a glass of brandy—as she felt faint. She murmured, 'My heart, you know,' when the stewardess brought it to her, and she smiled bravely at the two passengers on the other side of the gangway. She then sank back with her eyes closed, and stayed that way until they were airborne and lunch was served.

'Perhaps you would prefer just a little soup?' suggested the stewardess.

'How kind,' murmured Lady Cowder. 'But I believe that a small meal might give me the strength I shall need when we land.'

Kate listened to all of this nonsense with some amusement, tinged with dismay. A month of this and it would be she who would be the invalid, not Lady Cowder.

Lady Cowder was helped off the plane with great care, Kate following burdened with scarves, handbags and books. Once they were alone, Lady Cowder said sharply, 'Well, don't just stand there, Kate—find whoever it is who is to meet us.'

This was easily done, seeing that he was standing with a placard in his hand with Lady Cowder's name on it. A pleasant man, he went with Kate to collect their luggage, settled Lady Cowder in the back of the car and held the door open for Kate.

'Get in front, Kate,' said Lady Cowder. 'I need to be quiet for a time. I'm exhausted.'

Kate did as she was told, thinking thoughts best left unsaid, then cheered up in response to the driver's friendliness.

There was so much to see as he drove; her spirits rose as he pointed out anything which he thought might interest her and by the time they reached Bergen, she was ready to enjoy every minute of their stay there. He indicated the fish market, the shops, and the funicular to the top of the mountain behind the town, then asked how long they would be staying.

'Only two days. I don't suppose I'll have time to see everything, but I'll do my best.'

An optimistic remark, as it turned out.

The Hotel Norje, in the centre of the town, was everything anyone could wish for—even Lady Cowder gave her opinion that it was comfortable. She had a splendid room overlooking the Ole Nulle Plass—a handsome square opening into a park—and an equally splendid bathroom.

'You may unpack at once,' she told Kate, 'and phone for tea. You had better have a cup before you go to your room. I shall rest for an hour or so and dine later.'

Kate poured tea for both of them, unpacked Lady Cowder's luggage and disposed of it in cupboards and drawers, only too aware that in a couple of days she would have to pack it all again. She did it silently and competently, then went down to Reception to collect her room key.

Her room was on the floor above Lady Cowder's. It was nicely furnished, but lacked the flowers, bowl of fruit and comfortable chairs. There was no bathroom either; a small shower cubicle was curtained off in one corner. Kate unpacked what she would need for a day or so, showered, got into the mole crêpe and went back to her employer.

'Go and get your dinner. You can tidy the room while I'm in the restaurant, and wait here. I shall probably need some help with getting to bed; I'm utterly exhausted.'

Kate, her tongue clenched between her splendid teeth,

went down to the restaurant. Obviously Lady Cowder didn't intend to eat with her housekeeper.

Not that Kate minded—she was hungry, and ate everything set before her—soup, cod, beautifully cooked, and a dessert of cloud berries and cream. She sat over her coffee, oblivious of the admiring glances cast at her. Despite the sombre dress, her lovely face and magnificent person made a striking picture. Indeed, several people wished her good evening as she left the restaurant, and she answered them with her serene smile.

She paused at the reception desk to ask about sending letters to England, accepted a free postcard, wrote on it then and there and left it for the receptionist to post, with the promise of paying for the stamp in the morning. She would have liked to have phoned her mother, but she had only a small amount of English money. She would have to go to a bank in the morning and change some of it.

Lady Cowder greeted her crossly. 'What a very long time you have been, Kate. Had you forgotten that I was waiting for your return until I could go to dinner?'

Kate, mellowed by good food and the friendly glances she had received, said cheerfully, 'You could have come down to the restaurant, Lady Cowder—there was no need to wait for me.'

Quite the wrong answer. 'See that someone brings me a warm drink when I return, and tidy the room and bathroom. I sent the chambermaid away. I can't find my travelling clock; you had better look for it.'

Kate found the clock, tidied the bathroom and sat down in one of the easy chairs to wait. She was going to earn every penny of that extra money, she reflected, but it would be worth it. She spent some time thinking about her plans for the future, and then allowed her

thoughts to dwell on Mr Tait-Bouverie. She was sorry
for him, having an aunt as disagreeable as Lady Cowder.
She wondered if his mother was like her. Perhaps that
was why he wasn't married. To have a mother like that
was bad enough, to be married to a woman of the same
nature would be disastrous.

Her musings were cut short by Lady Cowder's return.
She declared that she must go to bed immediately—
which didn't prevent her from wanting this, that and
the other before Kate was at last told that she might go.

In her room at last, Kate took a quick shower and got
into bed. Her last thought was one of thankfulness that
Lady Cowder was going to have her breakfast in bed and
didn't wish to be disturbed until ten o'clock. A splendid
chance to nip out directly after she had had breakfast
and take a quick look at the town.

Kate woke early and got up at once. It was a grey
morning, but that didn't deter her from her plan. She
went downstairs and found several other people break-
fasting. They greeted her pleasantly and waved her towards the enormous centre-table loaded with dishes of
herrings, cheese, bacon, eggs and sausages. It seemed
that one helped oneself and ate all one wanted. She piled
her plate, asked for coffee, and sat down at a table by
herself, only to be invited to join a group of young men
and women close by. They were on holiday, they told
her, on their way to the north of the country. When she
told them that she knew nothing of Norway, they told
her where to go and what to see.

'You are alone?' they asked.

'No. I'm travelling with an elderly lady—I'm her
housekeeper in England.'

'So you are not free?'

'No. Only for an hour or two when it is convenient for her.'

'Then you must not lose time. The shops will be open soon, but the fish market is already busy. Go quickly and look there; it is a splendid sight.'

It was an easy walk down the main shopping street, and well worth a visit. It wasn't just the fish, although they were both colourful and splendid, it was the flower stalls, bulging with flowers every colour of the rainbow. Kate went from one to the other and longed to buy the great bunches of roses and carnations, thinking how delightful it would be to buy a whole salmon and take it back home. Impossible, of course. She caught sight of a clock and hurried back in time to present herself in Lady Cowder's room.

There was no reply to her civil good morning.

'Go down to the desk and arrange for a car to drive us out to Troldhaugen—Edward Grieg, the composer, lived there—we will return here for lunch. Make sure that the driver is a steady man.'

Kate, not sure how she was to do that, decided to ignore it and hope for the best. Their driver turned out to be a youngish man who spoke excellent English and was full of information. Kate listened to every word, but Lady Cowder closed her eyes and asked Kate to give her the smelling salts.

They had to walk a short distance to the house, something which they hadn't known about. Lady Cowder, in unsuitable shoes, declared that the walk would tire her, but rather grudgingly agreed to Kate having a quick look.

There were other tourists there with their guides, but Kate, given a strict ten minutes, didn't dare linger.

All the same, when she returned to the car, she was expected to give an account of what she had seen. Kate suspected that when they returned to England and Lady Cowder met her friends again she would wish to recount her activities in Norway. A little knowledge of Grieg's house and Kate's impressions of it would be useful in conversation...

Kate didn't escape for the rest of that day. Lady Cowder had little desire to stroll around looking at the shops; certainly the fish market had no attraction. She intended to take the funicular to the top of Mount Floyen.

'It would, of course, be much nicer to go by car, but that would take time and probably not be worth the journey. Besides, I'm told everyone goes by the funicular.'

Kate held her tongue, afraid that if she ventured an opinion they might not go at all.

It was raining when Kate got up the next morning. It rained a great deal in Bergen, the friendly receptionist told her, but that didn't deter her from putting on her raincoat and tying a scarf over her head and hurrying out as soon as she had breakfasted. This was their last day in Bergen, and the chances were that Lady Cowder would refuse to go out at all.

The funicular was out of the question, so were the various museums. If she walked very fast she could get a glimpse of the Bryggen, with its medieval workshops and old buildings. She started off down the main street towards Torget and the Bryggen, head down against the rain, only to be brought to a sudden halt against a vast Burberry-covered chest.

'Good morning, Kate,' said Mr Tait-Bouverie. 'Out early, aren't you?'

She goggled up at him, rain dripping from her sodden scarf.

'Well, I never…!' She gulped and added sedately, 'Good morning, sir.'

Since he made no move to go on his way, she added politely, 'You don't mind if I go on? I haven't much time.'

He gripped her arm gently. 'To do what, Kate?'

'Well, Lady Cowder doesn't like to be disturbed until ten o'clock, so I want to see as much as I can before then.' She added hopefully, 'I expect you're busy.'

'Not until midday. Where are you going?'

She told him, trying not to sound impatient.

'In that case—' he lifted a hand at a passing taxi '—allow me to make up for the delay I have caused you.'

He had bundled her neatly into the taxi before she could draw breath.

'It is a little after half-past eight; you have more than an hour. Tell me, how long have you and my aunt been here?'

'We're here for two days; we go to Olden later today—for three weeks.'

'I shall be surprised if my aunt remains there for so long. It is a delightful little place, but, beyond the hotel, there isn't much to do. There are ferries, of course, going to various other small villages around the fiords, but I doubt if she would enjoy that.' The taxi stopped. 'Here we are, let us not waste time.'

For all the world as though I didn't want to see the place, thought Kate crossly, getting out of the taxi and ignoring his hand.

She said coldly, 'Thank you for the taxi, Mr Tait-Bouverie. I'm sure you have other plans…'

He took her arm. 'None at all, Kate.' He led her down a

wide passage lined with old wooden houses. 'Let us have a cup of coffee and you can recover your good humour.'

'I have only just had breakfast,' said Kate, still coldly polite. A remark which was wasted on him. The wooden houses, so beautifully preserved, housed small offices, workshops and a couple of cafés. She found herself sitting in one of them, meekly drinking the delicious brew set before her.

'They make very good coffee,' observed Mr Tait-Bouverie chattily.

'Yes,' said Kate. 'It's very kind of you to bring me here, but really there is no need...'

A waste of breath. 'Your mother is well?' he asked.

'Yes, thank you. The plaster is to come off very shortly.' Kate finished her coffee and picked up her gloves. 'I'd better be getting on. Thank you for the coffee, sir.'

Mr Tait-Bouverie said pleasantly, 'If you call me "sir" just once more, Kate, I shall strangle you!'

She gaped at him. 'But of course I must call you "sir," Mr Tait-Bouverie. You forget that I'm in your aunt's employ—her housekeeper.'

'There are housekeepers and housekeepers, and well you know it. You may cook divinely, dust and sweep and so on with an expert hand, but you are no more a housekeeper than I am. I am not by nature in the habit of poking my nose into other people's business—but it is obvious to me, Kate, that you are housekeeping for a reason. Oh, I'm sure you need the money in order to live, but over and above that I confess that I am curious.'

Kate said coolly, 'I'm sure that my plans are of no interest to you, s—Mr Tait-Bouverie.'

'Oh, but they are. You see, I can think of no reason why you should work for my aunt. I dare say she underpays you, certainly she works you hard. She may be my aunt, but I should point out that my visits to her are purely in order to reassure my mother, who is her younger sister and feels that she must keep in touch.'

'Oh, have you a mother?' Kate went pink; it was a silly question, deserving a snub.

'Indeed, yes.' He smiled faintly. 'Like everyone else.'

He lifted a finger and asked for more coffee and, when it had been brought, settled back in his chair. 'Are you saving for your bottom drawer?' he asked.

'Heavens, no. Girls don't have bottom drawers nowadays.'

'Ah—I stand corrected. Then why?'

It was obvious she wasn't going to escape until she had answered him. 'I want to start a catering business. Just from home—making simple meals to order, cooking for weddings and parties—that sort of thing.'

'Of course. You are a splendid cook and manager. Why don't you get going?'

It was a relief to tell someone about her schemes. For a moment she hesitated at telling this man whom she hardly knew and would probably not meet again on equal terms. But she felt reckless. Perhaps it was being in foreign places, perhaps it was the caffeine in all the coffee she was drinking.

'I'm saving up,' she told him. 'You see, if I can go to the bank and tell the manager that I've a hundred pounds he might lend me the money I need.'

Mr Tait-Bouverie looked placid, although he doubted very much if a bank manager would see eye to eye with Kate. A hundred pounds was a very small sum these days: it might buy dinner for two at a fashionable restaurant in London, or two seats for the latest play; it might be enough to pay the electricity bill or for a TV licence, but one could hardly regard it as capital.

He said in a kind voice, 'Do you have much more to save?'

'No. That's why I've come with Lady Cowder. She has said she will double my wages if I act as her companion while she is here.'

He nodded. 'I have often wondered, what do companions do?'

'Well, they are just there—I mean, ready to find things and mend and iron—and talk, if they're asked to. And buy tickets and see about luggage and all that kind of thing.'

'Will you get any time to yourself?' He put the question gently and she answered readily.

'I'm not sure—but I don't think so. I mean, not a day off in the week or anything like that.'

'In that case, we have just fifteen minutes to take a quick look around while we're here. There's a rather nice shop along here that does wood carvings and some charming little figures—trolls. Have you bought a troll to take home?'

She shook her head. 'Not yet...'

He bought her one, saying lightly, 'Just to bring you luck.'

They went back to the hotel by taxi presently, and when it stopped, Kate asked, 'Are you coming in? Shall I tell Lady Cowder you're here?'

He said unhurriedly, 'No, I must go to the hospital very shortly and later today I'm going to Oslo. No need to say that we met, since there is no chance of my aunt seeing me.'

Kate offered a hand. 'Thank you for taking me to the Bryggen and giving me coffee. Please forget everything I told you. I shouldn't have said anything, but I don't have much chance to talk to anyone. Anyway, it doesn't matter, does it? We don't meet—I mean, like this.'

He smiled down at her lovely face, damp from the rain. All he said was, 'I do hope you enjoy your stay in Norway.'

She didn't want to go into the hotel; she would have liked to have spent the day with him. The thought astonished her.

Chapter 4

Lady Cowder was sitting up in bed eating a good breakfast.

'They tell me it is raining,' she informed Kate. 'There seems no point in staying here. Go down to the desk and arrange for a car to take us to Olden. I wish to leave within the next two hours.'

It was a complicated journey—Kate had taken the trouble to read the various leaflets at the reception desk—involving several ferries, and quite a distance to go. But there would be no need to get out of the car, she was assured, unless they wished to stop for refreshment on the way. It would be prudent, decided Kate, to get the clerk to phone the hotel at Olden. She asked for the bill, asked if coffee could be sent up to Lady Cowder's room in an hour's time, and went back upstairs. There was all the packing to see to...

The rain stopped after they had been travelling for

an hour, and by the time they reached Gudvangen there was blue sky and sunshine.

'Tell the driver to take us to a hotel for lunch,' said Lady Cowder.

He took them up a hair-raisingly steep road. 'Nineteen hairpin bends,' he told them proudly, 'and a gradient of one in five. A splendid view is to be had from the top.'

'But the hotel?' queried Lady Cowder faintly. She had been sitting with her eyes closed, trying not to see the sheer drop on either side of the road.

'A splendid hotel,' promised the driver. As indeed it was. Once inside, with her back to the towering mountains and the fiord far below, Lady Cowder did ample justice to the smoked salmon salad she was offered. The driver had taken it for granted that he would have his lunch with his passengers, so he and Kate carried on an interesting conversation while they ate.

Olden, it seemed, was very small, although the hotel was modern and very comfortable. 'There are splendid walks,' said the driver, looking doubtfully at Lady Cower. 'There are also shops—two or three—selling everything.'

Lady Cowder looked so doubtful in her turn that Kate hastily asked to be told more about the hotel.

Presently they took the ferry, after another hair-raising descent to the village below, and crossed the Sognefjord to Balestrand to rejoin the road to Olden. Quite a long journey—but not nearly long enough for Kate, craning her neck to see as much as possible of the great grey mountains crowding down to the fiord. She was enchanted to see that wherever there was a patch of land, however small, squashed between the towering grey peaks, there were houses—even one house on its

own. Charming wooden houses with bright red roofs
and painted walls.

'Isn't it a bit lonely in the winter?' she asked.

The driver shrugged. 'It is their life. The houses are
comfortable, there is electricity everywhere, they have
their boats.'

Olden, when they reached it, was indeed small—a
handful of houses, a small landing stage and, a little
way from the village, the hotel. Reassuringly large and
modern, its car park was half-full. Lady Cowder, who
had had little to say but had somehow conveyed her
disapproval of the scenery, brightened at the sight of it.

Certainly their welcome lacked nothing in warmth
and courtesy. She was led to her room, overlooking the
fiord, and assured that a tray of tea would be sent up immediately, together with the dinner menu.

Kate unpacked, went down to the reception desk to
make sure that their driver had been suitably fed and
went to find him. He had been paid, of course, but Lady
Cowder had added no tip, nor her thanks. Kate handed
him what she hoped was sufficient and added her thanks,
knowing that Lady Cowder would want an account of
everything Kate had spent from the money she had been
given for their expenses. She would probably have to
repay it from her own wages but she didn't care—the
man had been friendly; besides, he had told her that he
had five children.

Her room, she discovered, was two floors above Lady
Cowder's and at the back of the hotel, its windows looking out towards the mountains. It was obviously the kind
of room reserved for such as herself: companions, Ladies' maids, poor relations. It was comfortable enough
but it had no shower, and the bathroom was at the end

of the passage to be shared with several other residents. She didn't mind, she told herself—and felt humiliation deep down.

She was to eat her dinner early and then return to Lady Cowder's room and wait for her there, occupying herself with the odd jobs: buttons to sew on, odds and ends to find, things to be put ready for the night.

She enjoyed dinner; the dining room was elegant and the food good. The brown crêpe hardly did justice to her surroundings, but she forgot that in the satisfaction of discovering that there were several English people staying at the hotel. Moreover, they looked to be the kind of people Lady Cowder might strike up a passing acquaintance with. Kate, straining her ears to catch their conversation, was delighted to hear that they were discussing bridge, a game her employer enjoyed.

She finished her coffee and went back to Lady Cowder's room, and listened with outward serenity to that lady's grumbles about a crumpled dress. Alone, she tidied up, fulfilled the odd jobs she had been given to do, arranged for Lady Cowder's breakfast to be brought to her in her room and then went to look out of the window.

The sky had cleared and the last of the evening sun was lighting the sombre mountains, making the snow caps that most of them wore glisten. But if the mountains were sombre, there was plenty of life going on beneath them. Passengers were going aboard a ferry, and she wished that she was going with them to some other small village, probably isolated except for the ferries which called there. Not that she sensed any loneliness amongst the people she had met so far—indeed, they seemed happy and perfectly content.

Who wouldn't be, she reflected, living in such glorious surroundings? As far as she could discover, communications were more than adequate; the driver had told her more in a couple of hours than any guide book could have done. She watched the ferry until it was out of sight round a distant bend in the fiord, and then she drew the curtains—Lady Cowder's orders.

Her employer was in a good temper when she returned. 'So fortunate,' she observed. 'There are several English people staying here, only too glad to make up a table for bridge. They tell me that this hotel is most comfortable; I am glad I decided to come here.'

After the first few days Kate agreed with her. A bridge table was set up each afternoon and she was free for several hours to do as she liked. She spent the first afternoon walking to the village, which was cheerfully full with visitors, its one shop bustling with tourists. It sold everything, she discovered, not only souvenirs but clothes and shoes, household goods and food. She bought cards to send home, walked to the end of the village and then retraced her steps, stopping to admire the smart men's outfitters displaying the latest male fashions—wondering when they would be worn in such a small community.

A ferry had just come in, and she spent some time watching the cars landing and the passengers coming ashore. There were plenty of people waiting to board, too, and she wanted very much to know where it was going. In a day or two, she promised herself, when she felt more at home in her surroundings, she would find out.

After that afternoon she got bolder. She went a little further each day, stopping to ask the way, discovering that English seemed to come as easily to the Norwegians as their own tongue. Greatly daring, she took the bus to Loen, a pretty village some kilometres away from Olden. She had no time to explore it, for Lady Cowder had told her that she must be in the hotel by five o'clock, ready to carry out her wishes, but at least, she told herself, she had been there.

She had suggested that Lady Cowder might like to hire a car and visit some of the neighbouring villages herself, only to be told that it wasn't for her to suggest what they should do.

'I should have thought,' said Lady Cowder, sounding reproachful, 'that you were more than grateful for the splendid time that you are having. Heaven knows, there is little enough for you to do.'

It wasn't a companion that Lady Cowder needed, thought Kate. A lady's maid would have been nearer the mark. Kate, who had a kind heart, felt sorry for her employer, being so incapable of doing the simplest thing for herself. Perhaps she had had a husband who'd spoilt her and seen to it that she never had to worry about anything.

'Very nice, too,' said Kate, addressing a handful of sheep peering at her from their pasture, which was sandwiched between two frowning mountains. 'But who on earth is likely to wrap me in carefree luxury?'

She walked on past the sheep, and along a narrow road running beside the fiord. She wished her mother could have been with her. Never mind the mundane tasks she was given to do, the indifference of her employer, the small—perhaps unintentional—pinpricks meant to put her in her place a dozen times a day; she was happy to be in this peaceful land. Just as long as the bridge parties continued each afternoon, life would be more than tolerable.

* * *

It was the following morning, when she went as usual to find out what Lady Cowder wanted her to do before she went down to breakfast, that she found that lady in a bad temper. She ignored Kate's good morning, and told her to pull the curtains and fetch her a glass of water.

'The Butlers are leaving today.' She spoke with the air of a martyr. 'There is no one else in this place who is willing to make up a table for bridge. I shall die of boredom.' She looked at Kate as though it was her fault.

'Perhaps there will be some other guests…'

'I have enquired about that—something you might have done if you had been here. There are no English or Americans expected. I intend to leave here. There is a good hotel at Alesund; the Butlers have stayed there and recommend it. Go downstairs to the reception desk and tell them that we are leaving tomorrow. Then phone the hotel and get rooms.'

She handed Kate a slip of paper with the name of the hotel and the phone number on it. 'I require a comfortable room; I hardly need remind you of that. Get a room for yourself. Those with a shower are cheaper, and it doesn't matter if it isn't on the same floor as mine. Now hurry along and do as I ask instead of standing there, saying nothing.'

Kate went down to talk to the clerk at the reception desk. Why had they come all this way? she wondered. Lady Cowder could have played bridge just as easily at home. She set about the business of smoothing Lady Cowder's progress through Norway.

Alesund was a large town, built on several islands, and the hotel was, fortunately, to Lady Cowder's liking. It had all the trappings she found so necessary for her comfort—a uniformed porter at its door, bell boys to see to the luggage, a smiling chambermaid and willing room-service. Her room, the lady was pleased to admit, was extremely comfortable—and there was a number of Americans and English staying at the hotel.

Kate unpacked once again, listened to a list of instructions without really hearing them, and went to find her own room, which was two flights up with a view of surrounding rooftops. It was comfortable, though, and she had her own shower. She hung up her few clothes and went down to make sure that Reception knew about Lady Cowder's wishes. She found some information leaflets, too, and took them back with her to read later.

Hopefully they would stay here for the rest of their time in Norway—they had been only nine days at Olden; there were still more than two weeks before they returned to England. Kate prayed that there would be an unending flow of bridge players for the next few weeks. Certainly, there were several Americans in the foyer.

She went back to Lady Cowder to tell her this, and was told to order tea to be sent up.

'And you can get yourself tea, if you wish,' said Lady Cowder, amiable at the prospect of suitable company.

Mr Tait-Bouverie, finding himself with several days of freedom between lectures, reminded himself that his aunt might be glad to see him. It was his duty, he told himself, to keep an eye on her so that he could assure his mother that her sister was well. At the same time he could make sure that Kate was having as good a time as possible.

It annoyed him that he was unable to forget her while at the same time remaining unwillingly aware of her. He reminded himself that his interest in her was merely to see if she would achieve her ambition and branch out on her own. She was a competent girl, probably she would build up a solid business cooking pies and whatever.

He drove himself to Olden, to be told at the hotel there that Lady Cowder had given up her room and gone to Alesund. So after lunch he drove on, enjoying the grand scenery, queueing for the ferries as he came to them, going unhurriedly so that he had the leisure to look around him. He had been on that road some years earlier, but the scenery never failed to delight him.

It was four o'clock by the time he reached the hotel at Alesund and its foyer was nearly full. He saw Kate at once, standing with her back to him, reading a poster on a wall. He crossed to her without haste, tapped her lightly on the shoulder and said, 'Hello, Kate.' He was aware of a deep content at the sight of her.

Kate had turned round at his touch and for a moment her delight at seeing him again was plain to see. Though only for a moment. She wished him good afternoon in a quiet voice from a serene face. She asked at once, 'Have you come to see Lady Cowder? I'm sure she will be delighted to see you…'

'Are you delighted to see me?'

She prudently ignored this. 'She plays bridge until five o'clock every afternoon.' She glanced at her watch. 'I'm just waiting here until she's ready for me.'

'Your free time?' He wanted to know.

'Yes, every afternoon unless there's something…' She paused. 'I've seen quite a lot of the town,' she added chattily. 'Walking, you know, one can see so much more…'

He had a mental picture of her making her lonely way from one street to the next with no one to talk to and no money to spend. He put a hand under her elbow and said gently, 'Shall we sit down and share a pot of tea? If you'll wait here while I get a room and order tea…'

He sat her down in a quiet corner of the lounge along-side the foyer and went away, to return within minutes followed by a waitress with the tea tray, a plate of sandwiches and a cakestand of tempting cream cakes.

'Be mother,' said Mr Tait-Bouverie. Kate, he could see, was being wary, not sure of herself, so he assumed the manner in which he treated his childish patients—an easy-going friendliness combined with a matter-of-fact manner which never failed to put them at their ease.

He watched Kate relax, passed the sandwiches and asked presently, 'Do you suppose my aunt intends to stay here for the rest of her holiday?'

'Well, as long as there are enough people to make up a four for bridge. I think she is enjoying herself; it's a very comfortable hotel and the food is excellent, and so is the service.'

'Good; I shall be able to send a satisfactory report to my mother. What happens in the evenings?'

He watched her select a cake with serious concentration.

'I believe there's dancing on some evenings. I—I don't really know. I dine early, you see, and then go and wait for Lady Cowder to come to bed.'

'Surely my aunt is capable of undressing herself?' He frowned. 'And why do you dine early? Don't you take your meals together?'

Kate went pink. 'No, Mr Tait-Bouverie. You forget—I'm your aunt's housekeeper.' She saw the look on his face and added hastily, 'I don't take my meals with Lady Cowder in her own home.'

'That is entirely another matter. So you don't dance in the evenings?'

She shook her head. 'I'm having a lovely holiday,' she told him earnestly.

A statement of doubtful truth, reflected Mr Tait-Bouverie.

It was two minutes to five o'clock. 'I must go,' said Kate. 'Thank you for my tea.' She hesitated. 'I dare say you would like to surprise Lady Cowder?'

'No, no. I'll come up with you. Is she in her room?'

'There is a card room on the first floor. I go there first…'

She sounded so unenthusiastic at the thought of his company that Mr Tait-Bouverie found himself smiling, then wondered why.

It had struck five o'clock by the time they reached the card room. Lady Cowder was sitting with her back to the door, but she heard Kate come in. Without turning round, she said, in the rather die-away voice calculated to win sympathy from her companions, 'You're late, Kate, and I have such a headache. I dare say you forgot the time.' She glanced at her three companions. 'It is so hard to get a really reliable…' She paused, because they were all looking towards the door.

Mr Tait-Bouverie, a large hand in the small of Kate's back propelling her forward, spoke before Kate could utter.

'Blame me, Aunt. I saw Kate as I arrived and kept her talking. I was surprised to find that you had left Olden, and she explained—'

'My dear boy,' said Lady Cowder in a quite different voice. 'How delightful to see you. Have you come all this way just to see how I was enjoying myself? I hope you can stay for a few days.'

She got up and offered a cheek for his kiss, then

turned to the three ladies at the bridge table. 'You must forgive me. This is my nephew; he's over here lecturing and has come to see me.'

He shook hands and made all the usual polite remarks, aware that Kate had returned to stand by the door, watching, ignored. She might have been a piece of furniture.

'We shall see you this evening?' asked one of the ladies.

'Certainly. We shall be dining later.' He turned to his aunt. 'At what time do you and Kate have dinner, Aunt?'

Lady Cowder looked uncomfortable. 'I dine at half past eight, James.' She smiled brightly at her bridge companions. 'I'm sure we shall all meet presently.'

She said her goodbyes and went to the door. Mr Tait-Bouverie, following her, slipped a hand under Kate's elbow and smiled down at her.

The three ladies were intrigued; his Aunt was outraged. Alone with him presently she said, 'You forget, James, Kate is my housekeeper.'

He agreed placidly. 'Indeed I do; anyone less like a housekeeper I have yet to meet.'

'And it is quite impossible to dine with her...'

Mr Tait-Bouverie's blue eyes were hard. 'Can she not manage her knife and fork?' he enquired gently.

'Yes, of course she can. Don't be absurd, James. But she hasn't the right clothes.'

'Ah,' said Mr Tait-Bouverie, and added reflectively, 'You and my mother are so different, I find it hard to remember that you are sisters.'

Lady Cowder preened herself. 'Well, we aren't at all alike. I was always considered the beauty, you know, and your mother never much cared for a social life. It has often surprised me that she should have married your father. Such a handsome and famous man.'

'My mother married my father because she loved him and he loved her. I see no surprise in that.'

Lady Cowder gave a little trill of laughter. 'Dear boy, you sound just like your father. Isn't it high time you married yourself?'

'I think that perhaps it is,' said Mr Tait-Bouverie, and wandered away to his own room.

Kate, summoned presently to zip up a dress, find the right handbag and make sure that Reception hadn't forgotten Lady Cowder's late-night hot drink, was treated to unusual loquacity on the part of her employer.

'My nephew has plans to marry,' she observed, already, in her mind's eye, seeing Claudia walking down the aisle smothered in white tulle and satin. 'He is, of course, a most eligible man, but dear Claudia is exactly what he needs—pretty and well dressed, and used to his way of life. The dear girl must be in seventh heaven.'

She surveyed her reflection in the pier-glass, nodded in satisfaction and glanced briefly at Kate. Not really worth a glance in that brown...

Mr Tait-Bouverie, dining presently with his aunt, behaved towards her with his usual courtesy, but refused to be drawn when she attempted to find out if he had plans to marry soon.

As they drank their coffee he asked idly, 'Where is Kate? Off duty?'

'Waiting for me in my room. I'm sure she is glad to have an hour or so to herself.' Lady Cowder added virtuously, 'I never keep her up late.'

They went presently to the small ballroom where several couples were dancing to a three-piece band. When he had settled his aunt with several of her acquaintances, James excused himself.

'But it's early, James,' his aunt protested. 'Do you care to dance for a while? I'm sure there are enough pretty girls...'

He smiled at her. 'I'm going to ask Kate to dance with me,' he told her.

Kate, leaning out of the window to watch the street below, withdrew her head and shoulders smartly at the knock on the door. Lady Cowder occasionally sent for her, wanting something or other, so Kate called, 'Come in,' and went to the door to meet the messenger.

Mr Tait-Bouverie came in quietly and shut the door behind him. 'If you could bear with a middle-aged partner, shall we go dancing?'

Kate stopped herself just in time from saying yes. Instead she said sedately, 'That's very kind of you to ask me, sir, but I stay here in the evenings in case Lady Cowder should need me.'

'She doesn't need you; she is with people she knows. I have told her that we are going to dance.'

'And she said that I could?'

Mr Tait-Bouverie, a man of truth, dallied with it now. 'I didn't hear her reply, but I can't see that she can have any objection.'

Kate had allowed common sense to take over. 'Well, I can. I mean, it just won't do.' And then, speaking her thoughts out loud, she added, 'You're not middle-aged.'

'Oh, good. You consider thirty-five still youthful enough to circle the dance floor?'

'Well, of course. What nonsense you talk…' She stopped and started again. 'What I should have said…'

'Don't waste time trying to be a housekeeper, Kate.'

He whisked her down to the ballroom at a tremendous pace and danced her onto the floor.

It had been some years since Kate had gone dancing, but she was good at it. It took only a few moments for her to realise that Mr Tait-Bouverie was good at it, too. Oblivious of Lady Cowder's staring eyes, the glances from the other guests, the brown dress, she allowed herself to forget everything save the pleasure of dancing with the perfect partner—for despite his vast size he was certainly that. He didn't talk, either, for which she was thankful. Just dancing was enough…

The music stopped and she came down to earth. 'Thank you, sir, that was very nice. Now, if you will excuse me…'

'Kate, Kate, will you stop being a housekeeper for at least this evening? You aren't *my* housekeeper, you know. The band's starting up again—good. And did I ever tell you that I shall wring your neck if you call me "sir"? I should hate to do that, for you are a magnificent dancer—big girls always are.'

Kate drew a deep breath. 'How very rude,' she told him coldly. 'I know I'm large, but you didn't have to say so…'

'Ah, the real Kate at last. Did I say big? I should have said superbly built, with all the curves in the right places, and a splendid head of hair.'

Kate had gone very pink. 'I know you're joking, but please don't. It—it isn't kind…'

'I don't mean to be kind. You see, Kate, I want to see behind that serene face of yours and discover the real Kate. And I'm not joking, only trying to get to know you—and it seems to me that the only way to do that is to stir you up.'

The music stopped once more and he took her arm. 'Let us take a walk.'

'A walk? Now? But in an hour Lady Cowder will go to bed.'

'We can walk miles in an hour. Go and get a jacket or shawl or something while I tell her.'

Kate gathered her wits together. 'No, no. Really, I can't! I'd love to, but I really mustn't.'

For answer he took her arm and trotted her across the room to where his aunt sat.

'I'm taking Kate for a brisk walk,' he told her. 'I'm sure you won't mind, Aunt. It's a pleasant evening and we shan't be gone long. Do you need Kate again before you go to bed?'

'Yes—no...' Lady Cowder was bereft of words for once. 'I dare say I can manage.'

'I'll knock when I come in, Lady Cowder,' said Kate in her housekeeper's voice. 'But if you would prefer me not to go, then I'll not do so.'

Lady Cowder looked around her at several interested faces.

'No, no, there's no need. Go and enjoy yourself.' She added wistfully, 'How delightful it must be to be young and have so much energy.' She smiled around her, and was gratified by the approving glances. She was, she told herself, a kind and considerate employer, and Kate was a very fortunate young woman. Poor James must be feeling very bored, but he was always a man to be kind to those less fortunate than himself.

They walked the short distance to the harbour, which thrust deep into the centre of the town, and walked around it. It was still light and quite warm, and there were plenty of people still about. Mr Tait-Bouverie sauntered along beside Kate, talking of this and that in a pleasantly casual manner, slipping in a question here and there so skilfully that she hardly noticed what a lot she was telling him.

On their way back to the hotel he observed, 'Since I'm here with a car I'll drive you to the nearest two islands tomorrow. You're free in the afternoon?'

Kate said cautiously, 'Well, I am usually—but if Lady Cowder wants to go anywhere or needs me for something...'

'Like what?'

'Well—something; I don't know what.'

He said softly, 'You don't need to make excuses if you don't want to come with me, Kate.'

She stopped and looked up at him. 'Oh, but I do, really I do. You have no idea...'

She paused, and he finished for her. 'How lonely you are...?'

She nodded. 'I feel very ungrateful, for really I have nothing much to do and I don't suppose I'll ever have the chance to come here again.'

'But you are lonely?'

'Yes.'

He began to tell her about the islands. 'Unique,' he told her. 'Connected by tunnels under the sea, and the islands themselves are charming. There is a small, very old church with beautiful murals; we'll go and look at it.'

At the hotel she wished him goodnight. 'It was a lovely evening,' she told him. 'Thank you.'

He stared down at her upturned face. He knew as he watched her smile that he was going to marry her. He could see that there would be obstacles in his path, not least of which would be Kate's wariness as to his intentions once he declared them. But he had no intention of doing that for the moment. First he must get behind that calm façade she had adopted as his aunt's housekeeper and find the real Kate. He was a patient man and a determined one; he had no doubt as to the outcome, but it might take a little time.

He said with cheerful friendliness, 'Goodnight, Kate. I'll see you tomorrow around two o'clock.'

Kate paused on her way to her room, wondering if she should knock on Lady Cowder's door—and then decided not to. She had said that there was no need, hadn't she? Besides, Kate hated the idea of the cross examination to which she would be subjected.

She stood under the shower for a long time, remembering her delightful evening. It was strange how Mr Tait-Bouverie seemed to have changed. He was really rather nice. She got into bed and lay thinking about tomorrow's trip. She would have a lot to write home about, she thought sleepily.

She was on the point of sleep when she remembered that Mr Tait-Bouverie was going to marry Claudia. If she hadn't been half-asleep already the thought would have upset her.

Lady Cowder wasn't in a good mood in the morning. Kate was sent away to press a dress which should have been done yesterday. 'But, of course, if you aren't here to do your work, what can one expect?' asked Lady Cowder, adopting her aggrieved, put-upon voice. Kate said nothing, seeing her chances of being free in the afternoon dwindling. She was aware that her employer disapproved of her nephew having anything to do with her, and would interfere if she could.

Kate had reckoned without Mr Tait-Bouverie, who took his aunt out for a drive that morning, gave her coffee at a charming little restaurant and drove to the top of Mount Aksla so that she might enjoy the view over Alesund.

'You're playing bridge this afternoon?' he wanted to know. 'Supposing I take Kate for a short drive? I want to visit a rather lovely old church, and she might as well come with me.' He added cunningly, 'It is very good of you to allow her to have the afternoons free. She seems to have explored the town very thoroughly.'

Lady Cowder smiled complacently. 'Yes, she may do as she likes between two and five o'clock each day and, heaven knows, I am the easiest mistress any servant could wish for. Take her with you by all means; this holiday must be an education to her.'

Mr Tait-Bouverie swallowed a laugh. His aunt had had a sketchy education—governesses, a year in Switzerland—and had never made any attempt to improve upon it. Whereas he knew from what Kate's mother had told him during one of his seemingly casual conversations, that Kate had several A levels and would have gone on to a university if her father hadn't wanted her at home to help research his book.

'Just so,' he said mildly, and drove his aunt back to the hotel.

Kate, brushing and hanging away Lady Cowder's many clothes, was quite startled when that lady came into her room.

'I have had a delightful morning,' she announced. 'And I have a treat in store for you, Kate. Mr Tait-Bouverie has offered to take you for a drive this afternoon. I must say it is most kind of him, and I hope you will be suitably grateful both to him and to me. Now go and have your lunch and come back here in case I need anything before I go to lunch myself.'

Kate skipped down to the restaurant, gobbled her food and hurried to her room. She wondered what Mr Tait-Bouverie had said to make Lady Cowder so amenable. Perhaps she could ask him; on the other hand, perhaps not. He was making a generous gesture and probably wasn't looking forward to the whole afternoon in her company. What on earth would they talk about for three hours?

She got into the jersey dress she hadn't yet worn. It was by no means new, but it fitted her and the colour was a warm mushroom—it toned down her bright hair nicely. Her shoulderbag and shoes had seen better days, too, but they were good leather and she had taken care of them. She went downstairs, wondering if Mr Tait-Bouverie had left a message for her at the desk. She had told him that she was usually free soon after two o'clock, but now that she saw the time she saw that she was much too early. It would never do to look too eager. She turned round and started back up the stairs.

'Cold feet, Kate?' asked Mr Tait-Bouverie, appearing beside her, apparently through the floor. 'I'm ready if you are.'

She paused in mid-flight. 'Oh, well, yes. I'm quite ready, only I'm too early.'

'I've been waiting for the last ten minutes,' he told

her placidly. 'It's a splendid day; let us cram as much into it as we can.'

Kate was willing enough. She was led outside to where his hired Volvo stood, ushered into it, and, without more ado, they set off.

'Giske first,' said Mr Tait-Bouverie, driving away from the town and presently entering a tunnel. 'I hope you don't mind the dark? This goes on for some time— more than a couple of miles—but it is used very frequently, as you can see, and is well maintained. Giske is rather a charming island—it's called the Saga island, too. We'll go and see that church, and then drive over to Godoy and have tea at Alnes. It's quite a small village but there's a ferry, of course, and in the summer there are tourists…'

His placid voice, uttering commonplace information, put her quite at her ease. She wasn't sure if she liked the tunnel very much—driving through the mountain with all that grey rock and presently, as he pointed out to her, under the fiord—but he was right about Giske. It was peaceful and green, even with the mountains towering all round it. There were few cars, the sun shone and the air was clear and fresh.

Kate took a deep breath and said, 'This is nice.'

The little church delighted her, so very small and so perfect, with ancient murals on its walls and high-backed pews. It was quiet and peaceful, too; she could imagine that the peace went back hundreds of years. Mr Tait-Bouverie didn't say much but wandered round with her, and when she had had her fill he took her outside to the little churchyard with its gravestones bright with flowers.

'It's something I'll remember,' said Kate, getting back into the car.

They drove on to Godoy then, through small villages, their houses beautifully kept. And when they reached Alnes they had tea at the small hotel opposite the ferry. By now Kate had forgotten to be wary and become completely at ease.

Mr Tait-Bouverie watched her lovely face and was well content, taking care not to dispel that.

Chapter 5

Kate, making a splendid tea, was happy to have some-one to talk to, to answer her questions, who was apparently as happy as she was. After a couple of weeks of no conversation—for Lady Cowder only gave orders or made observations—it was delightful to say what she thought without having to make sure that it was suitable first, and, strangely enough, she found that she could talk to Mr Tait-Bouverie.

'We should be going,' he told her presently. 'A pity, for it is such a pleasant day.' He smiled at her across the table. 'There's another very long tunnel ahead.'

'Longer than the other one?'

'Yes. But there's plenty of time; we are quite near to Alesund.'

'It's been a lovely afternoon,' said Kate, getting into the car, wishing the day would never end. In a little over an hour she would be getting into the brown crêpe dress, ready to eat her solitary dinner. She frowned, despising herself for allowing self-pity to spoil the day. Besides, there was still the drive back…

The tunnel took her by surprise; one moment they were tooling along a narrow road edged with thick shrubs, giving way to trees as they climbed the mountain beyond, the next they were driving smoothly between grey rock. True, the tunnel was lighted, and there was a stream of traffic speeding past them, but, all the same, she caught herself wondering how many minutes it would be before they came out into daylight again.

Mr Tait-Bouverie said soothingly, 'It takes less than five minutes, although it seems longer.' He added, 'You don't like it very much, do you? I should have asked you about that before we left the hotel. There are any number of other places to visit.'

'No, oh, no, I've loved every minute—and really, now we are in the tunnel, I truly don't mind. I wouldn't like to drive through it alone, though.'

He laughed. 'You're honest, Kate. Even if you don't exactly enjoy it, it's something you will remember.' He glanced at the dashboard. 'We're exactly halfway.'

The sudden sickening noise ahead of them seemed to reverberate over and over again through the tunnel—a grinding, long drawn-out noise accompanied by shouts and screams. And the lights went out.

Mr Tait-Bouverie brought the car to a smooth halt inches from the car ahead of him as other cars passed him, unable to slow their pace quickly enough, colliding inevitably. He could have said the obvious; instead he observed calmly, 'A pity about the lights,' and reached for the phone beside his seat.

Kate, who hadn't uttered a sound, said now in a voice which shook only very slightly, 'I expect someone will come quickly,' and thought what a silly remark that was. 'Were you phoning for help? You were speaking Norwegian?'

'Yes, and yes. Now, Kate, perhaps we can make ourselves useful. I'm sure everyone with a phone has warned Alesund, but the more helpers there are the better. Come along!'

He reached behind him and took his bag from the back seat. 'How lucky that I've my bag with me. I don't care to leave it at the hotel. Stay where you are; I'll come round and open your door, then follow me and do as I say. You're not squeamish, are you?'

It didn't look as though she would be given the chance to be that. She said meekly, 'I don't think so.'

'Good; come along, then.'

They didn't have far to go—a van had gone out of control and slewed sideways so that the car behind it had crashed into it, turned over and been pushed by another car against the wall, presumably with such force that the lighting cables had been damaged.

There were a great many people milling around, some of them already hauling people from damaged cars. Mr Tait-Bouverie, holding Kate fast by the hand, spoke to a man kneeling beside a woman whose leg was trapped under the wheel of a car.

'I'm a doctor; can I help?'

He had spoken in Norwegian and the man answered him in the same language, shining his torch on Mr Tait-Bouverie and then on Kate. 'English, aren't you? God knows how many there are trapped and hurt. I've told people to go back to their cars. There is a nurse somewhere, and several men giving a hand.' He glanced at Kate again. 'The young lady?'

'Not a nurse, but capable. She will do anything she is asked to do.'

'Good. Can she help the nurse? Over there with those two children? This young woman—if you could look at her? Tell us what to do—most of us have some knowledge of first aid....'

'Off you go,' said Mr Tait-Bouverie to Kate. 'I'll find you later.'

I must remember, thought Kate rather wildly, picking her way towards the nurse, to tell him that he is a rude and arrogant man.

Then she didn't think about him again; there was too much to do.

The nurse, thank heavens, spoke excellent English. Kate tied slings, bandaged cuts and held broken arms and legs while the nurse applied splints made of umbrellas, walking sticks and some useful lengths of wood someone had in their boot.

She was aware of Mr Tait-Bouverie from time to time, going to and fro and once coming to kneel beside her to find and tie a severed artery. The nurse had told her to apply pressure with her fingers while she fetched the doctor and Kate knelt, feeling sick as blood oozed out despite her efforts. Mr Tait-Bouverie didn't speak until he had controlled the bleeding. 'Bandage it tightly with anything you can find.'

He had gone again. Kate, feeling queasy, took the clean handkerchief she saw in the patient's pocket and did the best she could.

It seemed like hours before she heard the first sounds of help arriving. It had only been minutes—minutes she never wished to live through again. Even though help was on the way it took time to manoeuvre the cars out of the way so that the ambulances and the fire engines could get through. Everyone was quiet now, doing as they were told, backing out of the tunnel whenever it was possible, making more room.

She was suddenly aware that there was a man crouching beside the old lady she was trying to make comfortable.

'You are a nurse?' he asked in English.

'No. Just helping. I'm with a doctor—a surgeon, actually. Mr Tait-Bouverie.'

'Old James? Splendid. He's around?' He didn't wait for an answer, but began to question the old lady. He looked up presently. 'Concussion and a broken arm. She's worried about her handbag. She was thrown out of her car...'

'Which car? I'll look for it.'

It was an elderly Volvo, its door twisted, its bodywork ruined. Kate climbed in gingerly and it creaked under her weight. The bag was on the floor, its contents spilled. She collected everything she could see and began to edge out backwards.

'There you are,' said Mr Tait-Bouverie. He sounded amused. 'Even if you are back to front, I'm glad to see that you're none the worse for all this.'

He stopped and lifted her neatly the right way up, out of the car.

Kate said coldly, 'Thank you, Mr Tait-Bouverie. There was no need of your help.'

'No, I know, but the temptation was too strong.' He looked her over. 'You look rather the worse for wear.'

She started back to the old lady. 'Well, I am the worse for wear,' she told him tartly, and thought vexedly that he looked quite undisturbed—his jacket over his arm, his shirt-sleeves rolled up. His tie was gone—used for something or other, she supposed. He still looked elegant.

Kate, conscious that her hair was coming down, her hands were filthy and scratched and her dress stained and torn, turned her back on him.

He was there, beside her, exchanging greetings with the Norwegian doctor while she handed over the handbag and listened to the old lady's thanks.

'You're off now?'

'Yes. I must take this young lady back to my aunt.'

'Come to dinner while you're there. We'd love to see you again. How long are you here? Oslo, I suppose, and Bergen and Tromsö?'

'Tromsö tomorrow,' said Mr Tait-Bouverie, 'and back to England four days later.'

Kate had heard that, and was conscious of an unpleasant sensation under her ribs. Indigestion, she told herself, and shook hands politely when Mr Tait-Bouverie introduced her.

'This is not a social occasion, I am afraid, but I am delighted to meet you—may I call you Kate? Perhaps next time you come to Norway... Ah, here are the ambulance men.' He smiled goodbye, and turned his attention to his patient.

Mr Tait-Bouverie took Kate's hand. 'A hot bath and a quiet evening,' he observed as they made their way through the throng. Kate didn't reply. She would be lucky if she had time for a quick shower; Lady Cowder wasn't going to be pleased at having been kept waiting for more than an hour...

It took some manoeuvring to get out of the tunnel; cars were being backed, a way was being cleared by the police. It was all very orderly, even if it took some time. The road, when they at last reached it, had been closed to all but traffic leaving the tunnel.

'It's all very efficiently organised,' said Kate.

Mr Tait-Bouverie glanced sideways at her. Her beautiful face was dirty and her hair, by now, a hopeless russet tangle hanging down her back. He gave a sigh and kept his eyes on the road.

He had been in love several times, just as any normal man would be, but never once had he considered marriage. He had assumed that at sometime, somewhere, he would meet the girl he wanted for his wife, and in the meantime he immersed himself in his work, happy to wait. Now he had found her and he didn't want to wait. He would have to, of course. He wasn't sure if she liked him—certainly she wasn't in love with him—and circumstances weren't going to make the prospect of that any easier. Circumstances, however, could be altered...

They talked about the accident presently. 'It is a miracle that it didn't turn into a major disaster...'

'You mean if fire had broken out or there had been panic? Everyone was calm. Well, nearly everyone.' Kate added honestly, 'I would have liked to have screamed, just once and very loudly, only I didn't dare.'

'Why not?'

She looked away from him out of the window. 'You wouldn't have liked that—I mean, you knew you would go and help. I dare say you would have left me in the car to scream all I wanted to, but you had enough on your plate.'

'I wouldn't have left you alone, Kate. To be truthful, I rather took it for granted that you would help, too, in your calm and sensible way.'

Kate fought a wish to tell him that she had felt neither of these things—that sheer fright had stricken her dumb. She had felt neither calm nor sensible, only terrified. Although she had to admit to herself that having him there, quiet and assured, knowing exactly what to do, had given her a feeling of safety. Strange to feel so safe and sure with him...

Soon they reached the hotel, and he got out and opened her door and walked with her into the foyer. There were a lot of people there, gathered to hear news of the accident, and they stared and then crowded round them, anxious for details.

'You were there?' someone asked. 'We felt sure that you were. The young lady...?'

'Is perfectly all right', said Mr Tait-Bouverie placidly. 'But she does need a bath and a rest.'

He took her to the desk and the three receptionists there hurried to him.

'Miss Crosby needs a bath, a change of clothing and a rest. I'm sure she'd like a tray of tea before anything else.' He looked at Kate. 'What is your room number? There is a bathroom?'

'Well, no,' she mumbled awkwardly. 'But the shower's fine. I'm perfectly all right.'

'Of course you are, but you will do what I say. Doctor's orders.'

He turned back to the desk. 'Will you send a chambermaid with Miss Crosby to fetch a change of clothes from her room, and then go with her to my room so that she may have a most essential warm bath? Perhaps she will let me know if Miss Crosby is bruised or scratched and I'll deal with that later. She is to stay with her, and

I think that she might have dinner there. In the meantime let me have another room, will you?'

He said to Kate in what she could only call a doctor's
voice, 'While you are finding something to wear I'll get
what I need from my room. And here is the chambermaid. Go with her, and after your dinner go back to your
room and go to bed.'

Kate found her voice. 'Lady Cowder…?'

'Leave her to me.' He smiled then, and she found herself smiling back and wanting to cry. 'Goodnight, Kate.'

She lay in the warm bath and snivelled. She didn't
know why; she hadn't been hurt, only scratched and
bruised, and was tired from the heaving and shoving
and lifting she had done. But it was nice to have a good
cry, and the chambermaid was a kindly soul who found
plasters to put on her small cuts and grazes and presently
saw her onto the bed and urged her to have a nice nap.

Which, surprisingly, she did, to wake feeling quite
herself again and to eat with a splendid appetite the dinner that the good soul brought to the room.

Kate had half expected to have a visit from Lady
Cowder—or at least a message—but there was nothing.
She ate her dinner and, still accompanied by the chambermaid, went back to her own room. In a little while
she went to bed. It was a pity that Mr Tait-Bouverie was
going to Tromsö tomorrow; she would have liked to
thank him properly for his kindness. She spared a sleepy
moment to wonder what he was doing…

He was walking briskly through the town, not going
anywhere special, thinking about the afternoon and
Kate. His aunt had been vexed at the news that she would

have to manage without Kate that evening, declaring plaintively that the news of the accident had been a great shock to her, that she felt poorly and would probably have a migraine.

To all of which Mr Tait-Bouverie had listened with his usual courtesy, before suggesting that an early night might be the answer.

'I'll say goodbye now, Aunt,' he had told her. 'For I'm leaving early in the morning. I shall be back in England shortly, and will come and see you as soon as you return.'

'I shall look forward to that, James. I believe that I shall invite Claudia to stay for a while—she is such a splendid companion, and so amusing.' When this had elicited no response, she had added, 'How delightful it will be to see your dear mother again. She wrote to say that she will be returning soon. There is so much for us to talk about.'

Mr Tait-Bouverie considered his future with the same thorough care with which he did his work. Complicated operations—the kind he excelled in—needed careful thought, and there would be plenty of complications before he could marry his Kate. At least, he reflected, he would know where she was…

Kate hadn't expected sympathy from Lady Cowder and she received none. 'So very inconvenient,' said that lady as Kate presented herself the following morning. 'You have no idea of the severity of my headache, and all the excitement about the accident… It was most generous of my nephew to give up his room for your use, though really quite unnecessary. However, he has always done as he wishes.'

Kate, perceiving that she was expected to answer

this, said quietly, 'Mr Tait-Bouverie was very kind and considerate. I'm very grateful. I hope I shall have the opportunity of thanking him.'

'He wouldn't expect thanks from you,' said Lady Cowder rudely. 'Besides, he left early this morning for Tromsö. He will be back in England before us.'

Kate felt a pang of disappointment. Perhaps she would see him in England but on rather a different footing—the accident in the tunnel would have faded into the past, obliterated by a busy present. Thanking him would sound silly. She wondered if she should write him a polite note—but where would she send it? Lady Cowder could tell her, but she was the last person to ask. It was an unsatisfactory ending to what had been, for her, a very pleasant interlude, despite the fright and horror of the accident in the tunnel.

At least, Kate reflected, she had behaved sensibly even while her insides had heaved and she had been terrified that fire would break out or, worse, that the tunnel would fall apart above their heads and they would all be drowned. A flight of imagination, she knew. The tunnel was safe, and help had been prompt and more than efficient. It had been an experience—not a nice one, she had to admit—and despite her fright she had felt quite safe because Mr Tait-Bouverie had been there.

Waiting for Lady Cowder that afternoon, she wrote a long letter to her mother, making light of Lady Cowder's ill humour, describing the hotel and the town, the food and the people she had spoken to, enlarging on the beautiful scenery but saying little about Mr Tait-Bouverie's company. She wrote about the tunnel accident too, not dwelling on the horror of it, merely observing that it had been most fortunate that Mr Tait-Bouverie had been there to help.

She wrote nothing about her own part in the affair, hoping that her mother would picture her sitting safely in the car out of harm's way.

Her circumspection was wasted. Mrs Crosby, reading bits of the letter to Mr Tait-Bouverie, observed in a puzzled voice, 'But where was Kate? She doesn't say…'

They were sitting at the kitchen table, drinking coffee with Moggerty on Mr Tait-Bouverie's knee. He had arrived that afternoon, having driven down from London after a brief stop at his home. He'd been tired by the time his plane got in, and had hesitated as to whether it wouldn't be a better idea to go and see Kate's mother the following morning. But if Kate had written, the letter would have arrived by now and Mrs Crosby might be worried. He had eaten the meal Mudd had had ready for him and driven himself out of town, despite Mudd's disapproving look.

He was glad that he had come; Mrs Crosby had had the letter that morning and had been worrying about it ever since. He had been able to reassure her and tell her exactly what had happened. 'Kate behaved splendidly,' he told her. 'She's not easily rattled, is she?' He smiled a little. 'She didn't like the tunnel, though—too dark.'

Mrs Crosby offered Prince a biscuit. 'I'm glad she was able to help. Did Lady Cowder mind? I mean, Kate had to miss some of her duties, I expect.'

Mr Tait-Bouverie said soothingly, 'My aunt quite understood. Kate had her bath and her cuts and bruises were attended to, and she had an early night.'

'Oh, good. I shall be so glad to see her again, though it was most kind of Lady Cowder to take Kate with her.

It's years since she had a holiday, and she does have to work hard.' She paused. 'I shouldn't have said that.'

Mr Tait-Bouverie offered Moggerty a finger to chew. 'Why not? Being a housekeeper to my aunt must be extremely hard work. You see, people who have never had to work themselves don't realise the amount of work other people do for them.'

'Well, yes, I dare say you're right. Are you not tired? It was very kind of you to come all this way... When do you start work again?'

'Tomorrow, and I knew that once I got started it would be some days before I could come and see you.'

'I'm very grateful. Kate's all right, isn't she? I mean, happy...?'

He said evenly, 'We had a very happy afternoon together. We went dancing one evening...she is a delightful dancer...'

'She was never without a partner at the parties she went to—that was before her father became ill. What was she wearing? She didn't take much with her—she didn't expect... Was it a brown dress?'

'I'm afraid so,' said Mr Tait-Bouverie gravely. 'She is far too beautiful to wear brown crêpe, Mrs Crosby.'

'She hadn't much choice,' said Mrs Crosby rather tartly.

'It made no difference,' he assured her. 'Kate would turn heads draped in a potato sack.'

Mrs Crosby met his unsmiling gaze and smiled. Not an idle remark calculated to please her, she decided. He really meant it.

He went away presently, with Prince at his heels eager to get into the car beside his master.

Mrs Crosby offered a hand. 'Don't work too hard,' she

begged him. 'Though I suppose that in a job like yours you can't very well say no…'

He laughed then. 'That's true, but I do get the odd free day or weekend. I hope I may be allowed to come and see you from time to time?'

'That would be delightful.'

She watched him drive away, wondering if his visit had been made out of concern for her worry about Kate or because he really wanted to see her—and Kate—in the future. 'We shall have to wait and see,' she told Moggerty.

Kate quickly discovered that she was to pay for the few hours of pleasure she had had with Mr Tait-Bouverie. Lady Cowder declared that she was tired of bridge, and on fine afternoons a car was hired and she and Kate were driven around the countryside—Kate sitting with the driver since Lady Cowder declared that Kate's chatter gave her a headache.

Kate ignored this silly remark, and was thankful to sit beside the driver, who pointed out anything interesting and, before long, told her about his wife and children.

After several days of this the weather changed and, instead of going out in the afternoons, Lady Cowder stayed in one of the hotel lounges, playing patience or working away at a jigsaw puzzle while Kate sat quietly by, ready to help with the patience when it wouldn't come out, or grovel around the floor looking for lost bits of the puzzle.

Now she had only a brief hour each morning to herself, so the days stretched endlessly in long, wasted hours.

It was only during the last few days of their stay that this dull routine was altered, when Lady Cowder decided to shop for presents. She hadn't many friends—bridge-playing

acquaintances for the most part—and for those she bought
carved woodwork. But Claudia was a different matter.

'Something special for the dear girl,' she told Kate.
'She is so pretty; one must choose something to enhance
that. Earrings, I think—those rather charming gold and
silver filigree drops I saw yesterday. Of course, they are
of no value; James will see that she has some good jewellery when they marry…'

She shot a look at Kate as she spoke, but was answered with a noncommittal, 'They would be charming. I'm sure Claudia will be delighted to have them.'

'Such a grateful girl. You might do better to copy her
gratitude, Kate.'

Kate, with a tremendous effort, held her tongue!

The journey back to England went smoothly—largely
because Kate had planned it to be so. All the same, it
was tiring work getting Lady Cowder out of cars, into
the plane and out of it again and then into her own car.
She had complained gently the whole way home so that
Kate had a headache by the time they stopped in front
of Lady Cowder's house.

That was when her long day's work really started.
Safely home again, Lady Cowder declared that she was
exhausted and must go to bed at once.

'You may bring in the luggage and unpack, Kate, but
before you do that bring a tray of tea up to my room.
I'll take a warm bath and go to bed, I think, and later
you may bring me up a light supper.' She sighed. 'How
I envy you your youth and strength—when one is old…'

Seventy wasn't all that old, reflected Kate, receiving an armful of handbags, scarves and rugs. And Lady
Cowder lived the kind of life which was conducive to

looking and feeling a lot younger than one's years. She saw Lady Cowder to her room, got her bath ready and went downstairs to unload the boot.

Lady Cowder was in bed by the time Kate had put the car away and brought the luggage indoors.

'You might as well unpack my things now,' said Lady Cowder, sitting up against her pillows as fresh as a daisy.

'If I do,' said Kate in her quiet voice, 'I won't have time to get your supper.' She added woodenly, 'I could cut you a few sandwiches…'

Lady Cowder closed her eyes. 'After my very tiring day I need a nourishing meal. Leave the unpacking, since you don't seem capable of doing it this evening. A little soup, I think, and a lamb chop with a few peas—if there are none in the freezer, I dare say you can get them from the garden. Just one or two potatoes, plainly boiled. I don't suppose you will have time to make a compote of fruit; I had better make do with an egg custard.' She opened her eyes. 'In about an hour, Kate.'

Only the thought of the extra wages she had earned, enough—just—to make up the hundred pounds to show the bank manager, kept Kate from picking up her un-opened bags and going home.

She went to the kitchen, put on the kettle and made tea, then a little refreshed but still angry, she phoned her mother.

'I can't stop,' she told her. 'There's rather a lot to do, but I'll see you on Wednesday. I'm to go to Thame for some groceries on Thursday; I'll go to the bank then.'

Her mother's happy voice did much to cheer her up—after all, it had been worth it; the rather grey future held a tinge of pink. In a few months she would be embarking on a venture which she felt sure would be successful.

* * *

Later she carried a beautifully cooked meal up to Lady Cowder's room.

'You may fetch the tray when I ring,' said that lady. 'Then I shan't need anything more. I'll have breakfast as usual up here. Poached eggs on toast, and some of that marmalade from the Women's Institute. In the New Year you can make sufficient for the whole year; I cannot enjoy any of these marmalades from the shops.'

Kate said, 'Goodnight, Lady Cowder,' and received no answer. She hadn't expected one. She hadn't expected to be asked if she were at all tired or hungry, nor had she expected to be thanked for her services during their stay in Norway. But it would have been nice to have been treated like a person and not like a robot.

She ate her supper, unpacked her things, had a very long, too hot bath and then went to bed. She was tired, but not too tired to wonder what Mr Tait-Bouverie was doing. She told herself sleepily not to waste time thinking about him and went to sleep.

She was kept busy the next day; after a month's emptiness the house was clean, but it needed dusting and airing. Stores had to be checked, tradesmen phoned, the gardener had to be seen about vegetables, and Horace to be made much of. He had been well looked after but he was glad of her company again, and followed her round the house, anxious to please.

Lady Cowder, catching sight of him following Kate up the stairs, said irritably, 'What is that cat doing here? I thought he had been got rid of. I'm sure I told Mrs Beckett to have him put down before she left…'

'It's most fortunate that she didn't, Lady Cowder,'

said Kate in the polite voice which so annoyed her employer. 'For he is splendid at catching mice. All those small rooms behind the kitchen which are never used... he never allows one to get away.'

She uttered the fib with her fingers crossed behind her back. It was a fib in a good cause—Horace was a sympathetic companion and someone to talk to. That he had never caught a mouse in his life had nothing to do with it...

'Mice?' said Lady Cowder in horror. 'You mean to tell me...?'

'No, no. There are no mice, but there might be without Horace. A cat,' she went on in her sensible way, 'is of much more use than a mousetrap.'

Lady Cowder agreed grudgingly, annoyed to feel that Kate had got the better of her without uttering a single word which could be described as impertinent or rude.

Kate went home on her half-day, taking her extra wages with her, and she and her mother spent a blissful afternoon making plans for the future.

'I'll need a thousand pounds to start,' said Kate. 'I'll start in a small way, and then get the money paid off to the bank and get better equipment as we expand. I'll stay with Lady Cowder until I've drummed up one or two customers—the pub, perhaps, and that bed and breakfast place at the other end of the village. Once I can get regular customers I can branch out—birthday parties and even weddings...'

'It's something you can go on doing if you marry,' observed her mother.

'Yes, but I don't know anyone who wants to marry me, do I?' For some reason Mr Tait-Bouverie's face rose, unbidden, beneath her eyelids and she added, 'And I'm not likely to.'

She took care to laugh as she said it and her mother smiled in return—but her eyes were thoughtful. Mr Tait-Bouverie would make a delightful son-in-law, and he might fall in love with Kate. It didn't seem likely, but Mrs Crosby was an optimist by nature.

Before Kate went back that evening she arranged to call in the next day on her way to Thame. She wasn't to use the car—Lady Cowder considered that Kate could cycle there and back quite easily with the few dainties which she had set her heart on.

'I quite envy you,' she'd told Kate in the wistful voice which made Kate clench her teeth. 'Young and strong with the whole morning for a pleasant little outing.'

Kate said nothing. The bike ride was one thing, but shopping around for the special mushrooms, the oysters, the lamb's sweetbreads, the special sauce which could only be found at a delicatessen some distance from the shopping centre was quite another. But she didn't mind; she was going to find time to go to the bank...

Kate got up earlier than usual, for Lady Cowder expected the morning's chores to be done before she left, but still Kate left the house later than she had hoped for. It would be a bit of a rush to get back in time to get Lady Cowder's lunch. She stayed at her home only long enough to collect the hundred pounds, which she stowed in her shoulderbag and slung over her shoulder. It would never do to get it mixed up with the housekeeping money in the bike's basket, every penny of which she would have to account for.

It was a dull day, but she didn't mind that—this was

the day she had been working and waiting for. Now she could plan her future, a successful career... It was a pity that Mr Tait-Bouverie's handsome features kept getting in the way.

'Forget him,' said Kate loudly. 'Just because he was kind and nice to be with. Remember, you're a housekeeper!'

She bowled along, deciding what to do first—the bank or the shopping. Would she be a long time at the bank? Would she be able to see the manager at once? Perhaps she should have made an appointment. Another mile or so and she would be on the outskirts of Thame. She would go to the bank first...

She parked her bike and had turned round to take her shopping bag and the housekeeping money from the basket when she was jostled by several youths. They did it quite roughly, treading on her feet, pushing her against the wall, but before she could do anything they chorused loud apologies—presumably for the benefit of the few pedestrians in the street—and ran away.

They took her shoulderbag with them, neatly sliced from its straps.

It had all happened so quickly that she had no chance to look at them properly. There had been four or five of them, she thought, and she ran across the street to ask if anyone passing had seen what had happened. No one had, although they admitted that they had thought the boys had bumped into her accidentally.

So she went into the bank, calm with despair, and explained that her money had been stolen. Here she was listened to with sympathy, given an offer to phone the police, and told with polite regret that an interview with the manager would be pointless until the money was recovered. When a police officer arrived there was little he could do, although he assured her that they would certainly be on the look-out for the youths.

'Although I doubt if you'll see your money back, miss,' she was told.

She gave her name and address, assured him that she was unharmed and, since there was nothing else to be done about it, got on her bike and did her shopping. A pity that they hadn't taken the housekeeping money instead of her precious savings.

She didn't allow herself to think about it while she shopped. Her world had fallen around her in ruins, and she would have to start to rebuild it all over again. Disappointment tasted bitter in her mouth, but for the moment there were more important things to think of. Lady Cowder's lunch, for instance...

She cycled back presently, her purchases made, wondering how she was going to break the news to her mother. She would have to wait until Sunday. She rarely got the chance to use the phone unless it was on Lady Cowder's behalf, and she saw no hope of getting enough free time to go home until then. And she had no intention of telling Lady Cowder.

Back at the house, she was reprimanded in Lady Cowder's deceptively gentle voice for being late. 'It is so essential that I should have my meals served punctually,' she pointed out. 'I feel quite low, and now I must wait for lunch to be served. You may pour me a glass of sherry, Kate.'

Which Kate did in calm silence before going down to the kitchen to deal with the mushrooms and oysters. But before she did that she poured herself a glass of the cooking sherry—an inferior brand, of course, but still sherry.

She tossed it off recklessly and started on her preparations for lunch, not caring if she burnt everything to cinders or curdled the sauce. Of course, she didn't; she served a beautifully cooked meal to an impatient Lady Cowder and went back to the kitchen where she sat down and had a good cry.

Chapter 6

Kate felt better in the morning. The loss was a set-back, but with the optimism born of a new day she told herself that a hundred pounds wasn't such a vast sum and if she could save it once, she could save it a second time.

Her optimism faded as the day wore on; Lady Cowder was demanding, and for some reason sorry for herself. She declared that the journey home had upset her and went round the house finding fault with everything.

It was a blessing when the vicar's wife called after lunch to confer with her about the Autumn Fair. Lady Cowder prided herself on patronising local charity, and made no bones about telling everyone how generous she was in their cause.

She spent a pleasant afternoon telling the vicar's wife just how things should be done. Kate, bringing in the tea tray, heard her telling that lady that she would be delighted to supply as many cakes and biscuits as were needed for the cake stall and the refreshment tent.

'As you know,' said Lady Cowder in her wispy voice, 'I will go to any amount of trouble to help a worthy cause.'

Kate, with the prospect of hours of cake baking ahead of her, sighed.

The vicar's wife was only a passing respite, though; by the following morning Lady Cowder was as gloomy as ever. Thank heavens, thought Kate, that I can go home tomorrow.

Lady Cowder fancied a sponge cake for her tea. 'Although I dare say I shall eat only a morsel of it.' She added sharply, 'Any of the cake which is left over you may use for a trifle, Kate.'

Kate stood there, not saying a word, her face calm, and wearing the air of reserve which annoyed her employer. 'I'll have the turbot with wild mushrooms for dinner. Oh, and a spinach salad, I think, and a raspberry tart with orange sauce.' She glanced at Kate. 'You're rather pale. I hope you aren't going to be ill, Kate.'

'I'm very well, thank you,' said Kate, and went away to make the sponge cake. She hoped it would turn out like lead, but as usual it was as light as a feather.

She thought of Mr Tait-Bouverie as she worked. It was silly of her to waste time over him, but at least it stopped her thinking about her lost money.

Mr Tait-Bouverie stood at the window, looking at his aunt's garden. He wasn't sure why he had felt the urge to pay her a visit and had no intention of pursuing the matter too deeply. He had almost convinced himself that the feelings he had for Kate were nothing more than a passing infatuation, but when the door opened and she came in with the tea tray he had to admit that that was nonsense. Nothing less than marrying her would do, and that as soon as possible.

However, he let none of these feelings show but bade her a quiet good afternoon and watched her arrange the tray to please his aunt. She had gone delightfully pink when she'd seen him, but now he saw that she looked pale and tired. More than that—unhappy.

She left the room as quietly as she had entered, not looking at him again, aware of Lady Cowder's sharp eyes, and he went to take his tea cup from his aunt and sit down opposite her.

'I'm sorry to hear that you found the journey home tiring. Kate looks tired, too. Perhaps you should have broken your trip and stayed in town for a night.'

'My dear boy, all I longed to do was get here—and indeed the journey was so fatiguing, getting to the airport and then the flight. You know how nervous I am. And then standing about while the luggage is seen to and the car fetched—and then the long drive here.' She added sharply, 'Kate isn't in the least tired. She's a great strapping girl, perfectly able to cope—and after a month's idleness, too. I'm glad to see that she hasn't taken advantage of your kindness to her at Alesund.'

Mr Tait-Bouverie gave her a look of such coldness that she shivered.

'Of course, I'm sure she would do no such thing,' she said hastily. 'Such a reserved young woman.' Anxious to take the look of ferocity from her nephew's face, she added, 'You will stay to dinner, won't you, James?'

Mr Tait-Bouverie, making plans, declined. After his absence from London, he pointed out, he had a backlog of work. He urged his aunt to take more exercise, volunteered to let himself out of the house and went round to the kitchen door.

Kate was sitting at the table. The ingredients for the raspberry tart Lady Cowder fancied for dinner were before her, although she was making no attempt to do anything about it.

Seeing Mr Tait-Bouverie had been a bit of a shock— a surprisingly pleasant one, she discovered. She had put down the tea tray and taken care to reply to his pleasant greeting with suitable reserve, but the urge to fall on his neck and pour out her troubles had been very strong. She reflected that she must like him more than she thought she did, not that her feelings came into it.

'But it would be nice to have a shoulder to moan on,' she observed to Horace, who was sitting cosily by the Aga.

'I don't know if you have a shoulder in mind,' said Mr Tait-Bouverie from the door. 'But would mine do?'

She turned her head to look at him. 'You shouldn't creep up on people like that; it's bad for the nerves.'

Indeed, she had gone very pale at the sight of him.

He came right into the room and sat down at the table opposite her.

'Did I shock you? I'm sorry. Now tell me, Kate, what is the matter? And don't waste time saying nothing, because neither you nor I have time to waste.'

'I have no intention...' began Kate, and stopped when she caught his eye. She said baldly, 'I went to Thame on Thursday to shop, you know, and I had the money— the hundred pounds—with me to take to the bank. I was going to see the manager. I was mugged by some boys. They took my bag with the money inside.' She paused to look at him. 'Fortunately the housekeeping money was in the basket on my bike, so I was able to do the shopping.'

She managed a small smile. 'I'm a bit disappointed.'

He put out a hand and took hers, which was lying on the table, in his. 'My poor Kate. What a wretched thing to happen. Of course, you told the police…?'

'Yes. They said they'd do their best—but, you see, no one really saw it happen. People were passing on the other side of the street but not looking, if you see what I mean.'

'You told my aunt?'

She gave her hand a tug but he held it fast. 'Well, no; there's no point in doing that, is there?'

'Your mother?'

'It's my free day tomorrow. I shall tell her then.'

'What do you intend to do?'

'Why, start again, of course. I'd hoped that I would be able to leave here quite soon, but now I'll stay for at least a year—if Lady Cowder wants me to.' Her voice wobbled a bit at the thought of that, but she added, 'A year isn't long.'

Mr Tait-Bouverie got up, came round the table, heaved her gently out of her chair and took her in his arms. He did it in the manner in which she might have expected a brother or a favourite uncle would do. Kind and impersonal, and bracingly sympathetic. It cost him an effort, but he loved her.

It was exactly what Kate needed—a shoulder to cry on—and she did just that, comforted by his arms, soothed by his silence. She cried for quite some time, but presently gave a great sniff and mumbled, 'Sorry about that. I feel much better now. I've soaked your jacket.'

He handed her a beautifully laundered handkerchief.

'Have a good blow,' he advised. 'There's nothing like a good weep to clear the air. What time are you free tomorrow?'

'I usually get away just after nine o'clock, unless Lady Cowder needs something at the last minute.'

'I'll be outside at half past nine to take you home. It might help your mother if I'm there, and it might be easier for you to explain. She's bound to be upset.'

'Yes.' Kate mopped her face and blew her pink nose again. 'That would be very kind of you, but are you staying here for the night? I didn't know—I must make up a bed…'

'I'm going back home now.' He gave her a kind and what he hoped was an avuncular smile. 'I'll be here in the morning. Perhaps we can think of something to help your mother over her disappointment. Now cheer up, Kate; something will turn up…'

'What?' asked Kate.

'Well, that's the nice part about it, because you don't know, do you? And a surprise is always exciting.' He bent and kissed her cheek. 'I must go. See you in the morning. And, Kate—sleep well tonight.'

She nodded. 'I think I shall. And thank you, Mr Tait-Bouverie, you have been so kind.' She smiled. 'You're quite right; there's nothing like a good weep on someone's shoulder. I'm grateful for yours.'

She sat at the table for several minutes after he had gone. He had offered no solution, made no hopeful suggestions, and yet she felt cheerful about the future. Perhaps it was because he had been so matter-of-fact about it, while at the same time accepting her bout of weeping with just the right amount of calm sympathy. Breaking the news to her mother would be a great deal easier with him there.

He had kissed her, too. A light, brotherly kiss which had made her feel…she sought for the right word. Cherished. Absurd, of course.

She got up and began to prepare Lady Cowder's dinner, then made herself a pot of tea, gave Horace his evening snack and sat down again to wait for Lady Cowder's ring signalling her wish for her dinner to be served.

It was a fine morning when Kate woke from a good night's sleep. A pity her nicest dress had been ruined in the tunnel she thought as she got into a cotton jersey dress. It had been a pretty blue once upon a time, but constant washing had faded it. As she fastened its belt she wished that she had something pretty and fashionable to wear, and then told herself not to be silly; Mr Tait-Bouverie wouldn't notice what she was wearing.

He did, however, down to the last button, while watching her coming round the side of the house from the kitchen door, the sun shining on her glorious hair, smiling at him shyly because she felt awkward at the remembrance of her tears yesterday.

He wished her good morning, popped her into the car and drove off without waste of time. 'Your mother won't mind Prince again?' he wanted to know.

'No, of course not; he's such a dear.' She turned round to look at him sitting at the back, grinning at her with his tongue hanging out.

'You have slept,' observed Mr Tait-Bouverie.

'Yes, yes, I did. I'm sorry I was so silly yesterday— I was tired…' She glanced at his rather stern profile. 'Please forget it.'

He didn't answer as he stopped before her home, but got out and opened her door and let Prince out to join them. By the time he had done that Mrs Crosby was at the open door.

'What a lovely surprise. Hello, darling, and how delightful to see you again, Mr Tait-Bouverie. I hope you've come to stay? There's coffee all ready—we can have it in the garden.'

She beamed at them both and stooped to pat Prince. 'You'll stay?' she asked again.

'With pleasure, Mrs Crosby. You don't mind Prince?'

'Of course not. He shall have some water and a biscuit.' She turned to Kate. 'Go into the garden, dear, I'll bring the tray...'

Mr Tait-Bouverie carried the tray out while Kate fetched the little queen cakes her mother had made, all the while talking over-brightly about Norway—indeed, hardly pausing for breath, so anxious was she not to have a long silence which might encourage her mother to ask about her trip to Thame.

In the end, Mrs Crosby managed to get a word in. She couldn't ask outright about the bank manager, not in front of their guest, but she asked eagerly, 'Did you have a successful trip to Thame, dear?'

'I've some disappointing news, mother,' began Kate.

'Won't they lend you the money? Wasn't it enough, the hundred pounds?'

'Well, mother, I didn't get the chance to find out. I was mugged just outside the bank. The police don't think that there is much chance of getting the money back—it was in my bag.'

Mrs Crosby put her cup carefully back into the saucer. She had gone rather pale. 'You mean, there is no money...?'

'I'm afraid not, Mother, dear. It's a bit of a blow, isn't it? But we'll just have to start again.'

'You mean,' said Mrs Crosby unhappily, 'that you must go on working like a slave for too little money for another year? More, perhaps.'

She picked up her cup and put it down again because her hand was shaking. 'Did you know about this?' she asked Mr Tait-Bouverie.

'Yes, Mrs Crosby. I saw Kate yesterday evening and she told me.'

Mrs Crosby said, 'I can quite understand what a relief it must be to have hysterics. Kate, dear, I am so very sorry. After all these months of work—and you've never once complained.' She looked at Mr Tait-Bouverie. 'This is rather dull for you. Let's talk about something else.'

He said in his calm way, 'If I might make a suggestion, there is perhaps something to be done…'

He had spent a large amount of the previous evening on the telephone after he'd returned home, but first of all he had gone in search of Mudd, who had been sitting in the comfortable kitchen doing the crossword.

'Mudd, do I pay you an adequate wage?'

Mudd had got to his feet and been told to sit down again. 'Indeed, you do, sir; slightly more than is the going rate.'

'Oh, good. Tell me, would you know the—er—going rate for a housekeeper? One who runs the house more or less single-handed and does all the cooking.'

'A good plain cook or cordon bleu?' asked Mudd.

'Oh, cordon bleu.'

Mudd thought, named a sum and added, 'Such a person would expect her own quarters too, the use of the car, two days off a week and annual holiday.'

Mudd looked enquiringly at Mr Tait-Bouverie, but if he hoped to hear more he was to be disappointed. He was thanked and left to his puzzle while Mr Tait-Bouverie went to his study and sat down at his desk to think. The half-formed plan he had allowed to simmer as he drove himself home began to take shape. Presently, when it came to the boil, he had picked up the phone and dialled a number.

Now he returned Kate's look of suspicion with a bland stare. 'No, Kate, it isn't something I've thought up during the last few minutes. It is something I remembered on my way home last night. An old lady—an extremely active eighty-something—told me some time ago that her cook would have to go into hospital for some time and would probably be away for several months. It seems the poor woman should have been there much earlier, but her employer was unable to find someone to replace her. She lives in a village south of Bath—a large house, well staffed... Kate, will you tell me what wages you receive?'

She told him, for she saw no reason not to.

'I believe that you are underpaid by my aunt. Did you know that?'

'Oh, yes. But I needed a job badly, and someone we knew offered us this cottage at a cheap rent. I know I'm not paid enough, but where would I find another job where we could live as cheaply as we do here?'

'Exactly. But if you could get work where you lived rent-free and were better paid, it might be a good idea to take a calculated risk. You would be able to save more money—no rent, nor gas or electricity. I'm a bit vague about such things, but surely there would be more scope for saving?'

'But it would be temporary. I might be out of work again...'

He raised his eyebrows. 'With Bath only four miles away?' He smiled. 'Faint-hearted, Kate?'

She flared up. 'Certainly not; what a horrid thing to say.' She added quickly, 'I'm sorry. That was ungrateful and horrid of me.'

She looked at her mother. Mrs Crosby said quietly, 'We have nothing to lose, have we? I think it's a marvellous idea, and I'm grateful to James…' She smiled across at him. 'You don't mind? You see, I feel that you are our friend…for thinking of it and offering us help.'

Kate got up and went to stand by his chair, and when he got up, too, held out her hand. 'Mother's right; you're being kind and helping us, and I don't deserve it. I feel awful about it.'

He took her hand in his and smiled down at her. 'I hope that I may always be your friend, Kate—you and your mother. And as for being kind, I don't need to trouble myself further than to write to this old lady and let you know what she says. She may, of course, have already found someone to her taste.'

All of which sounded very convincing in Kate's ear. As he had meant it to.

Kate took her hand away reluctantly. 'What do you want us to do? Write to this lady asking her if she will employ me?'

'No, no. I think it best if I write to her and discover if she has found someone already. If she has, there is no more to be said—but if she is still seeking someone, I could suggest that I know of a good cook who would be willing to take over for as long as is needed.' He looked at Mrs Crosby. 'Would that do, do you suppose?'

'Very well, I should think. We'll try and forget about it until we hear from you, then we shan't be disappointed.' She smiled at him. 'We can never thank you enough, James. I've said that already, but I must say it again.'

He went away soon after that, leaving them to speculate about a possible future. 'James is quite right,' said Mrs Crosby. 'If we can live rent-free think of the money we'll save. Even if the job lasts for only a few months we might have enough to get started, with help from the bank.'

'It's a risk.'

'Worth taking,' said Mrs Crosby cheerfully, and clinched the matter.

Kate heard nothing from Mr Tait-Bouverie for the best part of a week and then suddenly there he was, standing in the kitchen doorway, wishing her good afternoon in a cool voice.

Kate paused in her pastry making, aware of pleasure at seeing him.

'Are you staying for dinner?' she wanted to know. 'Because if you are I'll have to grill some more lamb chops.'

'No. No. I merely called in on my way back from Bristol. I have been sent by my aunt to tell you that I am here for tea.'

'I have just taken an apple cake out of the oven. Does Lady Cowder want tea at once?'

'I do have to leave in half an hour or so, if that is not too much trouble?'

He came further into the kitchen. 'I heard from the old lady I told you about. She will be writing to you. It will be for you to decide what you want to do, Kate.'

She smiled widely at him. 'You have? She will write? That's marvellous news. Thank you, Mr Tait-Bouverie. If this lady wants me to work for her I'll go there as soon as I've given notice here.' She added uncertainly, 'If she would wait?'

'Oh, I imagine so,' said Mr Tait-Bouverie easily. 'I

don't suppose another week or so will make any difference.'

He strolled to the door. 'I'm sure everything will get nicely settled without any difficulties.'

He had gone before she could thank him.

The letter came the next day. Kate was asked to present herself for an interview on a day suitable to herself during the next week, and she wrote back at once, suggesting the following Wednesday afternoon.

Getting there might be a problem—one solved by asking the son of the owner of the village shop to give her a lift into Oxford, where she could catch a train. It would be a tiresome journey, and to be on the safe side she told Lady Cowder that she might be back late in the evening.

Kate, hurrying down to the village to start her journey on Wednesday afternoon, felt mean about leaving Lady Cowder in the dark—then she remembered how that lady hadn't scrupled to underpay her...

Rather to her surprise, she was to be met at Bath and driven to her prospective employer's house, which was at a small village some four miles or so away. The man who met her was elderly and very polite, although he offered no information about himself.

'Mrs Braithewaite is elderly, miss, as you perhaps know. You are to see her first for a short interview and then have a talk with Cook. You are to return to Thame this evening?'

'Yes. I hope to catch the half-past-six train to Oxford, if possible.'

'I shall be taking you back to Bath. You should be finished by then.'

He had no more to say, and sat silently until he

turned in at an open gate and drew up before an imposing Queen Anne house set in a large garden. Its massive front door was flanked by rows of large windows, but Kate followed her companion round the side of the house and went in through a side door.

The kitchen at the end of the stone passage was large and airy and, she noted, well equipped with a vast Aga and a huge dresser, rows of saucepans on its walls and a solid table. There were chairs each side of the Aga and a tabby cat curled up in one of them. There were three people there—an elderly woman, sitting on one of the chairs, and two younger women at the table, drinking tea.

They looked up as Kate was ushered in, and the elder woman said, 'You're young, but from all accounts you're a good cook. Sit down and have a cup of tea. Mrs Braithewaite will see you in ten minutes. I'm Mrs Willett. This is Daisy, the housemaid, and Meg, the kitchenmaid. Mr Tombs, the butler, will see you before you go.'

Kate accepted a cup of tea, thanked the man who had driven her from the station and got a quick nod from him. 'I'm the chauffeur and gardener; Briggs is the name.'

'I'm very grateful for the lift.'

He shrugged. 'It's my job. You don't look much like a cook, miss.'

She was saved from answering this by Mrs Willett, who got to her feet with some difficulty, saying, 'Time we went.'

They went along a lengthy passage and through a door opening into the entrance hall. They crossed this and Mrs Willett knocked on one of the several doors opening from it. Bidden to come in, she stood aside for Kate to go in and then followed her to stand by the door.

'Come here.' The old lady sitting in a high-backed chair by the window had a loud, commanding voice. 'Where I can see you. What's your name again?'

'Kate Crosby, Mrs Braithewaite.'

'Hmm. I'm told you can cook. Is that true?'

'Yes. I can cook.'

'It's a temporary job, you understand that? While Mrs Willett has time off to go to hospital and convalesce. I have no idea how long that will be, but you'll be given reasonable notice. Dependants?'

'My mother.'

'There's Mrs Willett's cottage at the back of the house. She's willing for you to live there while she's away. Bring your mother if you wish. I take it you have references? I know Mr Tait-Bouverie recommended you, but I want references as well.'

Kate had a chance to study the old lady as she spoke. Stout, and once upon a time a handsome woman, even now she was striking, with white hair beautifully dressed. She wore a great many chains and rings and there was a stick by her chair.

'I'm a difficult person to please,' went on Mrs Braithewaite. 'I'll stand no nonsense. Do your work well and you will be well treated and paid. You can start as soon as possible. Arrange that with Mrs Willett.'

Mrs Willett gave a little cough which Kate rightly took to be a signal to take her leave.

She thanked Mrs Braithewaite politely, bade her good day and followed Mrs Willett out of the room.

'There, that's settled, then,' said the cook in a relieved voice. 'You've no idea how many she's interviewed, and me just dying to get to hospital and be seen to.'

'I'll come as soon as I can. I have to give notice where

I'm working at present. I'll write to you as soon as I've got a date to leave, shall I?'

'You do that, miss. What's your name again? Not married, are you?'

'No. Would you call me Kate?'

'Suits me. I'll tell the others. Come and see the cottage, and there's time for another cup of tea before Briggs takes you back. And you've still got to see Mr Tombs.'

The cottage was close to the house—a small, rather sparsely furnished living room opened into a minuscule kitchen and a further door led to a bathroom. The stairs, behind a door in the sitting room wall, led to two bedrooms, each with a single bed, dressing table and clothes cupboard.

Kate said, 'We have our own furniture where we are at present. We'll store it, of course, but would you like us to bring our own bed linen—and anything else to replace whatever you would like to pack away? We're careful tenants…'

Mrs Willett looked pleased. 'Now that's a nice idea, Kate. Bring your own sheets and table linen. I'll put anything I want to store away in the cupboard in the living room.'

'There's just one other thing—we have a cat. He's elderly and well-behaved.'

'Suits me, so long as he doesn't mess up my things.' Mrs Willett led the way back to the house. 'Mr Tombs will be waiting to see you…'

Mr Tombs was an imposing figure of a man. Middle-aged, with strands of hair carefully combed over his balding pate, he wore a severe expression and an air of self-importance. He fixed her with a cold eye and expressed the wish that they would suit each other. 'The kitchen is, of course, your domain, but all household matters must be referred to me,' he told her pompously.

Later, in the car being driven back to her train, Briggs said, 'You don't have to worry about Mr Tombs; his bark's worse than his bite.'

'Thank you for telling me,' said Kate. 'But I shan't have much to do with the house, shall I? And the kitchen, as he said, is to be my domain.' She added, 'I think I'm quite easy to get on with.'

That sounded a bit cocksure. 'I mean, I'll try to fit in as quickly as possible, and I hope that someone will tell me if I don't. I shall do my best to do as Mrs Willett has done.'

'No doubt. We're all that glad that Mrs Willett can get seen to. She's waited long enough.'

Presently he left her at the station and she got into the train and spent the journey back making plans. They would have to start packing up, and the furniture would have to be stored, but they would be able to take some of their small possessions, she supposed. There was the question of telling Lady Cowder, too.

Kate spent a long time rehearsing what she would say. By the time she reached Oxford she was word-perfect.

Jimmy from the village had promised to meet her, and he was waiting.

'Any luck?' he wanted to know.

'Yes, I've got the job—but don't tell a soul until I've given in my notice, will you?'

'Course not. Coming back here when the job's finished?'

'Well, I don't know. Perhaps, if we can have the cottage back again.'

He left her at her home with a cheerful goodnight and she quickly went indoors to tell her mother. 'I can't stop,' she told her. 'I'll tell you all about it on Sunday. I've got the job. I'll have to give in my notice tomorrow.'

She kissed her mother, got on her bike and pedalled back to Lady Cowder's house. It was late now, and she would be hauled over the coals in the morning in Lady Cowder's gentle, complaining voice. She let herself in, crept up to her room and, once in bed, lay worrying about the morning. She expected an unpleasant interview and the prospect allowed her only brief snatches of sleep.

Her forebodings looked as if they were going to come true, for when she took in Lady Cowder's tea that lady said, 'I wish to speak to you after breakfast, Kate. Come to my sitting room at ten o'clock.'

Kate, outwardly her usual quiet, composed self was very surprised to find Lady Cowder looking uneasy when she presented herself. She didn't look at Kate, but kept her eyes on the book on her lap.

'Yesterday I had a long talk with my god-daughter, Claudia—Miss Travers. As you know, I am devoted to her. She told me that her mother is going to live in the south of France and is dismissing her staff at her home here in England. Claudia is upset, since their house-keeper has been with them for some years and is, in her opinion, too elderly to find another post. Claudia asked me—begged me—to employ this woman.

'Claudia is a sensible girl as well as a strikingly pretty one—she pointed out that it will be easier for you to obtain a new post than their own housekeeper, and suggested that you might consider leaving. She is quite right, of course.' Lady Cowder looked up briefly. 'So be good enough to take a week's notice as from today, Kate. I will, of course, give you an excellent reference.'

Kate restrained herself from dancing a jig; indeed, she didn't allow her surprised delight to show. Lady Cowder's discomfiture was very evident, and Kate added to it with her calm, 'Very well, Lady Cowder. Have you decided what you would like for lunch today? And will there be your usual bridge tea this afternoon?'

'Yes, yes, of course. I have no appetite—an omelette with a salad will do.'

Kate shut the door quietly as she went, and then danced all the way down to the kitchen, where she gave Horace the contents of a tin of sardines and made herself coffee. She couldn't quite believe this sudden quirk of fate, but she was thankful for it. It was a good sign, she told herself; the future was going to be rosy. Well, perhaps not quite that, but certainly pink-tinged.

She would have to write to Mr Tait-Bouverie and tell him that his help had borne fruit. She knew where he worked as a consultant, for her mother had asked him, and she would send a letter there.

She composed it while she assembled Lady Cowder's coffee tray. She wasn't likely to see him again, she reflected, and felt decidedly sad at the thought. 'Which is silly,' she told Horace, 'for we quite often disagree, although he can be very kind and—and safe, if you know what I mean. Only I wish he wasn't going to marry Claudia…'

She wrote the letter that evening and gave it to Mrs Pickett to post when she went home. It had been surprisingly difficult to write; things she wanted to tell him and which would have sounded all right if she had uttered them looked silly on paper. She considered the final effort very satisfactory, and had stamped it with the feeling that she had sealed away part of her life instead of just the envelope. She had no reason to feel sad, she reminded herself, and the concern she felt for his forthcoming marriage to Claudia was quite unnecessary—in fact, rather silly.

Mr Tait-Bouverie read the letter as he ate his breakfast the following morning. Reading its stiff contents, he reflected that Kate must have had a bad time composing it. It held no warmth but expressed very correctly her gratitude, her wish for his pleasant future and an assurance that she would endeavour to please her new employer. No one reading the letter would have recognised the Kate who wrote it—but, of course, Mr Tait-Bouverie, with a wealth of memories, even the most trivial ones, tucked away in his clever head, knew better. He read it again and then folded it carefully and put it into his pocket. Kate might think that they would never meet again but he knew better than that.

Chapter 7

There was a great deal to do during the next few days, but Lady Cowder rather surprisingly told Kate that she might go home each evening after she had served dinner and cleared away the dishes. Kate had arranged to go straight to her new job, and her mother would follow within the week, after seeing their furniture put into store and returning the cottage key to its owner.

The owner of the village store had turned up trumps with an offer to drive Mrs Crosby to her new home with most of the luggage and Moggerty, so that Kate needed only her overnight bag and a case.

It was all very satisfactory, although her remaining days with Lady Cowder were uneasy, partly because Claudia had arrived unexpectedly, bringing with her the woman who was to replace Kate. She was a thin, sour-faced person with a sharp nose and grey hair scraped back into a bun. She followed Kate round the house on a tour of inspection, answering Kate's helpful remarks with sniffs of disapproval.

'I'll not have that cat in my kitchen,' she told Kate. 'The gardener can take it away and drown it.'

'No need,' said Kate, swallowing rage. 'Horace is coming with me, and may I remind you that until I leave I am still the housekeeper here.' ·

Miss Brown drew herself up with tremendous dignity, then said, 'I am sure I have no wish to interfere. It is to be hoped that your hoity-toity ways don't spoil your chances of earning a living.'

With which parting shot she took herself off to complain to Claudia, who in turn complained to Lady Cowder. That lady, who was guiltily aware that she had treated Kate badly, told her god-daughter with unexpected sharpness to tell Miss Brown to be civil and not interfere with Kate.

'Kate has been quite satisfactory while she has been with me, my dear, and she will be going to another job in two days' time.'

The next morning when Kate took up Lady Cowder's breakfast tray she waited until that lady had arranged herself comfortably against her pillows before saying quietly, 'Miss Brown doesn't want Horace in the house, Lady Cowder. May I take him with me?'

'The kitchen cat? I suppose so, if he'll go with you. Can he not be given to the gardener or someone? They'll know what to do with him.'

'They'll drown him.'

Lady Cowder gave a shudder. 'Really, Kate, must you tell me these unpleasant things just as I am about to have breakfast?'

When Kate said nothing and just stood there, Lady Cowder said pettishly, 'Oh, take the cat by all means. It is most unfair of you to cause this unpleasantness, Kate. It is perhaps a good thing that you are leaving my employ.'

She wasn't an unkind woman, although she was selfish and self-indulgent and lazy, so she added, 'Take the cat to your home this afternoon. Miss Brown can get our tea.'

Kate said, 'Thank you, Lady Cowder,' and went back to the kitchen to tell Horace that he would shortly have a new home. 'Where you will be loved,' she told him cheerfully, so that he lost the harassed expression he had had on his whiskery face ever since he had encountered Miss Brown.

Kate took him home later and, being an intelligent beast, knowing upon which side his bread was buttered, he made cautious overtures to Moggerty, explored the garden without attempting to leave it and settled down in the kitchen.

'Nice company for Moggerty,' observed Mrs Crosby.

Two days later Kate left Lady Cowder's house. It was still early morning, and Lady Cowder had bidden her goodbye on the previous evening. She had given Kate an extra week's salary, too, at the same time pointing out that her generosity was due to her kind nature.

'My god-daughter told me that I am being unnecessarily generous,' she pointed out to Kate. 'But as you will no doubt agree, I have been most liberal in my treatment of you, Kate.'

Kate would have liked to have handed the money back, only she couldn't afford to. Lady Cowder, waiting for grateful thanks and assurances of her generosity, frowned at Kate's polite thanks.

'Really,' she told Claudia later. 'Kate showed a lack of gratitude which quite shocked me.'

'Well, I told you so, didn't I? Brown wants to know at what time she should serve lunch…and I must go back home this afternoon.' She added carelessly, 'Have you heard anything of James lately?'

Lady Cowder looked thoughtful. 'No, I have been seeing quite a lot of him during the last month or so, but not recently. He's in great demand and probably working hard.'

Mr Tait-Bouverie was indeed working hard, but he still found time to think about Kate. He was aware that he could have made things much easier for Kate and her mother by driving them to their new home himself, but he had kept away. His Kate, he reflected ruefully, was suspicious of any help which smacked even slightly of charity. Besides, she was quite capable of putting two and two together and making five…

He would have to wait until she was settled in before paying a visit, so he took on even more work and at the weekends, if he happened to be free, went down to Bosham with Prince and spent the day sailing. He had a dear little cottage there; Kate would like it, and he would teach her to sail.

He came home late one evening after a long day at the hospital, and Mudd, meeting him in the hall, observed gravely that in his opinion Mr Tait-Bouverie was overdoing it.

'With all due respect, sir,' said Mudd, 'You are wearing yourself out; you need a wife.'

Mr Tait-Bouverie picked up his case and made for his
study. 'Mudd, you're quite right. Will it make you happy
if I tell you that I intend to take a wife?'

Mudd beamed. 'Really, sir? When will that be?'

'As soon as she'll have me, Mudd.'

Kate, getting ready for bed in Mrs Willett's cottage,
presently laid her tired head on the pillow. It had been a
crowded day; not least of all her arrival, her rather sol-
emn reception by Mr Tombs followed by a brief five
minutes with Mrs Braithewaite and then tea with the
rest of the staff and finally going to bed in the cottage.

Mrs Willett had left that very afternoon to go straight
to the hospital, leaving everything very neat and tidy,
and all Kate had to do was go to bed, close her eyes and
sleep until her alarm clock went off at half past six the
following morning. But despite her tiredness, she allowed her thoughts to stray towards Mr Tait-Bouverie.
She wondered sleepily what he was doing and wished
that she could see him again.

'You are more than foolish,' said Kate loudly to herself, 'you are downright silly. Forget him.'

So she went to sleep and dreamed of him.

During the next day, and those following it, Kate
made several discoveries. Mrs Braithewaite was old and
crotchety, and she expected perfection, but she never
failed to thank those who worked for her. Kate, used to
Lady Cowder's demands, was thankful for that. The rest
of the staff, even Mr Tombs, were friendly, anxious to
put her at her ease and show her where everything was
kept. Mr Tombs expressed the wish that she would find

her stay with them a happy one, and that she was to con-
sult him if any problem should arise.

As to her work, she was kept busy enough running
the house, being careful not to upset Daisy or Meg or
the two cleaning ladies who came each day—and besides that she had the stores to order, menus to discuss
with Mrs Braithewaite and the cooking to do. She was
free each afternoon for a couple of hours and free, too,
once dinner had been served to Mrs Braithewaite and
the rest of the staff had had their supper.

Her mother had followed her within a few days and
the little cottage, decorated with a few of their personal
ornaments and photographs, had taken on the aspect of
home. Up early in the mornings, feeding Horace and
Moggerty, taking tea to her mother and drinking her
own by the open door leading to the little garden beyond
the cottage, Kate was happy. It wasn't going to last; she
knew that. But while it did she was content.

Well, almost content. Despite her best efforts, she
found her thoughts wandering far too often towards Mr
Tait-Bouverie. She hadn't expected to hear from him
again, but all the same she was disappointed. Unable
to forget the matter, she asked her mother, one day, in
what she hoped was a casual manner if she thought he
might find the time to phone them. 'Just to see if we've
settled in,' Kate explained.

'Most unlikely,' her mother had said firmly. 'A busy
man like him. After all, he has done all he could for us
but that doesn't mean to say that he has to be bothered
with us. He helped us and that's that, Kate.'

Mrs Crosby glanced at Kate's face, unwilling to agree
that she had been disappointed, too. She had thought,
quite wrongly, it seemed, that Mr Tait-Bouverie had had

more than a passing interest in Kate. Well, she had been
wrong; he had done an act of kindness and that was that.
She went on cheerfully, 'I've been looking in the local
paper—he was quite right, there are several hotels adver-
tising for cooks or housekeepers. You'll get a job easily
enough when we leave here. I shan't like that, will you?
You're happier here, aren't you, Kate?'

'Yes, Mother. It's a nice job and Mrs Braithewaite is
rather an old dear. I know she's strict but she's not mean.
Compared with Lady Cowder she eats like a bird, although Mr Tombs tells me that she entertains from time
to time on a lavish scale.'

Kate and her mother had been there just over two
weeks when Kate, going off duty for her afternoon
break, walked out of the kitchen door and saw Mr Tait-
Bouverie. He was sitting, very much at his ease, on the
stone wall by the door but he got down and came to
meet her. His, 'Hello, Kate,' was casual in the extreme,
which had the immediate effect of damping down her
delight at seeing him.

She bade him a good afternoon in a severe manner
and started to walk across the wide cobbled-stone yard,
and he fell into step beside her. 'Pleased to see me, Kate?'

Of course she was, but she wasn't going to say so.
She didn't answer that but observed in her calm way, 'I
dare say you have come to see Mrs Braithewaite—you
did mention that you knew her.'

'Of course I know her; she's one of my aunts. Are
you going to invite me to your cottage?'

Kate stood still. 'Certainly not, Mr Tait-Bouverie.
You know as well as I do that it's not possible.'

'You mean old Tombs will take umbrage?' He loomed

over her, too close for her peace of mind. 'He taught me
to ride my first bike. I used to stay here when I was a
small boy.'

Kate was momentarily diverted. 'Did he? Did he, really? How old were you?'

She remembered suddenly that she must remain aloof.
Grateful and friendly, of course—but aloof... 'You will
excuse me if I go? I have only an hour or so, but I have
several things that I want to do.'

He nodded. 'Wash your hair, rinse out the smalls,
bake a cake. Stop making excuses, Kate; I asked if you
were glad to see me?'

She stood there, rather tired from her morning's work,
her hair not as tidy as it might be. He studied the curling
tendrils of hair which had escaped, and only with difficulty stopped himself from taking the pins out and letting the whole gleaming mass fall round her shoulders.

Kate had her eyes fixed on his waistcoat; that seemed
the safest place. She said quietly, 'Yes, I'm glad to see
you, Mr Tait-Bouverie.'

'Good. Has our friendship advanced sufficiently for
you to call me James?'

'No! I mean—that is, it wouldn't do.'

'It will do very well indeed when we're alone.'

'Very well,' said Kate. 'I'll tell Mother that I have
seen you, we—she talks about you from time to time.'

'I've visited your mother. While you were slaving
over a hot stove I was drinking coffee in the cottage
with her.' He saw her look. 'When I come here I look up
the entire household. Tombs would be upset if I didn't
spend half an hour with him, and I like a word with
Daisy and Meg, and old Briggs. We had a pleasant chat,
your mother and I. She is full of plans for your future.'

Kate nodded. 'Yes. You were quite right—there are plenty of jobs in Bath. When I leave here we'll find something there. Just as soon as—as it's possible, we'll look for somewhere to live and I can start…'

'That is still what you have set your heart on doing, Kate?'

She said soberly, 'Yes. Then we shall have a life of our own, won't we?'

'What if a man should come along and sweep you off your feet and marry you?'

'I'd like that very much, but since it isn't likely to happen…'

'Will you promise me to tell me when it does?'

He spoke lightly and she smiled at him. 'All right, I do promise.' She added hesitantly, 'Lady Cowder told me that you are to be married.'

'Did she, indeed? She is, of course, quite right.' He held out a hand. 'I'm going to have a chat with Briggs. I'm glad that you are happy here, Kate. Goodbye.'

She offered her hand and wished that he would never let it go. But he did, and she said a quiet goodbye and went on her way to the cottage. He had said goodbye, she reflected. She wouldn't see him again and this was hardly the time to discover that she was in love with him.

Her mother was in the small garden behind the cottage, with Horace and Moggerty curled up together beside her.

'You're late, darling,' she said. And then, when she saw Kate's face, 'What's the matter?' she asked. 'Something has upset you?'

'I met Mr Tait-Bouverie as I left the house. He—he was wandering around talking to everyone. He said he'd been to see you.' Kate took a slow breath. 'He said goodbye.'

'Yes, dear. He's going back to town this afternoon. We had coffee together—what a nice man he is, and so interested in our plans. He's off to America in a couple of days. He certainly leads a busy life.'

Indeed he led a busy life, Kate agreed silently. A life in which there was no place for her. He would become more and more successful and marry Claudia, who would arrange his social life for him, and see that he met all the right people. She would be good at that, ignoring his work and having no interest in it. He would be unhappy... Kate sighed—such a deep sigh that her mother gave her a thoughtful look.

'You're happy here, Kate? I know it isn't for long, but if all goes well we should be able to start on our own before the winter. I intend to get a job—part-time—so that I can look after us both while you get your catering started.'

That roused Kate from her unhappy thoughts. 'No, Mother, you're not to go out to work. There'll be no need—we can manage on the money I'll borrow from the bank. With luck I'll get one or two regular customers—hotels in Bath and small cafés—and we'll manage.'

They would too, Kate reflected. She would make a success of her cooking and catering and she and her mother would live in comfort for the rest of their lives. She would also forget Mr Tait-Bouverie...

As it happened that wasn't difficult to do, for the following morning she was summoned to Mrs Braithewaite's sitting room. She had seen very little of her since she had arrived to work for her, but she hadn't

expected to—Mr Tombs relayed his mistress's require-
ments from day to day, and only occasionally had Kate
been bidden to the old lady's presence.

'Not the sack,' thought Kate aloud, assuming her calm
housekeeper's face and tapping on the door.

The old lady was sitting by the window, guarded
from draughts by numerous shawls and scarves. She said
tetchily, 'Come in, do, Kate. I hope you have your notebook and pen with you. There is a great deal to discuss.'

Kate advanced into the room and stood where her employer could see her. She said, 'Good morning, madam,'
and produced her notebook and pencil without comment.
Presumably a special dinner...

'It is my birthday in two weeks' time,' said Mrs
Braithewaite. 'I shall be eighty-three years old and I intend to celebrate the occasion. I shall give a buffet luncheon for—let me see—about sixty or seventy persons.
I do not require you to cook those tiresome morsels on
biscuits, and bits and pieces. You are to do ham on the
bone, and a whole salmon, of course—two, perhaps?
Cheese tartlets, a good round of cold beef, chicken... I
expect you to embellish these and add anything else suitable. Sweets, of course, something which can be eaten
elegantly without trouble—possibly ice cream, which
you will make yourself. What have you to say to that?'

'May I add suitable accompaniments to the main
dishes, madam? And may I make out a menu and let
you decide if it suits you?'

'Do that. I want it this evening, mind. If you need
extra help in the kitchen, say so. Tombs will see to that.'

Mrs Braithewaite was suddenly impatient. 'Go along,
Kate, you must have work to do.'

Tombs was waiting for her in the kitchen. 'This

is to be a great occasion,' he told her solemnly. 'Mrs Braithewaite has many relations and friends. You will let me know if you need help, Kate, and please come to me for advice if you should need it.' His tone implied that he was quite sure that she would.

Kate thanked him nicely, aware that he was doubtful as to her capabilities when it came to such an undertaking. She had no doubts herself. She went back to her work and that afternoon she went over to the cottage, told her mother and sat down to assemble a suitable menu.

She presented herself later in Mrs Braithewaite's sitting room and handed her a menu and two alternatives.

Mrs Braithewaite adjusted her lorgnettes. 'What is a toad-in-the-hole?' she wanted to know.

'A morsel of cooked sausage in a very small Yorkshire pudding. They can be eaten in the hand.'

The old lady grunted. 'The salads seem adequate. See that there is enough of everything, Kate. And desserts—sorbets, of course, ice creams, Charlotte Russe, jellied fruits, trifle… Very well, that should suffice. Send Tombs to me, if you please.'

So for the next two weeks Kate had more than enough to do, keeping her too busy to think about anything other than food. There was an enormous freezer in the kitchen, so she was able to prepare a great deal of food in advance, and, although Mrs Braithewaite had said nothing about it, she baked a cake—rich with dried fruit, sherry and the best butter. She had wisely consulted Mr Tombs about this, and he had given it his blessing. Indeed, the kitchen staff had been consulted as to its decoration, to be undertaken at the last minute.

Kate's days were full; it was only when she laid her

tired head on the pillow that she allowed her thoughts to dwell on Mr Tait-Bouverie. She supposed that he would come to the luncheon if he was back in England, but she was hardly likely to see him. She was unlikely to stir out of her kitchen.

Tombs had assembled casual help from the village to do the waiting, and she would remain in the kitchen and make sure that the food was transported safely upstairs to the big drawing room where trestle tables were to be erected, suitably swathed in white damask and decorated with the flowers that the gardener was cherishing for just such an occasion.

Mr Tait-Bouverie was back in England. His aunt's invitation was waiting for him when he returned from a weekend at Bosham, where he had spent a good deal of time thinking of good reasons why he should go and see Kate. Now the reason was most conveniently there.

He accepted with alacrity and Mudd, removing the well-worn and quite unsuitable garments which Mr Tait-Bouverie delighted in wearing when he was at Bosham, reflected with satisfaction that such an occasion would make it necessary for his master to be clothed in the superfine suiting—exquisitely tailored—the pristine linen and one of the silk ties which Mudd found fitting for a man of Mr Tait-Bouverie's standing.

'Just for luncheon, sir?' he wanted to know. 'Will you be staying overnight?'

'No, no, Mudd. I'll drive back here during the afternoon. It's a Saturday, isn't it? I'll go down to Bosham and spend Sunday there.'

Mudd nodded gloomily. He would do his best with the unsuitable garments, but that was all they would ever be in his eyes. He asked hopefully, 'You will be wearing the grey suiting, sir?'

Mr Tait-Bouverie, thinking about Kate, nodded absently. 'I'll need to leave the house early tomorrow morning, Mudd. Breakfast at seven o'clock?'

Mudd, his feelings soothed by the prospect of sending his master well-dressed to his luncheon date, assured him that breakfast would be on the table at exactly seven o'clock.

'Dinner will be ready in half an hour, sir.'

'Good; I'll be in the garden with Prince.'

He wandered around with Prince, enjoying the twilight of the early autumn evening, allowing his thoughts to dwell on the satisfactory prospect of seeing Kate again. He would have to go carefully...she was a proud girl, and stubborn. His pleasant thoughts were interrupted by Mudd, coming to tell him that Lady Cowder was on the phone.

'Dear boy,' cooed his aunt, 'you're back in England. Tell me, are you going to your aunt's luncheon party? Her birthday—just imagine, eighty-three and giving a party. I have been invited, of course, although we scarcely know each other. I mean, she is on your father's side of the family, isn't she? Of course, I have accepted, and begged to bring dear Claudia with me. May we beg a lift from you? And if you would be kind enough to drive us back after the party...?'

Mr Tait-Bouverie was a truthful man, but sometimes a lie was necessary. Certainly it was now—to spend several hours in Claudia's company was something he had no wish to do.

'Impossible, I'm afraid,' he said briskly. 'I shall be going, but only if I can fit it in with my work. Surely

Claudia can drive you there and back? That is, if she accepts the invitation. She will know no one there, I presume?'

'She knows you,' said Lady Cowder, and gave a little titter. When he didn't have anything to say to that, she added, 'Oh, well, I thought I might ask you; I forget how busy you are. I do hope that we will see you there and have time for a chat. Claudia is always talking about you.'

Mr Tait-Bouverie said, 'Indeed,' in a cold voice, and then, 'Forgive me if I ring off; Mudd has just put dinner on the table.'

'Oh, how thoughtless of me, James. Tell me, before you go, how is your dear mother?'

'In splendid health.' And when he had no more to add to that, Lady Cowder rang off herself.

He was eating his breakfast the next morning when his mother phoned. 'James, I do hope I haven't got you out of bed? I'm back... I know I'm not supposed to be here until tomorrow, but there was a seat on the plane and I thought I'd transfer. Can I come to your place and tidy up before I go home?'

'Mother, dear, stay just where you·are—I'm on my way to work, but Mudd shall fetch you at once. You'll stay here as long as you like. I'll be home later today and Mudd will look after you. Did you leave everyone well in Toronto?'

'Splendid, dear. The baby's a darling. I'll tell you all the news when I see you.'

'Go and have breakfast or coffee, my dear; Mudd will be as quick as he can.'

He put down the phone and found Mudd at his elbow. 'Mrs Tait-Bouverie is back, Mudd. Will you take the

Rover and fetch her from Heathrow? Take Prince with you…no, on second thoughts he had better stay at home. It's Mrs Todd's day for cleaning, isn't it? She'll keep an eye on him. Mother is sure to have a great deal of luggage.'

'Mrs Todd has already arrived, sir. I will inform her of what has happened and go immediately to the airport.'

Mudd spoke with his usual dignity, refusing to be hassled by the unexpected. Mr Tait-Bouverie swallowed his coffee and prepared to leave his house. 'Splendid, Mudd. And think up one of your dinners for this evening, will you?'

'I have already borne that in mind, sir,' said Mudd.

There was a hint of reproach in his voice, and Mr Tait-Bouverie said at once, 'You're a paragon, Mudd. I would be lost without you.'

Mudd, aware of his worth, merely inclined his head gravely.

Mrs Tait-Bouverie was sharing a sofa with Prince when her son got home that evening. He was tired; his outpatients clinic had been larger than usual, and he had interrupted his ward round in order to see a badly injured child brought into the accident room.

His mother offered a cheek for his kiss. 'You've had a long day, James.'

'Yes, Mother, but it's so nice to come home to you…'

'You should be coming home to your wife.'

He sat down opposite to her and picked up the glass Mudd had put on the table beside his chair. 'Something I hope to do.'

Mrs Tait-Bouverie put down her glass of sherry. 'James, dear, you've found her…?'

'Yes.' He glanced at his mother—a tall woman, a little given to stoutness, but still good-looking, and with a charming smile. She dressed beautifully to please herself and was always elegant.

He went on, 'She has a lovely face, and quantities of russet hair. She is tall, as tall as you, and she has a delightful voice. She is cook-housekeeper to Aunt Edith Braithewaite.'

'Why?' asked his mother.

'Fallen on hard times after her father died. She lives with her mother.'

'Not one of those beanpole girls playing at earning her living?'

'No, no. She has no money.' He grinned suddenly. 'And she has what I believe are described as "generous curves".'

His mother accepted a second glass of sherry. 'She sounds exactly right for you. Has she agreed to marry you?'

'Certainly not. I imagine that she is unaware that I'm in love with her. Certainly she treats me with a cautious politeness, which is a bit disconcerting.'

'When shall I see her?'

'We are invited to Aunt Edith's birthday luncheon. She will be in the kitchen, of course. We must contrive a meeting.'

'When is this luncheon to be?'

'Ten days' time. Will you stay until then?'

'No, my dear. I'd like to go home and make sure that everything is all right. Have you managed to go there at all?'

'Twice. It's too far for a day's drive; I managed weekends. Everything was all right. You could easily stay here, and I'll drive you up to Northumberland after the party.'

'I think I'd like to go home first. I'll get Peggy to drive me down. Did you see her while you were there?'

'Yes. She seems very happy. I'm to be an uncle again, I hear.'

'Yes. Isn't that splendid? Your sisters have given me several grandchildren, James. It's time you did the same.'

He smiled at her. 'All in good time, my dear. Here is Mudd to tell us that dinner is on the table.'

Two weeks wasn't long in which to plan and prepare the kind of luncheon Mrs Braithewaite insisted upon giving. Kate sat up late at night, writing copious notes and then assembling everything she would need. A good deal could be prepared well ahead of the day, but catering for seventy people was a challenge. Luckily the staff, led by a self-important Mr Tombs, were delighted with the idea of such a social gathering and went out of their way to help Kate—Tombs going so far as to drive her into Bath so that she could choose what she needed for herself and then stow it away in the huge freezer until she needed it.

All the same, even with so much willing help, there was a lot to do. Kate enjoyed it, though. Cooking for Lady Cowder had been a thankless task, but now, as she made tartlets and pork pies, cooked the hams to an exact pinkness, coated chicken breasts in a creamy cheese sauce, made lobster patties and crisp potato straws, she felt satisfaction.

On the day previous to the luncheon she stayed up until the small hours, making bowls of mouthwatering trifle, puréeing fruit to mix with gelatine and turn out into colourful shapes. And the cake... She had baked that days ago; now she iced it, decorated it with the roses she had fashioned so carefully and set a single candle amongst them.

Mr Tombs had advised that. 'Mrs Braithewaite hasn't

enough breath to blow out one candle, let alone eighty-three,' he had told her seriously.

The great day dawned with a clear sky, although there was an autumnal nip in the air. Luncheon was to be served at one o'clock, and Kate and her helpers were up and about before the sun was up. The tables had to be set up, draped with damask, decorated with flowers and set with plates and cutlery, glass and napkins.

They ate a hasty breakfast and Kate assembled what she would need for dinner that evening. There were to be guests staying on—ten people, close family of Mrs Braithewaite—and she had been warned to send up a four-course meal. Rack of lamb with suitable accompaniments, a sorbet, Charlotte Russe and, for starters, mushrooms in a garlic and cream sauce. For the kitchen staff she had wisely made a vast steak and kidney pudding which could be cut into and kept warm if need be.

The guests began to arrive at around noon and Mr Tombs, Daisy and Meg went upstairs to take coats and hand around sherry. Kate, a little nervous now, put the finishing touches to the cake and put on a clean pinny. Now was her chance to nip up to the drawing room where the buffet had been arranged and make sure that everything was just as it should be.

She paused on the threshold and sighed with satisfaction. The tables were loaded with food but they looked elegant. The flowers were perfect and the hams on their vast dishes, surrounded by dishes of various salads, looked mouthwatering. The cake, of course, was to be brought in at the end of luncheon, to be cut by Mrs Braithewaite and handed round with champagne. Kate nodded her bright head, well satisfied.

Mrs Tait-Bouverie, just that minute arrived and strolling round the hall while James put the car away, paused to look at her. Even from the back Mrs Tait-Bouverie knew who she was. There weren't many heads of hair like hers—besides, James had described her very accurately. Mrs Tait-Bouverie wandered a little nearer, and when Kate turned round to go she was pleased to see that he had been quite right about Kate's looks, too. A beautiful creature and plenty of her, thought his mother. She said pleasantly, 'May I take a peep, or is it to be a surprise at one o'clock?'

Kate smiled at her. 'Well, yes, I suppose it should be. Mr Tombs said that no one was to go into the room until then. I'm the cook, and I came to make sure everything was as it should be.'

Mrs Tait-Bouverie surveyed the colourful display. 'It looks magnificent. Caterers, I suppose?'

'Well, no,' said Kate matter-of-factly. 'It's all been done here. We all helped.'

'But who did the cooking?'

'I did—only I couldn't have done it without everyone's help. I'd better go—and if you don't mind I'll shut the door...'

Which she did, and with a polite murmur went back to the kitchen. Mrs Tait-Bouverie strolled back to the entrance to meet her son.

'I've been talking to your Kate,' she told him. 'She's everything you said of her, my dear, and I suspect a lot more besides. She had no idea who I was. You'll go and find her before we leave?'

'Yes. There should be plenty of opportunity. The house is packed with people; we had better join them.'

Chapter 8

Mr Tait-Bouverie following his mother, entered the smaller drawing room, where his aunt was sitting receiving her guests. A slow business, as she insisted on opening each present as it was offered to her. She greeted Mrs Tait-Bouverie with a peck on the cheek and turned to James.

'So you found the time to come?' she observed, and added slyly, 'Your Aunt Cowder is here with that girl... wanted to know where you were.'

He bent to kiss her cheek and she added wistfully, 'I should like to see you married, my dear.' She chuckled. 'Not to Claudia, of course.'

He said, 'Since it's your birthday, I believe it very likely that you will have your wish granted.'

He offered his gift, suitably wrapped and beribboned,

and, leaving his mother with the old lady, wandered off to greet family and friends.

It wasn't long before Lady Cowder saw him.

'James, how delightful. You managed to get here, after all.' She pecked his cheek and added archly, 'Claudia is so looking forward to seeing you.'

Claudia, James saw at a glance, was dressed to kill—her make-up had been applied by a skilled hand and her blonde hair had been arranged in a fashionable tangle which, while in the forefront of the current mode, did nothing for her... Mr Tait-Bouverie shook hands, said everything necessary for good manners, and excused himself, giving his aunt a vague reply when she wanted to know when he would be returning.

'Of course, he knows everyone here,' said Lady Cowder soothingly to Claudia, and wished uneasily that the girl would at least disguise her peevishness with a smile.

The last of the guests having arrived, drinks were handed round, a toast was drunk to their hostess and Tombs announced that luncheon was being served from the buffet.

This was a signal for a well-mannered rush to fill plates while Tombs carved the hams and Daisy and Meg and the girls pressed into service from the village saw to it that everyone was served.

When that was done everyone settled down to eating and gossip, having their plates replenished from time to time and drinking the excellent wines Mrs Braithewaite had provided. That lady was seated in some state at a table at one end of the room while an ever-changing stream of people came and went to exchange a few words with her. Everyone was, in fact, fully occupied, and Mr Tait-Bouverie had no difficulty in slipping away unseen.

The house was quiet once he had left the drawing room, gone down the staircase and through the baize door at the back of the hall to the kitchen. He opened its door quietly and paused to enjoy the sight of Kate, fast asleep in one of the shabby armchairs by the Aga.

She had kicked off her shoes and slept like a child, her mouth slightly open, confident that she had the place to herself for an hour or more. The last of the food had been carried upstairs and there was nothing for her to do until Tombs came to tell her to make the tea which some of the guests, at least, would undoubtedly want. So she slept dreamlessly, aware of a job well done.

Mr Tait-Bouverie trod silently across the kitchen and sat down in the equally shabby chair opposite her, quite happy to wait. He had dismissed a strong wish to kiss Kate awake, and contented himself with watching her tired, sleeping face.

Presently she opened her eyes, stared at him unbelievingly for a moment and, Kate being Kate, asked, 'Was I snoring?'

Mr Tait-Bouverie stayed where he was. 'No,' he said placidly. 'What time did you get up this morning, Kate?'

'Me? Four o'clock—I had to finish icing the cake. How did you get here?'

'I came down the stairs. Shall I make us a pot of tea?'

'That would be lovely…' She stopped and sat up straight. 'I'm sorry, Mr Tait-Bouverie, did you come with a message, or want something? I'm sorry I fell asleep.'

He perceived that any rash ideas he might have had about asking her to marry him would have to be ignored for the moment. A pity, for he saw her so seldom, and now, with plenty of time in which to tell her of his feelings, he would have to waste it making tea. He smiled at the thought.

'No, no, everything is going splendidly upstairs. I came to see if you were still quite happy here.'

He got up, opened up the Aga and put the kettle on, found a teapot and the tea and two mugs, whistling quietly as he did so—a sound which Kate found reassuring and in some strange way comforting.

'A very successful birthday party,' said Mr Tait-Bouverie. 'Have you had lunch?' And when she said that she had not, he asked, 'Breakfast?'

'Well, I didn't have any time…'

'As a small boy,' said Mr Tait-Bouverie in a voice so soothing it would have reduced a roaring lion to tears, 'I was taught to boil an egg, make toast and butter it— my mother being of the opinion that if I could master these arts I would never starve.'

He had found the bread and the eggs and was busy at the Aga. 'Is your mother well? I must go over to the cottage and see her before we leave.'

Kate's tired brain fastened on the 'we'. 'Oh, you came with Claudia, I expect.'

The fragrant smell of toast made her twitch her pretty nose, and she didn't see his quick glance.

'No. I came with my mother. She's back from Canada, and came down from Northumberland. She and Aunt Edith are close friends.'

He placed a plate of well-buttered toast on the table and dished up an egg. 'Come and eat something.' When she had sat down at the table he poured the tea, a strong brew capable of reviving anyone not actually dead.

Kate ate her egg, polished off the toast and, imbued with new energy by the tea, got to her feet.

'That was lovely, thank you very much. I mustn't keep you, Mr Tait-Bouverie.' She popped a crumb into her mouth. 'I'm very grateful, but I mustn't keep you. It was most kind...' She stopped herself saying it all again.

She didn't quite look at him, and it was an effort to remember that she was the cook and must behave accordingly.

He made no attempt to leave. 'You have made your plans for the future?' he wanted to know. 'I am told that Mrs Willett will be returning in another few weeks, but I'm sure you will find something in Bath until you are ready to start on your own.'

'Yes. I shall start looking round in a week or two. Bath seems a very pleasant place. Mother has been there— to look round, you know. I'm sure I'll find something.'

They were standing facing each other and she said again, 'Don't let me keep you—you're missing the party.'

When he didn't move, she added, 'It's a success, I hope? Mrs Braithewaite was so anxious that it should go off well. I hope she had some lovely presents—it's quite an achievement to be eighty-three and still have so many friends to wish one well...'

She spoke in her cook's voice, saying anything which came into her head, because if she didn't she might fling herself at him and pour out all her hopes and fears and love for him. She added, 'I must start the clearing up...'

'Of course. I'm glad you are happy here, Kate. I must go back upstairs and have a word with friends I haven't seen for some time.'

She nodded and answered his goodbye in a voice as cheerful as his own. It was pure chance which had caused them to meet again, she told herself when he had gone, and chances like that seldom happened twice.

Claudia was there, upstairs in the drawing room, looking, according to Daisy, quite lovely. Kate began to stack dishes, put away uneaten food and set out cups and saucers for the tea that the staff would undoubtedly be wanting later.

As for Mr Tait-Bouverie, he crossed the courtyard behind the house and paid a visit to her mother.

She greeted him warmly. 'Is it any good offering you coffee?' she asked. 'I expect you've had it already. Is the party a success?'

'Indeed, it is. A magnificent banquet; Kate can be proud of herself.'

'It was hard work,' Mrs Crosby said eagerly. 'But you see, James, that she could make a career out of her cooking, once she can get started?'

'If that is indeed what she wants.' He took the mug of coffee she offered him. 'Mrs Crosby—you're tired, or not feeling well…'

She said far too quickly, 'I'm fine.' And then, catching his eyes, 'Well, it's just this silly little pain; it comes and goes. Even when it's not there I know that it is, if you see what I mean.' She smiled. 'It's nothing; really, it isn't…'

'Does Kate know?'

'No, of course not. She has had enough to think about for the last two weeks—up at dawn and going to bed at all hours. I'll go and see a doctor when the festivities are over.'

'This pain,' said Mr Tait-Bouverie. 'Tell me where it is, Mrs Crosby.'

She told him, because suddenly he wasn't James but a

kind, impersonal doctor asking her questions in a quiet voice.

'I would not wish to alarm you, Mrs Crosby,' he told her. 'But I think that you should go to a doctor and allow him to examine you.' He smiled suddenly. 'Nothing serious, I do assure you, but from what you tell me I should suspect a grumbling appendix, which nowadays can be dealt with in a few days. Do you have a doctor?'

'No. I expect I can find one in Bath.'

'Allow me to arrange a check-up for you—I've a colleague in Bath who will see you. I'll phone him this evening and let you know when he can see you.'

'If it's necessary. I don't want Kate worried.' She added, 'You're very kind. You help us so often.'

'I'll let Kate know and reassure her.' He put down his mug. 'I must go back to the party.' He stood up and took her hand. 'Mrs Crosby, if you or Kate need help will you let me know? Phone my house. Even if I'm not there, my man will see that I get your message.'

He loosed her hand, scribbled in his pocket book and took out the page. 'Here is the number.'

Mr Tait-Bouverie wasn't a man to waste time. At home that evening he phoned his colleague in Bath, made an appointment for Mrs Crosby and picked up the phone to tell Kate.

She was making a last round of the kitchen, making sure that everything was ready for the morning. Daisy and Meg had already gone to their beds and the helpers from the village had long since gone. Mr Tombs had bidden her goodnight, expressed himself satisfied with her efforts and gone upstairs to check windows and doors and lock up. He had looked at her pale face and said kindly, 'You did a good job, Kate. Mrs Braithewaite was pleased.'

Kate was on the point of leaving the kitchen when the phone rang. She went to answer it, wondering who it could be, for it was used almost solely to order groceries and receive calls from tradespeople. Mr Tait-Bouverie's voice, very calm in her ear, took her by surprise so that she had no breath for a moment. When he said her name for a second time she said, 'Yes, it's me.'

'You're tired, but this is most important. I went to see your mother this afternoon. I'm not sure, but from what she tells me she may have a threatening appendicitis. Nothing to worry about, provided it's nipped in the bud. I've arranged for a Dr Bright in Bath to see your mother on Monday afternoon. He'll examine her, and if he thinks it's necessary he'll have her in hospital and take her appendix out. It's a simple operation and she will be quite fit in a few weeks.'

He was silent, and Kate said angrily, 'Why wasn't I told? How ill is Mother? I had no idea, and now you're telling me all this just as though it's not important, as though she's got a cold in the head or cut her hand...'

'Forgive me, Kate. You are always so sensible and practical, and I thought that I could tell you without wrapping it up in soft talk and caution.'

'Well, you're wrong. I've got feelings like everyone else—except you, of course. I don't suppose you feel anything except pleasure in nailing bones together and dancing with Claudia. You don't know about loving...' She gave a great sniff and hung up, then snatched up the phone again, appalled at what she had just said. 'No, no. I don't mean a word of it...'

The line was dead, of course.

To find a quiet corner and have a good cry was out of the question; Kate locked the door behind her and went to the cottage. Her mother gave her a guilty look as she went in and Kate said at once, 'Mr Tait-Bouverie has just been phoning me, Mother.' She spoke cheerfully and managed a smile, too. 'I had no idea that you weren't feeling well—I should have seen for myself...'

'Darling, you had more than enough to think about. Besides, I'm not really ill. What did James say?'

Kate told her. 'I expect there'll be a letter in the post on Monday morning. I'll ask Mrs Braithewaite if I can have the afternoon off and we'll catch the bus in after lunch. A Dr Bright is going to see you, and if he thinks he should he'll refer you to the hospital. We can't make any plans for the moment until we know what's to happen.'

Kate put her arms round her mother. 'I'm sorry, Mother, dear—it was very brave of you not to say something.'

'This birthday party was important, Kate. Once you start on your own you may find it useful; a lot of the guests are local people, and news gets around in the country.'

'None of that matters while you're not well, mother. I'm going to make us a warm drink and you're going to bed. We'll know more on Monday.'

There was a letter on Monday morning, giving the time and the place where Mrs Crosby was to go and, what was more, Tombs himself took Kate aside after breakfast and informed her that Mrs Braithewaite, having been appraised of Mrs Crosby's indisposition, had ordered Mr Briggs to drive them both to Bath and bring them back.

Kate stared at him, her eyes wide. 'Mr Tombs, however did Mrs Braithewaite know? I've certainly not told her—I intended to do so this morning…'

'As to that, Kate, I am quite unable to say,' he told her severely, mindful of Mr James's express wish that the source of the arrangement should be kept secret.

'I've talked to my aunt, Tombs,' Mr Tait-Bouverie had continued. 'And she has agreed to sending Briggs with the car, so not a word to a soul.'

Tombs had assured him that he would be as quiet as the grave.

So Kate and her mother were driven in comfort to see Dr Bright, a youngish man, who examined Mrs Crosby and then told her in his pleasant voice that she should go into hospital as soon as possible and have her appendix out.

'Which hospital?' asked Kate. 'You see, we don't actually live here…'

'Ah—as to that, I think things could be arranged. You are acquainted with Mr Tait-Bouverie, are you not? He is an old friend and colleague of mine—and an honorary consultant at our hospital; there should be no trouble in finding a bed for you for a week or ten days—and you are an emergency, Mrs Crosby. I should like you to come tomorrow and be seen by the surgeon there—also a colleague of Mr Tait-Bouverie—and he will decide when he will operate. The sooner the better. The operation is simple, but nonetheless necessary.'

When Mrs Crosby hesitated, Kate said, 'You are very kind, Doctor. If you will tell me where Mother has to go and at what time…?'

'Would you wait while I arrange a bed?' said Dr

Bright, and ushered them back into the waiting room, to emerge in ten minutes or so.

'Bring Mrs Crosby to the hospital at two o'clock to-morrow afternoon. She will be seen then, and admitted.'

He shook hands with them both, said that he would be seeing Mrs Crosby again very shortly, and went back to his surgery and lifted the phone.

Kate was surprised at the amount of willing help she was offered when she told Mr Tombs the result of their visit to the doctor. She had expected him to grumble, even make it difficult for her to go with her mother to the hospital the next day, but he had been helpful. She was to go with her mother directly after lunch and stay until she was quite satisfied that Mrs Crosby was comfortable, and she had seen the surgeon.

'But dinner,' said Kate. 'I may not be back in time to cook it.'

'You have the morning,' Mr Tombs reminded her. 'Prepare a dish which Daisy or Meg can warm up. They are quite capable of cooking the vegetables. Unless Mrs Braithewaite asks for a special dessert, you will have time in the morning to make a trifle. She is partial to trifle.'

Kate thanked him and started to cook that evening's dinner, and make a steak and kidney pie for the staff supper. She made two; one would do for the next day. She had seen her mother safely back to the cottage and left her to pack a case and get ready for the next day. She hated leaving her alone, but Mrs Braithewaite had been kind so far, and so had Mr Tombs, but she was still the cook with a job to do.

Briggs took them to Bath the following day. Tombs had taken Kate aside while she was getting the breakfast and told her that Mrs Braithewaite had herself suggested it. 'And when you are ready to return, she wishes you to telephone to me and I will instruct Briggs to fetch you from the hospital,' said Tombs at his most pompous.

It was a surprise, too, when Mrs Crosby was taken to a small room opening out of the women's surgical ward. Kate said anxiously to the sister, 'Is there some mistake? I mean, Mother's on the NHS—we can't afford to pay— and this is a private room, isn't it?'

Sister smiled. 'It is the only bed we have free,' she explained. 'And of course you won't have to pay for it. Your mother will be here for a week or ten days at the most. Is there someone to look after her when she goes home?'

'Me,' said Kate. 'I'm a cook; we have a little cottage close to the house. I can manage quite well as long as Mother can be left while I work.'

'It should be perfectly all right.' Sister patted Kate's arm. 'You mustn't worry; I'm sure Dr Bright told you that it is a simple operation, and only needs a short stay in hospital. I'll leave you to get your mother settled in and then, if you will come to my office, I dare say Mr Samuels will see you. He's the surgeon who will operate.'

He was quite a young man, Kate discovered, and he told her that he would operate on the following day. Possibly in the afternoon. 'I'll get someone to let you know, then if you wish to see your mother you will be able to do so.'

'I'm not sure if I can get away. You see, I'm a cook and there's dinner to prepare. I've been given a lot of free time already...' Kate added anxiously, 'If I phoned, would someone tell me if everything was all right? I'll come if I possibly can...'

'Don't worry if you can't come,' he assured her. 'We'll

keep you informed, and I'm sure Sister will let you visit whenever you can manage it.'

So Kate bade a cheerful goodbye to her mother and phoned Mr Tombs, who told her to wait at the hospital entrance until Briggs came to fetch her. 'I trust everything is satisfactory, Kate?' he added.

Kate said that, yes, it was, and thanked him once again. 'Everyone is being so helpful,' she told him.

Mr Tait-Bouverie would have been pleased to hear that. He had spent time and thought and hours on the phone, persuading and explaining, shamelessly taking advantage of his consultant's post at the hospital. Because he was well liked by his colleagues—and Tombs hid a lifelong devotion to him—he had succeeded in his plan. Only Mrs Braithewaite had demanded to know why he should be taking so much trouble over her cook's mother.

'I'm sure Kate's mother is a very pleasant person,' she had stated. 'But, after all, Kate is the cook, James.'

'She is my future wife.' Mr Tait-Bouverie heard the old lady gasp. 'So, dear Aunt Edith, will you do as I ask?'

'Does she know?'

'No.'

Mrs Braithewaite chuckled. 'She is an excellent cook and a very pretty girl, and it's time you settled down. Come and see me when you have the time, James; I dare say you have some scheme in that clever head of yours.'

'Indeed, I have. And I'm free tomorrow.'

'I shall expect you!'

The operation was a success. Kate was called to answer the phone just as she had sent Mrs Braithewaite's lunch up on Daisy's tray. Sister was reassuringly cheerful. 'Your mother is back in bed and sleeping peacefully.'

'I thought it was to be this afternoon.' Kate did her best to keep the wobble out of her voice; it was silly to want to cry now that everything was all right.

'Mr Samuels decided to do your mother at the end of his morning list.' Sister had hesitated before she spoke, but Kate was in no state to notice.

'Please give Mother my love when she wakes up, and I'll come when I can. Would this evening be too late?'

'Come when you can,' said Sister comfortably. 'Your mother will probably be asleep, but if you visit her you'll feel better, won't you?'

Kate put down the phone. She was crying, although she had tried her best not to. Everything was all right, Sister had said, but she longed to be with her mother—just for a minute or two. Just to make quite sure...

Mr Tombs came to a silent halt beside her, and she blew her nose and sniffed back the tears. 'That was the hospital, Mr Tombs. Mother is back in her bed and everything is fine. Sister said so.'

'We are all relieved at the good news,' said Tombs, looking suitably serious. 'I will inform Mrs Braithewaite and I suggest that you go and have your dinner with the rest of the staff, Kate.'

He went on his dignified way and Kate went back to the kitchen, to be cheered by the kind enquiries she had from Daisy and Meg and the daily woman from the village. She couldn't eat her dinner, and only drank the strong tea Daisy gave her, her head filled with rather wild plans to go to Bath and see her mother. This evening, she reflected, once dinner had been served, she would get a taxi. No one would object to that, and she would be back before Tombs locked up for the night.

She got up and went along to the fridge; preparations for dinner needed to be made and Mrs Braithewaite wanted scones for her tea.

Tombs came looking for her. 'I have informed Mrs Braithewaite of your mother's operation, Kate. I am to tell Briggs to drive you to the hospital at half past seven this evening.'

Kate put down the dish of Dover sole she was inspecting. 'He will? I may go with him? How very kind of Mrs Braithewaite. I was going to ask you if it would be all right for me to get a taxi once dinner had been served, Mr Tombs.'

She smiled, wanting to cry from sheer relief. 'I'll have everything quite ready if Daisy or Meg won't mind dishing up.'

'They are glad to help you, Kate. If you wish to telephone the hospital you have my permission to do so.'

There wasn't much time once Kate had cooked dinner, so she hurried over to the cottage, tore into a jumper and skirt and shabby jacket, tied a scarf over her hair and, anxious not to keep Briggs waiting, went quickly to the other side of the yard where he would be ready.

'Sorry I'm late, Mr Briggs,' she told him breathlessly. 'It's been a bit of a rush.'

'Just you sit and catch your breath, Kate. It's a nasty old night—going to rain; chilly, too. Your ma's in the best place, I reckon.'

Certainly, Kate thought as she got out at the hospital entrance, it looked cheerful, with lights shining from every window. She paused to poke her head through the car window. 'I'll not be long, Mr Briggs. Will you be here, or shall I meet you somewhere? The car park?'

'You come here, Kate.'

He drove away when she had gone inside.

Kate went to the reception desk and waited impatiently while the girl phoned the ward. She was to go up, she was told. She could take the lift, or the stairs were at the back of the hall.

She raced up the stairs two at a time and then paused to calm down before she pushed open the ward doors. A nurse came to meet her and led her through the ward and into the short corridor onto which her mother's room opened.

'Your mother's fine, but tired,' said the nurse, and smiled and left her.

Mrs Crosby, comfortably propped up with pillows, was rather pale but almost her usual cheerful self. She said happily, 'Kate, dear, how lovely. How did you get here?'

'Briggs brought me, Mother. How lovely to have it all over and done with. Are you comfortable? Does it hurt? Are you being well looked after?'

'I'm being treated like a film star, and I'm only a bit sore. I'm to get out of bed tomorrow.'

Kate embraced her parent rather gingerly, and pulled up a chair.

'So soon? Do you want anything? I'm not sure if I can come tomorrow, but I'll be here on Friday—it's my day off, and I can get the bus. Do you want any more nighties? What about books? Fruit? I couldn't bring flowers; there wasn't a shop open.'

She took her mother's hand in hers. 'Mother, dear, I'm

so glad that they discovered your appendix before it got too bad. I'll ask if I can see the surgeon and thank him.'

'Yes, dear, such a nice man. But it's James we have to thank. He knew what to do.'

'Yes, yes, of course. I'll write and thank him, shall I?'

She remembered what she had said to him on the phone and blushed hotly. It would be a difficult letter to write. And it would serve her right if he tore it up without reading it.

She didn't stay long; her mother was already half-asleep. She bent and kissed her, and went back down the ward and tapped on Sister's office door.

Sister was there, sitting at her desk, and so was Mr Samuels. Mr Tait-Bouverie was there too, lounging against the windowsill.

Kate stopped short in the doorway. She said 'Oh,' uncertainly and then, 'I'm sorry—I didn't know...'

'Come in, Miss Crosby,' said Sister briskly. 'You've visited your mother?' When Kate nodded, she added, 'Well, since Mr Samuels is here I expect he'll tell you that everything is just as it should be.'

Kate transferred her eyes to his face, careful not to look at Mr Tait-Bouverie after that first startled glance.

'Your mother is doing well. Nothing to worry about. A nasty appendix; we caught it just in time. She'll be up and about in no time.' He smiled nicely. 'Of course, you know Mr Tait-Bouverie, don't you? Lucky he got the ball rolling, so to speak.'

Kate cast a look at Mr Tait-Bouverie's waistcoat. 'Yes, I'm very grateful. Thank you very much, Mr Samuels. And Sister. I'm being taken back—someone's waiting for me—I'd better go. I'll come again as soon as I can.'

Mr Tait-Bouverie hadn't uttered a word. Now he said quietly, 'I'll drive you back, Kate.'

'No.' Kate spoke loudly and too quickly before she could stop herself. She felt her face grow hot. 'What I mean is,' she added lamely, 'Mr Briggs is waiting for me.'

'He went straight back to my aunt's house. If you're ready?'

He stood up and went to the door, and she saw that there was nothing else to do but go with him. Mr Samuels was smiling, and so was Sister…

She thanked them both once more, shook hands and went past Mr Tait-Bouverie, who was holding the door open for her.

Halfway down the stairs she stopped. 'You arranged everything, didn't you? Mother being operated upon so quickly, having a private room, Briggs driving us to and fro…'

'Yes.' He had stopped beside her, his face impassive.

'I didn't mean a word of it,' she burst out. 'All that about you not having any feelings. I—I was taken by surprise and frightened for Mother, but that's no excuse.' She took a couple of steps down. 'You don't have to take me back; I feel awful.' She stopped again and added fiercely, 'You must know how I feel, calling you all those awful things, and you still helped Mother. If you never want to speak to me again I'd quite understand.'

He said placidly, 'What a silly girl you are, Kate.' He made it sound like an endearment. 'True, I have satisfaction—not pleasure—in nailing bones together, as you put it. And I do enjoy dancing—but not with Claudia. And, contrary to your opinion of me, I do know how to love.'

They had reached the bottom of the staircase. Kate's tongue ran away with her. 'If you're going to marry Claudia you ought to enjoy dancing with her,' she said foolishly.

'Why, yes, I suppose I should,' he agreed. 'Now come along; the car is round in the consultants' car park.'

She went with him, silent now. He had called her a silly girl and she supposed that she was—and if that was what he thought of her, she had indeed been silly to fall in love with him. She got into the car and answered his casual observations about her mother in a stiff little voice.

At the house he got out of the car with her, walked her to the kitchen door, opened it, bade her a cheerful goodnight and waited until she had gone inside before walking to the front door.

Tombs, on the look-out for the car, was waiting to open it for him. Mr Tait-Bouverie greeted him with a gentle thump on the back. 'I have just returned Kate to the kitchen,' he told him. 'Mrs Crosby is doing very well. Is my aunt in the drawing room?'

'Yes, Mr James, and there's coffee and sandwiches. You're no doubt hungry...'

Mrs Braithewaite was sitting by the fire, swathed in a shawl and with her feet on a stool. She looked decidedly elderly sitting there, but there was nothing elderly about her voice.

'Come in, James. I must say, this is a fine time of day to call on me. I should be in bed...'

He bent and kissed her cheek. 'Aunt Edith, you know, and so do I, that you're never in bed before midnight.'

'An old woman of my age...' she began, and then went

on, 'Oh, well since I'm here…pour yourself a whisky and you can give me one, too…'

He poured a small drink for her, added ice and gave himself a more generous drink. 'You shouldn't be drinking spirits at your age,' he told her mildly.

'At my age I'll drink anything I like!' she told him. 'Sit down; where's Kate?'

'I would suppose that she has gone to her home.'

His aunt chuckled. 'Was she surprised to see you? Did you sweep her off her feet?'

'Oh, she was surprised. But it hardly seemed the right moment to behave with anything but the utmost circumspection.'

'Oh, well, I suppose you know best. How's your mother?'

'Very well. Aunt Edith, when is Mrs Willett returning?'

'Hah! I might have known you had some scheme up your sleeve. In two weeks; it seems she has made great progress. She will come back here, of course, and your Kate will have to go.'

'Splendid. It will be too far to take Mrs Crosby up to Mother's. I intend to offer her the cottage at Bosham. When Kate leaves here, she will join her there…'

'Will she? She might not want to, James. Aren't you taking a lot for granted?'

'Possibly. It's a calculated risk, isn't it? But she will have nowhere else to go.'

'You're a prize catch, James—good looks, money, well liked, well known in your profession, comfortable ancestral home, even if it is in the north, fashionable house in town, cottage at Bosham. I'm surprised that Kate hasn't flung herself into your arms.'

'Kate doesn't care tuppence for any of that,' said Mr Tait-Bouverie. 'She's proud—the right kind of pride—and she's in love with me and won't admit it because she has this bee in her bonnet about Claudia, Lady Cowder's god-daughter. She has this idea that I'm on the point of marrying the girl. The last thing I would ever do. Lady Cowder has put it about that we are to marry, and Kate believes her.'

'But surely you told Kate?'

He shook his head. 'No. There is a great deal that I have to tell Kate, but only at the right moment.' He sat back in his chair. 'And now tell me, how do you feel? All the excitement of your birthday party must have shaken you up a little.'

He drove himself back to London presently, and he thought of Kate every inch of the way.

Chapter 9

Mrs Crosby made an uneventful recovery, and, although Kate was unable to visit her everyday, twice during the following week Briggs took her in the car in the evening when her work was done. She spent her days off in Bath, seeing her mother in the morning and afternoon. Mrs Crosby was out of bed now, walking about, and looking, truth to tell, better than she had done for some weeks—and she listened to Kate's plans with every appearance of interest.

'Mrs Willett is coming back in a week's time,' Kate told her. 'So I shall be leaving very soon now. I've been looking in the local paper; there are several jobs I thought I'd try for. Whichever one I'm lucky enough to get will have somewhere where you and Moggerty and Horace can live with me. Once we're settled I'll go to

the bank—there's enough money saved for me to ask
them for a loan. Isn't it exciting?'

Her mother agreed, reflecting that Kate didn't look
in the least excited—nor did she look happy. The temptation to tell her of Mr Tait-Bouverie's visit was very
strong, but she resisted it. Not that he had said much, only
that she and Kate weren't to worry about their future.

'I can't think why you're doing this for us,' Mrs
Crosby had told him.

He had smiled a little. 'Oh, but I think you can, Mrs
Crosby. If you will leave everything to me…' he had said.

She had nodded. Before he'd taken his leave of her
he had bent and kissed her cheek.

Mr Tait-Bouverie, home late from the hospital, was
greeted by Mudd with the promise of dinner within half
an hour—and the information that Miss Claudia Travers
had telephoned. 'She wishes you to join a few friends at
the theatre tomorrow evening, sir, and would you phone
her back as soon as you returned.' Mudd managed to
sound disapproving. 'I informed her that you would
probably be late home.'

'Splendid, Mudd. Come into the study, there's a good
fellow…'

Once Mudd was seated opposite him, with the desk
between them, Mr Tait-Bouverie said, 'Mudd, the mother
of the young lady I intend to marry has been ill. I think
it would be a good idea if she were to convalesce at
the cottage at Bosham. Mrs Squires sees to the place
when we're not there, doesn't she? Do you suppose she
would go each day and cook and clean and so on while
Mrs Crosby is there? It may be necessary for you to go
down from time to time and make sure that everything

is as it should be. She will be joined by her daughter very shortly.'

'You won't be going down yourself, sir?'

'Oh, very probably, but I can't always be sure of getting away.'

'You mentioned that you would be getting married,' said Mudd.

'Yes, indeed—once I can persuade Miss Crosby that she wishes to marry me.'

Mudd looked taken aback. Mr Tait-Bouverie had been the target of numerous young ladies for a number of years, all of them ready to fall into his lap at the drop of a hat. Here was a young lady who needed persuading. Mudd reflected that she must be someone out of the ordinary. As long as she didn't interfere in his kitchen…

'I shall notify Mrs Squires of your wishes, sir,' said Mudd. 'If you could give me a date? She will need to make beds and air the place and get in food.'

'It might be as well if you go down yourself and make sure that everything is just so, Mudd. Thursday week— eight days' time.' Mr Tait-Bouverie was lost in thought. 'If I can manage a day off I'll drive you down early in the morning and leave you there, then go on to Bath and collect Mrs Crosby, bring her to Bosham and drive you back here with me.'

'Miss Crosby?' ventured Mudd.

'She won't be free for another day or so. I'll fetch her then.'

Mudd went away then to prepare the dinner, leaving Mr Tait-Bouverie sitting there with Prince's great head on his knee, lost in thought. When the phone rang he lifted the receiver and heard Claudia's shrill voice.

'James, didn't you get my message? Why haven't you telephoned me?'

Mr Tait-Bouverie said smoothly, 'Yes, I had your message, Claudia. I'm afraid that it is a waste of time including me in your social activities—indeed, in any part of your life. I feel that our lives are hardly compatible. I'm sure you must agree.' Because he was a kind man he added, 'I'm sure that you have a host of admirers.'

Claudia snapped, 'Yes, I have, and they're all young men,' and slammed down the receiver.

Mr Tait-Bouverie put down the phone, quite unmoved by this reference to his age. 'When I'm seventy,' he told Prince cheerfully, 'our eldest son will be the age I am now.'

Prince rumbled an answer and blew gently onto his master's hand, waiting patiently for Mudd to come and tell them that dinner was on the table.

Mrs Crosby was to leave hospital the following day and Kate had packed a case of clothes to take to her. Mr Tombs had told her that she might have the time off to take them during the evening. 'But see that you are back in good time,' he had told her. 'One must not take advantage of Mrs Braithewaite's generosity.'

So Kate, carrying the case, got into the car with Briggs and made her way to her mother's room. 'Will you be all right?' she asked Briggs anxiously. 'Where will you wait? I may be half an hour at least...'

'Don't you worry your head, Kate, you come back here when you're ready.'

Her mother was sitting in a small armchair, and it struck Kate that she looked guilty—but she looked excited too.

She kissed her parent and asked, 'What's the paper

and pencil for? Are you making lists?' She opened the case. 'I brought your tweed suit and a woolly, and your brown shoes; you won't need a hat. I'll unpack them and leave the case to put your nightie and dressing gown in when I come to fetch you.'

She glanced up, saw her mother smiling at someone behind her and spun round. Mr Tait-Bouverie, immaculate as to person, pleasantly remote as to manner, was standing just inside the door. He shut it quietly and said, 'Hello, Kate.'

Kate said, 'Hello.' And then, 'Why are you here again?'

He put his hands in his trouser pockets and leaned against the door. He looked enormous. 'Your mother is going to convalesce at my cottage at Bosham. She will be well looked after by Mrs Squires, who takes care of the place for me. You will be able to join her as soon as you leave Mrs Braithewaite's.'

Kate stared at him. 'High-handed,' she said at length. 'That's what you are—arranging everything behind my back.' She rounded on her mother. 'You knew about this, but you didn't tell me...'

'Well, darling, it seemed best not to, for I thought you would object.'

'Of course I object. I can take care of you at the cottage...'

'I understand that you will be leaving there within the next few days,' observed Mr Tait-Bouverie pleasantly. 'Have you found somewhere else to go?'

When she didn't answer he added, 'Kate, your mother will need a little while to get absolutely fit. The cottage is empty; a short while there will give you time to find another job. No one will bother you, you can go job hunting knowing that your mother is in good hands.

'I knew that you would dislike the idea simply because it was I who instigated it, but you will see nothing of me. Stay there until you have found something to your liking and move out when you wish to. I am sure that you agree with me that your mother's health is more important than any personal feelings you may have.'

Beneath the pleasant manner was a hint of steel. He had, reflected Kate crossly, managed to make her look selfish. She said stiffly, 'Very well. If you think that is the best thing for Mother, we accept your offer. It is most kind of you, if you're sure that it will be quite convenient? I'll ask for my free day and take Mother to Bosham. But Mr Tombs will want a day's notice, so if Mother could stay here for another day?'

'No need. I'll drive her there myself tomorrow morning, see her safely in and go on back to town. You will be free very shortly, I take it?'

'Yes.' She saw that wasn't going to be enough and added, 'Mrs Willett comes back in two days, and I'm to go three days later.'

Mr Tait-Bouverie, who knew all that already, nodded. 'Splendid.' He went to Mrs Crosby and took her hand. 'I'll be here for you about ten o'clock tomorrow. You've been a model patient.'

He went away quietly with a brief nod to Kate, who watched him go with her heart in her boots. Nothing could have been more polite and thoughtful than his manner towards her—and nothing, she reflected bitterly, could have been so uninterested. She thought fleetingly of Norway—they had been friends then. Of course, he would never understand that it was loving him that made it so difficult to accept his kindness, knowing that he didn't care for her in the least.

Her mother's voice roused her. 'Isn't it marvellous?' she wanted to know. 'It gives us a breathing space, doesn't it, darling? There's just one thing—would you be able to send on some more of my clothes? I've only got one of everything in the case, haven't I? And the nightie and the dressing gown here.'

'I'll ask Mr Briggs to bring me back. If I go home now I can pack a few things and bring them straight here. I'll bring the rest with me when I leave. Mother, what about Horace and Moggerty?'

'Oh, James said he'd deal with that...'

'How, Mother?'

'I've no idea, but if he says he will do something he does it, doesn't he?'

All the same, thought Kate, I'll have to make sure. She emptied the case, told her mother that she would be back as soon as possible and sped down to the hospital entrance. Mr Briggs was nowhere to be seen, but Mr Tait-Bouverie was. He took the case from her, took her arm and popped her into his car before she had time to utter a remark.

'Mr Briggs,' she managed. 'I must see him—he's got to bring me back—Mother's clothes—you don't understand...'

'Briggs has gone home. I'll drive you back and wait while you pack whatever your mother needs. No need for you to come back here; I'll see that she gets them.'

She could think of nothing to say as he drove her back. She would have to apologise; she had been absolutely beastly to him. If he had been angry it would have been easier... She tried out one or two suitable speeches in her head but they didn't sound right—but until she had told him that she was sorry it was hard to behave with the same friendliness which he had shown. It would be much easier if she didn't love him so much…

He went with her to the cottage and sat patiently with the cats on his knee while she flung things into the case. As well as clothes she grabbed her mother's modest make-up, more wool for her knitting, a writing pad and more shoes. She carried it down to the sitting room and found him asleep. Somehow the sight of him made it easy; there was no need for speeches.

'I'm sorry,' she said. 'I've been horrible to you, and you've shown us nothing but kindness, and I feel awful about it. I hope you'll forgive me.'

He had opened his eyes and was watching her. He wasn't smiling, and he looked politely indifferent. He said coolly, 'You have made such a colossal mountain out of a molehill that you can't see the wood for the trees, Kate. Rather a mixed metaphor, but really true.' He got up. 'Is this all that your mother needs? Have you any message for her?'

'No, thank you. There's a note in the case.'

Kate watched him walk to the door. He had said that he wouldn't be going to Bosham while they were there— she wouldn't see him again and he hadn't said that he'd forgiven her, had he? She swallowed back tears and wished him goodbye in a polite voice.

He didn't answer that, but said, 'Don't worry about the cats; some arrangement will be made for them.'

He had gone before she could assure him that she would take them with her when she went.

When she was sure that he had gone she sat down at the table in the kitchen. Horace and Moggerty came and sat with her, and presently she got up and fed them, made a pot of tea, drank it and went to bed. She was still the cook, and had to be up and about by seven o'clock.

Although she was tired she slept badly, but once her day had begun she worked her way through it in her usual calm and unhurried way. It was as they were finishing their midday dinner that Tombs, who had been called away, returned and told her that he had received a telephone call from Mr Tait-Bouverie to say that Mrs Crosby was installed in the cottage at Bosham and was well.

'I have ascertained the telephone number, should you wish to speak to your mother. You may use the kitchen telephone, Kate, after six o'clock.'

It was almost eight o'clock before she found the time to do so. She smiled at the sound of her mother's cheerful voice. It had been a lovely drive to Bosham, said Mrs Crosby, they had stopped and had coffee on the way and the cottage was delightful, and so comfortable. Mrs Squires had been waiting for them with James's man, Mudd.

'Such a nice person, Kate, and so efficient. I have a lovely room, and Mrs Squires is sleeping here until you come. James and Mudd went off just before tea, back to London. Mudd told me that James has a house there.' Mrs Crosby was bubbling over. 'Kate, he's thought of everything. The local doctor is coming to make sure that I am well, and he's left me his phone number.'

'I'm glad everything is so delightful, Mother. Take care, won't you? I'll be with you in four days. I'll find out the best way to travel. Train to Chichester, I expect, and then a bus...'

'Oh, I dare say,' said Mrs Crosby airily. Much later it

struck Kate that her mother had shown very little interest in her journey. It was going to be an awkward one,
what with the luggage and the cats…

Mrs Willett, well again and eager to resume her place
in the household, took over the cooking from Kate at
once. 'You'll need to pack up,' she pointed out. 'I must
say you've kept the cottage very nice, and Mr Tombs
told me that Mrs Braithewaite was very satisfied with
your work.'

Kate replied suitably and, given a free afternoon,
began the task of packing the two suitcases she would
have to take with her—watched with deep suspicion by
Horace and Moggerty, who got into the cases each time
she opened them. 'You're coming with me,' she assured
them, and wondered where all of them would finally end
up. Chichester sounded nice; if they could find a small
house there… She would have to go to the bank, too,
and if she could get the money she wanted she would
begin the slow process of building up the home catering
business. Kate sighed. There was a lot to do before she
could get started. 'But at least we've saved more money
than we expected to,' she told the cats, 'and if I can get
a part-time job to start with…'

The last day came. She was to leave in the early afternoon and take a train from Bath—an awkward journey,
but she had worked it out carefully. She had her breakfast, made sure that the cottage was exactly as Mrs Willett wanted it to be, and, bidden by Tombs, went to say
goodbye to Mrs Braithewaite.

'You're a good cook,' said that lady. 'They say the

way to a man's heart is through his stomach,' she chuckled. 'I wish you well, Kate.'

Kate thanked her. She wanted to point out that it wasn't only men she intended to cater for—birthday parties, family gatherings, even weddings were what she aimed for—but there was no point in saying so. She said goodbye in her quiet manner and went down to the kitchen. They would be having their morning coffee, and she could do with a cup.

So, it seemed, could Mr Tait-Bouverie, sitting there with a mug in one hand and a hunk of cake in the other. He put both down as she went in, watched the surprised delight in her face with deep satisfaction and got to his feet.

'Good morning, Kate. I'll drive you down to Bosham; I'm on my way there now.'

She had wiped the delight from her face and found her voice.

'I've booked a taxi...'

'Tombs has cancelled it. I'll go and say goodbye to my aunt while you have your coffee and then collect your things and the cats from the cottage.'

Mrs Willett chimed in. 'That's right, dear, you sit down for five minutes. Mr James will let you know when he is ready.'

Kate sat. There really wasn't much else she could do without making a fuss. There would be time enough to tell him what she thought of his high-handed actions once they were in the car.

Once they were on their way, with the cats on the back seat and the luggage in the boot, she found it difficult to begin. She mulled over several tart comments as to his

behaviour, but they didn't sound right in her head and
would probably come out all wrong if she uttered them.

'I'm waiting,' said Mr Tait-Bouverie.

'Waiting for what?'

'The tart reprimand I feel sure is quivering on your
lip. Oh, and quite justified too. I have no business to interfere with your life, I ride roughshod over your plans,
I turn up without warning and order you about. I am, in
short, a tiresome fellow.'

Which was exactly what she had intended to say herself. She thought how much she loved him even when he
annoyed her. He had been kind and helpful and, more
than that, they had been friends. He might be going to
marry Claudia—although how he could love the girl
was something she would never know—but she thought
that he liked her...

'Well, you do arrange things, don't you?' she said.
'I mean without saying so, but I expect that's because
you're used to doing it at the hospital. I've been ungrateful and snappy. I'm sorry.'

'Good. We understand each other. Try calling me
James.'

'No,' said Kate. 'How can I do that when I've cooked
dinner for you?'

'Do you mean to tell me that when my wife cooks my
dinner she will refuse to call me James?'

'Of course not. This is a silly question.' She added,
'Can Claudia cook?'

'Most unlikely, but Mudd, my man, is capable of that.'

She didn't see his smile.

It wasn't any good; she couldn't go on being vexed
with him. Anyway, it was a waste of time for he had an
answer for everything. Presently she found herself tell-

ing him of her plans, comfortably aware that he was listening—indeed, was making helpful suggestions.

She was quietly happy, even though she knew that the happiness wouldn't last. Each time they had met she had told herself that she wouldn't see him again, but there had always been a next time. These few hours together really would be the last. He had said that he wouldn't be going down to the cottage while they were there, and why should he? He had his own busy life and his marriage to plan. Her heart gave a painful twist at the thought.

She was enchanted by Bosham when they reached it, and when he stopped outside the cottage she stuck her head out of the window to take a better look.

'It's yours? It's lovely. Couldn't you live here always? It's not very far to London, is it?'

'No, but it's too far to travel there and back every day. Besides, I have a very pleasant house in London.'

He had got out and opened her door and she stood outside beside him, looking around her. It was, in Kate's opinion, quite large for a cottage, but it had a thatched roof and a number of small windows, and a solid door in a porch. Although summer was long over there were chrysanthemums and late roses, and a firethorn against one wall, vivid scarlet against the grey stone.

The door had opened and Mr Tait-Bouverie took her arm and urged her up the short path. Mudd was there, waiting for them, bidding them good day and casting a sharp eye over Kate. Very nice too, he considered, and ushered them into the narrow hall.

'Mrs Crosby is in the sitting room,' he informed them. 'Mrs Squires will serve lunch in half an hour, sir. I will see to the luggage and the cats.'

Mr Tait-Bouverie gave Kate a small shove. 'The sitting room's there, on the left. Go on in. I'll come presently; I must speak to Mudd.'

So Kate went in through the half-open door and found her mother waiting for her.

'Kate, dear. Oh, how lovely to see you. I've not been lonely for one moment. Mrs Squires is marvellous, and there's so much to do—and Mudd came this morning, and Prince too. You're all right? Mrs Braithewaite was pleasant? And the others? And did you have a good trip?'

Kate hugged her mother. 'Mother, you look marvellous. Are you all right? Was the doctor pleased with you? Are you eating well and sleeping?'

'Yes to that, my dear. I never felt better. I still get a bit tired, but that's normal. Another two weeks and I shall be better than I've been for a long time.'

Kate took off her coat, looking around her. The room was low-ceilinged and quite large, with a wide hearth with a brisk fire burning. The walls were cream, and there was a number of pictures. She would look at those later. The furniture was exactly right—deep armchairs, a wide sofa on either side of the hearth, and little lamp-tables—antiques, just as the bow-fronted cabinet against one wall was antique. There was a beautiful sofa-table with a bowl of chrysanthemums on it, and a charming little desk in one corner.

'It's perfect,' said Kate.

Mr Tait-Bouverie came in then, with the cat baskets, and Prince prancing beside him. To Mrs Crosby's expressed worries that Prince would eat the cats up Mr Tait-Bouverie said placidly, 'They'll be quite safe,' and let them out. Prince sat, obedient to his master's quiet voice, while Horace and Moggerty prowled cautiously round the room and presently climbed into a chair and sat, eyeing Prince, who lay down, put his head between his paws and went to sleep.

They drank their sherry, then, and Mrs Crosby and Mr Tait-Bouverie carried on a pleasant conversation about nothing much—and if they noticed that Kate had very little to say they didn't comment upon it.

They had lunch presently, but they didn't linger over it; Mr Tait-Bouverie had to return to London, taking Mudd and Prince with him, so that the cottage seemed suddenly very empty. Kate, watching the car disappear down the lane, reflected that he had said nothing about seeing them again. He had bidden her mother a cheerful goodbye, and when Kate had begun to thank him for driving her down and waved her thanks aside with a brief goodbye which had left her downcast. She deserved it, of course; she had said some awful things to him. She went red just remembering.

The rest of the cottage was just as perfect as the sitting room. Her bedroom wasn't over large, but the bed and the dressing table were dainty Regency, and the curtains and bedspread were pale pink and cream. The pink was echoed in the little armchair by the window and the lamps on either side of the bed. Her mother's room was larger and just as pretty. 'The loveliest room is at the back,' said Mrs Crosby. 'It's large with its own bathroom; I peeped in one day.'

Her mother was happy. After the places they had been living in, this must remind her of the house she had had when Kate's father had been alive. Kate would have to find work quickly and postpone her catering once more; with a decent job they could afford to live in a better house. There was the money she had saved—some of it could be used to pay rent...

'I shall go to Chichester tomorrow,' said Kate. 'And find an agency.'

'Darling, you've only just got here. James assured me that there was no hurry for us to leave. It's too late in the year for him to sail and he has a great deal of work, he told me.'

'Did he say when he was getting married?' asked Kate casually.

Her mother hesitated. 'Well, no, dear, not exactly.'

Kate said quickly, 'I'll feed the cats. They seem to have settled down nicely. Mrs Squires won't mind if I go into the kitchen?'

'Of course not, Kate. Now you're here, she said she would just come for a couple of hours in the mornings and then for an hour or so to see to the dishes after lunch. She'll be glad not to have to come out in the evening now it's getting dark early.'

It seemed a suitable arrangement. 'I'll come whenever you want me,' Mrs Squires told Kate the next day. 'If you're wanting to go away and don't like to leave your mother, just you say.'

'Thank you, I might be glad of that. I must go and look for a job. I thought Chichester...'

'As good a place as any,' said Mrs Squires. 'There's a good agency in the High Street, and plenty of hotels and big houses in and around the town.'

Kate didn't go to Chichester. The weather was bright but chilly, and her mother wanted to explore Bosham. 'I'm quite able to walk,' she declared. 'And it is such a delightful little place. Besides, I want to hear your plans.

If you could find somewhere cheap where we could live, you could start cooking…but do you have to go to the bank first?'

Mrs Crosby spoke with an overbright cheerfulness which caused Kate to give her a thoughtful look. Kate had had a wakeful night. She must face the future with common sense and set aside her dreams of starting a catering business. Seeing her mother so happy in the charming little cottage, living the kind of life they had led when her father had been alive, she realised that she must plan and decide on a different future.

She said now, 'There's plenty of time to make plans, and it's a good day for a walk. Shall we go down to the harbour?'

Her mother's face lit up.

They had a very happy day, exploring the little village at their leisure. There weren't many people and they spent a pleasant half-hour having coffee in a small café empty of other customers. 'A bit quiet,' said the owner, 'but it's busy enough at the weekend—they come down to overhaul their boats and do a bit of painting and such. Staying long, are you?'

'A week or so,' said Kate cautiously.

'Very nice it is at Mr Tait-Bouverie's cottage. Keeps it nice, he does, and always has a friendly word. Got a lot of friends here.' She added, 'Mrs Squires is my sister-in-law.'

On the way back Kate said, 'Perhaps we had better be a bit careful what we say in front of Mrs Squires, but I suppose in a small place there's always a bit of gossip.'

That night, lying in bed wide awake, Kate thought about their future. She discarded the idea of finding work in Chichester—it was too near the cottage and Bosham, and there would be the risk of meeting James when he spent his weekends there. He would have Claudia with him… She wouldn't be able to bear seeing them together. She would have to think up a good reason for moving away where she would never see him again.

Tomorrow, she promised herself, she would get a copy of *The Lady* and look for a job—preferably in the north or along the east coast. She would have to give her mother a good reason for that, too. She could see now that there would be little chance of her starting up on her own, not for several years.

Not that it mattered any more—the future unrolled before her with no James in it. She thrust the thought aside and concentrated on a possible move to a job which would be suitable. There was her mother to consider, and the cats. They would need a roof over their heads and a decent wage. If she abandoned her catering plans there wouldn't be the need to scrape and scrimp. They would go out more, buy new clothes—enjoy life!

Having made these suitable arrangements, Kate had a good cry and fell asleep at last.

She awoke very early and, rather than lie there thinking of the same unhappy things, she got out of bed and looked out of the window. It was a grey morning and still not light. A cup of tea would be nice, and she might go to sleep again. She didn't wait to put on her dressing gown but crept barefoot down the stairs and into the kitchen.

Mr Tait-Bouverie was sitting at the kitchen table, the teapot beside him, a slice of bread and butter in his hand. He looked up as she paused in the doorway and said, 'Good morning, Kate,' and smiled at her.

Kate's heart beat so loudly and so fast that she thought

he must surely hear it. She drew a difficult breath. 'How did you get in?'

He looked surprised. 'I have a key.'

'Is something the matter? Do you want something?'

'Nothing is the matter. I do want something, but that can wait for the moment. Would you like some tea?'

She nodded. 'Yes, please.'

He got up and fetched another mug from the dresser. 'Then run upstairs and get a dressing gown and slippers. You look charming, but you distract me.'

Kate said, 'Oh,' and fled back to her room and wrapped herself tightly in the sensible garment she had had for years. It concealed her completely, and would never wear out. At least it covered the cheap cotton nightie she was wearing.

She went back downstairs, feeling shy. Mr Tait-Bouverie's glance slid over her person with the lack of interest of someone reading yesterday's newspaper, so that she felt instantly comfortable. She sat down by the Aga and, since she longed to look at him, she kept her eyes on Prince, snoozing comfortably between Moggerty and Horace.

Presently she asked the question which had been on the tip of her tongue. 'Is Claudia with you?'

He looked amused. 'No.'

'She knows you are here?'

'No. Why should she?'

'Well, if it was me,' said Kate, throwing grammar to the winds, 'I'd want to know.'

'Well, shall we throw Claudia out of the window, metaphorically speaking? She's no concern of mine. I can't think why you've dragged her into the conversation.'

'We weren't having a conversation. And how can you

talk like that about her when you are going to marry her?' She added defiantly, 'Lady Cowder said so.'

'One of my least likeable aunts. I have no intention of marrying Claudia. I don't like her, Mudd doesn't like her, Prince doesn't like her...'

'Then why are you here?'

'Because I have something to say to you. On several occasions I have tried to do so and each time I have been thwarted. Now you are in my house, in my kitchen, and I shall speak my mind.'

Kate got up. 'I said I was sorry, and I am. I didn't mean any of the things I said...'

'Well, of course you didn't.' He had come to stand very near her, and when she would have taken a prudent step back he folded his great arms around her, wrapping her so close that she could feel his heart beating under her ear.

'I've been in love with you for a very long time now, my darling, and I have waited for you to discover that you loved me, too—and that hasn't been easy. Such a hoity-toity miss, hiding behind her cook's apron...'

'Well, I am a cook,' said Kate into his shirt-front, and then, because she was an honest girl, she said, 'But I do love you, James.'

He put a gentle finger under her chin, smiling down at her. He kissed her then, slowly and with the greatest of pleasure, for this was the moment he had waited for. Kate kissed him back and then paused to ask, 'Mother! What about Mother...?'

'Hush, my love. Your mother and I have had a little talk. She is happy to live here with Mrs Squires to look after her. We shall come down whenever I'm free. You won't mind living in London? I have a house there, a pleasant place.'

Kate reflected that she would live in a rabbit hutch as long as she was with James. 'It sounds very nice,' she said.

'Oh, it is.' Hardly a good description of the charming little house overlooking the river.

Something in his voice made her ask, 'James, are you rich?'

'I'm afraid so. Don't let it worry you, my love.'

Kate stared up at him. 'No, I won't—it doesn't matter in the least, does it?'

'No.'

'Although, of course…' began Kate.

Mr Tait-Bouverie kissed her silent. 'Will you marry me, Kate?'

'Well, yes—of course I will, James.' She smiled at him. 'Ought we to sit down and discuss it? The wedding and so on?'

'With all the will in the world, my dearest girl, but first of all…'

He bent his head to kiss her, and Kate, in a happy world of her own, kissed him back.

* * * * *

WE HOPE YOU ENJOYED
THIS BOOK FROM

◆ HARLEQUIN

SPECIAL
EDITION

Believe in love. Overcome obstacles. Find happiness.

Relate to finding comfort and strength in the
support of loved ones and enjoy the journey
no matter what life throws your way.

6 NEW BOOKS AVAILABLE EVERY MONTH!

"Gracie, will you look at me?"

Stifling a sigh, she turned her head to face him. Those melty brown eyes were full of self-recrimination and regret.

"I'm sorry," he said. "I never should have touched you. I'm too old for you, and I'm not any kind of relationship material, anyway. I don't know what got into me, but I swear to you it's never going to happen again."

Hmm. How to respond?

Too bad there wasn't a large blunt object nearby. The guy deserved a hard bop on the head. What was wrong with him? No wonder it hadn't worked out with Marjorie. The man didn't have a clue.

But never mind. Gracie held it together as he apologized some more. She watched that beautiful mouth move and pondered the mystery of how such a great guy could have his head so far up his own ass.

Maybe if she yanked him close and kissed him, he'd get over himself and admit that last night had been amazing, the two of them had off-the-charts chemistry and he didn't want to walk away from all that goodness, after all.

Yeah, kissing him might shut him up and get him back on track for more hot sexy times. It had worked more than once already.

But come on. She couldn't go jumping on him and smashing her mouth on his every time he started beating himself up for having a good time with her.

No. A girl had to have a little pride.

He thought last night was a mistake?

Fair enough. She'd actually let herself believe for a minute or two there that they had something good going on, that her long dry spell manwise might be over.

But never mind about that. Let him have it his way. She would agree with him.

And then she would show him exactly what he was missing. And then, when he couldn't take it anymore and begged her for another chance, she would say that they couldn't, that he was too old for her and it wouldn't be right.

Don't miss
Their Secret Summer Family *by Christine Rimmer,*
available May 2020 wherever
Harlequin Special Edition books and ebooks are sold.

Harlequin.com

HSEEXP0420